CROW CUT COVE: SEASONS

An AllensRusk Press Book
Nashville, TN

D.M. MARTIN

This is a work of fiction. All the characters and events portrayed in this book are either fictitious or are used fictitiously.

CROW CUT COVE: SEASONS

ISBN-13: 978-0-9672246-7-1
ISBN-10: 0-9672246-7-5

Kindle ISBN-13: 979-8-88589-161-5

Published by AllensRusk Press
P.O. Box 100213
Nashville, TN 37224

Printed in the United States of America

Library of Congress Control Number: 2022903535

Thanks, Rose!

Thanks, Sharon!

FOREWORD

My memory of events is so non-linear. That's the reason I have my notebooks, however, I have discovered that I didn't consistently date events. Now, I have no clue why, so I only have a rough estimate of the dates of some events. When there is a time span of months between dated entries, memory and my journal fight a battle which neither wins.

Every seven years, one's cellular structure is completely renewed/copied with lethal and non-lethal errors entrenched within to be repeated or scrapped in the next cycle, along with the next generation of errors. If there is such a thing as a seven year cycle, I am entering another one. And my mindset, my feelings remind me of another cycle that began in the year I married. A year of emotional flux. So much has changed and so much is still the same.

I have to return, in memory to that time, because the solutions, especially the organic unconscious solutions that I came up with… I need them now. The winters are bright, cold, gray, dark, silent, or mostly silent with the gunshot cracks and booms of widow makers shearing from their anchoring trees punctuating the silence at irregular intervals. Summers are dry, with a faint or strong odor of burning forest permeating the air. Fires are endemic. No one bothers to replant the trees. Where thick forests towered…now there are random patches of green spindly shrubs and fire flowers dotting the blackened mountainside for their season. Otherwise, in aerial photographs, one sees only the blackened mountainside waiting for the next fire to seek and destroy the meager new growth that struggles to survive. The wildlife is hungry and gardens and pastures are barricaded with native stone walls.

I have a birth daughter and son. I ask myself too often in these pages how I could possibly be a birth mother. Juston was needed practice. Now, he wants to return. To him, this is a place of safety…home. He wants to marry and raise his children in the place he calls home. I'm discouraging him; Josh is encouraging. I think Juston has a child's view of this place. Josh and I protected him from the worse the mountain offered. He argues that cities are no better.

Joshua and I are arguing. Maybe that's why I am searching for the notebooks that chronicled that first year. I feel like I'm in an emotional time warp and I don't know how to return to the present.

The Paper has been awarded a number of commendations. Some deserved; some for lack of competition. I have a loyal following, but most people get their news online. So far, I have refused an online presence which Cinda says is slow suicide. Her mantra is monetize, monetize, monetize. However, internet and phone service is not consistent or reliable. We get the most reliable service in the mid-spring before the fires begin and after the fire season which varies from late fall to midwinter. Last year's award was an investigative piece with graphics created by Rachel.

Rachel didn't want to do the graphics, but she is a starving artist who needed the money. I laughed at her description of herself. Rachel is very talented and has shown her work in the United States, Canada, and Brazil, with private showings in Ghana, Nigeria, Ivory Coast, and the Islands. Artists need a patron and she is lucky…her brother is her patron. They're arguing because her current *friend* is living with her. He's a musician and has steady gigs, but he has no money sense and his managers are fleecing him…but they're his friends.

Next year, we will be empty nesters. Drujo (Andrew Joshua, but Zeezee insisted that we call him Drujo because everyone should have a family name and a public name) will be in college. Is that the true reason for the arguing? Zeezee's opinion is that I am menopausal and should cool out in Kentucky. Zeezee's surprisingly agile arthritic fingers are into everything and she usually has advice that makes sense. However, I don't feel like writing and one of my nieces is hiding out there, recuperating from her latest failed relationship.

Vonnie Pearl is a doting grandmother, but she knows, because I told her, that I will kill her and curse her corpse if she harms my children and I would burn her body so that she would never be buried beside her beloved Andy.

Brer Rabbit no longer sleeps on the couch or in the warmest spot he could claim for his own. Josh asked if I wanted another cat…was that the beginning of the arguments? I didn't scream at him, but my expression must have. I have never wanted a pet. He foisted Brer Rabbit on me because he thought I would like the company. In his mind, there was something unnatural about a woman living alone, with nothing tangible to nurture. However, Brer Rabbit and I came to an understanding and he became part of my universe. Never did realize that he was a cat, except once. He dropped a dead mouse on my right foot and swished his tail and cat stared me for his due praise while I swallowed a scream and found myself telling him how proud I was of his accomplishment. He promptly appropriated his favorite spot on the sofa and cat stared me while I stood frozen, looking from the mouse to him. How did he get out and what possessed him to kill a mouse and bring it to me kept circling through the same neural path in a loop that wasn't broken until I heard Zeezee's snicker. She calmly removed the mouse by the tail from my foot and tossed it into the trash.

Brer Rabbit's sole purpose in this earthly existence was to be taken care of according to his most particular specifications. When I found Brer Rabbit, warm from the fire, but stiff in death, he appeared to be cat smiling me and not a Cheshire cat grin, but one of deep contentment. I think he wanted me to know that he was well-pleased with his existence and me as his chosen minion.

But that was before Rikki (Aurelia Charzette named for three of her great-grandmothers, but known as Rikki) left for college. Had the arguments began at that time? Rikki noticed on one of her breaks and asked why we were arguing. I shrugged which led her to ask Josh. That led to me and Josh arguing, which was interrupted when Drujo barged in and told us we needed to get it together or divorce. I remember thinking…how could he possibly have heard us and Josh saying…*We were quiet arguing*…like he had read my thought.

Later, Drujo explained that it wasn't that he heard, but that he felt, sensed the negative change in the ambient vibrations permeating our home (that's how he talks) that meant his two most favorite people in the world were arguing.

Who told Juston? Finally, some order to the notebooks of that first couple of years. Juston will visit this weekend and I can't lie to him. So I have to find a truth before he arrives.

CHAPTER 1

I wish I could pretend that I love the mountains, but can one really love the place that has taught one to respect fear? I think the most these mountains can ever expect from me is respect. When I think like this on days when I see no one but the people who say I am family, she stands mirage-like, gazing at me so sadly. I then shake myself back to the reality of the noisy printing press that shares the front room of the old home place with me. I often wonder who she is and why she visits me. I look at her in those instances and see someone who reminds me of Zeezee, but I know she who visits is somehow of me. What does she mean? Sometimes what she is saying is clear—*went to the mountains to hide my face…the mountains cried out* ***no hiding place***. An old song…where could I possibly have heard it? She is adamant that I discover the meaning and I don't know where to begin.

Part of me would like to belong to these mountains. Another part of me wants to run. I keep my gun close at all times. I am startled by the whispered fall of a leaf. As I search for the source of that faintest of rustle, I know in my heart that I have not claimed these people or this place as my own.

Soon I will find out what these mountains are like in the winter. Zeezee says she doesn't like to think of winter. Winter comes early in these mountains. First, there is the teaser snow that dusts the mountains like the powdered sugar on a gingerbread house. That snow comes anywhere from late September to mid-October. Then, there is an Indian summer that usually lasts until mid-November. That is when the tourists come in hoards to enjoy the trees with their leaves of gold, yellow, orange, red, and purple. A hard frost heralds the end of the tourist season.

This year is different. A blizzard roared through the mountains on the day after Josh and I returned from our honeymoon. There is still snow on the ground two weeks later.

Zeezee has inspected her stash of material and today we will travel to Knoxville for more. *Keep busy and don't think you are trapped. Always have a project, she advised. I will teach you to quilt, maybe, even to crochet.* I suppose I am Zeezee's project for this coming winter. I have no talent for or inclination to learn what she desires to teach me. I have told her that I cannot be what I am not. She refuses to listen. She is determined that her grandson shall be content, no…he shall be happy, and that her daughter can be appeased. My contentment and happiness, she firmly believes is with Joshua. I have decided that as long as her teachings do not interfere with the newspaper, I will cooperate.

I hate it. I hate the mountains in winter. My first winter and there has been more snow this year than in the past thirty years. There has been more ice, not the same thing as snow, by any means, than in the past twenty years. *Weather changing*, Zeezee said with a shrug. My question to myself is—do I love Josh enough to stay or do I love him enough to take me and my discontent far from these cold, white mountains? I don't particularly like being married either. Compromise is difficult and frustrating. I can understand his point of view—does that mean I have to find this midpoint, neither of us is happy with, in order to co-exist?

And I keep dreaming of her—the one who reminds me of Zeezee. Why is she almost smiling? Why does she no longer speak? Why does she gaze at me so intently? What else must I do in the garden?

We can do this. That's what Josh had said that night as we held each other on the steps of Mr. P's burned cabin. And in the light of that silvery moon, I could only agree. We could.

My sister and brother coerced our father into attending my wedding. Patrice's idea…the wedding…not mine. Mama had wanted Patrice and me to wear her wedding dress when we married. On each of our fourteenth birthdays, she had showed us the dress of cream silk with a row of pearls on each of the long sleeves and then had returned it to storage. Mama's grandmother and mother had made the dress. Mama had sewn the pearls on the sleeves—real pearls that she had saved for after carefully selecting each one. She had told us the story so many times—twenty pearls—ten for each sleeve. They had to be the same size and color. The jeweler had despaired of ever having twenty pearls to satisfy my mother. Mama said the jeweler sold the pearls to her at a discount because he never wanted to see her again. After showing the dress to me and before returning the dress to storage, Mama had snipped the pearls from the dress and had a jeweler make a necklace. Mama gave the necklace to me. She wore it to some function and I was the only one who noticed it. However, as Patrice was quick to point out, she didn't want the necklace—the pearls weren't big enough and, at the time, no one was wearing pearls. Mama had given me the necklace with the understanding that if Patrice wanted to wear the wedding dress that the pearls would be resewn to the dress for that day.

Patrice had been unable to fit into the dress when she married and had only worn what was left of the veil under protest. In one of her rare introspective moods, Patrice had admitted that she did not want to wear the dress or the veil. She didn't want to jinx her marriage.

I tried on the dress and it only needed altering in the bust as my mother was a D cup and I was barely a B cup. After the dress was altered, on the night before my wedding, under the supervision of my aunts, I sewed the pearls onto the sleeves. Aunt Maline tried on the veil and she and Aunt Leda pronounced the repair satisfactory. As long as Josh did not mind having a wedding, I did not care. I sensed that he was relieved. Josh didn't want an elaborate wedding, but he wanted more than a civil ceremony. Josh believed that marriage was a contract that should be publicly acknowledged and privately sealed. He had asked if I understood. I told him that I did, but I did not. I mean, I understood the words, but not his meaning.

If only Patrice and Franklin hadn't coerced Dad into attending my wedding. He refused to participate in the ceremony and sat on the front row, frowning his displeasure. Patrice thought I would be upset that he did not walk me down the aisle. I was not. He was not giving me to Joshua. I had agreed to this marriage and I would publicly acknowledge the agreement I had made. At the reception, Dad told anyone who cared to listen that I would be home before the winter was over and that I would then want the job with the County that was no longer available.

Before the wedding, Josh tried to talk to him, to tell my father that he loved me and that he would be the best husband he could be. Dad, of course, not only refused to listen, but also said some things that I shall never forget. Patrice says I should forgive him, because, after all, he's the only father we have, but he is still trying to persuade Franklin and Patrice to side with him.

The memory of his rants has drowned out any joyful memories of my wedding.

I look at these words that I wrote three years ago and I find myself re-feeling the disconnectedness. Now, I have some understanding of my younger self. I had not stocked up on notebooks with the intention of keeping a journal, but that is the use I made of some of them. I had no one to talk to of my feelings, and I am sure that even if I had, I would not have talked about my true feelings. None of my feelings made sense to me as they were so contradictory. I now know that at each of my life passages I have felt the same, but the intensity of my feelings, at that time, is still unsettling to me.

The time has come for me to come to terms with that time, that first year of marriage. I have a decision to make and I will not make the correct decision if I do not understand who I was at that time.

CHAPTER 2

Lanetia wore a down-filled coat, two sweaters (one wool cardigan and one cotton pullover), and silk thermal underwear. Still, the cold seeped in. She could see the smoky tendrils of her breath and, for a moment, the ridiculous fact that she was cold distracted her from the copy she was proofreading.

Lanetia had finally given in to the vagaries of the antique printing press. The printing press worked well when the room was cold. If the temperature was above fifty-five degrees, the printing press balked and caused more frustration than it was worth. That was why she now had a printer in Chattanooga who was already hinting that when winter came to the mountains that he might not be able to deliver the paper. Lanetia was determined to print the anniversary issue on the old printing press, so she continued to experiment with it, hoping that she would know enough by June to do so.

So far, the Paper did not lose money. The Paper didn't make any money, but it certainly hadn't caused her to dip into any of her savings. The Paper usually disappeared within a couple of days from the racks she had set up in Sycamore, Tiny Town, Salyna, and the gated subdivisions. People didn't mind paying fifty cents for the weekly Paper and now there was a somewhat lively discussion going on in the Letters to the Editor about the lack of road maintenance. Lanetia grimaced to herself—what road maintenance? Grotman County was too poor to buy or maintain salt trucks and the State wanted to forget that Grotman County existed, especially after the events of the summer.

She could not concentrate on the copy. But going to the house was not an option. Vonnie Pearl would be there. Always with that look on her face—*I know you will tell Josh what I tried to do. I know you'll take him away.* Vonnie Pearl had seemed to age overnight until she appeared to be older than Zeezee. Zeezee had tried to coax Lanetia to talk about that day, but so far Lanetia had kept her promise. *How long though before Josh wishes for a time before Vonnie Pearl's unpredictable moods and headaches? Before me?* Josh was always asking what and why and saying you have to let me help.

Lanetia wished she knew what she felt toward Vonnie Pearl.

"Nesha, turn on some heat. It be cold," Cinda complained as she and Juston noisily slammed the front door.

"School out already?"

"Early . . . more snow. I be . . ."

"Am, say I am and it is," Lanetia corrected.

"Why?"

"So you can help me proofread."

"The computer does that," Cinda shot back, always ready to spar with her sister-in-law.

"I make A's in English. I'm at home now."

"I know you do. Practice…practice…practice. You know context. The computer does not. Juston, how was school?"

Juston had a tendency to let Cinda talk for him. By now, he and Cinda knew the question was for him. There wasn't a hint of the frightened little boy of the summer. She and Juston, before dark came so early, would walk in the woods and talk until there was a companionable silence between them. Most times Cinda accompanied them. Juston said that he didn't mind because no one really talked to them except Lanetia. Now, he and Cinda, on the way home after being dropped off by the bus, would stop off at the old home place to talk. Lanetia had thought Juston might have wanted to join the elementary school's basketball or football team, but he was adamant in his no. *They're way bigger than me, he had pointed out.*

"I got a hundred on a pop quiz in Science and I read my book report. I got an A on that, too. Mrs. Rellson wouldn't call on me in Geography. She kinda told me in a nice way that I was showing off."

"You want me to talk to her?"

"Maybe if she does it again. What does she mean when she says I have advantages the other kids don't?"

"Miz Thomason told me the same thing," Cinda chimed in. "She said not everybody has a lawyer living with them and a brother who's an engineer. She said she expected me to do well."

"Maybe I should speak to both of them." They both said no and exchanged an expression that said she wouldn't understand. Lanetia nodded. She remembered. A small town and only one or two of her classmates' parents were college graduates. None had parents who were teachers. They had been bullied…very discreetly. Their mother wouldn't permit them to fight or to report the bullies. *Ignore them* had been their mother's mantra. *In high school, you won't have to deal with them.* How had she known that none of those bullies would be in the college prep classes or any of the extra-curricular activities they had participated in?

A college education was not a priority for the mountain born. Most of the teachers had been recruited from Knoxville, Chattanooga, and Johnson City. "You two may have some advantage, but it's up to you to use what you have for and to *your* advantage. However, your teachers shouldn't be making such comments. Tell me, if they continue to do so." Juston slowly nodded. Sometimes, Juston was as stubborn as Lanetia. Lanetia had already talked to Mrs. Rellson once about her making fun of Juston's accent. *Juston's mother was from Minnesota. He lived there until he was seven. He does not have a southern accent,* Lanetia had told the teacher. *If you cannot teach a child who does not speak with a southern accent, I shall take this matter up with the principal and, if he does not know that your comments are inappropriate, then I will speak to the superintendent and, if necessary, to the School Board.* So far, there had been no more comments about Juston's accent, but now this. The teacher's conduct added up, in Lanetia's mind, to a subtle undermining of Juston's love of learning.

"Go to the house. I'll be there in a few minutes. I really want to finish proofing this week's letters to the editor."

"Josh say…he don't understand why you always experimentin' with this old press. I kinda like it. It smells creative when you run it. Miz Thomason wants you to come to school again," Cinda said, interrupting herself. "But this time she wants you to talk about being a lawyer. I have a note somewhere," she said, talking more to herself than to Lanetia as she dumped out the contents of her backpack on the table. "Did I put the note in my Social Studies book? I left that in my locker. No, here it is in my Science book. She sealed it so I couldn't read it. What's it say?"

"Give me a minute to read the note. Put your books back… I'm sure you have homework. Your school is having a career day. She wants Josh to come, too."

"Yeah, he always comes."

"Did Rachel go to the house?"

"I guess. Ain't nowhere else for her to go. She depressed."

"I can't say I blame her. I can't concentrate. I'll walk with you. Juston, check the back door. I moved some boxes to the back porch and I don't think I locked it."

Zeezee and Lanetia sat under the bright light of a floor lamp, guaranteed to mimic sunlight. Lanetia had not only ordered the lamps for the old home place, but also for this corner of the living room that she and Zeezee used for sewing, the girls' bedroom, and her and Josh's sitting room. *This house is too full of shadows.* Josh had frowned at Lanetia's assessment, but had agreed with her solution.

Lanetia thought any beneficial affect was probably more of a placebo effect than a real cure. However, they had all noticed that the lamps made a difference. Rachel tried to pretend to be depressed, but Rachel would be doing her homework and singing. Rachel! The lamp that had been intended for their bedroom was in Joshua's office. He had ordered two more lamps, but they hadn't arrived. Now, if only Vonnie Pearl would use one of the lamps he had ordered.

As always, Cinda and Juston lay on pillows at their feet, reading when they weren't teasing each other.

"Tiny stitches, Nesha."

"This is as tiny as they get. Remember, this is for me. To say, yes, I made a quilt top, all hand-sewn… I…"

"No excuse, tiny, tiny stitches so the pieces will stay together."

"Once your friend…what's her name?...Miz Treena?...quilts it, won't it stay together?"

"Take it out. You got to concentrate. Look at your stitches in this piece. That be the way all them stitches should look."

"Zeezee, this is no fun…not anymore. You want perfection; I just want to do it."

"Then do it right. There be the door openin'. I never seen such a one for findin' somethin' to do. Black dark out, startin' to snow, why can't he come in where it be warm?"

"Zeezee, I ain't payin' you no mind. Nesha, your mail," Josh said as he dropped some letters in her lap on top of the colorful quilt square. Lanetia was grudgingly picking out the stitches with a seam ripper. Zeezee was watching closely to ensure that she actually picked out the stitches. Zeezee had lectured Lanetia more than once about impatiently ripping out the seams. *Look at the holes in the material you done caused, Zeezee would point out. Now, we got to cut some more pieces.*

Joshua longed to touch Lanetia, but dared not. If Vonnie Pearl was in the room, as she was now, Nesha would withdraw and he hated that. But she wouldn't tell him why. Later on, when they were alone, Lanetia would respond. *I should be able to touch my wife in front of my mother.*

What had happened that day at Mr. P's cabin? He'd known something was very wrong when his mother had burst into the kitchen with an apron full of berries, tears streaming down her face. She'd gasped out about finding Mr. P's son's body. He'd called the Rangers and the Highway Patrol. Then, when he'd asked her where Nesha was, she'd looked terrified and muttered something about Old P's shack.

"Career Day," Lanetia was saying. "Ms. Thomason wants us there at two. Write it in your appointment book, because I think you wanted to do something next week, but you hadn't decided when."

"Fix the Co-Op's air conditioning unit. I just got the part in." He pulled out his appointment book, pleased that she had remembered. Nesha listened. *Why doesn't she think I will listen to her?* "Letter from Mona. Gonna read it?"

"Later. I know why she's writing. Don't put anything in an e-mail that you might have to explain to people you would rather not explain to," Lanetia said, with a hint of a smile at his frown.

"What she want you to do?"

"It's not really her. She doesn't even like this governor. He wants me to be on the committee that's overseeing the renovation of the prison into a museum. Mona's pushing. I don't want to be bothered. I don't know anything about museums…"

"Miz Thomason says it'll bring in tourists and tourists spend money," Cinda interrupted as she hooked her legs around one of her brother's legs, hoping for a tickle.

"Fall on you…smushed Cinda," Josh said, patting her cheek. "What you readin'?"

"African Folk Tales. Nesha says me and Juston be woefully ignorant about our ancestors. Didn't even know they were my ancestors. I like Anansi. He's funny. He tricks everybody."

"Yeah, that old spider…"

"You know about him? Why you never tell me?" Cinda demanded.

"Never thought about it. You always wanted me to read Sleeping Beauty and Cinderella. You give them the Brer Rabbit books?" he asked, as he sat on the floor next to Cinda and settled back his head touching Lanetia's knees.

It was something else they shared—a college course where one read Brer Rabbit stories. The two professors couldn't have approached the subject more differently—Nesha's professor, a professional storyteller, was interested in the emotion of the story. Joshua's professor, who had a doctorate in English, was only interested in analyzing the stories and their place in the folk history of the United States.

"Dinner's ready, if anyone interested," Vonnie Pearl announced as she got up to go into the kitchen.

Josh looked at Lanetia who was suddenly very interested in picking out the uneven stitches in the quilt piece. Nobody moved. Sometimes, dinner wasn't a pleasant meal. Sometimes, Vonnie Pearl would taunt Lanetia as though daring her to say something. And, the more Lanetia ignored Vonnie Pearl, the more frantic her taunts would become until Josh put a stop to it for that day.

"You gonna let her persuade you?" Josh asked, tapping the letter on Lanetia's lap.

"I haven't decided. It's not something I feel drawn to."

"Rachel, you come on down," Vonnie Pearl called out from the bottom of the stairs.

"Let's eat and we can talk about it later." Please, his eyes pleaded with hers. *Don't say you're not hungry.* Lanetia nodded.

"Last summer was the first summer since I've been back that we didn't have a booth in the square to sell Zeezee's quilts, pickled peaches, crocheted doilies, and whatever else she decided to make over the winter. We made a little money, but after Deacon Harmond got his percentage…wasn't much left. One year, Zeezee knitted afghans. She say she never want to see another afghan. Ain't made none since. I was talkin' to Carl who owns the Co-op. He want to know if you'd do a story on him. He been around for a long time and he liked the story you did on Mr. Holzer before he left for Florida. Also, the ads you do…people been noticin' and he swear he gettin' more business."

"How much snow? I didn't listen…"

"Let me get you warm." He noticed her hesitation, but she got up from the sofa and came to bed. "You not smilin' today. Anything the matter?"

"No, sometimes I feel as though I can feel the weather changing. Today, I feel kind of caged in, like the animals at the zoo must feel. Winter was never my favorite season."

"Caged… We can leave. Is that what you want?"

"No, it's winter everywhere in the Northern Hemisphere and the Southern Hemisphere is a little too troubled."

“That’s not what I meant. For once, don’t change the subject.”

“Josh, love, it’s moot. I will not discuss…”

“Why not?”

“Because I love you. This is where you must be. We could leave, but we’d both always know that you left when you were needed the most. Nothing’s over. Don’t you know there are a hundred Sheriff Dardens out there just waiting to be elected? He should be in prison for a very long time and so should two of his deputies. The infrastructure is here. Someone will try to use it.

“Your land… Someone else will try to steal it. It’s a legacy… your legacy and you actually care about it. It’s not something you visit every once in a while. It’s a part of you.”

“You are, too. I need to hold you just like I’m doing now and to talk. It’s not just talk, is it, Nesha,” he asked, tipping her chin up, just so he could look into her eyes.

CHAPTER 3

On days like today, when the snow or ice had piled high from the night's precipitation, Lanetia would get up with Joshua and helped him clear a path to the barn. She knew he marveled at her insistence. Lanetia had learned that if one lived in a place, one should know how to run it. She had never lived on a working farm and she was glad she hadn't. The chores were boring, repetitive, and labor intensive. She helped feed the cows, lay down fresh straw, and she was getting pretty good at milking the cows. Joshua had noticed that she didn't like doing any of it. He'd asked her to stay in the house and she'd just continued to get up and help.

On this morning, they cleared the path of the fresh snow that continued to fall from the gray sky. The snow wasn't expected to stop for two more days. They'd be snowbound. Wasn't any use clearing the driveway until the snow stopped falling for more than a day or two. Sometimes, Joshua would stop what he was doing and survey his surroundings. He would wrinkle his nose and glance at Lanetia. Lanetia thought he was trying to see the barn as she saw it—animals, stink of their waste, now that he couldn't put them out to pasture, and dark shadows that menaced in their eerie movements that reminded one of a shootout at high noon in the old West.

"I'll get the bale of hay. You move the cows to the milking area. Okay?"

"Okay," Lanetia agreed, but her thoughts were elsewhere, planning her day or her escape…both equally crowded her imaginings on these cold dark mornings.

By the time Joshua returned with the hay, Lanetia had not only moved the cows to the milking area, but had started mucking out the big stall where they had been. "I'll do that."

"You milk. You do it faster than I can. Now I know why your garden grows," Lanetia said, laughing to herself. The waste and hay she was raking out into a pile behind the barn was used as fertilizer for the vegetable garden. Everything Josh grew was organic. Josh's father had farmed organically, using non-genetically modified seeds, long before it was popular.

Joshua didn't laugh. *Mary, Mary, quite contrary, how does your garden grow?* Dad. Dad...that's what Dad would say, all the while smiling at his private joke.

"You don't like that nursery rhyme, do you?"

"It's okay." He'd never told her what his father had said. What he had understood too late.

"Your father liked it. He said…"

"How you know what he say?" Joshua said, more sharply than he intended.

"Kaemon said that your father's pet name for your mother was Mary because she was so contrary."

"Oh, I didn't know that." *He thought I did. But I, like most kids, didn't concern myself with hearing things like that.*

Lanetia reread Mona's letter. Have you ever thought about running for District Attorney? The DA that serves Grotman County will be retiring either next year or the year after, maybe earlier. His assistant is almost as old as he is. We had to completely bypass him in the Grotman County investigation because of his association with Bond and Warfordy. We can't prove that he was paid off by the sheriff, but we believe that is what happened. Being on the prison renovation committee would get your name into the public consciousness in a positive way. That with the Paper… Great job. Bet you didn't know I get a weekly copy from an acquaintance, since you won't sell subscriptions. Where do you get your crossword puzzle? It stumps me sometimes. You could be elected. Don't frown. I know you're frowning.

“Rachel, have you finished the crossword puzzle for this week?” Rachel looked up from the computer. She probably had on more layers of clothes than Lanetia.

“Just about. I don’t think we can use the puzzle it be creating. I don’t recognize a lot of the words.”

“Look in the OED. If the words aren’t there, maybe another theme. What about…” Lanetia reread Mona’s letter. Is this something I want to do? I need to talk to Josh. Why must I talk to Josh? You’re married—that’s why you have to talk to Josh. Why am I arguing with myself? Is this something I want to do? Finally, Rachel interrupted the internal circular argument.

“Nesha, they in here, but the first thing it says is archaic. There be ten clues with these archaic words.”

“Too many. If the crossword aficionados are too frustrated, there’ll be letters to the editor about the puzzle. What about archers as the theme?” Lanetia said, thinking out loud. “Sagittarius might come up as one of the answers. Try that.”

Rachel liked helping with the newspaper. Usually they worked on the crossword puzzle together. They decided on a theme and the computer program would create the puzzle.

Lanetia sighed. The article she was writing about the trial was not going well. The jury had been deliberating for a week.

Now, the jury had asked for instruction on the charges. Even if the jury found in the sheriff's favor, the indictments in the Special Task Force's case were pending. The politicos had let it be known that they wanted the Special Task Force's case fast-tracked so that it would be over before the elections next year. The sheriff's lawyers had already asked for more time as they claimed it would take them more than six months to sift through the evidence the Special Task Force had generated in its investigation. It was too legalistic for the Paper's audience. How do you dumb down the events that had led to the trial, the trial itself, and jury deliberation? Lanetia laughed out loud as she drew an oval and dressed it up with a bowtie.

"What's so funny?"

"How is this for a story—Humpty Dumpty sat on a wall. Humpty Dumpty had a great fall. All the king's men and all the king's horses couldn't put Humpty together again."

Rachel giggled. She got it. "Ain't nobody around here would appreciate that. Maybe Josh. But you put that under that headline—Justice and Sheriff Darden—most folk will think you just lost it. Nesha, I read that letter to the editor in the Tennessean and the editorial that said the same thing. Does Sheriff Darden belong in jail? If you and me had a done what he did, we'd be in jail. Why doesn't he belong in jail?"

"Well, the argument is look at the good he did for Grotman County. During his tenure, there were no murders, at least not of anyone who resided in Grotman County, real estate development flourished, burglaries and robberies were virtually non-existent. In making the County safe for the bad guys, he made it safe for its residents. Everyone benefited. So, his friends feel like he should pay a fine and be barred from ever holding public office—that would be sufficient punishment."

"But I read in the Tennessean that he had two Swiss bank accounts."

"Two Swiss bank accounts and three in the Grand Cayman Islands. Those accounts will probably be forfeited. That case is separate from the criminal trial." Lanetia frowned at her lopsided Humpty. Good…could good, lasting good, come from evil? That was a question for the philosophers.

"I don't like it. Maybe, just maybe, I want a family. If you a DA, you ever gonna want a family?"

"I hadn't thought about it that much." Lanetia pretended to stroke Brer Rabbit who was in her lap, purring loudly. Brer Rabbit looked more like a black raccoon than a cat. All he did was eat and sleep and protest as only he could if his bowl was not as full as he knew it should be.

"I have. You and me—our baby. Girl or boy, both, it don't matter. If it was money, I could say whatever you want…just tell me I'll get it for you. But it's not money. Makes it hard for a man when his wife wants what money can't buy. If you were DA, you'd go after those criminals who'd come to use the infrastructure that's waiting to be used. I remember, Nesha. I know somebody has to. Does it have to be you? The Paper's not enough, is it? I don't guess a baby would be either. Whatever happened between you and Ma—you need to tell me, so I can fix it. I can't fix a thing if I don't know what's broken and somethin's broken real bad between you two."

"Please don't bring up Vonnie Pearl. We're discussing Mona's letter. Let's stay on topic."

"If you want me to say go for it, I can't do it. I can't protect you if you do that," he said so softly that she almost couldn't hear him even though he stood by the window in their sitting room, looking out into the darkness.

"I appreciate that you want to protect me. Josh, how could we thrust a baby into the middle of this? I can't hover over a baby, hoping…" She stopped, suddenly afraid of saying too much.

"Hoping what, Nesha? Middle of what, Nesha? Talk to me."

She wanted to scream at him—*hoping your mother doesn't harm our baby because she hates me. She's crazy enough to do it. I know it, but you don't. I hope you never do.* "Hoping, that's what mothers do—they hope." It was the best she could do and it wasn't enough. And that was when she remembered a professor in a philosophy class saying that hope was not left in Pandora's Box as a passive last resort. Hope, in and of itself, is a futile response to an active evil. Hope was left to activate the fight or flight response. And, in the face of an active evil, subterfuge and flight were the survivors' response. Lanetia avoided Joshua's intense gaze, as he seemed to be trying to read her thoughts.

Joshua kneeled in front of her. "Cat, you and me can't both be in Nesha's lap. Scat." Brer Rabbit opened one eye and turned his face to Lanetia's stomach. "Don't mind me. You never have. Why start now? Nesha, fathers hope, too."

Later that night, a howling gust of wind startled Nesha awake. Before she slipped back into sleep, she remembered Joshua's words. Then, she had smiled. Now, in her sleep haze, she realized that Joshua had not been talking to Brer Rabbit.

"You like Nesha's SUV better than your truck?" Juston asked, as they delivered the newspapers. Juston liked collecting the money and restocking the newspaper bins.

"More comfortable," Josh grunted. Sleet pelted the windshield…

During the week before their wedding, Lanetia had shown Joshua some of her favorite places in and around Nashville. One day, after coming back from an antique store that specialized in vintage lace (Neither of the sisters would discuss the veil that even Joshua knew was only tacked to the tiara. As Lanetia had snipped the long, oddly placed stitches, Joshua had asked her what had happened. Lanetia had shrugged and changed the subject. Joshua found out later that Patrice had not liked the tiara that the veil was attached to and had hired an incompetent seamstress to alter the veil.), they'd stopped by Franklin's condo, as he was going to dinner with them. Joshua had noticed the Mercedes in the driveway, but thought it was Franklin's. They'd rented a van for the drive to Nashville, but on that day, they had borrowed Patrice's car. Patrice was using the van to haul decorations. Patrice was with Franklin, when Franklin, late as usual, arrived. Joshua liked Patrice. Patrice asked to see the lace and agreed the lace was an excellent match, especially the color.

Joshua also liked Patrice's on again-off again husband, Larmont. Lanetia's Dad liked Larmont. Probably because he was the principal at one of Nashville's magnet schools. Joshua had stayed with Larmont who had his own house, while everyone else stayed with Patrice. They'd stood around talking about nothing, until Patrice asked Lanetia about her car. He'd quickly understood Patrice wasn't talking about Hoopty. Lanetia hadn't sounded too concerned when she said she would sell it and get something else. That's when the argument started. Franklin and Patrice wanted to do something with the car and Lanetia was adamant in her no. Finally, Lanetia had said, *it's my car. I paid for it. I will do with it as I please. You two need to get a life or at least an understanding of personal property. I don't need a tax write off. If you do, invest in a fish farm. You'll never have to worry about paying taxes. What do you think you're going to do with a Mercedes in the hills of East Tennessee? Franklin had demanded. I'm not going to do anything with it in the hills of East Tennessee. It will be gone from your driveway in the morning. End of story. Let's go eat.*

Joshua didn't get a chance to ask Lanetia about the car until the next morning. Patrice dropped them off at Franklin's condo. *I have an errand. Want to come?* Joshua was surprised that the seats in the Mercedes were not leather covered. Patrice's and Franklin's cars had leather covered seats. Lanetia drove to a CarVerse Boutique. *I researched SUV's. This SUV is not made any more, but it has good reviews for its handling in hazardous road conditions.* Lanetia had shown him a picture of the SUV she wanted. Joshua had quickly read the review underneath the picture. The salesman had frowned when Lanetia had shown him the picture.

By chance, Joshua had heard the appraiser talking about Lanetia's car to the salesman. *I know someone who's been waiting for this model without leather seats. He'll pay top dollar and look at that mileage! What does she want for it? Trade, the salesman said. But, we don't have what she's looking for. I don't think the model she wants was ever sold in the States. I heard her say she'll try Global Auto Reclamations next. We can find exactly what she wants, the appraiser had declared. We have franchises in twenty states. Look in Montana, Michigan...that area. Call them. We can get a car here in three days max. I've got a buyer for her car. Make a deal. Got it?*

The salesman had found the vehicle Joshua was now driving at a CarVerse Boutique located in North Dakota. It hadn't even been prepped for sale. Joshua had thought Lanetia might not get a fair trade, but she'd already priced the Mercedes. They'd held a whispered conversation about the value of her car and the suggested retail of the SUV. Then, Joshua had negotiated the deal. Lanetia had gotten this SUV and cash.

"Wow, we made it up that hill and didn't slide once! This is my kind of truck. We can go anywhere. But, then you're a good driver. You'll teach me, right?"

"You bet. Got your money pouch ready? Take this can of Freeze-Not in case the key don't turn in the lock. Nesha don't want you out in this cold for a long time." Juston was a pro. He knew how to walk on the iced snow. He assessed the lock, squirted it with the Freeze-Not, and, within two minutes, he was back in the truck. He dumped the coins into a moneybag that was almost half full of coins. He entered some numbers into the spreadsheet displayed on the laptop and held a thumb's up to Joshua. Joshua carefully maneuvered the truck down the slippery hill. Only three more deliveries to make. Then home.

"It's been so long since I've worn a suit, it feels wrong. Does it look okay?"

"You look fine. You losing weight?"

"No, my dear. I'm building muscle."

"Told you to stay in the house."

"You don't like muscle?"

"You heard any complaints?"

"Miz McCory, Mr. Marlowe, come in. I've been on the lookout for you because we've moved Career Day from the cafeteria to the gymnasium. I want to take you through the school because the sidewalks are too icy to be safe. Salt's not helping at all. Just frozen salt water as there's been no sun today. The Principal fell this morning, but thankfully she wasn't hurt. My aide couldn't get in today. Pipes froze," Mrs. Thomason explained. "I'm having to meet people and tend to my class. Can you find your way from here?" At Joshua's nod, she rushed back the way they had come.

Joshua minded that Lanetia did not use his name. But as Zeezee said, why should she. Lanetia, to hear Zeezee tell it, had done the right thing.

Lanetia had debated and debated whether or not she could be Mrs. Joshua Marlowe or Lanetia McCory Marlowe or Lanetia A. Marlowe. Finally, she had folded and re-folded the forms for the change of name for social security and her driver's license and dropped them in the trashcan. She had added up the pluses and minuses and the minuses had won, and the only minus that really mattered was Vonnie Pearl. Taking the name Marlowe could be taken to mean that she had forgotten…that she and Vonnie Pearl had some commonality of interest that would bind them to a common purpose…that somehow she was like Vonnie Pearl.

They were the only African-American presenters. Afterwards, they each sat at a table with a backdrop about their respective professions made by the fourth and fifth graders and answered questions. They were there until the last bus had gone. It was only three thirty and it was as dark as night outside. Another storm was brewing.

"I saw Rachel; where'd she go?" Lanetia looked around before gently shaking Cinda who had fallen asleep with her head against Lanetia's shoulder. Juston was sitting beside Joshua, looking sleepy, but still awake.

Just then, Rachel came in, holding hands with a tall boy whose hair was plaited in thick braids. Lanetia noticed Joshua sizing up the boy.

"Josh, this be Amare. He live about three miles from here. Can we take him home? His parents just moved here from Atlanta. They with that new store that just opened up in Tiny Town."

"I think I met them. Is your last name Knollton?"

"Yes sir. My dad can come get me if …"

"No problem. You walked with Rachel from the high school?"

"Yes sir. It's kind of slippery. I didn't want her to fall."

"I guess I'm gonna have to carry Cinda. She too sleepy to walk. Excuse me. Nesha, don't pick her up. I'll get her. She too heavy for you to be carryin' around. Rachel, introduce your friend. They the ones I told you about…just moved here to manage the Dollar for More Store," he reminded Lanetia as he picked up Cinda.

"Seems like a nice boy, Rachel," Josh commented as he watched Amare enter the unlit brick house about a mile out of Tiny Town. "His parents must still be at work. The store doesn't close until six."

"Didn't you say they're openers?" Lanetia asked.

"Uh-huh," Josh grunted. He was concentrating on the ice and snow covered road, navigating the deep ruts caused by traffic up and down this treacherous mountain road. If one didn't straddle the ruts, one could get stuck in an icy rut, with no traction.

"What's that? Aren't they stayin'?" Rachel asked, too casually.

"Openers rarely stay with a store long term," Lanetia explained. "Their specialty is opening the store and ensuring that the store has the optimal mix of merchandise for a particular location and properly trained employees. They might stay with a store for a year. Usually it's around six months."

"He didn't tell me that," Rachel said, pouting a little.

"He didn't tell you that he and his parents moved around a lot?" Lanetia asked, wondering why Rachel had said nothing about Amare.

“Yes, I guess he did,” Rachel conceded. “He doesn’t like school.”

“Why?”

“He say there ain’t nobody to hang with. We don’t have a huge Black population, not like Atlanta.”

Animals forced one into a routine. Animals had to be fed and cared for each day, no matter how one felt. Lanetia was glad Josh only had the cows and chickens. Josh was talking about breeding one of the cows, but that was for the spring. For a moment, Lanetia admired the solar energy collectors that glinted off the side of the hill above the old homestead. Beside the solar energy collectors were two windmills. On this snowy, gusty day the vanes of the windmill were turning furiously.

Electricity, the energy she took for granted, was an iffy proposition in these hills. As more people lived year round in the gated communities, it was becoming a hot potato issue at the electric co-op’s meetings. She hadn’t written an editorial about the increasingly antagonistic meetings and it was because of the solar energy collectors and the windmills. If the electricity was out, as it had been for the past two days, Josh flipped a switch and they had the electricity needed for all the buildings on the property.

The batteries weren't that efficient. Josh was constantly tinkering with the batteries to improve their efficiency. That was the reason for the windmills—if the sun wasn't shining, there was the wind and, for the last week, there had been gusting winds along with the snow.

"Hold up, Nesha," Zeezee called from somewhere behind her. "Hold up, 'til …" The rest of what she said was lost in a swirl of snow and the whistling and moaning of the wind. "What you doing out in this mess?" Zeezee huffed. "I went to the old home place and you wasn't there. Couldn't you just sit with Josh while he watchin' that football game? Girl, it be Thanksgiving. It be about the only day he will sit down and relax and do somethin' he enjoy. Why you take that enjoyment away? That ain't you."

"If he did it before I came, then I'm certain I'm not part of the enjoyment," Lanetia retorted, her words as harsh as she intended. "You shouldn't be out in this. It's way below zero and cold makes your arthritis worse. I'm on my way back to the house."

"No, you ain't. You gonna walk back to the old home place and, like most days, we ain't gonna see you 'til dark. Today be Thanksgiving. We hostin' dinner, because ain't nobody got electricity but us. Josh keep offerin' to install… But you can't make a horse drink. Leastways, Josh got most of them to buy stoves run by propane like the heaters, but the propane got to last 'til the truck can make it back up here, which from the weather reports, ain't gonna be any time soon. So we get the company." Zeezee muttered the last as though the idea of company didn't enthuse her too much.

"Don't you like Josh to cuddle up with you? In the evenin' when we sittin' around, I been noticin' you act like he ain't there unless he make you notice him. Why you do that?"

"I'm not comfortable with public displays of affection." *Leave it alone, Zeezee.* But she wouldn't—Zeezee was on a mission. She perceived that Josh wasn't happy and she was going to do something about it.

"You like Josh, right? He ain't done nothin' to make you dislike him?"

With a sigh, Lanetia turned to look at Zeezee. The wind driven snow swirled around them. "We'd best get back. Zeezee, this isn't about Josh."

"Then who it be about? Why ain't you thinkin' about havin' me some great-grandchildren? Why you ain't eatin'? You can tell Josh all you want to that it be muscle. I ain't blind. You beginnin' to look like you did when I first met you…all bones. You was roundin' out nicely."

"I'm adjusting."

"To what? Why you don't let Vonnie Pearl teach you about the house?" *There... I said my daughter's name and even through all the layers of your clothes and mine, this wind and the snow and we ain't even touchin', I feel your withdrawal.*

"I have no desire to starch curtains or iron handkerchiefs."

"She know the way Josh like his food cooked."

"Then she best be around a long time to cook it just the way he likes it," Lanetia snapped back. "I'm not his maid."

"No, you his wife. What be wrong with the name Marlowe? Why you won't let anyone call you Mrs. Marlowe?"

"It causes confusion." *Zeezee leave it alone! Please.*

"You think it caused confusion when Vonnie Pearl married Andy?"

"Vonnie Pearl was very young. That's her identity. How do you think she would feel if she answered the phone and someone asked for Mrs. Marlowe and it wasn't for her? My way avoids a lot of unnecessary... What's that moving in the woods? See... Can't really see... A deer?"

"Lordy, Nesha," Zeezee said, brushing snow from her eyelashes, "that be one of the cows. How'd it get out of the barn?"

"Stupid cow, we shut the door and prop a piece of two by four against it. The wind must have blown the door open."

"Guess…"

"Why?" Lanetia questioned, anticipating what Zeezee was about to say. "Why would you tell Josh? You said this is his time to watch the football game. I can get the cow into the barn. All I need is a stick, but this branch will do," she continued. She reached up and broke off the tip of a low hanging branch. "Zeezee, go back to the house. The driveway… You can always tell where the driveway is," she said impatiently, pointing to the huge pine trees that someone had deliberately planted along both sides of the driveway.

Zeezee blinked the snow out of her eyes. *Where my eyes been all these years? I ain't never noticed them pine trees. But, then, I don't remember comin' out in winter much over the last twenty years and certainly not to walk down the driveway.* "My arthritis ain't been so bad since you got those lamps. I been readin' about them. That light do make you feel better. And, you right, we call on Josh to do every little thing. Make a man tired. You got the switch. I can help."

"It's too cold for you."

"Let that cow wait for a second. It ain't goin' nowhere. In the spring, you got to go to church. I been thinkin' on this. Sometimes you got to do what you don't want to. If goin' to church will keep the peace, then… No, you listen. Just listen to what I been thinkin' on," Zeezee pleaded, as she again felt Lanetia's withdrawal. "Josh be a deacon; his wife need to be there. You got a place in this community and… It be only two Sundays. Ignore what Pope say."

"There are some things that are non-negotiable," Lanetia said, carefully moving nearer to Zeezee so that she and Zeezee were almost nose to nose. "I didn't go to church before I met Josh and I'm not going now. Zeezee, Josh didn't ask you to do this, did he?" The scarf that was Zeezee's head went side to side. "I didn't think so. Before we married, Josh and I had a lengthy discussion about religion and spirituality. We agreed that we would have a spiritual union, but that it wouldn't be grounded in any religion. I acknowledged that he believed his path to spiritual wholeness to be through organized religion. I agreed to respect his path. He acknowledged that I believed my path to spiritual wholeness was through mindful experience. He agreed to respect my path. Just…I don't know…Josh's path and mine have converged…our path. But some of our individual paths are parallel and will never meet. We know and respect that.

"Zeezee, I want you to understand. I do not believe any religion can contain or guide my spirit. What you ask would imprison my spirit. I believe my spirit deserves more than fines and penalties in this life she has chosen."

"Well, that be that. Ain't never heard it put quite like what you sayin' but it do make some kind of sense to me. Kind of remind me when I was in the Islands. We'd be singin' and dancin' in a cove, with the soughing of the sea, a lullaby in the background, and sometimes I'd hear them talkin' like you talkin'. I always wondered how they knew so much. They went to church, but out there…what was in church didn't exist. Scared me until…Fayth…that was her name…said I'd never forget it…told me there was no reason for our spirits to worship fear. Better to worship a grain of sand, than to worship fear. But, I always had to come back here and, somewhere in the comins and goins, I forgot what she told me. People think you crazy if you don't do what they do. So you just reminded me of what I forgot. I won't ask again."

"I suppose Juston is getting a mixed message," Lanetia continued. Zeezee shrugged or maybe the gust of wind caused the movement of the too big coat to imitate a shrug. "I allowed Vonnie Pearl to take Juston to church. I went to church. I want Juston to understand the ignorance being spewed from that man and his ilk and I want him to have the common sense to reject it. Otherwise, he would be home with me. Zeezee, I want peace. I'd rather have peace, but, if that's the way to keep the peace, then let there be war. I'm hoping that the people who attend that church are civilized."

"You hopin' for a lot," Zeezee snorted in derision at Lanetia's presumption. "You do it your way. I done had my say and like I said…I think I understand."

"Josh married his whore and now he has to re-gain the respect of the church members, who, when you really think about it, have no religion. And horrors, the whore owns the County newspaper," Lanetia laughed, only then realizing what Zeezee was really talking about.

"Wouldn't have put it that blunt, but that pretty much sums up them hypocrites," Zeezee said with a grimace that might have been due to the swirling snow.

"Where'd that cow go?" Lanetia peered through the whiteness for a glimpse of the dun colored cow.

"Nesha, this snow gettin' pretty heavy. If we wander off the driveway…too easy to lose our way. We can't afford to lose that cow."

"Do you know what Josh named that cow? I can't tell the difference."

"Me, neither, Child. There be Bessie, Lottie, and Dunnie. Take your pick. I be from Atlanta."

Lanetia doubled over with laughter. She knew the cows' names; she just didn't know which cow was which. Her laughter was whipped from her by the gusting wind. She pulled her scarf more closely to her face. Zeezee seemed to have trouble standing in the wind that now whipped the branches of the trees back and forth. Stupid cow must have heard something familiar because it was ambling toward them. For some reason, it stopped under a maple tree whose branches were weighed to the ground with snow and ice. Lanetia swished the branch she held and sighed as she sank into a waist high drift of snow by the side of the driveway. The cow was obviously smarter that she was. Lanetia used the branch to prod the reluctant cow to the driveway. She, then, assessed Zeezee's clothing. *Should've done this before*, she chided herself. Zeezee had on Lanetia's long down filled coat that she wore in the mornings when doing chores with Josh. Her face and neck was muffled in a long scarf that she was rearranging now that she had finished talking. One of Cinda's stocking caps with a multicolored pompom was pulled down as far as it would go and she wore a pair of old boots. Lanetia took Zeezee's arm and they slowly made their way to the house, with the cow leading the way.

At the house, Lanetia made Zeezee go inside and she continued to the barn. Every once in a while, she could see the blurred outline of the barn. *Are all the stupid cows out?* But no, the other two cows were huddled together, languidly chewing their cud. Snow was piled in the doorway. Lanetia kicked enough of the icy mess out of the way, so the cow could get into the barn. *Okay, Lanetia, shovel out the doorway so you can close the door.* The heat lamp that Josh had rigged to keep the barn a little above freezing was no match for the frigid wind that was blowing through the barn.

Lanetia had almost finished shoveling the snow from the doorway when Josh appeared. He held out his hand for the shovel. Lanetia hesitated and he gestured again. Josh said something, but the rattling of the tin-roofed barn from the gusts of wind made it impossible to hear. Josh slapped his thigh with his right hand and again held out his hand. Lanetia decided to fight another battle and gave him the shovel. As soon as Josh finished clearing the doorway, he stepped into the barn where she stood protected from the icy blast of the wind and shut the door. "What you think you doin'? What do you think you doin'?" He repeated. "Answer me."

"Josh, I'm not Vonnie Pearl and I'm not your sisters. Do you agree?"

"Yeah, you my wife. I ain't seen you all day. Our first Thanksgiving. You could've helped Ma and Zeezee with the cookin'. You could've spent some time with me. I'll ask again…what you doin'?"

"Shoveling ice from the doorway in order to close the door."

"No, that ain't what you doin'."

"Then you know something I don't." They glared at each other for a long minute.

"We got people comin' to dinner. You need to be dressed."

"If I were you, I'd say thank you."

"I ain't got a thank you in me, because you ain't helpin' me. Maybe yourself; but not me. Come on. Cows be fine. I'll fix the door tomorrow. Can't even find that piece of two by four in all this snow and ice." There were some concrete blocks left over from building the foundation of the shed that was beside the barn. Josh closed the barn door and placed a concrete block against the door to ensure that it stayed closed.

As long as one didn't need to drive down the mountain, the people who lived in Crow Cut Cove could get around. Dinner was at four and there was a crowd by three. Roberta was there. Seems she had come to visit her parents. Lanetia had met Roberta once before. Roberta had said Lanetia wouldn't stay and Joshua would be back with her by fall. Roberta was very pretty in a gypsy kind of way. She was dressed in bright red…a red delicious apple red, and she matched from head to toe as she had a colorful, mostly red, scarf wound through her braided hair and her boots were a reddish brown.

Lanetia studied her own outfit—a brown blazer, with matching trousers and a black silk/mohair blend turtleneck. She could count the number of casual dresses that she owned on one hand. Even on this bitterly cold day, all the other women wore dresses. *Is this something else I have to consider? But I don't fit in with the women or with the men, so why try? Roberta was entertaining or, should I say, openly flirting with Josh. Roberta doesn't even know Josh well enough to sense he's too angry to respond. She thinks since he's not saying anything that he approves. She doesn't see that almost imperceptible wavy line creasing his forehead.*

I could care less about who's ill and who hasn't visited whom. So, Roberta, you can sing and dance. Enjoy yourself. Why do they look at me? Am I supposed to make a scene? I've never liked parades and the televised Thanksgiving Day parade is more interesting than Roberta's show. When can I leave? Why must I be polite? What was I doing last Thanksgiving? The tornado... Franklin and I helped the Aunts and Kaida clean up. All those old trees uprooted... Two sheds and a barn...all gone. You could stand where the barn used to be and see the path of the tornado. Nothing was harmed on either side of the path of destruction. When I talked to the aunts yesterday, they said it was sixty-five degrees. Why can't I be like Brer Rabbit. He'd had the good sense to do a walk through, then swish his tail and disappear. A tug on her arm interrupted her reverie.

"Josh is ready to bless the food so we can eat," Juston whispered to her. "He wants us to stand up."

For a moment, as she stood up, Lanetia's and Josh's eyes met—he was livid.

After the mercifully short prayer, Zeezee pulled her aside. "Girl, you was doin' the same thing that drove that Pope crazy that Sunday. You know it drive Josh into some kind of rage. He was already angry, then you sit as far from him as you possibly could and get that half-smile on your face. Can't nobody touch you when you go to that place…wherever it be. What you tryin' to do? You see that Roberta?"

"Zeezee, she was very entertaining, don't you think?"

"Have you lost your mind?" For a moment, Zeezee was speechless. Lanetia's expression said she was making something out of nothing. Zeezee took a deep breath. "Nesha, that woman be sittin' on Josh's lap and you lost in some world of your own makin'. Nesha, this the real world. It ain't pretty. People hurt you to get some gain for themselves. You livin' in this community, you need…"

"Must…need…got to…those are the words I hear from you and Josh. Zeezee, there are very few real musts, needs, and got tos. I'm not hungry." Lanetia turned and went up the stairs.

Zeezee stared at her retreating back. *If this keeps on, we gonna lose her. And I be beginnin' to think she want to be lost.*

"Nesha…"

"Juston, go back downstairs and eat your food," Nesha ordered, without looking up from the book she was pretending to read.

"Me and Cinda brought you some food. Those people aren't being very nice."

"They're just being people. Not nice; not un-nice. Thank you both."

"Can we stay with you, Nesha? There ain't any room downstairs."

"May...may we…and isn't, Juston…isn't any room." Juston frowned and shrugged. "Okay, move those two chairs to the desk," Lanetia said, nodding toward two side chairs, "and I'll clear the desk."

"Nesha, that Roberta…"

"Cinda, Roberta was being Roberta."

"Why didn't Josh stop her?"

"Maybe because it's a snowy Thanksgiving. People have been cooped up in their houses for the past week and people need some release. Everyone is laughing and having a good time. When neighbors get together, that's the way it should be."

"You weren't laughing, Josh wasn't laughing, Zeezee wasn't laughing, Cinda, me, and Rachel, we weren't laughing," Juston observed. "She wasn't funny."

"Entertaining doesn't necessarily mean funny. People like to participate in drama and the drama Roberta was acting in has entertained people for ages."

"I didn't like it. She was making fun of you."

"Yes, she was."

"Ain't you supposed to do somethin' when somebody make fun of you?" Cinda asked, frowning.

"Aren't… You can, but it usually doesn't work. Ignoring, in the long run, is the only response that really works."

Outside in the hallway, Josh was listening. He had a plate of food in his hand. Lanetia was right, but then she usually was. He opened the door. "I brought you some food, but I see them two beat me to it."

"Thanks. I'm sure it won't go to waste."

"You comin' back downstairs?"

"I don't want her to," Juston said. "I don't…"

"Juston, they just bein' people."

"But…"

"The kids be lookin' for you two."

"I'll be down after I finish eating. How's that?" Compromise. Make the effort. Why didn't he understand that she didn't belong downstairs? Why couldn't he say that he understood her point of view? He wouldn't. He couldn't, wouldn't understand past his view of the ideal husband and wife. She had thought of the words to express some of what she felt and she would have said them, but for Cinda and Juston who weren't even pretending not to listen, not only to their words, but also to the undercurrents between the two of them that were saying more than words ever could.

"Fine. That be just fine."

CHAPTER 4

I am holding an ice cube to the tip of my nose. A voice is asking why are you doing such a silly thing. A nosebleed another voice suggests. The ice is not melting and a huge yellow sun shines, but I am not sweating, nor do I feel its warmth. Wake up…yet another voice says. One of the voices protests, but the voice that says wake up is insistent.

Cold… Lanetia, as if in a dream, searched for and found her old, red terry cloth robe that lay across the foot of the bed for added comfort for her feet. For a moment, she stared at Josh's back. Angry…Josh was angry. They had never promised not to go to bed angry and Josh slept, armored in his emotion. Lanetia considered in that moment whether or not she cared that they had never made the promise and that Josh was angry, even in his sleep. She decided she did not. She briefly wondered if his dreams were as angry as his rigid body indicated. Anger created a welcome space between them. One day I will exploit his anger for and to my advantage. I know and accept that about myself. I am lucky. Josh does not snore. Tonight, his anger made it easy for her to slip out of their room. Lanetia shivered and tied the sash of the robe. For a moment she reveled in its tattered comfort. Josh frowned whenever she wore it. He had bought her a robe. It was red, but he didn't understand the comfort she felt when she wrapped her old, patched robe around her. This robe had seen college, law school, private practice, and Nashville. This house with the starched curtains was not hers, but this robe was.

She peeked in on Rachel and Cinda and then Juston. Rachel and Cinda were buried under their quilts. Juston's left hand was outside his covers. She arranged the covers, so he too was buried under the quilt. She checked their bathrooms and turned on the cold water to drip.

Lanetia rarely went into the kitchen, but she was shivering. Tea…with lots of honey. A nightlight on the exhaust vent dimly lit the kitchen. She filled the small tea kettle and swayed to music that only she heard.

"I'll have me some of that if you don't mind." Lanetia stiffened. *Vonnie Pearl—what was she doing up?* "There be enough water for two cups. Won't take long to boil." Vonnie Pearl set a dainty china cup and saucer beside Lanetia's mug. "You and me need to talk."

"About what?" Lanetia surprised herself. The question came out neutral and not aggressive and confrontational.

"No reason for what happened today except you settin' yourself above the people in this community. They don't like…"

"No. We don't need to talk," Lanetia interrupted. *How dare you chastise me? Moral hypocrite. Church on Sunday; murder on Monday. I'm insane to be living in the same house with you.* She turned to face Vonnie Pearl. Vonnie Pearl stepped back when she saw and felt Lanetia's cold hostility.

"I done… Everything I done was to protect my family. I ain't gonna let you tear us apart. I done told you this."

"Yes, you have. Why are you telling me again? I understood you the first time." Lanetia didn't try to hide the impatience that sneeringly mocked Vonnie Pearl's attempts to explain.

"You can't keep ignorin' me. We in this house together."

"Watch me." The words were a boast, a taunt, a call to arms. "The water's boiling." Lanetia busied herself finding a potholder. She filled Vonnie Pearl's teacup with hot water.

"Take your tea and go to bed, Vonnie Pearl," Zeezee spoke from the darkness of the dining room. She stood at the swinging door. Lanetia could just make out the smoky tendrils of her breath. "I heard you get up. Put some more water in that tea kettle, Nesha.

Go to bed, Vonnie Pearl. You done your dirt. Whatever it was, you really done it this time."

Vonnie Pearl dropped a teabag into the cup and left, stopping only to warn Lanetia with a look that said Josh is my son. Lanetia moved deeper into the shadows as she was not sure that she could control the revulsion that fought within her to be expressed. Zeezee warmed her hands in the heat rising from the stove. "Two spoonfuls of honey in my cup," Zeezee said, as Lanetia spun around the Lazy Susan. Zeezee chose a teabag from the tea caddy. "I heard you get up and check on the kids. I would've done it, but I just couldn't make myself get up. I was all warm and cozy and I was driftin' back to sleep when I heard Vonnie Pearl. She been mutterin' about talkin' to you since you and Josh came in from the barn. I need to know what Vonnie Pearl done. It gonna eat at us and tear us apart—the very thing she don't want. You can keep on ignorin' her, just like you ignored them fools today, but it ain't healthy. Josh told me what you told the kids and you right. They'll eventually go their way, but it be different when you dealin' with family. Especially, family you live with."

"Maybe you should've asked your daughter to stay. I have no answers to your questions."

"Funny, she don't either."

“What…” Josh began, startling both of them.

“Boy, you scared me.”

“Zeezee, I didn’t mean to scare you. What you two doin’ standin’ in the dark drinkin’ tea and not wakin’ me up? This house be freezin’. Pipes could freeze…”

“Nesha’s got the water runnin’ in the kids’ baths. I got mine runnin’. Water runnin’ in the kitchen… How the pipes gonna freeze? It can wait ‘til mornin’ which ain’t too far off.”

Josh ducked an answer to his grandmother. “Cup of tea?” Lanetia nodded. Vonnie Pearl always hung his favorite mug on a hook beside the stove. He liked the hazelnut tea, with lots of milk and one teaspoon of raw sugar. Josh had first tried the sugar in his coffee and decided he didn’t like it, then he’d tried the sugar in his tea and he was hooked. Lanetia handed the mug to him and he took a cautious sip, before winking at her.

He reached out his other hand toward her and she cuddled up to him. “You cold?”

“Not now…just awake.”

“You and Zeezee arguin’ or discussin’?” He took another sip and looked from the one to the other.

"Neither. Zeezee asked me a question and I didn't have an answer. The State is taking over Bond's bank. Bond has had a stroke and is in a rehabilitative facility. Word is he will be transferred to a nursing home. There should be no disruption in service and, surprisingly, the accounts are in order."

"Zeezee, were you askin' Nesha about the bank?"

"No, but it don't matter. Nesha did answer part of my question. I'm goin' back to my quilt. I'll check on Vonnie Pearl."

Joshua thoughtfully finished his tea. Nesha wasn't the least bit tense. It was as though they were deciding whether to have peas or green beans for dinner. Nesha didn't play games; she wasn't going to talk about whatever Vonnie Pearl was upstairs crying about. "You never did tell me what your family did at Thanksgiving," he said, just to break the silence.

"Nothing much. Thanksgiving was never a big holiday for us—not with teachers as parents. Sometimes, Patrice and I cook if our aunts are away. Franklin and some friends might come to dinner. We usually visited the aunts that you met at the wedding. Since Franklin left for college, Dad visits his family."

"So you just don't like the people here?"

"I neither like nor dislike them. Why the third degree?" Lanetia looked at him, almost smiling. He couldn't read her.

"What do you miss most about Nashville?"

"I'd have to think about that... Maybe...my classes. I taught Legal Writing at the Community College and I taught tennis at one of the community centers. I guess I should do the museum thing. Last fall...a couple of friends and I curated a show for the Bontemp Museum. We collect Black Memorabilia. I collect advertisements featuring Auntys and Mammys; Tanya collects figurines; and Diné collects furniture. Our collections kind of overlap. Miss it? I don't know if that's the right question. I miss the opportunity to do things and not be thought odd. In a place like this, one has to decide whether to follow one's muse or to fit in. Mr. Holzer told me that. It's like you said, seems like a long time ago...too many eggshell feelings."

"Well, Zeezee, you ain't out in this cold for your health. Why you out here?"

"Last night... Nesha... What she say?"

"Exactly what she say. No games. I asked her about what you think might be botherin' her. It don't. Somethin' Ma did bothers her. End of story. You get Ma to talk?"

"If I ask her, she get one of her headaches. That gas line never busted before."

"When the last time we had cold like this for this long?"

"Twenty, maybe thirty years…I heard on the radio. You don't need to be out here fixin' on it. The wood stove heat the house. Feel like a furnace inside. Only reason you got this propane is cause you hate choppin' wood. Don't say nothin' until *I* be finished. You done chopped enough wood from them storm trees that fell in the last couple of years to last for five years. Hush…you don't say nothin' Leave this be. We don't need it. Now, say what you have to say."

"Nesha already been out here fussin' at me. She send you? I see her peekin' around the corner. She makin' sure you tell me what she already done told me?"

"What if she did? She right. This ain't your area of expertise. I repeat…the house ain't cold. Can't you regulate the heat comin' from that old stove?" Josh nodded, but it was just to placate Zeezee. He had no intention of doing anything but making sure the fire did not burn out. He'd wanted to get rid of the old stove, but his Dad had said it would come in handy. They'd hadn't had to use the wood stove for over five years and there was plenty of wood from the storm felled trees. "You listenin' to me?" Josh nodded again and began to fill in the very small hole he'd dug in the partially frozen earth. Zeezee would fuss until he came in.

"We got electricity. Let that gas line be before you blow us and you up."

"The gas turned off. Just wanted to see if I could fix it. McGillicuddy say the pipe probably busted near the house. The ground ain't as froze near the house and he say the pipe been failin' near the connection to the buildings. McGillicuddy say he don't have the right kind of pipe to fix it and, even if he did, with his workload, he wouldn't be able to fix it for a couple of weeks.

"Josh, don't neither one of us need to be out in this weather."

"Alright, I hear you. I'm quittin'. You satisfied?" he grumbled and said it louder so that Lanetia, who again had peeked around the corner of the house, could hear. He heard the door close as he patted the last of the hard clumps of earth into hole. "I ain't gonna be in a cold house until spring, so get used to it bein' hot. That wood stove was made to put out the heat."

"You just bein' contrary," Zeezee said, just as Lanetia opened the porch door. She waved to them as she headed around the house.

Where she goin' in this mess?"

"Why you ask me that? You know where Nesha goin'. Now, who be fussin'? Sun up to sun down…the old home place.

She writin' an article about the Bank and another one about how people copin' with the cold. She also ain't comin' to the house for lunch. She never do. Anything else you know, but still just have to ask?

"Another thing—Sunday… She ain't gonna get up to hear you read from the Bible. It be history and it ain't her history."

"You two are just too alike. You sure she ain't kin to you?"

"She better not be; she married to you."

"Ma, where everybody?"

"Your headache gone?" Vonnie Pearl nodded, as she looked out the living room window to the snow covered deserted yard. She retied the curtain sash and checked the other to make sure the bows matched. "The kids sleddin' down by the old home place. Josh in his office. Why?"

"I got to tell you somethin'. Josh… I heard him readin' to the kids about David and Bathsheba. You know how David sent Uriah to his death so that he could have Bathsheba. You remember that story?"

"Sure. Their first born son died for his father's sin. Guess his mother's, too. From what happened later on in the story, I don't think she had any problem with how she got her position."

"Ma, it ain't funny."

"You never did have a sense of humor."

"I asked Dick to kill Nesha." Vonnie Pearl spoke quietly as though she didn't want to be heard.

Zeezee, who had been busy quilting... Time froze. "When you do that?" was all she could think to say, as she stared at the brightly colored material. Zeezee could not look at her daughter.

"This summer. I was gonna take her to his camp. He was gonna kill us all. I asked him to kill her first."

"She know? How she know?"

"I couldn't go through with it. And he couldn't do it no way. He dead from that snakebite. Probably would've died from that gunshot wound. Ain't you gonna ask me how I met him?" Zeezee waved her right hand in the air. That satisfied Vonnie Pearl. "Before Andy... I was in the Cee Bee in Salyna. He come up and introduced himself. He told me I was gonna suffer, just like you made him and his mama suffer. I told Andy. He already knew who he was. Andy said he would know who his true enemy was if he could find out who was lettin' Dick out of that mental institution. Andy wouldn't tell me what you done. I had to figure that out for myself.

"That be why you like that Nesha? She just as whorish as you was? Don't matter. I be tired of the headaches. I be tired of bein' punished. She say she won't ever like me, that she won't take Josh away. I see it in her eyes, Ma. She ain't gonna stay and, if she don't stay, Josh ain't gonna stay. Ma, I just want us to be together."

"Vonnie Pearl, I ain't gonna apologize for what I done. Sometimes love take you places, you wasn't raised to go. What I done was right for me." *David... That story...* "Vonnie Pearl, don't you tell Pope what you just told me." Zeezee felt as if a chasm had opened and she was one step from tumbling in. From Vonnie Pearl's expression of relief, she had guessed correctly.

"But I got to confess."

"Go in the woods and confess to a tree. Don't you tell Pope. You want it all over two Counties?"

"He a man of God. He…"

"He a ignorant, petty, trash talkin' devil. You hear me… You hear me like you ain't never heard me before—just because you think his mouth open and shut like a Bible, don't mean his words ain't evil. Four people know about what you tried to do—one be dead, so that leave us three… That be all that need to know. If you feel the need to confess, you come talk to me."

"What about my soul?"

"David prayed. He didn't go out and make no public confession."

"He talked to his priest."

"I know, baby, but we ain't got no priest. You got to see Pope for what he be. He jealous of Josh and will do anything to bring ruin to him. If he do, Josh **will** leave. You got to see that, Vonnie Pearl. You got to understand. Some men just say they got a message from God. Pope one of them. He just want to be in people's business so he can hurt them. Why you think Miz Flora stopped church? Why you think I stopped church?"

"Rev. Pope say you two like the witch of Endor. You talk to the devil and the devil tell you things."

"But it wasn't no devil who told us that Nesha was at that clinic with the girls and that she was huggin' on a man? That wasn't no devil? But I ain't judgin'. That be for a higher power. Take it to God, Vonnie Pearl. Don't take it to no man of this Earth."

For the first time since Vonnie Pearl had wandered into the living room, their eyes met. Zeezee saw a hint of calm in the wildness. Why had she never seen it before? Nesha saw it. Nesha knew what was there. If I knew what she knew, I wouldn't want no babies either, Zeezee admitted to herself. Nesha was in a precarious position. Zeezee dropped the quilt to the floor. “You feel like startin’ dinner?” Vonnie Pearl nodded. Soon there was the clatter of pans and Vonnie Pearl singing…something she had not done for months.

If Nesha hadn’t married Josh, then Vonnie Pearl wouldn’t have even the hint of the illusion that things might work out. Nesha was willing to give Vonnie Pearl that chance. Does that boy have any idea how much she loves him? Did I have any idea how much she loves him? I been thinkin’ all kinds of wild things because…

What did I do wrong? I tried to protect Vonnie Pearl. Cousin tried to protect her. P never wanted to hurt nobody, least of all his wife. Like P said, his father needed the woman’s name and money to advance his business. And, at the time, P didn’t care. She was in love with him; he was just with her. I was sixteen when we met. With his long black hair and pecan colored skin, he looked like the Indian braves in the movies. My mama always said you could choose who to love. I remember my sister screamin’ at her that it wasn’t true. She didn’t marry the boy she was so in love with. Daddy said he’d kill them both. After that, she married that boy who wasn’t no good, but Daddy approved of his family.

I birthed Vonnie Pearl when I was eighteen. I couldn’t go home. My Daddy told me never to darken his door with no bastard child. I had to take him at his word, because he barred the door to Purlie when she got pregnant. When she married the baby's father, before he would speak to her, he made her stand in front of all those awful people and confess her sins. Didn't make her husband, just Purlie. Like Purlie told me...she only did it for her husband. He wanted to be a deacon.

Hellfire and damnation—that be what he preached every Sunday. He had all this love, but none for his wife or children. Nesha asked me what I be made of. Should've told her the truth... I don't know. I always been too scared to know. He wouldn't even let me see Ma when she was dyin', even though I could hear her callin' my name. The only thing I could do was get that angel marker for her grave after he died. Purlie might still be among the livin'. I got to find out if any of their children be like Vonnie Pearl. Then I can think on what to do.

CHAPTER 5

Zeezee, did not have on coat or a scarf, just the sweater she wore around the house and one of Cinda's stocking caps that barely covered her ears. "I'm trying to write an article. You're not dressed for this weather," Lanetia fussed as Zeezee discarded the cap in the chair by the kerosene heater. Zeezee's eyes searched the room as though someone might be hiding in a corner or behind a chair.

"I be fine. Guess it be so hot in the house, I don't feel the cold. Stop what you doin' and listen to me good."

"I'm sorry she told you," Lanetia said, when Zeezee paused, searching for the words to continue. "It's not your fault, if that's where this is going. Vonnie Pearl made her choices."

"Nesha, you listen to me. I thought of somethin'. You do that genealogy. See if any of my family still livin'. I can't help Vonnie Pearl if I don't know what happened to my family. You know I be right. I can't tell Josh. I ain't never told him about my people."

“Drink this. It’ll warm you.” While Zeezee had been talking, Lanetia had turned up the heat and made hot chocolate on the hot plate. The windows were streaming water that was almost instantly refreezing. The lights blinked. “I must be pulling too much electricity. The batteries don’t last as long in this cold weather.”

“You’ll do it?”

“For you. Because the information will help you.”

“I know they say don’t keep secrets from your husband, but unless he asks you directly, I want this between us. I don’t know the words to tell him what his Ma wanted done to you. When I know what happened to my sisters and brothers, I’ll find the words. I’ll tell him. I’ll tell him I done lived a lie.”

“I consider it your secret, so it’s not mine to tell. Zeezee, as soon as spring comes, you know she will tell Pope, don’t you? For her, it’s all in that so-called good book. She must confess her sins.”

“She didn’t tell before. She might not.”

“She’s having bad dreams and headaches… Her dreams scare her and the headaches linger. She doesn’t understand that it’s all internal…a guilty conscience…and not some avenging god punishing her for an evil act. She doesn’t see the evil in Pope and she doesn’t understand how jealous Pope is of Josh.”

"What ya doin', Josh?" Cinda asked, as she hovered at the door of his workshop, waiting for an invite. Josh nodded. As always, Juston was close behind her. During the weeks before Christmas, Cinda always tried to find her presents. This year she had enlisted Juston's help. They'd looked in the attic and in all the closets and found nothing. Rachel had told Cinda that sometimes Vonnie Pearl would hide their presents in Josh's workshop.

Josh held up the picture he was framing.

"That's when you and Nesha stayed at that bed and breakfast after you got married." Juston talked fast, just so he could say it before Cinda did. Cinda playfully poked him with her elbow.

"Not in my workshop," Josh warned. "There be too much here for you to hurt yourself on. Don't tell Nesha…please."

"We're not babies. We know how to keep a secret," Cinda promised, her voice full of meaning that was not lost on Josh.

"Ain't none of your secrets here. So don't come lookin' when I ain't here. Books?"

"Nesha's lettin' us take a break. I be glad when school starts again. We ain't been to school but two days since Thanksgiving. Juston said he saw Presten when you was out deliverin' newspapers and he ain't picked up a book. Nesha done called our teachers and they done told her what we supposed to be studyin'. They even e-mail her stuff for us to do."

"Then I know two students who won't be behind when school start, whenever that be. It just stop snowin' to start again and this ain't even winter. Look at it come down."

"Josh..." Juston began hesitantly. Josh glanced at Juston who was frowning, obviously worrying over what he wanted to say.

"Uh-huh."

"Mr. McGillicuddy won't fix anybody's gas line. You gave the pipe you had to him."

Josh interrupted him. "I did not give it to him. He bought it. He and I talked to the manufacturer and that pipe I was savin' for who knows what could be used to patch the gas lines. I asked around to the folks who needed their gas lines patched and they said no."

"He didn't want any bad press," Juston said, continuing as though he had not heard. He was that upset because he did not understand why people were saying ugly things about Lanetia.

"Well, he got what he didn't want. You saw the story."

"Why won't he use the pipe to fix everyone's gas line?"

"Nesha talked to him before she did the story. But like she said, he between a rock and a hard place—he can't get the type of pipe he need for the gas line. I happened to have somethin' that would work, but in the spring the gas lines he repaired will have to be replaced."

"Why can't he put in what he has stacked at his business?"

"Regulations. Pipe not rated for these conditions and if he put it in the ground and it fail, he could be sued. We may never have another season like this for another thirty years, but the pipe he been usin' just won't hold up as everyone is findin' out. Juston, he used the pipe I sold him to fix the gas lines at the clinic in Tiny Town and at the old folks' home on Cherry Hill. He didn't fix ours because I figured we could make it with the wood stove for the rest of this winter. Good thing he didn't because he needed all of it to repair the gas lines in those two places."

"You could've kept it for us. We suffer, too," Juston challenged, still trying to work out for himself, why Josh hadn't kept the pipe for their neighbors to use.

"Like I said, I asked them. If McGillicuddy had some pipe left over, he wouldn't have used the pipe to fix their gas lines unless they signed an agreement not to sue him. They wouldn't do that. The old folks' home and the clinic signed the agreement. Some folk suffer because of their own short-sightedness."

"Everybody say we get special treatment," Cinda said.

"Juston, Cinda, folk talk. What they think, what they say just ain't true. We kept that wood stove. We warm, even though our gas line was not repaired. They could've kept theirs. They didn't. They were modernizing and didn't see no need to keep the old. I have to admit, I wouldn't have either. My Dad never could bear to throw away somethin' when nothin' was wrong with it. At the time, I said to myself that eventually I would talk him around to my way of thinkin'. Now, I see his wisdom.

"Let me tell you about people talkin'. I went to college. Folk talked. I came back. Folk talked. Nesha came. Folk talked. We married. Folk talked. Can't stop folk from talkin'. When they want help, you try to help them. That's all a body can do. And try not to hold any grudges," he added as an afterthought. "Let it go," he advised. "If you do your homework and don't fuss, maybe I can talk Nesha into lettin' you watch a movie this evenin'. Franklin sent a box of movies. I picked it up today."

Lanetia sat at the desk in their sitting room finishing an article on the school system. There was only one high school in Grotman County and two elementary schools. None of the schools were open. Not only were the roads impassable, but also the schools had no heat and the water pipes had burst when there had been a sunny day between snow storms. How were the children to pass the required standardized tests if they had only two solid months of schooling? How could one expect them to test on grade level? What about the federal funding based on the number of days the children attended school?

Lanetia had talked to the school superintendent and either he was ignorant of the issues or just didn't care. Lanetia was of the mind that he was ignorant and he didn't care. But, to be sure, she asked Josh. "Baylin in over his head. Last spring, the State almost took over the schools. The school system is on notice that if the students don't do better on the standardized test, then the State will take over. Instead of tellin' the County that he needed buses that could navigate these roads in all kinds of weather, the schools' renovated, and more teachers…experienced teachers, not these this-is-a-way-to-pay-off-my loans teachers, he told them the Black kids were draggin' down the scores because they didn't come to school.

"Of course, he got mad when I did a statistical analysis showin' that the small number of Black students couldn't lower the scores. That was just before you came. Baylin wanted to put a school up here for the Black kids. Tell you the truth, I wasn't against it until Baylin laid out his plan to put them on some kind of track which would've deprived the kids of a high school diploma. He be the worst kind of racist. Always doing somethin' for you that turn out to be the worst thing you could've wished on yourself. There used to be a school…by the church. Been torn down for years. Some folk would like to have it back. I would, but not on the terms he be offerin'. He tell you any of that?"

"No. Zeezee told me some. I read some back issues of the newspaper…that told me some. Now, you're telling me more. The Department of Education has had it with Baylin. My source tells me the Department wants him out. I'll sleep on this article. I want to say too many things that are not politically correct. Was everyone okay?" Josh and Juston had gone visiting that afternoon to make sure everyone had kerosene, wood, food. The phone lines were down again because of snow laden tree limbs breaking and taking the lines down with them.

"I got everybody supplied, but folk gettin' kind of crazy, sittin' in their houses with nothin' to do. I gave out the homework, but I don't think any of the kids will do it. They got the attitude…you only do schoolwork when you go to school. I know the kids complain, but I heard Rachel talkin' to Ma and she was sayin' she was glad she was busy because it made the day go by faster."

“I saw D’Arton’s bruises. Did his mother take her frustrations out on him or did he fall?”

“His mama. That be why I brought him to stay the night. Give them a break from each other. Did I tell you that his father be Mericus?” Lanetia nodded. “You know how to get in touch with him? Maybe, if he doin’ okay, he might do somethin’ for D’Arton.”

“I have a phone number…somewhere. I’ll call him. I’ve been thinking, if the weather clears, I’d like to go to Atlanta. I listened to the weather. There’s no ice on the Interstate. The back roads are another story. Mother Nature isn’t cooperating.” Josh grimaced, then shrugged. Mother Nature hadn’t cooperated for months. Blue skies…he’d forgotten that the sky could be blue, with not a gray, threatening cloud in sight.” You okay with that?”

“I ain’t invited?”

“Only if you want to go. I want to do some shopping.”

“That you can’t do in Knoxville, Chattanooga, or Nashville?”

“I could, but I want to go to Atlanta. There’s this jewelry outlet store in Atlanta I like to go to. For Christmas, I ordered Rachel and Cinda charm bracelets and this store has unusual charms, sold only in the store. A silversmith from upstate Georgia makes the charms. I called the store and he's made some gold ones. Look at these." Lanetia spilled the contents of a small, yellow drawstring bag into his hand. "The owner was really helpful. She took my order over the phone and she doesn't usually do that. I'd like to get them some more. Something the matter?" Josh shrugged, his expression closed. "Hold the charms in your hand and I'll attach them to the bracelets." Lanetia held up one of the bracelets. "Every three links?" Josh counted the charms and nodded. "I thought we agreed…"

"Yeah, we did. You want to stay overnight?"

"No, this weather is too unpredictable. If there's a lull, I could get up, help with the chores, and do a turnaround trip. If you went, I could drive down and you could drive back or vice versa."

"May have to be after Christmas. You mind?"

"No."

"D'Arton, I cannot permit you to disturb Cinda, Juston, or Rachel while they're studying. If you do not wish to study, then you may put on your outdoor clothes and go outside for a walk or you can go upstairs and take a nap."

"Why they got to study? We on break. You don't have to study if school ain't in." He reiterated his defiance by tossing a wadded up piece of paper in Juston's direction.

"You really don't know why you have to study or . . ."

Her question caused D'Arton to frown. "I ain't got to study at home," he muttered.

"D'Arton, you were one of the students held back last year, weren't you?" At his sullen nod, Lanetia continued. "Cinda wasn't held back. She wasn't passed because her last name is Marlowe. During the breaks in the school year, she had to study. Josh talked to her teacher and got her lessons. He's done the same thing this year. Don't you remember him coming to your house and giving your homework to your mother?" D'Arton sullenly nodded again. "You were supposed to study. Didn't he offer to help you with what you didn't understand?" D'Arton stared at the crumpled paper in front of him and a single tear wet the paper.

"You live in a community and a society that that has no use for you, except as an inmate…in a prison. Do you know what the white churches are doing? Since the snowstorm, the last of October, there have been tutors available for the children who attend those churches. Parents drop their children off at the Baptist church and they stay most of the day. They aren't playing; they aren't watching television; they're studying. When school opens, your teacher won't be starting where you left off. She'll do a hurried review, but she'll be starting with the last lesson they finished at the church and you'll be left behind again. I wrote an article on the role of the churches in educating the youth of the community when the schools are closed because of the weather.

"The Cove doesn't have a functioning church during the winter. Josh offered to hold school in our home, but no one wants to do that. Yet, your parents want you to pass. Well, you won't. And no one will cry a tear because you don't. As I said before, you'll be fodder in the criminal justice system, keeping some white guard employed. You're eight; sorry; we don't have the luxury of waiting to decide whether or not we'll play by their rules.

"When too many of us figure out their rules and how to use them to our advantage, they will change the rules. That's the way it works. You will not disturb these three. They have plans for their future." Lanetia pretended not to see the tears streaking D'Arton's cheeks and her expression dared the three who were staring at her to offer him any comfort. She gave D'Arton another work sheet of math problems and pushed the pencil toward his hand. D'Arton picked up the pencil and began to work the addition and subtraction problems. She eyed Rachel, Juston, and Cinda in turn and they each bent over their respective lesson.

"Nesha, come help me in the kitchen," Zeezee called out.

“Zeezee, I’m busy,” Lanetia said, as the swinging door swung closed behind her.

“What you said need to sink in. D’Arton smart, but his mama didn’t finish high school. She was held back. You seen what Mericus was up to,” she said in a whisper so the children in the next room couldn’t hear what she said. “When Josh was comin’ up, if he didn’t understand somethin’, Andy would take him to the teacher’s house. Didn’t matter if it was times like this with the snow. If Josh said he didn’t understand, Andy was at that teacher’s house, tellin’ him or her, that his boy did not understand and to explain it to him and he’d teach his boy. Josh was the only child in this community to graduate when he was supposed to. Josh and, now, you doin’ the same thing for them three. The parents in this Cove just keep sayin’ the same tired things they been sayin’…*Those Marlowe kids pass just because their name is Marlowe. If I had a gone to college, they’d treat my kids like the Marlowe kids. And with him marryin’ Miss I-Ain’t-From-Here, they ain’t never gonna fail them kids.*

“They don’t see you or Josh supervisin’ the kids all mornin’ and afternoon, makin’ sure they do their lessons, makin’ sure they readin’ and not lookin’ at television or playin’ video games. And, if they see it, they think we puttin’ on a show for them. They think you printin’ the lesson plans for all the grades in your Paper cause there ain't nothin' else out there to fill up the space. They still don't understand that if Baylin put a school up here that the diploma the kids would get wouldn't be accepted at the colleges and them with the jobs don't have to accept it, either. It'd be called a Certificate of Attendance. What good that gonna do these kids?

"To this day, I don't think Vonnie Pearl understand why I made her finish high school. That be why I took over raisin' Josh. Andy understood. He finished high school and he almost completed that two year business school when the Army came nosin' around. Andy had some kind of reputation around here, but, then, he grew up in Detroit. There was a part of Andy that would just as soon shoot you as to look at you. And listenin' to John, his granddad, only ingrained it in him more. Nobody messed with Josh or Rachel.

"I remember one of Rachel's teachers told her she was stupid. Andy went to the school board and got that teacher fired. Said he would sue them, the teacher, the State, and got himself this crazy Black lawyer out of Chattanooga, Alton Aleston—you heard of him?"

"Zeezee, he was one of the best Civil Rights Attorney in the Country."

"He be crazy. Him and Andy used to sit in the dinin' room at the same table those children sittin' at and you should've heard them talk. Anyway, that school board held out for two weeks. Then, that teacher was gone. I wish you could've known Andy. He would like you. You ain't very tactful, but... *Thanks, Zeezee.* You welcome. But maybe you could go around with Josh after Christmas and talk to the mamas. Ain't that many daddies around and maybe you can intimidate them into makin' their children study so they won't fail."

"After Thanksgiving, do you really think they'd listen to anything I say?"

"I do. Even Minnie, who can't stand you, cause you uppity, say you got class. Consensus be that Roberta made a fool of herself. Josh should've gotten himself one of them SUV's years ago. Make life a lot easier. That SUV a lot more comfortable than his old truck. You mind him drivin' it all the time?"

"What? Zeezee, slow down...SUV?"

"You mind him drivin' it all the time?"

"No. I don't like driving on icy roads, steep inclines, roads with no guard rails and abysses on both sides of the road. I'll do it if I have to. I think Josh likes it."

"Yeah, Andy was like that. Just had to get out to see what there was to see. Well, Vonnie Pearl ain't scared to ride with Josh in that SUV. Josh can drive pretty scary in that old truck and me and Vonnie Pearl don't usually go no place when the weather get like this. But that SUV make it different somehow. Tomorrow, when we go grocery shoppin' in Salyna, I be goin' to see Flora. Today, Josh took Vonnie Pearl to the bank in Tiny Town. I don't think none of us gonna go stir crazy this year.

"D'Arton's mother, she usually a good mother, but in winter, folks get strained. You doin' all you can some days to keep warm. You take this warm oil out to the porch. Make the house smell so good when we make this hair oil. I was kind of worried about money this year since we didn't have a booth last summer and you can't expect somebody to sell your wares like you do. But Nina done told so many of her friends, I been makin' a batch every week. And you got those friends of yours in Nashville and D.C. to sell it in their beauty shops. Always have a backup. Will a day or two help?" she asked, giving the oil a final stir.

"I did think about reporting her, but I thought better of it. He'd certainly be a lost child if the State ever took custody. And the whites have the same problem. That's one of the reasons that the churches open up when school is out because of the weather.

You know about the child who was killed a few years back."

Zeezee nodded. "The father just snapped."

CHAPTER 6

Lanetia stared at the picture—Judge Samuel Samson Guin's purple elephant. The bed and breakfast in rural, bucolic southern Tennessee, in a valley, that was almost in Mississippi, was supposed to supplement his retirement income. So far, it had only caused him to work as a substitute judge more often than he liked. She and Josh had not planned to go away, but the day she and her father had signed the documents to transfer Juston's custody to her, and the judge, after speaking to Juston, had signed the order that she had ready for his signature, Judge Guin had seen them and had stepped out of his empty court room to say hello.

She'd met Judge Guin at the Atlanta airport on the way back from Ghana. There was a tornado to the north of Nashville. There wouldn't be a flight to Nashville until the next day. She and Janine had rented the last car from the only rental company at the airport that was still open for business. Judge Guin had heard them talking about the best route to approach Nashville and had hesitantly approached them about sharing the car. Lanetia had heard his name, but as he was retired, she had never met him. Judge Guin and his wife were returning from Burkino Faso where they had been shopping for art to add to their collection.

Her father had told Judge Guin why they were there and that Lanetia was getting married. Judge Guin had enthusiastically offered the B&B for a weekend getaway. She had agreed to ask Josh, thinking he would say no. She didn't want to leave Juston. His therapist said he was progressing and she didn't want any setbacks. But Josh had said yes.

The B&B was almost completely surrounded by a lake and, on that September day, the leaves weren't yet showing their fall colors. She and Josh had rowed to the side of the lake that edged a stand of hardwood trees. There, they had dropped the anchor and he had handed her a rod and reel. She'd studied the water and chosen to fish next to a fallen tree whose hazy outline she could just make out in the depths of the brownish water. The cook had said they could catch their supper. Josh caught three trout and she caught crappie, most of which she released. They had walked and walked, bathed in the calming green and murmur of the woods on the far side of the lake. The leaves whispered forget and for a time a smile was a shared experience, with no under or overtones of lack or want or violence. It was the rest she had needed after a summer of emotion that would never make logical sense. And, for that weekend, she was secure in her decision.

But a part of her knew even then. That person, standing there smiling, holding hands with the man she truly loved, she should have known even then that love could not, would not conquer her feelings for this place.

"You…like it?" Josh asked, trying to read her expression as she, for a too long moment, deliberately avoided looking at him. She'd gotten him three solar batteries made by a German company that he wouldn't buy because they were expensive. Josh had tacked an article about the batteries on the wall in his workshop. The article was three years old and the note on the invoice informed them that the company had been bought and the batteries would no longer be available. Josh said the batteries were ahead of their time. He couldn't believe that Lanetia had read that yellowed, creased article.

"More than you'll ever know. I have the perfect place for it. At the old home place where I can look at it and remember." Lanetia told her lips to smile. She could smile at the memory of that weekend idyll. The now of her existence inhibited her smile. "You liked the B&B, didn't you?"

"I did. I liked the company even better. We needed that peace. You remember the Thursday hike?" Josh was smiling at the picture, remembering.

"To a grotto. We didn't do much hiking."

"We'll keep that to ourselves. Okay?"

"Useful. Blackmail…" Joshua leaned closer…

"Ma said y'all need to stop makin' out," Rachel interrupted from the doorway. The door was ajar so Brer Rabbit could enter after his morning visit with Mabel. "Can I come in? Are y'all decent?"

"You already in and if we wasn't decent, you'd know it. What you want?" Josh snapped.

"Don't snap at me. Daylight… Save it," Rachel snapped back. "Phone's workin'. You'd know if you didn't have your phone unplugged. Nesha's dad is on the phone."

"Thanks, Rachel."

"He still sound as mean as ever. He even say Merry Christmas mean. And is it a male thing?" she demanded. At their puzzled looks, she continued. "Juston's been polishing his bike all morning. A new bike. Why?"

Lanetia laughed. Rachel had been trying to persuade Juston to play a new video game and he was only interested in his bike. Josh smiled and pointed her out of the room. Rachel admired her charm bracelet for a moment and left just in time to catch Cinda sneaking out of their room with one of her Christmas presents. Lanetia plugged in the phone while Josh shushed Rachel and Cinda.

Josh, then, settled into the couch. Within a minute, Lanetia's expression had changed to the expression that said more than any words…I do not have to like, but I must respect. But it was a respect tinged with a mixture of cynicism, boredom and, maybe, even hate. He never wanted Nesha to look at him like that. Obviously, Mr. McCory had not called just to say *Merry Christmas*.

But why was he calling? Lanetia had called him two days ago...a conference call. That's what Lanetia's family did when they did not have their Christmas dinner...usually on the day after Christmas. After the weather cleared, they would set a date.

I can't make the man like me. Larmont said that Mr. McCory hadn't liked him either, not at first. He said the more problems he and Patrice had, the more Mr. McCory appeared to like him.

"Man's warped," Larmont had warned. "But what do you expect after he fought his way out of that little no-name southern crossroads? His father was a sharecropper; his mother a maid at the big house. They wanted more for their youngest son than the life they lived. His mother died for lack of medical care...antibiotics they couldn't afford. He promised on his mother's grave that he'd get out and he did. His father, brothers, and sisters gave him what help they could and, in return, he's always been there for them.

"He was hard on his kids. They had to excel in anything they did. They were a reflection of him. Their mother was also first generation college, but her people owned their land. Made a huge difference in attitude. White people couldn't ever really bother them. Patrice said when the whites acted foolish, her mother's people just withdrew and let them be fools. Their grandfather made the best moonshine, if you want to call it that, in a five County area, and, sooner or later, his customers came back. I'll tell you about the moonshine, because they never will. He had a recipe...used this fruit you never heard of—medlar. There's a medlar orchard behind the home place in Kentucky. I think the fruit is nasty, looks nasty... I can't bring myself to eat the fruit, but the Aunts make a jelly that's addictive. Lanetia and the Aunts make a batch of the liquor every other year and bottle it in rum bottles and use it as the liquid ingredient in their Christmas cakes, in a

barbecue sauce that will make you want to eat your fingers, and anything else they think needs a secret ingredient.. They label the bottles they give away—Royal Lee's Liquor. Royal Lee is their granddad. If I don't get my mother a bottle or two for Christmas, she tells me to get myself to Kentucky and beg like a dog if I have to. Means it, too. So, if you see Lanetia with a rum bottle, it ain't rum. Little family history. Where was I? Father...okay, got my train of thought... Patrice said their mother never really understood what drove their father. They owned land, they both were teachers—she never understood why that didn't satisfy him.

"Their father's goal was to always have enough in case someone needed help. He taught and he leased his land and the government crop allotments to area farmers. At one time, he owned a little juke joint, but had to get rid of it when he became principal of the Black High School. Then, he bought a convenience store...always something on the side. He doesn't trust anyone, not even his children. Which is why he's a politician to be reckoned with. He knows the value of being a big fish in a small pond.

"Lanetia came back to Nashville because of Franklin. He was failing medical school and he could've gone to jail for beating up his girlfriend. You'd think it was Patrice and he who were really close, but it's him and Lanetia. Lanetia knows where all his

buttons are and she knows just the order to push them in. Lanetia paid off his girlfriend, so she wouldn't press charges. Franklin had this thing for ghetto women. Then, Lanetia took him on a Black Networking Cruise. Those cruises were popular then. Don't hear about them anymore. She told him she didn't want him to be like the people he met on the cruise, but she wanted him to understand the aspiration to be something. The hope that I, the child, can do better than my parent. Sinking low...do nothing but stand and gravity will take you lower than low. Understand, gravity has no hold on hope. That's what she told him. There, standing in the middle of all the fakery, she told him to be authentic. It wasn't about their Dad or their Mother, it was about what he decided to do with what he had been given.

"After the cruise, she accompanied him to the medical school to assist him in pleading his case before the Retention Committee. He got back in on probation. Franklin graduated at the top of his class. About the car...Franklin honestly thought he was doing Lanetia a favor. Patrice just thought it would be a feather in her cap at her sister's expense. I love Patrice, but she can be in her own world. At least, Lanetia will come out of hers occasionally to take a survey to make sure everything is in its place.

"Aura?— they were best friends in law school. To hear Mr. McCory talk, she was one of those high yellow Blacks who had no

idea what it was like being Black. But, both of her parents were darker than I am and I ain't light. Happens. Aura's grandmother was the product of a rape—white man her father worked for. It wasn't that. Sometimes all your supports just seem to go missing. That's what happened. When Lanetia left D.C., Aura was engaged to be married. Then, her fiancé left her for some white woman, the daughter of a judge, he thought could advance his career. Like Lanetia said at the time, a comedy...tragi-comedy of events that spun out of control so fast that one could either, laugh, cry, or commit suicide. Aura chose suicide. Aura didn't talk to anyone, just took a bottle of barbiturates. We play all these games. Seems like the woman was just using him to get back at her father and, when she got tired of that, she divorced him and got him disbarred.

"When Lanetia was in D.C., she was in private practice. Lanetia called it a schizoid practice—they were getting to be known for their Civil Rights litigation, but it was the real estate practice that paid the bills. They specialized in the art of gently gentrifying neighborhoods. Neighborhoods they represented are all up and down the East Coast and they were just getting everything in place to really do some great things when Franklin did his thing. Then, she came here, went to work for that corporation, and you saw her fold into herself. Not an enriching place for a professional who doesn't look like them.

"Anyway, Patrice is very competitive with Lanetia. The veil? Don't believe anything Patrice says about the veil. Patrice does not like old stuff. She knew that seamstress would destroy it. That seamstress had no idea how to work with fragile fabrics and didn't care to know. The seamstress was supposed to carefully detach the thingy from the veil and attach the thingy Patrice had chosen. If Patrice had really wanted the veil handled correctly, she would have asked Aunt Leda. That woman can sew. Aunt Leda somehow made a veil from the mess and told Patrice she would wear the veil or nothing at all. All of them had worn the veil. They all had different dresses made by their mother and grandmother, but the lace for the veil was a shawl or something given to their great-grandmother by their great-grandfather. Only when Aunt Leda married did their grandmother decide that it would be reincarnated as a veil.

"You'll notice that Aunt Leda and Aunt Maline are polite to Patrice, but that's all. They like Lanetia and Franklin. Lanetia listens to them...she's written a family history...she'll do stuff with them. Aunt Maline said Patrice is like her son Detrick, selfish and self-involved.

"What else... Don't come between Franklin and Lanetia. Their mother asked Lanetia to look after Franklin. She spoke to each of them before she died. Patrice won't say what her mother

told her. Franklin won't say what else his mother said and Lanetia has never said a word. But we do know she asked Lanetia to do that. Otherwise...Lanetia would never have returned to Tennessee."

Maybe it wasn't hate. Maybe it was just a deep abiding anger. "What did he say other than *Merry Christmas*?" Josh asked as soon as she hung up the phone.

"I have to see my father. I'd rather you didn't come. You can take me to the Interstate and Franklin will meet us at the exit. That way you can keep the SUV. The newspaper is bundled for delivery and I should be back by the middle of next week."

"You leavin'…now?"

"No, tomorrow. Franklin will be at the exit around eleven."

"You can talk to me."

"About what?"

"Why you leavin'? What about the New Year?"

"What about it? I'm going to the old home place. I need to do some things I was going to do tomorrow."

"It be Christmas." Lanetia did not respond. Christmas…just another day, with things happening that needed taking care of. Why did Josh want to make special what was not?

Juston…Cinda…Rachel…each in their own way were Christmas skeptics. Each had viewed their ornament with cynicism. She'd heard them wondering aloud to each other…*why would I ever have a Christmas tree?* Let's give them to Ma was Cinda's solution. *She'll keep them in the attic.*

"She say anything?"

"Zeezee, she ain't said a word. He called; next day, she gone. I know he her Dad. And that Franklin…he acted like I didn't exist. Rush, rush, get her suitcase in the car. I got a pat on the cheek. She tell Juston somethin'?"

"Just that it didn't involve him; be a good boy; she'll call or e-mail every day; stuff like that."

"Why ain't I good enough for Lanetia?"

"I wouldn't worry about them. Lanetia married you. They ain't gonna sway her. You done seen that."

"You say that like I should be worried about somethin'. What?"

"I didn't mean it like that."

"She didn't want me to go with her."

"Boy, did it ever cross your mind that she might be protectin' you from that father of hers?"

"I can protect myself."

"I don't know. He want his way and he used to gettin' it. He see people as things to be manipulated. I knew a white man like him once. They… Nesha know what she doin'."

Lanetia did not feel like she knew what she was doing. "You sold out the Black community of Rendshaw. Why are you so concerned with the fallout? You never have been in the past."

Her father tried to intimidate her with *the stare*. When they were children, that stare had scared them into silence as they waited for him to pronounce their punishment. Lanetia glanced at her father and the glance said more clearly than words ever could—*I know what you're doing. I'm not a child. I am not intimidated.* "Dad, you said there was an emergency?"

Her father tapped the cigar that he dared not light. If he did, Lanetia would get up and walk back to those mountains. She hated cigar smoke. He'd never been able to smoke around her—Lanetia had asthma. "I have cancer. I have maybe six months to a year."

"Really. Is that an emergency?"

"Did you hear me?"

"Yes."

"Then how do I make this right? I don't want Rendshaw to be my legacy. I've done a lot of good in this community. This community has benefited. Eventually people forget, but…"

"You don't have eventually…for once."

"It's your name, too. I notice you don't use your husband's name."

"Dad, is Rendshaw a done deal?"

"All but the bulldozing. Their land has been bought."

"Fair market value?"

"Lanetia, this is business. No, they didn't get fair market value. They were paid a reasonable price."

"How much of the property did you own?"

"I started buying property five years ago when the road was first proposed. I got it voted down."

"Who's not happy?"

"I think it's the cemetery that they're unhappy about. It would have to be relocated. The County has offered some property for the cemetery. The dead don't care."

"You're dealing with the living. That cemetery has been there since 1867. Why not reroute the road?"

"It's four lanes with a median. That's the only solid piece of land through that particular part of the County. Caves. Remember, this County is pocked with caves. Feds would never knowingly permit highway funds to be used if the road was built on top of caves. Unfortunately, some idiot at the newspaper wrote an article about the topography of this area."

"I don't see how I can help you." Lanetia began. Her father held up his hand. Lanetia stared into the distance. His crafty, satisfied expression meant trouble, if not for her, then somebody. *My response is what matters, she reminded herself.*

"The property I bought is in your, Patrice's, and Franklin's names." Lanetia sat back and gripped the upholstered arm of the chair. For a moment, she didn't recognize the feel of the chair that had been in the same place in the same room since she could remember. She hadn't noticed...new upholstery...new color. The cushioned chair felt hard and unforgiving. *Breathe, Lanetia, breathe.* "Still think you can't help?" Lanetia sighed. A game. How many times had he said that politics was a game and an effective politician was the one in control of the rules of the game?

"Let me tell you now, before you die. I do not know why I have you as a father. In some past life, I must have really screwed up. Do you know how to care for anyone? Is it all about who, today, you can manipulate? I can wish for a different father, but, then, I wouldn't be me, would I? That will always be my dilemma. Why couldn't you have been content? Not with what you believe is wrong, but…"

Her father stopped fiddling with the cigar. "I know what you mean," he interrupted, not wanting to hear the question he had asked himself and had never found a satisfactory answer to. "I equate content with nice. A nice person wouldn't have had the money to pay your tuition to all those expensive schools or to finance your first year of private practice. In this country, being nice equates with weak. I am a Black man in a society that does it best to put me behind bars; a society that doesn't want me to have a job, not even digging ditches; a society where I, as a man, have never been respected. You remember Robert Brainerd?" Lanetia nodded. "He was nice. He played by their rules. I watched them take his business from him…bankrupt him… Now, it's theirs. All that work and he's in a nursing home. He had a stroke. He can't talk. I visit him sometimes. His eyes… Always the same question. *What did I do wrong?* He did everything just like they told him. He always said I didn't know how to trust. He didn't see them letting him have a little bit in order to gain his trust and, then, his business. I told Rawlins, you remember him…buys up all the decent farmland…that if he wanted my store, he could have it after

I burned it to the ground. Since then, he has never tried to mess with me.

"Did you know you're the only one who paid me back? That was our agreement. You honored it. More than your sister or brother ever did. But, you know about not being nice. That ghetto whore… Did you know she went to the police and told them she was afraid for her life, but she couldn't tell them why. She was talking about you. I just heard the story in the past year… She didn't once mention that your brother had put her in the hospital until the police told her they couldn't do anything to you. You hadn't broken any laws. By then, she didn't have any credibility. She'd told the hospital admitting staff that she'd tripped and fell down some stairs. I always meant to pay you the money you paid to that ghetto whore. Since then your brother's had decent female friends. Ones with some home training. You might persuade your brother to marry Dessa. Her father works for the Post Office and her mother works for the State. They taught her self-respect. She has a good job in the hospital's lab. Talk to him."

"Why aren't Patrice and Franklin here?"

"Why? So Patrice can wail and Franklin, I guess he's a little better now, he'll ask all the correct medical questions. Well, I've been to the Mayo Clinic. I have my answers. You're a lawyer. I want you to do what lawyers do. Figure out a way so that I do not suffer the consequences of my actions. I'm not exactly a client. I don't intend to pay you a dime. You'll get yours when I die."

"Maybe you should hire a lawyer. And keep your money. I've done pretty well without it."

"Not the point. Someone has to take care of the family. Like the Juston business. That's you. I am not a fool. Neither Patrice nor Franklin has any business sense."

"I don't know your family."

"I never wanted you to. It's all about environment. Where I came from… I didn't want my children to have any excuse. You can't go back to where I came from. Hard to go back to something you've never known—way I looked at it. All that hopelessness. Juston is adjusting well. Patrice didn't understand that the boy needed stability. Neither here nor there. There're only a few cousins and nephews and nieces in that place. Most have moved away. They'll come to my funeral; you'll meet them then."

"Maybe you should make other plans."

"That Cove place, just like the place I came from. Full of ignorance, backwards…white people just run over them like they don't exist, jealous of anyone who has more than they have or who wants more than they have. I didn't raise you to be lost in that. I raised you to be doing what you were doing before Franklin got in his mess. You can go back. You still own a stake in that law firm."

"I don't want the same things you do. Never have."

"Mrs. Yarborough has your room ready. You'll take care of her."

Lanetia didn't nod. *Why would you order me to take care of your lady friend?*

Lanetia's father had pointed her to the keys to his runaround car—an old Cadillac—when she'd asked to borrow a car to visit the Aunts. Lanetia didn't know how he managed it. None of his cars or trucks, no matter how old, had a dent or a scratch.

Josh had been distant and cold when she'd talked to him. He'd listened to her instructions regarding the newspaper and hadn't asked a question. *I know what to do* had been his cold response when she had asked him if she had forgotten anything. Juston and Cinda had just wanted to know when she was coming home. Not my home had been her thought as she had reassured them that she would be home the next week, if not sooner.

Cemeteries can be moved, but not next to the old city dump. That was what was making people angry. So there has to be another piece of property that would be acceptable. The road was coming. From reading the articles and the letters to the editor in the local newspaper, people were not against the road. Most had been paid more money for their property than they had ever had before, so they felt compensated. No one wanted to propose an acceptable location for the Black cemetery. No one wanted to admit guilt or culpability. Just some dead Black people. That's how her father felt.

I wonder what else he has bought in our names? Why does he still think he owns us? Just pawns to be used when needed and, then, carelessly discarded as expendable.

Lanetia drove aimlessly around Nashville before doing what she had promised herself never to do. She parked across the street from her former home and, in her mind, visited every room and every tree and shrub that she had planted. The current owners had draped the house and the evergreen shrubs with too many Christmas lights for her taste. One shouldn't mourn the loss of a thing, but she did. She had invested a lot of herself in making this house her home.

She could finally admit to herself that she felt homeless. Vonnie Pearl's home…that was what the house in Crow Cut Cove was…Vonnie Pearl's home. Would she ever think of Vonnie Pearl's home without thinking of starched ecru cotton curtains, with ruffled valances?

She didn't want to see who currently lived in the house that garishly blinked at her. The too bright security lights at the storage facility made the dark winter evening seem even darker. She was looking for something small. Something no one would notice. Something that she had bought for herself. She opened a trinket box that was packed in a box filled with small pictures that had once formed a collage on her living room wall. The only thing in the trinket box was a necklace. She sat on a box, trying to remember when she had bought it and what outfit it matched. Black and gray beads with a shark's tooth pendant… Why would I buy… Then she remembered. Sitting on a North Carolina beach with Estelan. I love you…and he had unfastened the necklace he always wore and kissed her neck as he fastened it around her neck. I love you…

Then, not two months later, a call from a defiant, hostile Franklin. She had tried to return the necklace to Estelan. She knew what that necklace meant to him. He had refused. You love me, but you made a promise you must keep. You honor our love by keeping my gift to you. It is no longer mine. What is given in love cannot be returned. That night, after he had left, she had cried and cried… Until then, she had not known she had that many tears in her. The only reason she still had a stake in the firm was because Estelan had insisted that he could not afford to buy her share. She had always thought she would return, but the years had passed, almost without notice.

For a moment, she relived the devastating hurt when Estelan had told her he was dating. Neither of them could sustain a long distance relationship, especially when Frankie had been so needy and she had to fight with herself not to run. At that time, talking to Estelan had only caused a depression which had increased her anger against a world that had no happiness or even contentment for her.

She had half-heartedly responded to Byrd's overtures. After three months, he'd given up and she and Janine had traveled to four countries in West Africa.

Estelan was married…had a daughter. She put the necklace in her coat pocket. She finally chose a wall plaque carved in Ghana…the symbol meant life… If asked, she could talk about her trip to Ghana.

For another moment, memories of Estelan overwhelmed her and she leaned against a stack of boxes, idly rubbing the dark wood of the carved symbol with the hem of her tee shirt. Estelan spoke English with that island lilt that could never be successfully imitated. She had met him during one of her wide-eyed walks through Greenwich Village. He had noticed her undisguised naiveté and had followed her until she stopped to admire the work of an artist who was painting the scene that was so alive around them. In that meeting, her world had expanded. We, of the islands, love to travel. We grow up on a speck of land where sea to shining sea can be seen from any high point on the island, he had said, laughing, just for the joy of laughing.

I must always live near the salt water, Estelan had announced one day while they were walking along the Potomac. When I was three days old, my father dipped me in the sea…on the rough side…nearest Africa and presented me first to the homeland we never knew, then to our present home, and last to the universe for then my path would be of my own making. All the while my mother wrung her hands on the shore. My son will face many challenges, he told her, as he placed me in her arms. I want him to always know there is more to us than this island.

About six months later, he left…to work his way around the world on some tramp boat. I did not see him again until I was sixteen and he walked back into my life for a glorious week. He gave me a sack full of money and said it was money for college. He threatened to hunt me down if I spent the money on anything other than college. I believed him. He gave me the name of a bank in Florida and I was to speak to a man named Telman James. No other.

Telman James is a cousin. My great-grandfather never married. There were a number of women who he loved deeply and completely for the season of their love. He always planted a crop before the season ended. What a beautiful crop... My cousin explained the family tree and I dare not marry anyone from the Islands, for my great-grandfather traveled the Caribbean. My cousin invested the money my father gave me. After all this time, the money still takes care of me. I have not seen my father since that time. I have a fierce love for that man and a fiercer love for my mother. My mother says my father is the only man she ever loved. She, however, was content with my stepfather. Before the man I call Papa married my mother, he had to agree to accept me as his own. If ever he did not, then she would leave. I love him, too, as a father. He told me when I left for college that he could never have treated me otherwise, for I was the son of the only woman he had ever loved.

Telman James had retired six years ago. He had invested the money her father had given her to finance that first year of practice. He still dabbled in investments when he wasn't walking the beaches of his island retreat. When she had written to tell him of her impending marriage, he had sent a card, telling her to be happy with her choice. I wished for you to be kin to me, but it was not to be. Invest this money I give you as a wedding present in your newspaper. When you have been married for two years, come for a long visit and bring your man. Be happy…that is my wish for you.

Things move in and out of one's life…broken, misplaced, lost. Things must be enjoyed for the season they remain in one's life. Do not cling. Let things ebb and flow as the sea. The sea can bring the new and take away the old. Think of yourself as the sea.

Lanetia showed the plaque to Janine who remembered the market where they had haggled over the prices of this plaque and cloth that was being woven as they haggled. As they remembered, Lanetia knew what to do with all the cloth she had bought over the years. Zeezee could use the cloth.

Janine and Rico were engaged. Lanetia sipped a lemony herbal tea as Janine talked about her plans. Would she be matron of honor? Lanetia nodded. Janine had asked her was she happy. You haven't said two words since you came. Why not? Don't look surprised. I know you and I've been talking and talking trying to get a feel for how you are doing. I am not unhappy. I feel as though I am unmoored. It's an adjustment. I want my marriage to work. I am challenged. You remember…we would sit in a café and talk for hours. Well, not only are there no cafés in those mountains, but when one does say something, one has to be very careful of what one says and to whom one says it.

On the Interstate, a solution came to her. If the Cemetery Board disapproved the site, then the County would be forced to buy another parcel of land. I met the lawyer who represented that board. He did a seminar for the Library during their yearly Genealogy Workshop called...The Rights of the Dead. What was his name? Kevin...Kevin Connerly... I wonder if he still works there? There has to be a choice of sites. I wonder if any of the property around the church in Rendshaw is suitable and who owns it. Register's Office tomorrow, if I get back in time.

The County has the funds to finance a reburial celebration after the site is accepted. Can I do this in a week? Or just do enough and let Dad run with it? Another feather in his non-existent cap. And his legacy, in his mind, will be intact.

Aunt Leda was even sicker than Kaida, her daughter, had said. "Why didn't you tell me?"

"Mama doesn't want anyone to know. You know diabetes. You lose one leg... She hates being a double amputee. She has neuropathy in her right hand and sometimes can't hold a fork. She feels so helpless and Mama was always on the go and she frets about me. I tell her that I don't mind. My life crashed and I would have gone crazy if I hadn't moved here to be with her."

"She looked so well at my wedding. I knew she was a brittle diabetic, but I thought the pump had helped."

"It did...does. Lanetia, Mama was adamant that I not say anything. She wouldn't let me tell Jelly Bean and Tasha until the day before her operation. They cussed me and I didn't blame them. She...we were so happy that you had found **the** *man. How's that gorgeous man you married?"*

"Fine."

"If you don't want him, send him to me. I am not proud."

Lanetia finally laughed. "What can I do?"

"When she wakes up, visit a while and tell her how good she looks. Lanetia, she loves to hear you talk about the mountains. When she would visit me in Denver, we'd hike and just soak up the scenery. She has good memories of mountains. It's still early, even though it's midnight dark outside. Supper is about ready. Please, don't tell Miss or Mrs., whichever she is today, Histrionics. I don't care if Patrice is a nurse. She has about as much empathy as a rock. Why is she always competing with you?"

"She's the eldest. Eldest, in her mind, has certain prerogatives. She says she's back with Larmont and they're trying to have a baby."

"You know what that's about. Beat you to the punch. She ought to stop it. Where'd you find this fruit you brought us?

Because of all the storms, the produce around here has looked horrible."

"I came the long way through Nashville and stopped at this place called Fruits of the World. *You pick out the basket, the fruit, and the fillers, like boxes of raisins and little bags of nuts. I bought the single serve packets of the candy that Aunt Leda likes. Thanks for telling me about the store that caters to diabetics."*

"Thank you for picking up my order. Usually, I enjoy the drive, but with this fickle weather, I don't want to be stranded in Nashville. Aunt Maline can't do everything that needs to be done...not alone.

"Mama likes your newspaper. Tell her about the latest intrigues in Grotman County."

"Oh, come on, you have not read my Paper."

"Yes, we have. Uncle Franklin sends us a copy every week."

"You're kidding. Where would he get a copy? I don't sell subscriptions. I just sell the Paper in Grotman County."

"You know your Dad. If there's a way to do something, he will do it."

"You've been busy," Franklin McCory commented. He didn't like her plan, not one bit, and his voice conveyed his disdain. "I'm not buying that property. I wished you'd talked to me before you rammed your request through the Cemetery Board. We had them on our side. They had agreed to a variance."

"Not any more. The property next to the old city dump is not suitable for a historic cemetery. I did not ram. I merely pointed out the obvious. Why open up the possibility of a delay in a road project that will bring jobs to an economically depressed area when there are landowners willing to sell their property for use as a cemetery? You're the one who wants a legacy. I've identified three landowners who are willing to sell, if the property is used as a cemetery. The County has discretionary funds...but a donation from a concerned citizen... You're the politician. I've been here longer than I intended, so that's the plan. You do with it what you want. I own a newspaper that requires my attention."

"How did you manage to put out the Paper from here?"

"The wonder of computers." *And Josh who had driven to Chattanooga to pick up the Paper.*

"I suppose I have to tell Patrice and Franklin. I've asked them to come tomorrow. Then, Franklin can drive you to that place in the mountains."

The next day, at the news, Patrice immediately started sobbing loudly. Franklin studied his father for a moment. “Did the Mayo Clinic suggest an experimental drug that’s in human trials? It’s specifically for slow growing melanomas like you have.”

“Yes. Have you read about the side effects of that drug? No thanks. Lanetia, get a cold washcloth for your sister. I think she’s hyperventilating. Would have been nice if one of you had decided to have some children. Maybe, after I’m gone, you’ll bring them to the cemetery for a visit.” That comment caused Patrice to wail even more loudly if that was possible. “Do everybody a favor,” their father said to Franklin, pointing his unlit cigar at Patrice, “at my funeral, dope her up.”

“Why are you so cruel?” Patrice managed to hiccup out.

“I’m not cruel; I’m pragmatic. No one wants to hear your distress, whether real or pretend. Take some Valium and sit quietly so people can hear my Eulogy. That’s all I ask of you.”

“Maybe I won’t come.”

“That’ll work. Franklin, you drive Lanetia back to that place. Obviously, she hasn’t had enough of it…yet. I’m tired.”

“Why do you always know first? I’m the eldest. Why didn’t he tell me?”

"Patrice, no one wants to hear your wailing."

"Don't have to worry about that from you. You have no feelings for anyone and it's a wonder that man you married hasn't realized it."

"Why didn't he say something when I dropped you off two almost three weeks ago?" Franklin wondered out loud.

"Maybe he would've, but I seem to remember someone in an awful hurry. Hi, Dad. Got to go. Rounds. Bye. Do I remember correctly?"

"Be sarcastic with someone else. And, shut up, Patrice. Go home and cry on Larmont's shoulder, not on my leather seats."

"Oh, yes, by the way, Aunt Leda is very ill. Both legs have been amputated…below the knee. I've gone to see her a couple of times. She's willing herself to die. You might want to visit. Aunt Maline is depressed."

"Do you have any good news?" Patrice asked, turning to look at her sister who seemed to be nonchalantly staring at the snow-covered scenery whizzing by.

Lanetia turned to look at Patrice. "Sorry to spoil your day."

"Am I glad to see you!" Juston almost knocked her down as he threw his arms around her.

"My turn!" Cinda insisted. Lanetia pulled her into her side and gave her a one-armed hug.

Franklin wasn't in as big of a hurry as he had been when he had picked her up. He helped secure her suitcase and the three plastic tubs of fabric onto the luggage rack on top of the SUV. "Y'all mind?" Without waiting for an answer, he gestured for her to follow him to the old phone booth that had no phone. Franklin gingerly leaned against it, but it was sturdy, despite the cracked glass and the doorless opening. The rays of the early afternoon sun glinted off the mounds of blackened snow that surrounded the gas station. "What's happening?"

Lanetia knew what he meant. "Franklin, ask Dad if there's anything you can do for him. Accept his answer. But don't stop asking him the question. I'll call more often. Please visit the Aunts. Don't take Patrice."

"I'm not stupid. Why do you have to be in the boondocks?"

"This phase of my life is here. You'd better get going. Dad likes Dessa." Franklin raised an eyebrow. "Don't be shocked. Be careful. The roads are still icy, especially the bridges."

"You're serious? Dessa?"

"Very much. Think about it. Drive…"

"Lanetia," he interrupted. "I'm a good driver. Trust me."

"Call me when you get home. The phones are working. At least once a week…check. Tell him…for now, that he's part of your rounds. Think like a physician on this. You do not permit a patient to control what you think is best for the patient. The patient may not accept your advice, but you're there to give it. I did a little research. The pain from that type of melanoma can be excruciating. Do that for me?"

He nodded. He squinted against the glare of the snow. "Does Dad think that I'm competent?"

"He does. But he wants to do things his way. You can help him do things his way. That's important to him." She hugged him. "Drive safe, Frankie."

"Franklin…if you please."

Lanetia smiled at him. He smiled back and nodded. They understood each other.

CHAPTER 7

Zeezee, sat in the front seat, beside Josh who had barely nodded at Lanetia. *She's protecting me*, Lanetia thought. "I'll sit in the back with the kids. They can bring me up to date." D'Arton was actually doing his homework; school was opening next week; McGillicuddy had found a supply of pipe that could be used to repair the gas lines…

As soon as they got home, Josh had to finish the day's chores. Zeezee had cooked a wonderful dinner that Lanetia thoroughly enjoyed. Vonnie Pearl did not eat with them. She said she had a headache. Mrs. Yarborough cooked well enough, but she had high-blood pressure and did not use salt, not even a pinch, and she refused to use herbs. Didn't know anything about them and didn't want to. "What did you say, Juston?"

"I got a letter from my grandfather. He wanted to know if I'm being treated right. And there was fifty dollars in the letter." At her questioning look, he continued. "I got it today. By the postmark, he sent it before Christmas. I guess I have to write him back?"

"You guess right. Make sure you thank him for the money. And, as I'm sure you have plans for the money, tell him how you'll spend it."

"But I don't. I don't need fifty dollars. I never spend all of my allowance. I guess I'll put it in my savings account."

"There're some stamps and envelopes on my desk upstairs."

Brer Rabbit twined himself around her legs as she put away her things. Finally, she sat on the sofa and he leaped into her lap…a heavy black ball of fur and purr. Franklin called, just as she began to doze. After she spoke to him, she dumped Brer Rabbit out of her lap. A walk…

Coat, scarf...hat… Where is my hat?

"Where you goin'?" Josh said, startling her and Brer Rabbit, who arched his back and hissed as he backed between her feet. Josh must have just come from outside, for he brought a hint of the cold into the room with him.

"I thought I'd walk to the old home place and smell the place. It seems I've been gone for a long time."

"Nesha…"

She dropped the coat and held out her arms.

"So how do you feel… Your father, your aunt…" Josh asked. It was two in the morning, but neither of them was sleepy. They were getting to know each other all over again. It felt right to be curled up together, talking and touching.

"Kind of like the rug has been pulled from under my feet. After Mama died, the Aunts were always there to call about stuff. All of us would spend part of the summer with the Aunts. I don't know how I feel about Dad. He's tackling this illness on his own terms and that's what's important to him."

"Don't you want to visit more often?"

"I'm conflicted about that. We don't have that much to say to each other. Mrs. Yarborough practically lives there. She thinks we're horrible children because we don't visit. Yet, Dad doesn't particularly want us there."

"Zeezee …" *Huh?* "Zeezee been sendin' the Paper to your Dad, Mona, and anybody else who asked. She be your subscription service. She got quite a list."

"Why?"

"People call here and ask for you. You ain't here and she get to talkin' to them. She tells them to send her the postage and she'll send them the Paper. I been takin' the box to Old Bob, but I didn't know what was in it. She got the Paper all packed up and addressed and Old Bob put the postage on it and charge her account. She even send a copy to Mr. Holzer. He be on her list."

"If it makes her happy… But I had a reason not to take subscriptions."

"I know that; you know that; Zeezee just proud of you. Like me."

"Thanks. I'm glad we're together."

"Me, too."

"I don't ever sleep this late. Some coffee. The cows probably…"

Zeezee interrupted his spiel. "Cows been milked, fed, stall cleaned; chickens fed. Me and Nesha. Nesha mostly. You just sit there and eat breakfast. And don't be so amazed, you won't be able to digest your food properly. And before you ask, Nesha at the old home place. She got a Paper to put out."

"Maybe I should go back to bed. Kids ain't up? That clock say eight."

"I heard Nesha get up and, after I fussed at her for a little while, we decided to let you sleep in. You two done circled back to the way you was this past summer—she skinny and you a zombie.

Be a shame you got to have a living will, power of attorney for this and that just to die with dignity." She placed a plate filled with eggs, sausages, and biscuits in front of him.

Before answering, he spun the lazy susan filled with jams and jellies to choose the blackberry jam. "He could've waited until after the New Year. I wanted us to be together for that. He been knowin' about his condition for six months."

"But he had a sick spell Christmas Eve, and I agree with Nesha…it scared him. Josh, she had to go. If you wasn't here and one of us was ill, you'd come. Her aunt probably won't last the winter. That wear at you, Josh. I hear them kids finally gettin' up. Feel like a short order cook—I want scrambled, I want fried, I want boiled. We done spoiled them kids."

If I laugh, she'll fuss at me all mornin'. I best hold it in, Josh thought, but he couldn't help his shoulders shaking, just a little. Things felt normal—for the first time in almost three weeks, things felt normal.

The wind howled through the trees on the hillside behind the old home place. Inside, Lanetia and Zeezee only heard the beat of African drums as Zeezee danced through the backroom where Lanetia assembled the newspaper. Fabric of different weaves and bright primary colors was draped over chairs and the long table. *I*

see me some quilts. I do see me some quilts. Zeezee touched the fabric, a knowing touch that sensed the different textures and which fabrics would look best paired together. "Nesha, you right. There be no way to describe such beauty. I see patterns. First, I got to get organized." Nesha pointed to the photo album that Zeezee used to keep track of the fabric she bought. Swatches of fabric filled the album. Each swatch had notes underneath, setting forth yardage, ideas for use, when used, the pattern of the quilt it was used in, and any other information that Zeezee thought was relevant. Zeezee had a small bookshelf filled with the albums and her quilting books. "You got everything here for me? Scissors?" Nesha nodded. "Then, I'll get to work and catalogue the fabric. Leave me be. You work on the Paper. I'll be cuttin' and taggin' this material until dark. I'll put it back in the boxes, 'cept this piece. I'm takin' this with me," she said, fingering a fabric of multi-hued purples. "This be the border of a quilt I started ten years ago. Never could find the right material. Shoo… Close the door. I be warm enough. You got the kerosene heater goin'. Turn up them drums."

Lanetia smiled, then grimaced at the computer. Who wanted to write an article about highway maintenance when the drums of Africa were heating up one's blood?

The next day, an arctic front settled over the mountains. The door to the old home place blew open and paper soared across the room. “Zeezee, calm yourself.” Lanetia knew something was wrong. Zeezee was trying to say something, but no words were coming out. Lanetia had to lean against the door to close it. “Why are you out in this weather? I’ve made tea. Honey?” Zeezee nodded. Zeezee sipped the hibiscus tea, and when she set the cup on the table, she idly stirred the tea, before speaking.

“I don’t know what to do. I laid that material on the end of my bed. This mornin’ it wasn’t there. Thought it was on the floor, under the bed. Then I got busy with the mornin’ chores. Had to find that low stool to sit on, so I could look under the bed. Wasn’t there. The hasp on the trunk, down… It’ll do that if you close it and it don’t catch. I always check it after I been in it because I done hit my knee on it more than once. In my trunk, cut up. Just cut up. Like somebody didn’t want me to use that material for nothin’. My border…your material. We know who done it. She in the kitchen singin’ some gospel song like she ain’t done nothin’. I couldn’t look at her. How’d I make that piece of work?” Zeezee lamented. “This weather ain’t helpin’ her. Say we gonna be snowbound for a week or more. That cat of yours hiss every time she look his way. Should listen to them animals. Maybelle stay in my room.”

"Is the material shredded or just cut up into pieces?"

"Cut into pieces."

"How small?"

"Small enough."

"Do you think we can sew the pieces together to form strips? Remember that strip quilting book you showed me…the crazy quilt?" Zeezee nodded. Strip quilting wasn't her idea of quilting, but, if there was a book on quilting, Zeezee had it. *Never know what technique might come in handy.* "Then, we sew the strips together until we have a piece or pieces large enough to do what you envisioned. We'll use the sewing machine."

"She'll just cut it up again." Zeezee looked lost. Why bother?—her expression said.

"Not if Josh says it's pretty." *That just might work.* "Is Josh in his workshop?" Zeezee nodded. "Relax. We can put this Humpty back together. Don't go out of the house half-dressed," Lanetia fussed. "This cold seeps into your bones and it's hard to remember being warm." Lanetia wrapped a long brown and orange wool scarf around Zeezee's neck and made a hood for her head. She wrapped her coat around Zeezee. Once outside, the arctic cold pierced through the two layers of thermal underwear, as though she wore nothing. Lanetia was shivering by the time they reached the house.

"Zeezee, go in the front door. You've been outside long enough. What can Vonnie Pearl do? I'll find Josh. Don't... Just give me my coat."

Lanetia sent the kids upstairs to finish their book reports. "The sewing machine will disturb them," she said at Zeezee's frown of disapproval. Lanetia understood. Vonnie Pearl wouldn't do anything crazy in front of the kids when she saw what they were sewing. They'd have to chance it. "Square the pieces to make them easier to sew together. Tell me when the strip is long enough and I'll start another."

"They readin' them AWB books?" *Uh-huh* "Took you a while to find somethin' that Rachel would read. You know, Cinda and Juston done start readin' them books, too. Wish there was more of them. I never heard of graphic novels before. I like the characters...Simon and Sirita Black and their three kids, Adriel, Malik and Shaylin. Father in the Air Force; Ma's an English teacher for people who don't speak English. They at the age where they curious about everything. Rachel was on the website and I saw where the author puts up a different story every couple of months written by kids who like the books. I think that would be a project for them three. ***Adventuring While Black***... I really like that title.

"There might be another one published in November. Author's real reclusive. She let them kids experience just enough and the parents explain just enough. Think she got an earful?" Lanetia nodded. Vonnie Pearl could not see what they were sewing from where she was making a cake, but she probably could hear them talking. Now, she had reluctantly turned on the mixer. "Them kids getting' a better education round this dinin' room table, than they gettin' at that school."

Lanetia had a pile of strips by the time Josh came in for the night. "Pretty," Josh said, picking up a strip and frowning at them. *Josh, don't ask why. Please...when you come in...pick up one of the strips of cloth and say it's pretty. Show it to your mother. Do it for Zeezee. Please.* "You two got a job sewing these tiny pieces into strips. Why you do that? Ma, pretty, ain't it?" he asked, showing the strip he held to Vonnie Pearl. Her eyes widened and darted from Zeezee to Lanetia. "Ma, you feel okay?"

"I got a headache. Supper ready. I got to go to bed." Zeezee stared at the stairs for a long moment before tapping Lanetia's hand. Lanetia and she had speculated...if Vonnie Pearl felt guilty about cutting up the material, she might confess about that and feel no need to confess any other misdeeds.

"We got to feed them kids. Start up again after supper, if you got the time. You ain't worked on the Paper…"

A winter of snow and ice and the gray of charcoal and steel had descended onto the mountains. The sun was a distant memory. Lanetia struggled to walk to the old home place. She had managed to get out the last week's newspaper. There would be no edition this week. The drive to the printer in Chattanooga was too treacherous. Today, Lanetia only wanted to pull a quilt over her head until spring. Instead, she had put on two pairs of thermals and escaped from the house.

Lanetia idly tapped the keyboard and found herself writing…an idea…after all this time. One of the many reasons that she had come to these mountains…to discover if she could write again. The stress of the job, knowing what was coming had frozen her ideas in an Antarctica in her mind, and now with a blizzard…an idea.

Lanetia abandoned the keyboard and found a spiral notebook and settled into her overstuffed thinking chair in the back room. She always wrote better with pen and paper. She turned up the kerosene heater and was soon in a doze, ideas flowing faster than she could write. Her pen, falling to the floor, startled her awake and, for a moment, the woman in the coral suit was standing there by the heater, clearer than she had ever seen her. *Joshua*…the woman in the coral suit said and pointed outside. Lanetia shook herself awake.

Joshua…outside… Where? What had Zeezee been fussing about? Well pump…Vinton. When she had left the house, Vinton's truck had been in the driveway, already partially hidden in a drift of snow.

Most of their homes were snug enough, but the sub-zero temperatures were taking a toll. Folks budgeted for propane and their budgets were depleted. They had well water, but the water in the wells was freezing and that was burning out the pumps. Lanetia hid the notebook in a box of the African fabric and turned off the heater.

Josh stared at his gashed, bleeding hand. He was so numb from the cold that he did not feel the pain. Deacon Vinton quickly clapped his hand over Josh's hand, closing the gash, but the dripping blood quickly turned the snow bright red. Josh shook his head when Vinton gestured toward his house. No need to mess up the house was his thought. It was his left hand; he could still drive. The truck's bed was still piled high with parts, now coated with inches of snow. The main thing was to stop the bleeding. He was just about to ask Vinton to get some tape when they saw headlights coming toward them.

The SUV stopped at the side of the house and a small figure struggled to hold the door open so she could get out. She could barely walk in the gusting snow and wind.

"How that woman of yours always seem to know when you got trouble?"

"Don't know."

"Not another woman around here would be out in this weather."

"Glad she not from here."

Lanetia reached them and took in the discolored snow that was rapidly being covered with fresh snow. Saw the hand being held closed. "Deep?" Josh could not really hear her words, but he knew what she was saying.

He nodded.

She gestured for them to come with her. The wind was whipping their words away too fast to be heard.

The first aid kit was under the driver's seat. They crowded into the front seats. "Mr. Vinton, move your fingers a bit, so I can tape the hand. Don't open your hand," she ordered Josh. Lanetia taped the hand so that the wound was closed, but it still bled. She wrapped gauze around it. Josh grimaced. His right hand was clenched in a fist. "As you warm up, the pain will be worse," Lanetia murmured, as she rummaged through the first aid kit. "The topical ointment won't help...not with a deep cut. Hold your hand up. Use your right hand to hold it. Might help to stop the bleeding." Lanetia glanced at Mr. Vinton, who was frowning. "Is your pump repaired?"

"Yes ma'am. Cable slipped. I'll put the cover on the well."

"You need help…the wind?"

"No, I can slide it in place. You…"

"We'll be fine. If there's a lull, we'd appreciate it if you drive Josh's truck to the house and tell Zeezee and Vonnie Pearl what happened. But don't worry if you can't." Deacon Vinton nodded.

Josh was soon aware that Lanetia was not going home. "Zeezee can fix this."

"No, she can't. The cut is too deep. You need stitches. Don't talk to me. I have to concentrate on holding this truck on the road."

The nurse-practitioner, who manned the clinic, was getting into his SUV when they drove up. Lanetia blocked his exit. He opened the door on Joshua's side and, without a word, unbuckled Josh's seatbelt and helped him into the clinic.

"You are so lucky," he told Josh, as he sewed him up. "How'd you get off the mountain in this weather? I guess I would've tried if I had a cut this bad, but I'd be afraid that I would be blown into a ravine and not found until spring." He gave Josh a tetanus shot and an antibiotic. "Your hand is going to really hurt, so I'm going to give you a painkiller. You cannot move this hand. Wear this sling, even in bed. You'll be uncomfortable, but the hand will be immobilized. The local I gave you will wear off in two to three hours. Take a painkiller at the first hint of pain. Are you staying in Tiny Town tonight?"

Lanetia, who was standing in the doorway, spoke up: "No, we're going home. Lull…no snow. Tomorrow's forecast more snow. The wind is still gusting but, for now, the clouds have thinned enough for the moon to appear. Can you give him one of those painkillers now? It might take a while." The nurse-practitioner nodded.

The snow and ice reflected the moonlight, causing an eerie brightness marred by dark shadows. Josh would nod off, then jerk himself awake. "Josh, I'm okay. Relax," Lanetia said more to reassure herself than him.

Studded tires… Before Thanksgiving, Josh had installed the studded tires. The tire shop in Knoxville had to order the tires from one of its branches located in Canada. Lanetia had read and re-read the brochure, wondering if Josh was being overly cautious. Now, Lanetia knew that he was not.

Lanetia drove in the middle of the road to avoid the ruts under the freshly fallen snow. *No one would be fool enough to be coming down or going up this road at this time of night.* Josh had stashed a winter safety kit in the storage area. Not overkill to have a thermal blanket, water, energy bars, kitty litter, chains, and flares. *Trick to drivin' on these roads in the winter is to stay out of the ruts. Keep both gas tanks full.* Josh had made her stop on the way to the clinic to top off the tank. That was the reason they had almost missed the nurse-practitioner.

The green LED display flashed 2:17 as she turned into the driveway. Lanetia shook from the cold. She had turned off the heat in the SUV. The thermal blanket was all Josh needed and she needed to be alert. Half-way up the mountain, it had started snowing again. She narrowly avoided Mr. Vinton's truck which was barely outlined in a drift of snow as she parked the SUV. Lanetia sat for a moment before she tapped Josh's shoulder. "You awake?" Lanetia felt his nod. "I'll come around to help you." They slowly walked to the house which was ablaze with light.

"What happened?" Vonnie Pearl demanded.

"Josh cut his hand. I took him to the clinic in Tiny Town. He's had a painkiller and he's kind of wobbly. Let's get him upstairs. Zeezee, goldenseal? A little on the stitches? The wound is still leaking and that should help."

"Girl, you can barely stand. Vonnie Pearl and me will get Josh to bed. Rachel, you make tea. Pour the water in those mugs that I fixed up and you give one to Nesha and bring the other one upstairs to me. You just sit, Nesha. I said sit. Somebody need to invent a cell phone that work in these mountains. The phone been dead this past week. Couldn't call nobody…so we just been worryin'."

Lanetia sat as though in a daze listening to the wind howl and the house creak and shake. The tea was calming, but the nightmare of the drive was still with her.

"Nesha, why didn't you stay in Tiny Town? Nesha, you listenin' to me?" Zeezee said, waving her hand in front of Lanetia's face.

"Zeezee, you can't milk the cows and feed the chickens and do the hundred and one things that need to be done here…every day. But you and me, we can do it. That's what happens to these farms. One day you just can't do everything that needs to be done and it all falls apart."

"I had to send Vonnie Pearl to bed. She never could stand to see Josh hurt. At least, we got Josh in bed. He be askin' for you. He not completely out of it. You need some help?"

"No."

CHAPTER 8

Lanetia leaned against the door of the barn. Sleet pelted the tin roof, causing a pounding din. The cows mooed and shifted in their huddle. Their enclosure had been mucked out. The cows were fed and milked. The milking area had been cleaned and sanitized. She had replaced the checklist and the permanent marker. Josh was meticulous. Each month's checklist was kept in a notebook in his office. The hay in the feeding corner had been replenished.

She had a basket full of eggs. The chicken coop was an old stone building built solely for the chickens by Josh's great-grandfather. No wild animal could get into the coop. Two heat lamps kept the interior comfortable for the chickens. She had replaced the straw strewn on the floor and fed the chickens. Josh had built a watering system, so that as long as the water in the tank did not freeze, the chickens and the cows had fresh water. Someone was trying to open the door. Lanetia sighed as she opened the door.

"Juston, what are you doing out in this weather? Get back to the house," Lanetia ordered. "You…"

"I came to help. You can't carry all this stuff by yourself," he said, gesturing toward the two covered pails of milk and the basket of eggs. "I can help. I would've been here sooner, but I had to argue with Zeezee. I was trying to wake up when you did. Is Josh okay?"

"Fine. Josh is fine. I do not…"

"In the morning, wake me up when you get up and I'll come with you. I'll take…"

"You take the eggs. I'll take the milk. I… Thank you."

"You're welcome. I'll come with you in the evenings, too. I'm from Missouri and my mama was from Minnesota. Sometimes, maybe mostly, before her parents died, when money was tight, we had to live with them. I didn't like that. We were the only African-Americans on the block and there were only two or three others in my classroom when I went to school there. Grandmama said if I stayed, I'd get used to it. Mama said there were some things a kid shouldn't have to get used to. Mama ran away when she was sixteen. She said there had to be a place on this Earth where there were people who looked like her. She got as far as Chicago before the police found her. She was asleep in the bus terminal. After that, my grandparents sent her to live with a cousin in Savannah. She didn't like it there either. She liked the cousin. She said, at night, the trees, which were draped in Spanish moss, looked like the monsters in your worst nightmares.

"All of that is just to say I know how to get around in the snow. Although, when you live in the city like we did, you don't get the full effect…like you do here."

"Do you miss Missouri?"

"No… I miss my mama and my daddy, but not as much now. I wanted to stay with my granddaddy, but he said he couldn't take care of me. He said he couldn't stop drinking, even for me. He said he had too much pain he needed to drink away. My mother's cousin offered to take me, but granddaddy said no. He said your father would take care of me. I'm lucky. I have some cousins… They're not so lucky."

"Juston, I want you to do chores. But, farms…the repetition…it gets old fast. But as long as you're volunteering, I accept your help. Let's walk faster." Just as they reached the house, golf ball sized hail pelted them.

They hurriedly took off their coats and boots, for the storage porch was cold…not as cold as outside, but cold enough for them to shiver. They kept slippers under the bench, so they wouldn't track up Vonnie Pearl's spotless floors.

"Nesha, before we go in. Can I ask you something? There's no one in the kitchen," Juston said, bending to peek into the kitchen through the window.

"Sure."

"Are you ever going to write some more of those books?"

"How?"

"Your dad sent the books to my granddaddy and he gave them to me. I'm just pretending to read them for the first time. Mama read them to me and I looked at the pictures, until I could read for myself."

"Juston, open the refrigerator. Zeezee will do whatever with the milk later on today. I'll leave the eggs on the table. I haven't been able to write for years. I do have some ideas. What's on the website is wishful thinking. Tani, my illustrator, maintains the website and she has hopes. But saying a thing doesn't always make it true."

"Your dad said if you couldn't write here, there wasn't no place you could write. He meant Mr. P's cabin. Not here," Juston explained at Lanetia's raised eyebrow. "He says this place will suck you dry."

"When…"

"I heard him talking to Franklin at your wedding." *Who*… "No one else heard. I'm a kid. If I'm quiet, people forget I'm around."

"I remember and now I must remember to remember that when you're around," Lanetia said, laughing.

◆◆◆

"Vinton said that I could build a solar array and a windmill on his place this summer. He say that he can't stand another winter like this one. He say even if another winter like this don't come for thirty more years, he want to be prepared. He also say that the Church need to buy an SUV and then one of us can take the kids to school and not depend on the bus that can't get up the mountain when the roads are icy. Nesha, why am I still in bed?"

"Because you lost a lot of blood and you cannot move that hand. Are you uncomfortable? What about another pillow under your arm?" Joshua shook his head in frustration. "Vonnie Pearl said that she remembers your father cutting himself really badly. She couldn't drive and she forgets who took him to Salyna. Back then, there was a hospital in Salyna. You won't be able to use that hand for a month or more. Just like when your father cut his hand or leg, she couldn't remember which—people managed. They have to if they want to survive. So, stop worrying. Rachel and Juston are helping. I'm afraid Cinda will be blown away, so she's not happy that she has to stay inside.

"Are you finished eating? A book? A magazine? The solar battery schematics you've been studying? The nurse-practitioner e-mailed me and said you can get up tomorrow, but not to do anything. He wants you to take the painkillers for two more days. Then, as you need them."

"I always saw my daddy helpin' anyone he could. I don't see myself doin' any different. I love you. We don't say that to each other enough. Why? I can't hear it enough from you."

"I love you, Josh, but I don't know if I could ever do again what I did last night. I feel drained." Josh reached for her hand and held it tightly. *You have my strength.* Lanetia twined her fingers in his. *I accept.*

"Storm endin'?"

"Tomorrow, the next day… The jet stream carrying that frigid polar air is not moving."

"Zeezee, I can wiggle my fingers. I always could wiggle my fingers."

"Keep wiggling them. You almost cut your hand in two."

"It ain't that bad."

"Yes, it is. Be useful. Find me that light blue thread in my sewing box. That nurse done a good job sewing you up. Been a week and all you do is walk… Walk from upstairs to downstairs…out to the storage porch…to the dining room, then you go to the front and open the front door. View ain't changed. Wriggle them fingers. First one, then the others…in sequence." Five minutes of finger wriggling finally satisfied Zeezee, who was quilting. "That nurse been e-mailin' Nesha. He said that he would recommend physical therapy. He wanted you to start doin' some exercises like wriggling your fingers 'til we can get off this mountain back to the clinic. You gonna wiggle them fingers for me when I say so. Helps things heal the way they supposed to.

"Nesha can't wait on you hand and foot. Don't interrupt me," Zeezee ordered, holding up her hand that held the sewing needle like a tiny sword. Josh pretended to back away. "She doin' some of what you did and all of what she do. The kids are really helpin'. I been surprised at Rachel. She done learned how to milk the cows. She and Juston milk the cows, feed the chickens, get the bales of hay. They real resourceful.

"If you need somethin', holler for somebody other than Nesha. Be considerate. Your Ma ain't doin' nothin' but talkin' about her headaches. Give her somethin' to do. You think if Nesha with you then she restin', but that ain't so. You just puttin' her further behind. I had Nesha tell the nurse that you had a little fever for a couple of days, but he don't think you got no infection cause the cut be healin' nicely. He want me to put a different kind of bandage on it. Part of the kit he sent back with Nesha. He figured we wouldn't be able to get back to the clinic and he put some extras in it. Come in handy cause both the Tidwells got the flu.

"Nesha took me to see them yesterday. Got to go back today. Told them to take the flu shot. No—government conspiracy. Backward…but with all the news about contaminated this and contaminated that…maybe they right. Nesha didn't take the flu shot because of Juston. Seems like his mama told him never to take it and Nesha knew better than to force him and he didn't want her to take it. Don't you start fussin'. Nesha just drivin' me. She don't go in. Nesha and me wantin' to see if that eucalyptus oil story true. Indians used it when they had the flu. See if it help.

"Nesha got a newspaper to get out. That printer finally agreed to meet her at some exit. You was goin' to reopen the mill.

You could be drawin' the plans for that. Josh, you know how to keep yourself busy. If we keep needin' so much, Nesha gonna run and she ain't gonna stop 'til she done wiped this place clean from her mind. And don't none of us want that," Zeezee warned.

"Juston, stop runnin' in the house," Joshua said. The slamming of the door had roused him from a near sleep. Juston slowed, but did not stop. "Hey, you hear me? What the hurry?" Joshua closed the book that was putting him to sleep and grimaced at the sketch he had drawn on the graph paper. He didn't think the book had it right. Surely, the electrical plant described in the book would not have the capacity that he envisioned.

"Zeezee told me not to linger, but to get on back before I left…"

"Why? I'll go…"

"No, she wants some herbs. Her and Nesha cooking something that smells really bad. I'm to get chili peppers, nutmeg, almond flavoring, cinnamon, and some hot sauce."

"Come again?"

"They're cooking. It smells horrible. And some flour, milk, baking powder, and salt. I think that's all. Can I go?"

“Tell Ma I’m cookin’ lunch,” Vonnie Pearl interjected, as she, with a frown, found a tote bag in which to put the ingredients to a dish that didn’t sound that appetizing.

“I think they’re gonna send us home for lunch. What they’re cooking on the hot plate really stinks. And they’re giggling over this mushy looking stuff and they’ve already told us we couldn’t have any because it wasn’t for little boys and girls. But that’s not the stuff that stinks. It just looks gross. Zeezee says she used to have a friend who made this stinky stuff. Nesha’s friend sent the fixings to her and a card that her and Zeezee keep giggling over and won’t let us see—women,” he said, with the age old exasperation of male confronted with enigmatic woman.

“Ma…you finished?” Vonnie Pearl nodded and handed the bag to Juston. “I’ll walk back with Juston,” Josh said.

Whatever they were cooking, Juston was right. It stank. Rachel and Cinda were sitting at the computer, playing a game, making faces at each other, and overtly watching Lanetia and Zeezee.

“I don’t remember the proportions,” Lanetia was saying when Josh and Juston came in. “Please close the door. It’s cold enough in here.” She looked up and saw Josh. She immediately started giggling.

Zeezee kept a straight face, but with difficulty. "You get my herbs?"

Juston nodded and gave the filled tote bag to her. He looked a question at Rachel and Cinda, who each, in turn, shrugged.

"You know Ma be cookin' lunch. What is this smell?" Josh asked, wrinkling his nose.

"Nesha and me, we be cookin' up a recipe. The kids be along for lunch. You come here to tell us that?"

"The smell?" Josh prompted.

"Fish."

"Dead fish on the riverbank don't smell this bad."

"Well, this fish be dead, just ain't on no riverbank. It be in this here pot. I think it be time to pour off the water again. I think I can remember how to make them johnnycakes. Nesha, after you pour off the water, debone the fish. Enough for you and me. Two cups of flour, but the batter can't be too thin. Got to have some body. My friend, Tallcat, that's what we called him—nobody could make johnnycakes like him. Put some of this fish stew on it or some jelly… We had us a good old time. Hadn't thought about him in years. That was the winter I spent in Jamaica. He was a dancin' fool and I kept up with him."

Joshua turned the opened can on the counter to read it—diced tomatoes. There were chopped green peppers and onions in a plastic bag. The card was on the counter by the plastic bag of green peppers and onions. He turned it over, stared at the picture, looked at his wife who was busy deboning fish, and then glanced at his grandmother who was shaking her head at him. "I don't suppose I should say anything about this porno card."

"Your name ain't on it. Don't let it concern yourself. Me and Nesha appreciate it. Don't we, Nesha?"

"What's the problem? It's very amusing." At his frown, she added: "I take it you don't think so. There's a remedy for that. You put the card back on the counter, the way it was, and go to the house for lunch. Me and Zeezee are having a good time. Zeezee"

"Can we talk outside, please, Nesha."

"It's cold." *Please.* "What? Fine." Lanetia grabbed her scarf and wound it around her head and neck before she followed him outside.

"My hand may be hurt, but nothin' else is," Josh began, then said hurriedly, his voice muffled through the scarf that Zeezee had thrown at him as he stepped out on the porch, "I don't think

Estelan be a female." He tried to arrange the scarf. Finally, Lanetia took pity on him and wound it around his neck.

"He's not. We used to work together. He FedExed the fixings for an island delicacy. The kids and I met the truck at the end of the driveway. The driver was not happy that he had to make a delivery up here. Problem?"

"Ex-boyfriend?"

"Yes."

"Why he contactin' you?" Joshua tried to tell himself to stop, but jealousy guided him. Lanetia wasn't jealous of Roberta. He had wanted her to be. In that moment, he wasn't so sure. What was twisting inside of him was torture.

"To inform me that the yearly distribution from the partnership in which I still hold an interest has been transferred to my account."

"He know you married?"

"He's married. Josh, I don't quite understand why we're having this conversation. I had a life… You had a life. What's in the past, stays in the past. We agreed to that."

"He send…"

"Your former lover practically did a lap dance in your lap in my presence. I did not make a scene. I did not ask you questions. I expect the same courtesy."

"Can I stay for your lunch? I like to try new things."

"Nesha, you can tell your friend that his present was effective. I know I was not the intended recipient. Fish stew and johnnycakes, with warm sea musk milk on the side. Very potent. You can stop gigglin'. One day… You and Zeezee… I…maybe I was a little depressed. I don't need no aphrodisiac. I don't think I'll ever need that with you."

"I never said you did. You said—I like to try new things. I like that about you. Are you sleepy?"

"Your lesson for today—dance. Franklin sent me a video of party dances. Josh took Vonnie Pearl shopping. Right?" Rachel nodded. "Let's have dance class. Pop in video. Turn up the volume. Stand on either side of me. I like this dance. Janine wants us to dance this after she dances with her father and husband, so I have to learn it. Remember, we did something similar at my wedding. It's based on the cha-cha." Lanetia demonstrated the cha-cha and added a few steps and a spin.

"Nesha, what you think you doin'?" Zeezee shouted over the loud music.

"I was sitting in front of the computer and I got to thinking that these kids never dance. I don't want Juston to be nervous on a dance floor and look like he's got a steel rod in his back. Come on, Juston, cha-cha."

"I know how to dance." Juston moonwalked across the living room and added a spin.

"Good. Listen to what the DJ says. First, he'll go through the steps really slow, then the music will gradually increase in tempo. Expand your repertoire."

Cinda stared at Lanetia's feet for a second, then at the video and decided she would join them. "I'll rerun the video. Slow…slow…then move to the beat. Come on, Zeezee. Remember Tallcat. Remember the limbo? How low can you go? You can cha-cha?"

"Girl, move aside, I was dancin' before you was born. Look at a pro cha-cha."

They were nearing the end of the fifth dance on the video. The music was loud and Zeezee, who had collapsed on the sofa after the second dance, was loudly critiquing their every move. They did not hear the gasps of surprise that came from the doorway. Vonnie Pearl and Josh were back early because they had decided to go to Tiny Town and not Salyna. Vonnie Pearl and Josh looked at the dancing foursome as though aliens had invaded their home.

"You cut off that devil music and stop doin' that devil dancin'," Vonnie Pearl yelled. Lanetia turned off the video and, without a glance at either Josh or Vonnie Pearl, went outdoors through the kitchen.

"Girl, one of these days, you gonna learn how to have a little fun," Zeezee said, shaking her head. "We been cooped up here for how long and you gonna have a hissy over some dancin'. Didn't you get none of me?"

Josh caught up with Lanetia as she came around the house, heading to the old home place. "Hey, you gonna catch pneumonia runnin' outside all sweaty, with your coat open."

"Couldn't you have stayed away for just a little longer? I am sick of both of your…"

"Don't put me in whatever pot you brewin' with my Ma. Far as I be concerned, you can dance all you want. You can listen to the music you want. But you remember one thing, Ma didn't have a childhood like yours. She was courtin' and havin' me."

"So we all suffer for her lost childhood. Your Dad didn't dance? Didn't like music?"

"Yeah, he did. Stop, so I can put your scarf on. Nesha…" Lanetia took the scarf and wound it around her head and neck. "Button up your coat." Lanetia stared at the buttons and made no move to comply. "Please. I know you angry.

"Part of the problem. Dad…" he explained at her frown of incomprehension. "After he was killed, she didn't want anything to do with music or dancin'. Like that had somethin' to do with what happened. Put this hat on your head." Since he was trying to put the hat on her head, Lanetia relented and slid the hat on top of the scarf. "I like it when you dance."

"Juston **will** know how to dance. I hope it's something he'll enjoy."

"From what I saw, I don't think he'll be holdin' up anybody's wall. Zeezee ain't gonna be able to move."

"Yes, she will. Movement is good for arthritis."

"I like it when you dance with me."

"Really? Josh, I know you know how to have fun…laugh…see humor in just living. Why did you have to side with Vonnie Pearl who, from what Zeezee says, has never had a sense of humor? Don't answer. I need to be alone. Thanks for the scarf and the hat."

Lanetia took her time taking off her coat and unwinding the scarf. For a moment, she hated the newspaper, snow covered mountains, impassable roads, and all the lacks…so many lacks. The weight of the lacks… She began to shiver. She turned on the kerosene heater in the back room. For the fiftieth time, she wished that Josh hadn't repurposed the fireplace for the kerosene heater. Leaping, crackling flames were a soother that she missed. All of her homes had fireplaces. Candle…she found a thick, peach scented candle and lit it.

In the past, the only way she had to forget the lacks was to write herself into a state of oblivion. The notebook was waiting for her, as was the flickering flame of the candle. As she opened the notebook, she remembered—present forgotten, but somehow enfolded in all of infinity. She reread the last paragraph. Not great, but not bad. At this point, it was the idea that mattered. The dialogue would come.

"Nesha…"

"Juston, I'm in the back room," Nesha called out. "Is something the matter?"

"Time to do chores. I brought your gloves and work boots. Smells good. Makes me think of last summer and Zeezee giving me peach slices and telling me I'd turn into a peach if I kept eating,"

"Thanks. I forgot the time. It's dark already. Shouldn't be surprised."

"You got it hot in here."

"Yeah, turn off the heater and blow out the candle."

"What are you writing?"

"Ideas. I wrote an outline. Now, I can get organized and do some research. You know, the characters remind me of you, Rachel, and Cinda. Cinda said she dreamed me. Maybe, I dreamed all of you." Juston looked at Lanetia as though she had lost her mind. "I know. Cows." Juston laughed.

Aunt Maline couldn't stop crying. The call had come as they were eating Josh's birthday dinner. Vonnie Pearl was telling the story of Josh's birth. She and Zeezee had stayed with Miz Flora in Salyna for three months because of the snow.

Somehow, Lanetia and Franklin coaxed Aunt Maline to take a sedative. Lanetia patted Aunt Maline's face with a hand towel. Aunt Maline appeared to be crying in her sleep. Lanetia sighed and pulled up a chair so she could sit with her. Aunt Maline hadn't taken her husband's and son's deaths this badly. She didn't need to be in this big, drafty house in the middle of nowhere by herself. But how to convince her? Aunt Leda and Kaida wouldn't be within shouting distance anymore.

Kaida was moving back to Louisville where she had lived before she had moved in with her mother. Kaida's daughter attended the University of Louisville and her son lived with her ex-husband who also lived in Louisville with his third wife.

Aunt Maline's only child, Detrick, had been murdered when he sold some cake flour as cocaine and the buyer hadn't appreciated the switch. Kaida had asked Aunt Maline to live with her in Louisville, but so far Aunt Maline had said no. *I have my house. There's plenty of room. She could live in the mother-in-law apartment or the downstairs bedroom. You've been there. Maya might move in with me, Kaida said, referring to her daughter. She wouldn't have to pay rent, but she's used to having her own place. And I still don't know if I like her friend. Something about him just makes me grit my teeth. And you can't say anything. She starts in with I love him and I want to slap her into Tennessee. Lanetia, no comment required. Let me get this out of my system. He's coming to the funeral with her. Why does every no talented hustler want to be a rapper? I listened to one of his raps and if he didn't say ho once, he said it a dozen times and that was in the two minutes I could make myself listen to. I was never so glad in my life that she caught some virus and couldn't be in the video. Her father didn't put his foot down until he saw the video. He told her no daughter of his was going to be naked on a video for everyone to see. He said that's a condition if she wanted him to pay any of her tuition. He said she cried and threatened and then he didn't hear anything more. Her brother said Maya told him, she was relieved. Maybe, she has some sense.*

Kaida thought Aunt Maline might listen to Lanetia. Lanetia had her doubts. Aunt Maline could be very stubborn.

"Nesha?" Josh said, placing a hand on her arm to bring her back to the room with him.

"There were three sisters, Leda, Maline, and my mother, Nella. They were three peas in a pod....eighteen months apart. Everyone took them for triplets. Aunt Leda went to Oberlin, Aunt Maline went to Howard, and my mother went to Tennessee State, because she didn't want to be far from home. She almost went to Fisk, but my grandfather read something in the packet of information that Fisk sent that he didn't like.

"Told her, he wouldn't pay a dime for her to attend Fisk. But he would see what he could do, if she went to Tennessee State. May have been A&I then. I forget when the name changed."

"She met your father."

"Not at Tennessee State. She was getting her Master's Degree in Education at Oberlin. Dad was a year ahead of her in the same program. He eventually got his doctorate from there. If Mama had lived, she would have gotten her doctorate. She was waiting for Franklin to finish high school. When will this winter be over?"

Joshua hugged her to him. The bedroom was cold. The space heater wasn't even warming the floor in front of it. Lanetia had on a flannel gown over thermals and Joshua had on thermals under his flannel pajamas. Joshua's injured hand ached from the cold.

"Your Aunt can't stay here. She can't keep this place warm."

"She never comes up here and downstairs is okay. Franklin found an old hot water bottle, which gave me the idea of wrapping a bottle of hot water in a towel. I put a couple of them in the bed, so the bed should be warm. I'm just restless. Get in the bed. This cold isn't good for your hand. You don't want to be able to tell the weather by the ache in your hand."

"Your Dad has decided not to be civil."

“Ignore him. His favorite child is pregnant. Knowing her, she’ll have a C-section to ensure the baby is born on her schedule.”

“Nesha, I don’t get your Dad, but I don’t think that Patrice is his favorite child. He keeps lookin’ at you when he talkin’. He seems to be askin’ or tellin’ you somethin’ and it seems to me he don’t think you listenin’.”

“I’ve told him and told him. If he wants to tell me something, come out and say it. I’m no good at innuendos. Never have been.”

“Well, he said, you didn’t need to be stayin’ with your Aunt. He wanted you to stay with Kaida.”

“Oh, that… He thinks Patrice will influence Kaida, Jelly Bean, and Tasha to sell. See, this is the old house. Aunt Leda built her house when she retired. It’s all their parents’ property. We have an interest through our mother. If enough heirs want to sell, then there could be a forced sell. Dad does not believe in selling property.”

“Why’d he want you to read this article about a cemetery? It’s all marked up, so you can’t make out the words.”

“He and the County bought some property for the Black cemetery that has to be moved because of road construction. He just wanted me to see the headline. He’s the good guy…again.”

"Josh, aren't you tired? Pull over at the next exit and I'll drive. You hear me?" Lanetia tapped his arm when he didn't respond. At her tap, he nodded, but didn't look at her. Whatever her father had said when they had talked after the dinner had angered him. She could tell by the way his right hand clenched the steering wheel and by the firm set of his lips. What had her father said? Josh shouldn't be driving. He'd had no problem with her driving to Kentucky.

"What did he say?" Lanetia asked, hoping he would not retort that she wouldn't tell him what his mother had done, as he had, the last three times she had asked.

"Road finally clear. No ice," was his response.

Lanetia sighed. The funeral—Kaida and Aunt Maline had a shouting match over Aunt Leda's dress. Aunt Maline couldn't believe that Kaida would bury her mother in a dress her mother hadn't liked and rarely wore. It hadn't even alleviated the tension when Kaida had shown Aunt Maline her mother's instructions and there it was in her mother's handwriting that this was the dress she had chosen. Lanetia had attempted to mediate the situation, but Aunt Maline would not budge. Finally, Kaida had agreed to the dress that Aunt Maline had chosen.

Jelly Bean, a well-known gospel singer, had collapsed during his solo and after being revived had insisted on singing his song from the beginning. Tasha had surprised everyone by, instead of asking Aunt Maline, telling her, that she was coming home with her. Aunt Maline had agreed. They'd cleared the houses of furniture and filled up three storage bins at the local storage facility. Aunt Maline had promised to visit Lanetia in the summer. After living in Chicago for thirty years, Aunt Maline did not like the cold.

As funerals go, not that much drama. No one was inclined to sell. But that would change when Aunt Maline was no longer with them. They decided to rent Aunt Leda's house. They discussed razing the home place, but no one had the heart to tear down the house where they had spent so many summers.

The night before, Aunt Maline had asked Lanetia if she would buy the property. Lanetia had not hesitated in saying yes. How would this angry man who drove so carefully and meticulously react to that?

What could her father have said to cause such anger? Even though her father hadn't been civil to Josh, he hadn't talked to him until after the home going dinner at the church. Think Lanetia—what was Dad talking about in the few hurried conversations they'd had? *Land—don't sell; Patrice—pregnancy suits her;*

Franklin—accepted into a program teaching robotic surgery; me—oh, shit, he said I was too thin and he muttered something about milking cows. Who told him I'd been milking cows?

Did I do something that stupid? No, I don't talk to him about the mountains. Did I let it slip to either Patrice or Franklin? When would I have done that? Zeezee—I have to talk to Zeezee about her conversations with Dad. Zeezee's trying to be friendly and Dad is pumping her for information.

"He said something about me milking cows, didn't he? Josh?"

"Somethin'."

"And that I was too thin."

"Somethin'."

"Josh…"

"Conversation, trust be two way. Your dad was talkin' to me. Let me deal with it." *My daughter…milking cows? Who do you think you married? A farmhand? My daughter knows how to work… Her mother and I taught all our children the value of work. Maybe you don't believe I have any influence over her. Know this…I will make your life a living hell if my daughter continues to look like a stick figure on a diet. Do I make myself clear?*

"He's my father. We agreed that we would each deal with our relatives if they caused an issue between us. I ask that you honor that agreement."

"He has not caused an issue between us. I'll let you know when he does."

"Zeezee, you can't have a conversation with my father." Zeezee pursed her lips, determined to do what she wanted to do. "He's not having a pleasant conversation with you..."

"How do you know?" Zeezee challenged. "Your dad and I don't even talk that much about you. We talk about these here do-nothin' people up here more than we talk about you."

"Do you see what's happening? Josh won't let me help. His hand will never heal properly. It may look healed on the outside but the inside is still healing. That's what the soft tissue scan showed. That's why it hurts like it does."

For a moment, Josh had scared her. She had never seen him so angry as when he had blocked the barn door and told her never to come to the barn again. I can do it. My wife don't need to milk cows. I can put food on the table for you. Work on your Paper, your quilt, but don't come to the barn no more. He had shut the door in her face.

Josh didn't understand her father's tactics and she understood them too well. And, for once, Zeezee was no help. In her estimation, a little pain never hurt a man.

Lanetia rebuttoned the coat she hadn't taken off and walked away from the house, oblivious that Zeezee was watching from the porch.

Zeezee met Josh as he came up the path with the sealed pail of milk. She took the pail of milk from him and walked with him to the storage porch. She sighed as she put the milk into the refrigerator.

"Get rid of the cows. They too much trouble and…"

"You always wanted to have fresh milk, so you could make butter and they ain't no trouble."

"Josh, we got to have some common sense. You got to have some common sense. Nesha's Dad want to split you two up. I know that. Nesha say I been givin' him ammunition without knowin'. She probably right. He a real smooth talker, make you feel real comfortable, like he been knowin' you forever. Flatter you… He know how to get the information he want. I told you, seem like a long time ago, that I be knowin' men like him. I forgot that knowin' and you payin' the price.

"You can't milk…"

"I just did," Josh challenged. Zeezee glared at him and he turned away. He could barely close his hand…his hand really hurt. The cold…and he had milked the three cows mostly one-handed.

"With how much damage to that hand? Take a painkiller. Lay down. Read a book. You think I don't know you hurtin'? You couldn't hide that you was hurtin' from Lanetia when you insisted on drivin' from Kentucky. What you tryin' to prove? The reason you don't have no problem with that ankle you injured is cause me and your dad insisted that you follow the doctor's orders and I fixed you up some herbs. With your hand, you ain't followin' the doctor's orders; you ignore me..."

"He said I couldn't take care of my wife."

"So you gonna let your pride take you down a path you don't need to go cause you done heard a lie?"

"Zeezee said I scared you this mornin'. I didn't mean to. Can we walk down the driveway to the road? I took a painkiller and it don't make me sleepy, just too restless to stand or sit in one place for more than a few minutes. Nesha, I got on those gloves you bought that keep your hands warm. Helps a lot. Please." Lanetia turned off the computer. She was spinning her wheels trying to write an article about the life cycle of trees in a forest. A non-profit group was planning to plant two thousand hardwood trees in the mountains in the coming year. Lanetia wondered why they were planting the trees when they agreed with the naysayers who said planting such a small number of trees wouldn't make a difference.

March had come in like a lion, but on this day, the lion was resting. The driveway was covered in packed snow and ice, with just a little melt that would refreeze during the night. The sun was trying its best to usher in spring, but Mother Earth hadn't decided to banish winter, not just yet. They were almost to the main road, before Joshua spoke.

"Mrs. Rellson wants to know why you ain't accepted her apology. She said she was overwhelmed. She's been censured by the principal and the school board and she's goin' to Diversity Training like you asked."

"We are not uppity Negroes and, so what if we were? I will not have Juston's love of self, learning, this world crushed by those prejudiced, ignorant white people who pass themselves off as teachers in this godforsaken County. I will homeschool him as I have been since October. Juston is my responsibility—not yours. Some of his teachers have been making snide comments all school year. I warned Mrs. Rellson and ignored the others. No more. They have their wish. He doesn't attend their school. They don't have to deal with a Black male child who makes better grades than their ignorant children."

"Cinda done flat refused to go back to school and Rachel ain't far behind. You gonna homeschool all three of them, plus Rachel's friend? His parents asked me if you would consider it. Said he was an honor student before they transferred here and that exposé you're doin' on the teachers' gradin' practices is gettin' everybody up in arms. First time the school board ever got a public records request. The State will take over the school system next year. How could we have known they was deliberately gradin' the Black children lower than they earned? Why they always think what they do don't have consequences?

"Nesha, you and me can homeschool the kids. The Knolltons can homeschool Amare. Most of the folk up here can't. They ain't got a high school diploma. State talkin' about firin' all the teachers and the principals.

"You not listenin' to a word I'm sayin'," Joshua complained.

"If you're asking me to send Juston back to that school, the answer is no. Josh, are you being blind, deliberately blind? I'm not well liked in this community. If they can't hurt me, they might try to hurt Juston. For now, I want Juston close. I don't believe there will be violence here because you're known as a very good shot who will shoot when threatened."

"Some of them know you a good shot. Vinton got to talkin' to McNeil about last summer, sayin' more than he should, and McNeil been spreadin' the word that you know your way around guns. I think they know you'll shoot back.

"I never thought I'd see Rachel milkin' a cow. She and Juston have a contest every mornin'. Cinda feel real important, gatherin' the eggs and feedin' the chickens. I guess I should've let them help before. I should've let them help this mornin'. Anger make you act foolish. Ma said she ain't milked a cow in her life. Ma leavin' it up to me to decide about the girls' schoolin'. I guess they gonna stay with you."

"If the Knolltons want me to, I'll homeschool Amare, too."

"I be talkin' about everything, but what I intended to talk to you about. I…I was thinkin' maybe to fix up the old home place for us. Gut the back and leave the front where your equipment is the same for now. Then you'd have your own place…"

"What does that solve?"

"Women like their own space."

"And men don't?"

"Your dad…"

"Knows how to exploit male pride. The question you should have asked and answered was—are we comfortable/committed to our relationship. Instead you've asked my father's questions and you don't even realize that the answers don't have anything to do with us."

"Why don't they?"

"My father isn't who we are or want to be. His answers may have worked thirty, forty years ago, but not today. But, now that I think on it, his answers didn't work when my mother was ill. We have to make it on our own terms, not his."

"So I should just accept you milkin' the cows?"

"If something needs to be done, one of us needs to do it. If I don't want to do something, I will tell you. I'm not too proud to pay someone to do what I can't or won't do.

"Josh, I'm not thin from too much work. For one thing, I never was curvy and soft like your mother or Roberta. I gained some weight this past summer, but I deliberately set out to get rid of most of it so I wouldn't have to buy any new clothes. Let me finish.

"My reason for not buying new clothes is, I think, legitimate. I have too many, for one thing, and I wanted to see what kind of clothes I needed for this place. And I'm very well fed."

"Half the time you don't eat. Especially if Ma's in one of her moods."

"Please…this conversation isn't about your mother."

"Yes, it is, Nesha. This conversation be about my mother and your dad."

"Why don't we discuss finances or religion?"

When Joshua raised his right eyebrow, she shrugged. Then, they both laughed.

CHAPTER 9

Atlanta—March, almost April, almost ninety degrees, ninety-five percent humidity. Mountains—March, almost April, forty-five degrees, ten percent humidity. Atlanta…heat…sweat…freedom.

Lanetia and Corina sat over their third cup of tea, catching up. "Are you sure that you want me and the kids to stay with you until Wednesday? I know you're on Spring Break, but…"

"McCory, no problem," Corina said, using Lanetia's last name as they had all through college. It was an after effect of pledging on the same line. "I can't go anywhere. Mickey's school is on Spring Break two weeks from now. Kahla's Spring Break was last week—you get the picture. If the school system did a half-way decent job educating boys, Mickey wouldn't be in a private school and they'd have the same school breaks. Then, when they got to high school, we'd all be on the same schedule and, in all probability, we still wouldn't go anywhere. I don't know what I would do if I had money for a vacation. Know what…I have to give a standing ovation to those nuns. They have that boy totally in line. Bless the nuns.

"Do you remember why I married that fool? Did any of you, my sorors, tell me to think twice before I married Mr. Party? I know…broken record. Did you see my daughter giving Juston the eye? Did you see Cinda give *he*r the eye? Should be an interesting week. I'm looking forward to helping you, but why can't the kids know?"

"Zeezee told her only child…" *Your mother-in-law?* "Uh huh… That she was orphaned at the age of ten and she didn't have any family. An elderly neighbor took her in and, when she was fourteen, she got a job as a baby sitter with this white family that moved around a lot. That's the story they know."

"Before I tell you what I found out, I have to read what you wrote. It's been over four years and not a word… Now, you have chapters for me to edit?"

"No, just to read. I have an idea, but I'm having a difficult time finding their voices. It used to flow. This is choppy…like I'm writing discrete chapters with nothing to connect them but the characters. No coherent plot as of yet. I'll give it to you when you go upstairs to bed. Ridnour, I promise."

“Okay. I’ll be up the rest of the night. Well, Zeezee might want to stick with her story…about not having any family. I looked up the names you gave me. This guy, Philamon, has to be her nephew or great-nephew, has one of those evangelical mega-churches. He’s so sanctimonious that he was quoting scriptures as he kicked his wife out and I mean kicked…physically kicked. She had him arrested and he is still quoting scriptures as to why the Lord is blessing him with this woman, his mistress, who he had installed in his mansion, notice the use of the past tense… Big scandal. I tried to call you, but you know how that went and then something else happened. How can you live in a place with such poor telephone connections and even worse Internet access? Don’t answer…seasons. Where was I?

“Anyway, wife went to court and got room and board and had him kicked out of the mansion. Girl, he is still quoting scriptures and those fools at his church are telling anyone who will listen… Stop…stop laughing, I got this story to tell… You’re gonna make me… What was I saying? That their man of God been done wrong. They knew that wife of his was the devil and she had been seen practicing voodoo.”

They were laughing so hard that the tears flowed. “Bed…” Corina finally got out.

Lanetia lay in bed, Corina's report on her stomach. The preacher was Philamon Winslow Goodman. His father was Philamon Goodman, also a preacher, and Philamon's father was Winslow, Zeezee's brother who was some years older than she. Goodman was Zeezee's birth surname. *I just liked the sound of Tallent. I had talent or so I thought. I was the youngest. Zylus, Emalia, Winslow, Camelia, Cardine, Todd, Purlie, and me. After the Reverend died...I didn't go to his funeral...I went back and made sure Ma had a tombstone. Reverend wouldn't buy her one...too cheap. Already courtin' before she was cold.*

That tramp put him in his grave in two years. She had a baby, but it didn't live. You don't lay yourself in bed with no man the very night his wife done died. She didn't last six months after him. Emalia told me that whatever took her... It was agonizing. Then I started movin' around so much, I just lost touch. I made up a story that suited me and lived the story. I been doin' it so long... I can't remember the last time I said them names. The Reverend Zylus Azorel Goodman and my Ma, Lorelia Pearl. I thought it be the prettiest name. I almost named Vonnie Pearl after my ma, but Cousin's name was Vonnie, so I named my baby Vonnie Pearl, after two of the finest women I ever knew.

Purlie was the only sibling still living and she was in an assisted living facility. Corina and Lanetia were both family history buffs. They had, each, created a family tree for a class project and, off and on, they would take trips to out of the way courthouses to further their genealogical research. Even in college, Corina had wanted to live in Atlanta. That was the reason she had married Mr. Party. Mr. Party was from Atlanta and he was her ticket to the city of her dreams.

As Corina said, the search wasn't difficult. She had all the names and where they had lived. It was mostly searching through old city directories. On Thursday, Lanetia's first day in Atlanta, they had found Zeezee's kin's current addresses.

The kids had begged to come. Corina had a friend who owned ***A Child's View of Atlanta*** *which offered tours of Atlanta and the surrounding area. Today, the kids were going sight-seeing. Lanetia and Corina were going to the assisted living facility.*

"On the way back, we'll stop at Derinda's store. She sells these really fancy Easter dresses. Cinda will hate you. Derinda says an Easter dress is not an Easter dress without a stiff underslip known in the good old days as a cancan. Why? Because it was starched to the point it felt like you were wearing a shredded tin can. Kahla hates me every Easter. I showed her a picture of me in my Easter dress and she said I should want to do better by her. Torture… Listen to this… She's eight. *Torture should not be perpetuated through the generations. Someone has to say enough is enough.* It won't be me. She looks such a little doll. She gets to wear tights. I wore anklets because my mother wore anklets…frilly anklets. I hated those socks. Child does not know the meaning of torture. I have to show you the dress I bought her. You have Cinda's measurements?" At Lanetia's nod, she continued: "Kahla's dress needed altering. I'll pick it up while we're there.

"Before I forget… The Charge Nurse at the assisted living facility says Purlie is not senile, but she doesn't talk much."

The on-duty Charge Nurse pointed to Purlie. Purlie was sitting in a wheelchair at a window, just staring… maybe at memories of her childhood. *It's the stink of disinfectant masking that old people smell. That's what Telman James had said about old folks' homes…death traps for the old, the forgotten, the lonely. If I sound bitter, I am. My children chose a house of death for me. I fooled them and bought this piece of paradise. They are not welcome here and they will have no inheritance. Not my initial plan, but they deserve nothing and they will only be informed of my death exactly one year after that momentous date. That will provide Estelan the time he will require to settle my estate.*

"Miz Purlie," Lanetia said, as she and Corina sat on the couch that was beside the wheelchair, "Nurse Lands said she told you that we were coming today. My name is Lanetia McCory and this is my friend, Corina Ridnour." Purlie slowly turned her head to stare at them. Nurse Lands had said that Purlie had cataracts and refused to wear her glasses. *She can't be seeing too much without the glasses. She just had the cataract in the right eye removed and it has healed nicely so if she would only wear her glasses... Nurse Lands had trailed off with a shrug.*

Lanetia held out her hand. Purlie kind of waved hers. *So, she knows we're here.* The brown of Purlie's left eye appeared to be gray, while her right eye was a vivid brown. She seemed unable to focus. "I guess you're wondering why we wanted to talk to you." A slow nod, but still no real interest. "Do you remember your sister Xexema? You called her Mazie." Finally, some interest…the hand that had waved so listlessly, clenched into a fist.

"Mazie been gone. Gone. Why you askin' about Mazie? Gone."

"Yes ma'am, Mazie left. Mazie sent me to look for her sisters and brothers…"

Purlie clenched her other hand. "I told you Mazie gone, dead, gone. Why you keep askin' about Mazie?" Lanetia noticed that Nurse Lands had started toward them at Purlie's obvious agitation.

"Miz Purlie, Mazie is alive."

"I think Miz Purlie has had enough," Nurse Lands said, as she placed a comforting hand on Purlie's thin shoulder. "Miz Purlie, do you need some medicine?" Purlie shook her head. "If you give me that letter, I'll read it to Miz Purlie…"

"Letter? Now, read it now," Purlie insisted.

"You want me to stay near?" Nurse Lands asked. Purlie nodded.

As Lanetia read the words that Zeezee had dictated to her, tears poured down Purlie's face. They sat in silence as Purlie cried into a towel given to her by Nurse Lands. "She too sick to come? She couldn't come see me herself? Why? Why? All these years… Why?"

"If you'd like, I can get her on the phone for you. We call her Zeezee. Nurse, do you have a landline we can use? The number is toll-free."

"Phone… Yes, of course. At the desk. I'll bring it to you. The cord is long enough to reach here, so Miz Purlie doesn't have to move. She likes the view from this window. Just press nine for an outside line. Lanetia searched through her purse for a stray business card for the Newspaper. *I hate changing purses,* she thought, as she searched through the compartment where the business card should have been. She found a card with the Paper's toll free number in the compartment where her cell phone should have been. Zeezee had promised to answer the Newspaper's line. Vonnie Pearl had promised Josh that she would not answer the Newspaper's line (a light flashed and the ring tone was different) and the line would then be answered by the answering machine. Zeezee mush have been in the kitchen. She picked up on the third ring.

A light had come on for Purlie. She talked to Zeezee for over an hour.

"She comin' to see me. She didn't know. I thought her dead. That was Ma's baby on the phone. She comin'. Go get her. I want to see her. I got things to tell her. You go get her."

"Miz Purlie, you just had a lot of excitement. Hi, I'm Nurse Trent. Nurse Lands left a sedative for Miz Purlie. It's time for her lunch and I'll give it to her after she eats, calm her down. Can her sister really come soon? It would mean so much to her. They have a lot of catching up to do. Miz Purlie, you're gonna like what's in your room. These ladies brought you some fruit and flowers. And I just know I can get your hair fixed tomorrow. How would you like that?"

Nurse Trent winked at them, but mouthed at Lanetia. *Please.* Lanetia understood. If Zeezee did not come, Purlie could sink into a depression.

"Where's your van?" Lanetia asked, blinking in the bright sunlight.

"We came out the front door. We went in the side door. So this way," Corina directed, after looking around to orient herself.

"I'm not taking the kids with me. Do you mind?" *No, McCory. They have home training.* "Thanks. I want them to have some fun. They complain and then ask me what I have planned for them in the same breath. We'll meet them at three and I'll get them settled at your place." Corina nodded. "I will be back tomorrow morning…early. By three at the latest."

"Zeezee can meet me at an exit. Let's get Kahla's and Cinda's Easter dresses. Then, the mall… Rachel has to have a dress for Easter, but she won't shop for it. She saw a dress in that flyer from last Sunday's paper that she liked. I'm glad I remembered to ask you to save the flyers. Please, let the store have that dress in her size.

"If I leave by six, I can be at the exit by nine. Soon as we get back to your place, we'll call Zeezee."

"Try the cell," Corina said. "If yours isn't charged, use mine. Side pocket on purse. Sometimes you can call a landline even if you can't call another cell phone." Lanetia nodded, but held up her cell phone. She'd charged the phone last night, but hadn't used it because of the kids. She'd bought a cell phone for the kids in case of an emergency. She'd told them about it on the way to Atlanta and they had argued for an hour about who should carry it. Last night, she had given the phone to Rachel and told her, as the eldest, the phone was her responsibility. Each of them had a camera. She'd compromised and given Cinda, who wasn't very attentive where money was concerned, five dollars. She'd given Rachel money with the explicit instructions that she was to give Cinda money to buy souvenirs. Juston was very good with money. He had stuffed his money in the front pocket of his jeans.

Vonnie Pearl answered the phone. Zeezee was sitting on the porch. Lanetia heard the front door open and close. "Is Vonnie Pearl listening? Just say yes or no." *Of course.* "Then, listen and call me back at Corina's if you can meet me at the exit…where the Daytown Inn is located. Leave a message."

Zeezee had everything in place by the time they returned to Corina's. *Meet me at ten at in the parkin' lot of the Daytown Inn. Flora's nephew will be drivin' his Jeep, so you won't miss us.*

Zeezee was silent most of the trip back to Atlanta. It wasn't until they passed the sign for the first exit to Marietta that Zeezee said anything. "There was a church we used to visit. It was somewhere near Marietta. This here Interstate wasn't here. Wasn't nothin' worth lookin' at for miles. And now…the Interstate and all these lights. Your friend don't mind?"

"No, she's excited. I think this is better. You talking to your sister," Lanetia explained. "She'll open up to you. Corina and I were just two strangers."

"And that preacher be my great-nephew? Got his own television show? Sound like the Reverend. There be evil in this here world. It might skip a generation, here and there. I guess you got to know where it be. I can't believe those children put their ma in a nursing home. Excuse me…assisted living facility. They know what she went through for them? Guess you can't ask your children to appreciate you.

"Even back then, it was different if you was in the city. Folks in the city didn't seem to take care of their people like the folk in the country. Sometimes, I wonder what the city done to us. Seem like it took what little good feelin' we had for others and squeezed it out on the concrete and concrete don't grow nothin'. Not even more concrete."

They didn't wake up anyone when they arrived at Corina's house. Zeezee must not have slept. She tapped the door to Lanetia's bedroom at six. She was dressed and ready to visit her sister. Lanetia left a note for Corina and said that she would call in about an hour.

Purlie told the Aide who came to wash her hair that Zeezee would do it. If this person was really her sister, she would remember. And Zeezee did remember…she didn't touch the birthmark that was on Purlie's scalp in the back. She parted Purlie's still thick hair to look at it as though to reassure herself that this woman was Purlie. Then, they talked, cried, and laughed until lunch.

◆◆◆

"Ridnour, everything's good." Lanetia pushed the honey across the table to Corina after adding two dollops to her cup of tea. She was half asleep. Zeezee was napping.

"McCory, you are conflicted. Some of what you wrote is really good. Some…you're venting. I marked what I thought was right for the book. I like that it's edgier. A suggestion…a book, with scattered illustrations, instead of a graphic novel. What you've written doesn't feel like a graphic novel. Can't explain it. Think about it." Lanetia shrugged. She hadn't been thinking in terms of a graphic novel when she had written the first book. Corina and Tani had thought of that format.

"I wish you hadn't kinda sorta based the mother on me. Okay, she teaches English as a second language, but she writes poetry. I haven't written a poem since Kahla…no…Mickey was born. Remember when we used to read at those clubs around and on campus? With Darly? She was brilliant, but too troubled for this world. I hear she's not doing well. She's had pneumonia…twice, I think."

"I've been trying to convince myself to visit. I haven't yet."

"Ditto for me. I can't imagine being in her presence and not hearing some acerbic remark that's right on target…even if I am the object of the barb. We'll get there." Lanetia could not agree that she would. There was a long silence as they each thought about Darly. Neither had ever hoped they could match Darly in talent or showmanship. "McCory, don't disappear like you have for the last few years. You just seemed to give up when you moved to Nashville. You were only taking that job until you passed the bar. Remember…you said the more you learned about Nashville, the less you wanted to begin another practice."

"I was mired in the mud and I couldn't find a path that led to dry ground," Lanetia confessed. "I resented everything about my life. I didn't want you to know that *me*." Corina nodded.

"I did that when my marriage was falling apart. Remember, you and Tani persuaded me to edit the first AWB book. We used to have so much fun…then life happened. Darly said when you finally fell in love, you would be challenged by the messiness." Lanetia nodded. *Love is like a river, McCory. The more you try to contain it, the more swiftly it flows to a destination you know not.*

Just go. You might have to swim against the current. Once you get to that destination, you might find a waterfall...go over it, because beyond is what you could not possibly have dreamed of. Doesn't matter what is there. Just go. We're playing with sex and calling it love. You want to know why I know so much and so little? I was raised by my grandmother. She was an angry woman. She birthed two daughters who both liked sex, but not the inevitable consequence. I spent as much time as I could with my grandfather. He lived next door. He would stand in the doorway of my bedroom and act out a bedtime story for me. There wasn't a shadow that didn't become some fantastical creature.

"Darly's performance piece...*State of Fugue*... Now, I understand it. *You think fugue, daze, stupor, catatonic, reverie, trance are* words *that mean the same state of being. I am here to tell you otherwise. Listen to my state of fugue...*" Lanetia recited. She stopped. She only remembered the beginning. Somewhere in a box, she had copies of Darly's stories and poems. Darly had been in grad school when her grandfather died and, at the funeral, Darly had collapsed. She'd never returned to grad school and she'd refused to see anyone.

"You always drummed to that piece because I couldn't bear to listen to it. I still hear Darly's voice in my dreams. Its raw intensity crawled under your skin and people would leave during the performance because they didn't want to hear the truth--I *am the dead who speak when all is quiet, when all is as you have wished and hoped it would be.*" Corina shivered. "I know what you're thinking…Darly said I had no understanding of clichés or of fairy tales and I…" Corina shivered again. "She was right," Corina said, after taking a sip of tea to chase away a chill that could never be caused by a drop in temperature.

"Remember…you'd have your sagas; I'd have my latest angst filled poem; and Darly would have a performance piece from outer space… No, that's not right…inner space…hers. There's a café that has an open mike on Saturday night. Let's go. I can get a sitter. My kids will be with their father." Corina grimaced. "She's my regular. The kids will be well taken care of. You can read anything. You could read what I marked as "vent". Some of it is really poetic. The meter is terrific. Your first performance piece. And I'll find my notebook and read one of my old poems. Old times?"

"Old times. She spoke truth. I remember her graveled voice, slinging words like stones…no ricocheting bullets that grazed and pierced and left you quivering…almost like you were in shock. Then, her honeyed voice that challenged you to remove each invisible bullet from where it was embedded and drop it to the floor at your feet. Only when the invisible became visible could you acknowledge your pain and fling it into the void, along with a single tear that was your soul's ache."

"Love's a bitch," Corina said, with a knowing nod. They clicked their mugs together to seal their agreement and in honor of Darly.

Later that afternoon, they picked up Purlie from the assisted living facility. Purlie may have taken a short nap, but she had been on the phone with her son who was to meet them at a strip shopping center. The shopping center was well past its prime. On the rusting marquee were the names of businesses: A-1 Title Loans, Provider Auto Insurance (Pay by the Week), Toady's Rent to Own, ABZ Pawn Shop, Mrs. Pones Home Cooking and Teree's Barber and Beauty Salon. However, the parking lot was mostly empty and the buckled, pitted, and cracked pavement attested to its neglect. Weeds were growing around the rusting streetlights and through the cracks in the pavement and the sidewalk. Corina parked the van where Purlie insisted her father's church had been.

There was nothing left of the neighborhood where Purlie and Zeezee had lived as children and Purlie as an adult. Even if one had a map of the old neighborhood, it would be difficult to get one's bearing as the current neighborhood had been re-platted with new streets. The developers, who bought the land, wanted no reminders of the neighborhood they had destroyed. Purlie remembered that they'd tried to fight the developers, but the County had condemned their property, paid them a little money, and told them to move on.

Once Purlie had oriented Zeezee, Lanetia, Corina and Zeezee got out of the van. Purlie watched from an open window as Zeezee pointed out where their home had been. "Just a shotgun house on Hackberry Street. It would've been over there." She looked to Purlie. Purlie nodded. "Where we standin' was the corner of Hackberry and Stable Street. Stable Street was named after the old stables that took up most of the block. You remember the fire when they burned?" She didn't even wait for Purlie's nod. "We talked about that…the flames looked like they was reachin' for heaven is what I remember the Reverend sayin'. Said it was punishment for all the evil that was goin' on. Said it was just God's mercy that no one got burned up."

"After you left, Deacon Wiggam built a barn. Had cows, pigs, goats, chickens. It was still there when they come and took our property. Mazie, I think I see Junior's car. See that maroon Cadillac stopped at the light? You be nice to Junior. I told him I would rather be in that home with Tabitha than in the same house with that woman he married. Tabitha and me got along real good. I just got to get used to her bein' gone. We was friends for forty years." Purlie removed her glasses and dabbed underneath her eyes with a tissue. Her roommate had died about six months ago.

"He done heard your name. When I talked to him on the phone, I made him remember. These glasses don't do me no good no more. But, I just can't see payin' good money for another pair until I get this other eye fixed. Just ain't no joy in getting' old."

"Sure, there be. Say what you want. Wear what you want. Do what you can. Sometimes you realize you done learned somethin' from your experiencin'. You know nothin' be forever, if nothin' else. Now that you done reminded me, I ain't gonna cuss out your boy. Why you never tell him about the Reverend and what he put you through when he found out you was pregnant?"

"You hush about that. Some things best left unsaid. I made us up a marriage date and don't you tell him no different. Y'all, too," she said, nodding toward Lanetia and Corina.

Zeezee shrugged. "If that be what you want. But I still can't believe that Winslow took over the Reverend's church. There wasn't no kind of evil doin' that he didn't do or tried to do. Him goin' to jail for killin' that boy was what put Ma in her grave."

"People change. While he was in prison, he got the call. It was his son that really built it up. And now his grandson done got one of those churches so big, you have to watch the service on the

TV. Too bad…he be Winslow all over again. Can't keep his hands off the women. You remember Winslow didn't care if they was pretty or not. Well, his grandson is picky. They got to be his definition of pretty.

"I forgot to tell you. Winslow wasn't never married to his son's mama. She was married. Her husband caught her with some man and chased them out into the street. She got hit by a car. Before she died, she told her sister who all the children's fathers were, so they wouldn't be courtin' their half brothers and sisters. Had it all written down. Woman had four children and only one by her husband.

"That husband took the one and left the rest with the sister. Winslow gave his son, Philamon, to Camelia to raise. She couldn't have no children after she lost that first one. The boy went to school to learn preachin'. He the senior pastor at Philamon the second's church."

"They changed the name of the church," Zeezee interrupted.

"They added to it. Used to be King Solomon's Church of the Holy Spirit, now it be King Solomon's Wisdom for the Ages All-Saints Church. Philamon the second said he was bein' modern, whatever that means.

"Now, Junior done real well for himself. He drove a bus for the City. He retired about five years ago. He own a little fish market. Make a real good fish sandwich and he use my recipe for his hush puppies. He keep that woman like a queen and she ain't never satisfied. One day I heard her talkin' about how Junior done heard the call. I got that boy alone and gave him a good talkin' to. Last I heard of a call. What you turnin' up your nose at? Your ways ain't changed a bit. You still got your head in the clouds."

Junior was the eldest of six children. From his wary assessment of Zeezee, one could tell he wasn't quite convinced that she was his long lost aunt. Zeezee frowned at him, then asked: "You still got that birthmark on your left cheek, shaped like a…"

"Hush, now, Mazie," Purlie snapped. "Don't you go embarrassin' Junior."

"Just let me say what I got to say."

"Junior, this your auntie, my baby sister, whether you believe it or not. She still got a mouth on her that don't know how to shut up. What you want him to call you?" she continued, trying to deter Zeezee from saying what her disapproving expression said must be said. Zeezee didn't answer fast enough. "She callin' herself Zeezee now, so you call her Auntie Zeezee."

Junior held out his hand. Zeezee patted it and Purlie erupted into laughter.

"You ain't changed. Remember… You done the same thing when you met Junior's father. He was good to me, Mazie."

"I ain't never disputed that."

"Junior and Grace are the only two here. My Zylus got himself killed, Luranne in Chicago, Stella in D.C., and Beka in California. Junior, I told you to bring Grace with you to meet your auntie."

"Ain't it enough I have to look after her? She's comin'. Deuce is bringin' her."

"Deuce be my grandson named after Zylus. He a high school football coach," Purlie explained as she pointed a warning finger at Junior that said heard, been hearing it…your auntie doesn't need to hear it.

"Purlie, wait 'til I meet your family before you tell me names. I got too many names swimmin' around in my head to remember who's who."

"If you hadn't run off, you'd know your people," Purlie shot back as if to say you deserve the headache you're getting and I will enjoy every moment of your misery.

"You two do kind of look alike or maybe it's just the way you talk. Ma said if there were any pictures of you, they burned when the Reverend's house burned to the ground."

"The Reverend wouldn't have kept my picture…"

"Shut up, Mazie," Purlie warned.

"Don't he know nothin'?"

"He know what I tell him."

"Mystery, always a mystery when Ma talks about the Reverend. Which one of you ladies is my cousin-in-law?"

Lanetia nodded and shook his hand. "Lanetia McCory."

"Everybody just calls me Junior."

"And this is my friend Corina."

"Junior, we was just lookin' at what become of where we used to live. You remember where our old house used to be?"

"About where that ABZ Pawn Shop is. You tell how Winslow stole everybody's share of the money…with that Philamon. Said he gave it to the church. The church of his pocket," Junior muttered.

"Ain't got that far. Over and done with. Let it rest."

Junior changed the subject. "You know Deuce is really into family history. Ma didn't bother tellin' Deuce that you changed your name. She said she didn't remember when he was askin' about her brothers and sisters. This afternoon…she remembered what you told her when you came back to buy your Mama's tombstone. Ma still had that receipt, but you signed your real name. I can see how you could lose touch. After the Reverend died, we moved around a lot.

"I got three boys. Deuce, the youngest. Bernard, the eldest, got in trouble and he's in jail. Jordan's a master gardener. He owns his own business." Junior grimaced as he said Jordan's name.

"Junior, Jordan ain't at your door askin' you for nothin'. Let that boy be."

"Maybe you can, but I can't. I…"

"Mazie, get his mind off that boy. Show him your grandson's wedding picture. Mazie's daughter got three kids. That's when him and Nesha got married this past year."

Zeezee had brought a large manila envelope full of pictures to show to Purlie. Purlie handed her the envelope and Zeezee found the wedding picture.

"He got the look of Todd. Don't you think?" Junior commented, as he read the names Zeezee had written on the back of the picture.

"A little. Todd had some sense. He wouldn't have let Winslow do what he did. But he got himself killed at that sawmill. Only had that one girl with that woman he wasn't married to. No tellin' where she is. But look at that little girl. Her name Cinda. That what you say?" Zeezee smiled. "She look like Ma. Look at them eyes."

"Now that you mention it, I do see a resemblance. But Rachel, this one here," Zeezee said, pointing to Rachel in the picture. "She act just like you. I have to catch myself and not call her Purlie."

"Mazie..."

"Ain't said a word."

"But you achin' to say somethin'. I feel it."

Junior interrupted. "Why don't you get her to promise? That's how you used to keep us from tattlin' on each other."

"Cause my baby sister ain't never been able to keep a promise. She told me once that if you tell her not to tell, that be the very next thing out of her mouth. All of us knew never to tell

Mazie anything we didn't want out in the street. Seems though, she done learned to keep her own secrets."

For the first time, Junior laughed.

He and Josh have the same laugh, Lanetia noticed. And the forehead... the same ripple.

"What a day. Chocolate or tea? The kids are speculating. Why is Zeezee here? Someone needs to tell them something. Did you hear Juston? He's going to be the type of guy the girls swoon over. *You're both very pretty.* And, he looked at both of them as he said it with that look that says I see you and only you. I told Mickey to listen to him. Then he says…*Now, can we play?* Not an argument for the rest of the evening." Lanetia laughed and pointed to the chocolate. In the distance, in the quiet of an Atlanta night, a carillon musically chimed midnight. "Why'd you look so surprised when you saw Grace?"

"Not her looks. The way she talks. Just like Vonnie Pearl. Did you hear her telling Zeezee her history? In and out of the hospital. This Reverend sounds like he was either bipolar or schizophrenic. Purlie said that he did whatever the voices, that he took to be God, told him to do. That's scary."

"I saw Deuce's eyes get big when his grandmother said that and I don't think Zeezee knew that. Did you see how fast Zeezee shushed her?" Corina commented. She stirred her tea without drinking it.

"What do you know about your parents at fourteen?" Lanetia emptied the packet of chocolate mix into a mug of hot water and absent-mindedly stirred the clumps that inevitably formed.

"That he beatin' you and everybody else for no reason," Zeezee interrupted from the doorway. "I could use some tea." Corina pointed to a mug on the counter, the canister filled with teabags, the kettle filled with hot water and the Lazy Susan with the condiments.

"I feel as though I know you, so you're not company."

"Thank you." Zeezee talked as she made her tea. "I don't see how I could forget bein' beat, but until Purlie said that about the voices…

"I ran, but Vonnie Pearl… You see it, Nesha. She just like that Grace. And Jordan, ain't he a picture? What happened? Look like them genes…no rhyme or reason. Skipped me, but…"

"Could have. But your father was never diagnosed, so we're just guessing."

"I think Rachel could be an artist. You see that stuff she made at the pottery place? I can't believe the things the children got available for them in a place like Atlanta. You think we can go to Philamon's church on Sunday? The service at eleven. From what Purlie say, he basin' everything he preach on the Reverend's sermons."

"Nesha, you ain't got to pay no babysitter. I be glad to baby-sit and let you two go out and have some fun. I was gonna stay with Purlie tonight, but I can't. I got too much buzzin' in my head. Go…have some fun. Lord knows ain't no fun to be had on that mountain."

Zeezee looked at them approvingly when they came downstairs. Both had on skinny jeans, red high heels, and red sweaters.

"Why on earth did you want to wear high heels?" Lanetia complained as they got into the van. She and Corina had always worn the same shoe size. At the end of the school year, neither could ever remember whose shoes were whose. Lanetia smiled to herself, remembering a time when she had a short, short afro, and wore huge gold or silver hoop earrings, and shoes with three to four inch heels.

"Because I never get the chance to wear them. I teach and I don't wear heels to work. I want nothing to get in the way, if I have to run. Don't laugh. I've had to run from some of those fool kids. That or I'd be in jail. I have this one class and they are the spawn of devils. I haven't figured out what language they speak. I can't take any more. I interviewed for a position in administration. I think I have it. They're trying to figure out the salary.

Corina squeezed the van into a parking space two blocks from the tiny, tiny club. "Feet only hurt when you think they will," Corina announced as she opened the door.

"Ridnour, tell that to my feet. I don't believe you. Two long city blocks…"

"Remember, feet don't hurt when you're looking cute, no such thing as cold when you know you're cute in that unlined leather jacket…" Lanetia laughed. In college, they had accepted that *cute* demanded sacrifices.

"I'm not reading if you don't," Corina warned, as she waved to the bartender. "He owns this place. He always saves me a table. Why can't I like him? He likes me. All I feel is fear. I come here to listen to the poets and to flirt with him. The ones who read try to out-dramatize each other, so don't expect anything from the audience. We'll be too tame."

"I'm ready. I'm kind of excited. I'm experiencing another waterfall, albeit a tiny one. Ridnour, we forgot to bring a drum."

Lanetia pointed to a drummer as they sat at a table with a red paper heart glued to a straw. Corina grimaced as she lightly tapped the red heart. “Is he too much like your Ex?” Lanetia didn’t expect a response as the waitress had elbowed her way to them. Two gin and tonics, each with two lime wedges,” Lanetia ordered for them before the waitress could ask.

“We can borrow a drum. He’s not like my Ex. He actually has three jobs. He works. Too much. I keep looking for the flaw…the deal breaker. So I flirt… I know that guy, sitting in the corner. He has a drum. We’ll drum for each other.”

Lanetia groaned to herself when Zeezee tapped her on the shoulder the next morning. She and Corina had not gotten in until three o’clock. Lanetia blearily stared at the clock. Eight o’clock. “Zeezee, service is not until eleven. The church is only forty to forty-five minutes from here.”

“You two want me to cook breakfast? You certainly don’t look to be in any shape to feed them children.”

“Please. I know Corina’s still asleep. Another hour…that’s all I ask.”

Deuce had decided to drive Lanetia and Zeezee to the church. Lanetia had tried to persuade Zeezee to watch the broadcast, but Zeezee wanted, as she said, to experience the service in the flesh, and Deuce said that he hadn't dressed up for nothing. They sat in the balcony where they had a good view of the pulpit and a giant video screen.

Deuce sat between them and they were listening to him as he pointed out who was who and how the service was conducted. They did not notice that the Senior Pastor was standing at the pulpit, not following the program, but seemingly staring into space.

"Deuce," he suddenly boomed into the microphone, startling them and the entire church, "who is that sitting next to you?"

Deuce, being a football coach, was not shy. "This is Auntie Mazie and her granddaughter-in-law."

"She's dead and you know it." Now, they saw themselves on the giant video screen. "Who is it? What are you doing? Who is it?"

Philamon the second and another pastor were urging Philamon to leave the stage. Someone else was pointing to a man with a camera, mouthing, *shut it off*.

"Who do you think it is?" Deuce questioned.

At the question, Philamon held up his hand as though to ward off an attack and collapsed against the pastor who had taken his arm to lead him from the pulpit.

"Was that on TV?" Zeezee asked.

Deuce nodded. "This is the service that's televised. I never knew Aunt Camelia. Do you look like her? Because that's who he thought you were."

"Some folk said we favored. I never thought we looked anything alike. You think he had a heart attack?"

"Out of guilt. Grandma always said that Camelia would never have approved of what he did."

"I thought it was his father," Lanetia interjected.

"Philamon had his hand in it. Maybe we'd better go. These folk get out of hand when their pastor gets upset."

"Well, now we know where Pope gets his sermons," Lanetia muttered, as she held the telephone away from her ear. "Zeezee, Zeezee, stop covering your ears and talk to your grandson. He's not listening to me."

"You doin' fine. Let him talk himself quiet. Why I gotta hold the phone? I can hear him."

"What if I hadn't answered the phone?" Josh was saying. "What if Ma had? What would she think? Her Ma on TV causin' some preacher to collapse? What is this about her bein' kin to that man? She ain't got no people. Why I gotta call all over Atlanta to find you?"

"Well…"

"Well, nothin'. Can't you talk?"

"We cannot talk at the same time."

"You doin' this on purpose?" Josh asked, exasperated. Lanetia could tell he was trying to contain his temper. This was the end result of lies about oneself. No one was happy, not the liar or the lied to.

"Doing what?"

"Nesha…"

"Your grandmother hasn't exactly told you her entire story. Just the part she made up."

"Made up? Where *is* she?"

"Sitting on the couch. She can hear you. She doesn't want to talk. She spoke to her grandnephew. Seems like she and her older sister, the one who raised his father… They look very much alike. I just saw a picture. They could be twins. Zeezee says she doesn't see it. I get the impression that she and Camelia weren't close."

"I hear her laughin'. She can't talk to me, but she sittin' there laughin'."

"Would you rather she be crying?"

"I'll be there this evenin'."

"Why? If you come here, your mother will know something's not right."

"Really? You two should have thought of that."

"He hung up on you, huh."

"Zeezee, the mint has spread to the basil."

"And we can't tell the difference," Zeezee finished. "That boy is comin' over after he leave the hospital. Turn on your cell. Call him in an hour. Josh should know you ain't used to keepin' that phone turned on. He just lucky we called the kids and told them we wasn't comin' straight home. Give him time to reflect. He won't be so upset and we'll direct him to Corina's. Bobbie Jean, I know I'm bein' greedy, but could I have me just another little slice of that chocolate cake?"

"Sure. But…you don't have diabetes?" Bobbie Jean was Deuce's wife and they had just finished eating dinner when Philamon called. Then, Josh's call had interrupted dessert.

"Like everybody else? No."

"You're not like the rest of Deuce's family. How long have you been away?"

"Not long enough. But I got to see Purlie. We was the two youngest. Always fighting with each other and gettin' into trouble."

Junior spoke up: "You still are. Ma's been laughin' all morning. She won't admit it, but she's been waitin' for Philamon to get his. I told her Philamon the second was comin' over, so she has commandeered the phone. She told me to plug my phone in somewhere, so she wouldn't miss a word.

"Who is that?" he continued, at the sound of a knock on the back door. Jordan chose that moment to peer at them through the window. "What is Jordan doing here? That's all we need. Philamon the second can't stand Jordan. I ain't gonna sit here and listen to him preach." Junior started to get up, but Zeezee tapped him on the shoulder.

"I'd like to talk to Jordan some more." Junior shrugged and nodded toward the door. Jordan gave a thumb's up. Junior muttered something they couldn't make out.

Today, Jordan's fingernails were painted a fiery red and his long permed hair was pulled back into a pony tail.

"I think I like you. A breath of the past come alive," he said, complimenting Zeezee, as he held her hand. "I think you're much prettier than Camelia, but I can see the resemblance. Oh, the drama. A long lost aunt. Collapse on television. When's Philamon the second arriving? And don't tell me he's not coming."

"He's on his way."

"Mrs. Snob coming? You must meet Eleanor. So light, she thinks she's white, but her parents are so Black. You all heard she's back. That court gave her too much money and the mansion. Miss Thing had to go. Deuce, maybe I will read the family history. This is my kind of story."

Pastor and Mrs. Philamon Winslow Goodman, II arrived in a chauffeured white limousine. Bobbie Jean met them at the door and brought them to the living room where Jordan was entertaining everyone with a story about one of his customers whose garden was used for more than just growing exotic tropical plants.

Pastor and Mrs. Goodman sat on the couch across from Lanetia and Zeezee who sat on the matching loveseat. Philamon the second said nothing to fill the uneasy silence that followed their entrance. If Philamon the second thought he was going to out stare his great aunt, he was mistaken.

"What do you want?" It was the wrong thing to say, as even he could hear Purlie's derisive snort of *ignorant fool* that came from Junior's cell phone.

"Want? What do you mean…want?" Zeezee asked. She looked beyond her great nephew. Then, she flicked a glance at him that said more than words ever could that she felt nothing but contempt for him.

Philamon the second was not prepared for his great aunt's total lack of awe of him. He asked for a glass of water as he wiped his brow with a white silk handkerchief. Bobbie Jean sat for a long second before she got up to get it.

"You've been away a long time. Why now?"

"Let me tell you somethin'. Why I be here is my business. You mind your business. Far as I be concerned, you are a stranger and no stranger asks me what I want. You asked to see me. What do you want?"

Philamon the second sipped some water, set the glass on the end table, and wiped his brow again. He looked around at his relatives and grimaced when he saw Jordan, but said nothing. "My father asked me to come. He has congestive heart failure. He's not well. He thinks you're his Mama Camelia. He's rambling…"

"Well, you seen me. We were havin' a tolerable time before you came."

"Don't you want to see my father?"

"Not particularly."

"He won't rest until he sees you. You may be his aunt, but I think he may be just a little older than you. There was such an age gap between the older kids and the younger ones. He said the Reverend…"

"The who? I know my father didn't say nothin' about me."

"I meant my grandfather."

"Winslow…drinkin', gamblin', whorin', lyin', stealin', murderin' Winslow. You call Winslow…Reverend?" Pastor Goodman flinched at Zeezee's contempt. "My father did a lot of things, but he never did none of that. The only person you call Reverend in my presence is my father. Call Winslow your granddaddy, but don't put the name Reverend on that piece of evil."

"He changed. After you left..."

"He found a way to steal money without goin' to jail. Said he was evil; never said he wasn't smart," Zeezee interrupted.

Philamon the second, looked around for help. He was sweating and his hand shook as he sipped the water. "He said that Mama Camelia didn't approve of something. Do you know what he's talking about?"

"Then he definitely don't want to talk to me. Me and Camelia had our differences, but she knew right from wrong." Zeezee folded her arms across her chest.

Philamon the second turned to Lanetia. "You must be my aunt's grandson's wife."

Lanetia nodded.

"I hear you own a newspaper."

"A very small weekly."

"I write a column on religion. It's been picked up by over one hundred newspapers. I like to get the Word out to as many people as possible. Just a nominal charge."

"No thanks."

"But… How long will you be in Atlanta?"

"Until Wednesday."

"On Spring Break?"

Lanetia nodded. Lanetia had a feeling the less this man knew of their business the better. His eyes never rested. They darted here and there. He was an uncomfortable person to be around.

"Deuce, either you or Junior could bring," he nodded toward Zeezee, "to visit Dad in cardiac intensive care. His doctor says you can come after 10:30 a.m. He's very weak… I'll be there around that time, so I'd appreciate if you'd come while I'm there."

Eleanor, who had been quiet, suddenly spoke: "Now I remember where I've heard your name. Didn't you speak at the National Convention at a workshop on neighborhood redevelopment?" she asked, looking intently at Lanetia.

"Yes. That was a long time ago."

"My chapter sponsored two of those neighborhood grants you talked about and we won an award from the City for the work that was done in those neighborhoods. You're not doing that any more?"

"No."

"You know everyone has skeletons in their family closets. The church is doing a lot of good. Some things are best left in the closet. You agree? Father Philamon said some things this morning that have to be explained rationally. People don't need to know everything.

"There's a prayer vigil going on right now. Sister Ibrahima is preparing so that she can lay hands on him."

An uneasy silence followed that statement. Purlie's laugh only deepened the silence. Junior whispered to his mother to be quiet.

Lanetia cleared her throat. Someone had to say something. "I'm sure Zeezee will consider visiting her nephew. If she does, it will be tomorrow after we visit the family cemetery. We were going today, but it's too late to drive to the country."

"That's a church project…the upkeep of the old cemetery. It's very quiet and peaceful. Philamon, I think we should be going. I promised your stepmother that we would return shortly. Ms. McCory understands our position."

"Why on earth would you come with Pope? You know what he is. You know that he's jealous."

“A ride. Like you say, he doesn’t have my—our—interests,” Josh corrected himself, “at heart. Between your old car and my old truck, I didn’t have much choice. He wants to meet that Rev. Goodman. All the way here, he be talkin’ about Rev. Goodman’s sermons and what a man of God he be.

“I thought we’d worked out the talkin’. We supposed to talk. Why’d you do this without tellin’ me?”

“Zeezee asked me to do some research on her family. Never thought I’d find this. Zeezee has her secrets…”

“Which she don’t mind tellin’ you.”

“Because I don’t have a stake in it.”

“What does that mean? You ***are*** my wife.”

“I mean I don’t have any preconceived notions. No matter what I found, I would tell her and she would make the decisions about the use of the information. I don’t like that man being in Corina’s home. He…”

“He gonna stay with his brother. From what he say, his brother live on the other side of Atlanta, goin’ toward Macon. Your friend mind me stayin’ or do I go to a hotel?”

“Josh, we didn’t do this to anger you or to upset your world.”

"But you always done that. From the first… We goin' to see this preacher tomorrow? The kids get the news before I do. What do they think about all this?"

"They don't know as much as you think. Somewhere, someway, I believe that children should be permitted a childhood. They know that Zeezee has reconnected with some relatives. No details. I'd like for you to get to know Corina. She's good people." Lanetia held out her hand. After a moment's hesitation, Josh took it and held it to his lips.

Zeezee peeked into the den. "You ready to hear sense? You got it all out of your system?" Zeezee asked, hands on hips, prepared for whatever Josh had to say.

"Zeezee, if you got sense to say, then I be ready to hear it. Let me tell Pope that the Reverend's father is really ill and this ain't a good time to meet him." Josh came back, sat on the couch and, for a moment, he closed his eyes as though he had seen enough for one day. He opened his eyes as Juston brought in a folding table and set it in front of him. Rachel and Cinda followed with the food and iced tea.

Corina waved as she left to pick up Kahla and Mickey who were visiting their father.

"Nesha said you were really hungry. This is what we had for lunch," Cinda announced. "You mad because we got some relatives you didn't know about before?"

"No, not mad, just kind of disappointed."

"Wasn't Nesha's secret to tell," Cinda said, raising her right eyebrow. Josh nodded and shrugged at the same time. "Zeezee been waitin' for you to come so we could all hear the story. So you just be quiet and let Zeezee talk. Okay?"

Josh raised his right eyebrow at his youngest sister, shook his head, and picked up the fork.

"Well, what you think?" Zeezee said, after finishing her story.

"Why do I remind you of Purlie? I don't look anything like her," Rachel said, standing to study herself in the mirror that hung on the wall behind the sofa.

"Rachel, it ain't about looks. It be your ways and her ways," Zeezee explained.

"But Cinda do have the look of your mother," Rachel continued, frowning at her reflection. "I look more like Daddy's people. I don't know about all these preachers. Ma might enjoy them. She's always goin' around talkin' about the Bible." *Stop primping, Rachel, Juston muttered.* Rachel sat on the floor with a flourish that said I shall pretend I did not hear that.

"May I have her picture?" Cinda asked. She had appropriated her great-grandmother's picture and, as everyone could see, she wasn't about to give it up.

"I'll have a copy made," Lanetia promised. "Tomorrow, I'll take these pictures to the drugstore and make copies. I think Deuce has some more that we might want. He's bringing his picture albums tomorrow night."

"What did Zeezee leave out?" Josh asked when they were alone.

"It's her story. Let her tell you. In her own way. In her own time. We're going to the cemetery tomorrow and then to see her nephew. We'll pick up Purlie from the assisted living facility on the way to the cemetery. The kids will be at the Aquarium in the morning and Rachel wants to go back to the pottery place. They'll be there until six. I've got to find the time to get those copies made."

"I guess I am tired," he said, as he turned his back to her.

To everyone's surprise, Deuce and Jordan showed up as they were eating breakfast. Lanetia hadn't expected them for another hour or so. Junior knocked on the door not ten minutes later. They drank some orange juice while eyeing Josh. Lanetia noticed Junior's nod to himself and, as soon as Josh had finished eating, Junior motioned for Josh to follow him outside to the patio.

Zeezee shrugged, but Lanetia could sense she was worried about the story Junior was telling Josh. Corina was dropping off the kids before going to work. "I cannot wait for tonight" was her comment as she left her home.

The cemetery was tucked between exurbs on a country road about thirty miles from Atlanta. Almost look-alike estate homes graced the uniform five acre lots. Junior opened the wrought iron gate with his key. They had been allowed to keep the cemetery because of a law passed when a powerful political family was on the verge of losing its family cemetery. No land designated as a cemetery could be bought by a developer. If there was no one to maintain the cemetery, the County had to. There was a black wrought iron fence around the three acres of land. "Hardly any room to bury anybody else," Jordan commented.

Purlie muttered back: "I think there be just enough room for **you**." She looked in the direction of her grandsons, but not at either one of them. She moved slowly with her walker, with Zeezee and her son by her side. "That be the tombstone you bought for Mama. You said you was buying the best. Look at the one

Winslow got for the Reverend. Already crumbling. Winslow wanted to be buried on the other side of the Reverend. Show everybody that the line was unbroken. Never did get married. Zeezee visited each of her brothers' and sisters' graves, sometimes stopping at the tombstones in between, asking Purlie who such and such was. Lanetia turned the volume of the micro-recorder as high as possible to record the ebb and flow of the conversation between Zeezee and Purlie. Joshua walked beside Zeezee and Zeezee told him a little bit about each person and Purlie filled in the details.

On the way to the hospital, Zeezee and Purlie were quiet and both appeared to be taking a nap. "Junior, what you been tellin' Josh?" Purlie asked, her eyes still closed, when he opened the door to help her out of the car.

"Just some family history so he don't get blindsided. When he meets Grace, he has to act a certain way or she'll get agitated, won't take her medicine and we'll be up all night cause she'll be out somewhere ramblin'. Just…told him how Winslow stole everybody's money. Family stuff.

"Stuff you might not have told him. He said now that we talked to him he understands a lot of what's been goin' on."

"Bet he does," was her response, and, now not only were her eyes closed, but also her expression.

Lanetia frowned to herself. Lanetia was in the SUV with Deuce and Jordan. She had opened the door to wait for Junior to get Purlie's walker from the car trunk and had heard what he said. Was Josh putting two and two together and getting five?

A cold rush of air greeted them as the automatic door shut behind them. Everyone's attitude seemed to be let's get this over with.

Lunch was being served to the patients who were able to eat. Huge stainless steel carts with stacks and stacks of trays filled the elevators. All that food and not one whiff of an appetizing aroma… Lanetia dismissed and quashed the nausea that threatened to overwhelm her. The hospital bustled with the ding of elevator bells, the clang of metal on metal, the whoosh of rubber wheels on vinyl tile, the ping of machinery attached to the patients, and hushed voices. CCU was so quiet that one only heard the occasional hum or ping of a machine. Nurses were sitting and standing at the half-moon station, observing patients through uncurtained windows, dealing with paperwork, and talking in whispers on the telephone. A man in work clothes and a woman curled in a blanket were the only ones in the waiting area across from the nurses' station.

A nurse, coming from a CCU room, came over to talk to them before they reached the nurses' station.

"I'm Mrs. Blackmon. Are you here to visit Rev. Goodman?" At their nods, she continued: "Only two at a time. He's very restless. Who is his aunt?"

Lanetia spoke up: "He has two aunts who are here. His Aunt Zeezee and his Aunt Purlie." She pointed them out.

"Well, maybe they can visit…"

"I think someone else from the family should go in with them. Junior—he knows you," Lanetia continued, singling out the one person she thought might not overly agitate Reverend Goodman. Junior sighed and nodded.

"Okay, but we never had much to say to each other. Is anyone else in there?" he asked the nurse.

"His son just took his stepmother to lunch. We discourage visitors at meal time, not that he ate anything, but his son said to let his aunt visit when she came."

Junior was helping his mother negotiate her walker into the room when, all of a sudden, Zeezee grabbed Lanetia's arm and leaned against her. It was Lanetia's turn to sigh. The nurse just nodded.

Josh wasn't about to let the nurse close the door, so the rest of the family crowded in the doorway.

Rev. Goodman appeared to be asleep, but he was mumbling and the thin blanket that covered him was crumpled. He had once been a handsome man, but too many rich meals and underhanded dealings had caused his face to wrinkle and sag in all the wrong places. His jaws had become jowls and he had more than two chins.

"Philamon, you awake?" Junior asked, after an awkward silence and a meaningful prod from his mother.

Philamon slowly opened his eyes and his eyes went straight to Zeezee. His eyes opened wide and Lanetia could see the fear in the gaze that would not leave Zeezee.

"I ain't Camelia and you wouldn't be so afraid of meetin' her again if you had done right with your life," Zeezee announced. Her tone made it clear that she felt no compassion for this nephew.

Philamon's breathing quickened and, if anything, even more fear radiated from him. Nurse Blackmon brushed past them to lay a hand on the Reverend's wrist. "You…"

"No," Reverend Goodman whispered. His eyes finally rested on Purlie who had the same you-a-piece-of-scum expression as was Zeezee's tone. "Daddy made me," he said, his wispy voice faltering.

Lanetia felt a surge of pity for this minister who was no minister in his heart. Even now, sick and near death, he could not take responsibility for his life's path.

"You know, Purlie, I think I might have seen him once before I left. Wasn't his ma named Tansy and she lived two streets over next to Deacon Paltrough?"

"You right. She and her husband moved here from Florida. He got him a job at that place that made feed sacks. She was supposed to be a housewife. He was always braggin' that he made enough money to take care of his wife. Wouldn't come to church. But he sure liked to drink and gamble. Probably where Winslow met him. Winslow could out-drink and out-gamble just about anybody. She had two boys before this one here. You remember how many you seen her with?"

"No, I just remember bein' over to Deacon Paltrough gettin' some of that tobacco for the Reverend. Remember he was the only one who could get it because he had a son who sent it to him from Cuba. (You right again. I done forgot that.) But he would've been maybe a couple of years younger than me because I remember askin' Camelia, remember she lived about five or six houses from there, about the boy who looked like a Goodman. Her sanctimonious self told me to shut up and don't talk trash and I ain't seen nothin' of the kind. She was always takin' up for Winslow. You ever figure out why?"

"Winslow wasn't all bad. He used to stop the Reverend from killin' us with that stick of his. Even after the Reverend kicked him out, if one of us needed a place to hide until the Reverend got over his spell, he'd always find us a safe place. The Reverend didn't beat you half as bad as he done us older ones. Why you think we was all tryin' to get out of there? Many a time, Mama shielded you and us from his blows, tellin' us all the while to pray 'til it passed. I can still hear her tellin' us that the Reverend was a good man."

"So Winslow just thought he was takin' what was his when he took all the money for the property?"

"No, him and Camelia had a big blow-up over it and she never let him forget that he done wrong. She let him educate this one here cause she couldn't afford to do it. By then, anything his daddy say, this boy do. She always told me that Winslow mesmerized the boy. She didn't approve. No, not one bit."

"Put to good…" Philamon whispered. "Didn't steal… The church…"

"I'm afraid you all will have to leave. Reverend Goodman is getting too agitated. It's about time for his medicine anyway."

The Reverend Goodman's fear-filled eyes followed them out.

"Zeezee, I ain't never known you to be so cruel," Josh said, as they waited for the elevator. "Would it have hurt to pretend some compassion?"

"Josh, he a preacher and he layin' there scared of death. Well, meetin' Camelia. What that tell you about him? He my nephew—may his god rest his soul."

"Mazie, you hush that devil talk. He your God, too. And God forgives us sinners."

"You sound like my daughter. You should come and visit."

"Mazie, Zeezee, whatever you callin' yourself. You stop and you look at me. The Reverend was sick in the head, sick. You hear me…sick. My daughter be sick in the head." Suddenly she stopped and repeated herself—"my daughter be sick in the head" and she looked a question at Zeezee. Zeezee barely nodded.

"Zeezee, ain't nothin' wrong with Ma," Josh said angrily. "Ma just never got over Dad being killed. Some folks feel things different, more, but she…"

"You keep tellin' yourself that. I ain't got that luxury."

"Why do you like me?" Lanetia asked, turning toward Zeezee who had picked up the cell phone to call Purlie. They had just finished eating and Lanetia was washing the pots and pans while Rachel and Mickey good-naturedly bickered about the correct way to put the dirty dishes in the dishwasher.

"Why you ask?"

"Josh doesn't like me very much—not on this day. But did he ever?" She asked the last question more of herself than Zeezee. Zeezee put the cell phone on the kitchen counter. For a moment, she listened to Rachel and Mickey. When she was satisfied that they weren't listening, she leaned against the counter before she answered.

"Like…I liked you from the first time I saw you. I liked that faraway look in your eyes that said you'd been places—some you didn't necessarily like—didn't matter, you would survive. I guess I recognized some part of me I was wantin' to recapture.

"You said it best—lettin' people into your space is hard. You in my space and I like havin' you there. Josh done had a lot to cope with in the past year, even more so than when his Daddy was killed. Ever since you came, nothin' but change, mostly for the better. Josh done told me what he thought of me. He ain't pleased with me. He'll work it out. We his heart. And his Ma ain't never gonna like it," she said, muttering the last. "I want to talk to Purlie for a minute, then we'll talk to Josh."

"Josh, I can't say what I come from ain't got nothin' to do with you. It do. I always told you…lies catch up with you, one way or the other. I needed to forget where I came from in order to make me a life. That make sense?" Zeezee was quiet and all they heard was the distant roar of traffic and the chirping of crickets. A bright green frog hopped from the concrete planter containing a fern and disappeared into the grass that edged the patio. Josh sat beside the red azalea. A fat black and yellow striped bee lazily buzzed in and around the flowers, making its last run of the day as dusk hovered.

"I done forgot how hot it be here. Your Ma need help. You done seen your cousin. If Andy was here, she might be all right. He made her feel real safe and secure. But he ain't. Your Ma gonna get us run out of our home if she confess to that Pope. You gonna put yourself, the kids, Nesha, me through that? What you thinkin'?"

"You should've told me what Ma tried to do. You should've told me what you suspected once *you* knew. Why you put this off on Nesha?"

"Cause Nesha could look at what she found…objectively …that's the word. She wouldn't sugarcoat nothin'. She'd make me a report just like she done and let me decide what to do with it. I know you strugglin', but wrap your mind around what be. Junior got us an appointment to see Grace's psychiatrist. He been askin' Junior if anyone else in the family had any problems and Junior been tellin' him no. Even though, three of his cousins drank or drugged themselves to death. Like he said, he didn't think it was unusual. I want the doctor to know the family history."

Dr. Beauchron was a graduate of Howard University Medical School and had studied at the Jung Institute in Switzerland, among other schools and hospitals. He had set aside an hour, but ended up canceling his afternoon appointments. No one had ever permitted him to talk to Purlie. Now, he had Purlie on the telephone and Zeezee in his office. Purlie knew all of her relatives and she knew what had been going on in their lives. Dr. Beauchron muttered more than once that he wished someone had told him this or that detail when he had first started treating Grace.

"I think you're on to something, Mrs. Tallent. It's based in our need for self-preservation. Your daughter doesn't like change and she has a great need to feel secure. I or someone else would have to examine your daughter to determine what would work for her—medication, counseling, or some combination of the two. Have you told her about her family?"

"I told her a little bit this morning before we came here. She's really into Rev. Goodman." *I be like you, Zeezee had told Lanetia. I don't watch that mess and, when she talk about it, I don't listen.* "She watch him just about every Sunday. Only reason she wasn't watchin' Sunday cause Josh had cut the power to work on some wiring."

"Excessive religiosity would fit in with the profile I'm creating. What you've told me will help me in treating your niece. I appreciate your candor. It's hard for us to bring up a past that we'd rather forget. But people have history and that history affects them… Subconsciously, it's there and so many of us haven't the words to vocalize what needs to be said."

Josh who had been quiet throughout the session suddenly asked a question: "It appears to be skipping generations. Me and my sisters don't seem to be troubled with…"

"Your grandmother says that your sister, Rachel…isn't it, appears to be depressed, especially in the winter. You have to understand, we need our sense of self-preservation, we need to feel secure, we need to express our spirituality… It's the extreme that causes us problems. So it's not about skipping generations, it's about how those needs are met or not met and that has a lot to do with the times we live in and how we react to the situations in which we find ourselves.

"If your question is about your children? *Josh nodded.* Knowledge is your friend and advisor. Like every parent, you will be teaching your child to cope with what life throws at him or her and getting them help if they need it. I wish there was some way to know how many of us have this type of history. What we went through in this Country was and still is psychological hell. We, as a people, collectively, have, by no means, recovered. And, we have demonized mental illness which makes it difficult for us to admit we need treatment."

"Deacon Vinton doin' the chores. If you don't mind, I'll tell Pope, I'll be drivin' back with you. He been callin'. You got the pictures made? I know the kids went, and you've probably been, but I haven't. I'd like to visit the MLK Memorial and walk around the neighborhood before we leave." Lanetia nodded. She'd thought she might be able to finish the article on things to do in the mountains in the spring. Josh had been quiet after their visit to Dr. Beauchron. Now, he couldn't stop talking about everything, but what he really wanted to talk about. "Rachel really likes that pottery place. Corina says there's a summer school at one of the colleges for high school age kids who be interested in art. She say Rachel be welcome to stay with her. Might be a good idea…the school. Corina printed off an application. I think if Rachel be accepted, she should stay at the college. Be a good experience.

Help prepare her for the real thing. Now, to find somethin' for Juston and Cinda."

"I don't believe that summers should be too organized. Can we talk about that some other time and talk now about what's bothering you?"

"What's that?"

"I can't live with someone who won't talk to me. I can be as silent as the next person. You know I can, but this… I may not have talked to you about some things, but it was for both of our protection."

"How?"

"What we know raises more questions. I sense you're having a difficult time assimilating Zeezee's kin…your kin… Is your mother like Grace? Will I pass this to my children? Will I be like Grace? I could see those questions flitting across your face when you were silent and I sense the same questions as you talk about something as innocuous as a visit to a tourist attraction."

"So…do we have children?"

"Josh, can you admit one simple fact? I think you know what I'm going to say. Your mother hates me. Josh, I don't think any amount of medicine or counseling will change that. I can't risk her taking out her hate for me on my child. Do you think my family stock is any better than yours?"

"Then we could leave. But…"

"Exactly…it's not that simple. You know it isn't. You can't run away from genes. You can't leave your family. I wish it were just us, but… We're talking about two different things. I'm confusing myself. I suppose hate could be caused by a mental illness. Maybe hate is a mental illness, but it's not genetic. It's environmental."

"Nesha, I don't need for you to rationalize my mother. She is like Grace. I can't will myself into blindness and I want to. Junior has to care for Grace and it be a job that never ends. When do we get to live our lives, do what we want?"

"Maybe that's what we're doing now, even though we don't see it. The doctor was right about one thing…knowledge. We'll cope. We'll deal with it…together."

"I can't sell the cows. They Daddy's cows." Josh patted the rump of one of the cows as he urged the cow from the barn into the pasture.

“Then let me help. I looked up the life span of organic cows which yours are, more so than not, and they can live up to fifteen years. Is your hand hurting?”

“No. Rachel and Juston do the milkin’. I got to get the crops planted. I need two hands to steer the tractor.”

“Teach me to drive the thing.”

“I don’t see any other way. I don’t like it. You got the newspaper and homeschoolin’ the kids. The principal of the elementary school stopped me at the grocery store. She said that Cinda and Juston will have to take the standardized tests. The tests start next week. Rachel won’t have to take any tests until next year. I talked to the principal at the high school. I didn’t want no surprises.” He continued, but it was as though he was talking to himself: “Dad never liked plowin”. He said Mother Nature didn’t need no plow to grow a tree. He tried and tried no till until one year he said this soil just too rocky. I got a family to feed. He told me the story. I was too young. I always remember him plowin’. He designed and built the plow that you call a contraption. Work better than any store bought plow on this rocky dirt. He fussed over this dirt like it was me or Rachel.” Josh stared at his left hand and grimaced as he flexed it.

“Josh, in the next couple of weeks, I want to go to Kentucky and do some things to the house.”

"Why you?" Josh still stared at his hand.

"Because I'm buying the property." Lanetia flicked a glance at Josh to gauge his reaction. She had been searching for the right time to tell him and there hadn't been *the* right time. Now, Josh stared into the distance before speaking.

"Why?"

"To keep it in the family. Aunt Maline asked me to buy it. I'm the only one with enough money who wants to buy it. My cousins will honor Aunt Maline's choice. They've all agreed. My sister and brother have agreed. Aunt Maline is afraid of what Jelly Bean and Patrice will try to do after she's gone. She doesn't want the property developed. She knows I will not do that. While I'm there, I hope to find someone to rent Aunt Leda's house. The acreage is leased to a local farmer. I've decided to fix up the old house and keep it as a family retreat. I've already had a contractor look over the house and I know what needs to be repaired. I've had a new heating and air conditioning system installed. When Franklin returns from Boston, he's agreed to supervise the renovations. While I'm there, Kaida wants to come. She'll choose the furniture she wants to keep."

"You got it all worked out." The tractor was parked in the aluminum utility building next to the barn. Different kinds of plows, seeders, and other farming equipment filled the cavernous building that was surprisingly clean and free of cobwebs. Josh got on the tractor and gestured for Lanetia to stand on the running board. He expertly backed the tractor out of the building.

"Josh, you buy property and you don't discuss it with me. You just bought the Felton's property that came up for sale for nonpayment of taxes. Josh, I own the local newspaper. I look at the public records every week. So, don't go there with me on this."

"Not the same. The Feltons' ancestor came with my great great. They all gone. All this property on Crow Cut Cove… My Daddy said it was important that we keep it and I honor my Daddy by what I do."

"As I honor my aunt." Josh shrugged. He didn't think they were doing the same thing. Lanetia had to be buying her family's property because she didn't trust him to provide her with a home. Lanetia sighed and changed the subject. "Will you reopen the mill?"

"Thinkin' on it. Went there yesterday. Still in good shape. I think I figured out the plans for buildin' an electrical plant at the mill site. Help to maintain a steady supply of electricity durin' the year. Have to lay an underground conduit." Again, Joshua flexed his left hand.

"No time like the present. Trade places with me," he directed, obviously resigning himself to a reality he did not like and wanted to avoid. "We need to start plowin'. Plant in May. We may still have another storm or two this month.

"Ma's not sayin' much. It be like a car. Brake…accelerator, clutch, but the center of gravity be different. Why you tensin' up? Relax," he placed his hand over hers and leaned over and kissed her nose. "Just do like I show you. You can't make no sharp turns with this tractor. It'll turn over. This ain't like my old truck. See the N for neutral; R for reverse; 1 for first gear, and 2 for second gear? Before you turn off the ignition, always shift to Neutral. Just like a car, key in ignition, turn it on. Relax. Tractor won't move. Disengage the brake. I am here. Relax. Depress the clutch and shift the gear into first. Ease off the clutch. Easy on the accelerator. Just need to practice until you know the feel of the clutch and the accelerator. You doin' fine. When you want to stop, depress the clutch and shift back to neutral, set the brake, and turn it off. Nothin' to it. See, you doin' it. Keep goin'. Slow. Don't need to shift the gears, unless you on the road.

"Ma look at the pictures; she look at Zeezee; then she look at the pictures some more.

"I talked to Junior. Him and Deuce comin' up in two weeks to get Zeezee. Seem like Aunt Purlie want that other cataract removed and she want Zeezee to be there. Zeezee plan on takin' Ma with her. She usin' Philamon's church as the lure."

"I think that's a good idea. The museum board is having its first meeting tomorrow. Why is the steering wheel so stiff?"

"You'll get used to it. Let's ride to the field and back. You can practice turnin' in the field and shiftin' into reverse. For a second…you looked so scared. Ain't nothin' to it, is it?" Lanetia nodded. Some things shouldn't be thought on too much. Just do. That knowledge was a long time coming.

"Answer that phone," Vonnie Pearl called out from the kitchen. "Probably for you anyway," she added, loud enough for Lanetia to hear.

Annoyed... Lanetia looked around for the kids. Never around… She answered the phone and checked the time. *I will be late.* "Kaemon… How are you? What? Really? You do know your nephew. I like your idea. Don't ask him. You know what he will say. That will be a nice surprise. Won't say a word."

The meeting of the museum board was one of the reasons Lanetia had dropped her affiliations with clubs, associations, and sorority. Each person had an agenda. Mrs. Heinrich Stoltz of the Stoltz millions, (she didn't seem to have a first name of her own) wanted her husband's name on something as he had given a substantial donation to create the museum; Dylan Modran, ex-prisoner, wanted them to keep it real, whatever that meant; Hayden Hamilton, the Governor's regional representative, wanted the museum to happen under this administration; Dolly Goans, Tri-County rep, wanted a four-lane highway from the Interstate to the prison museum with a by-pass around Tiny Town; and Lanetia McCory, citizen representative, wanted nothing more than that the meeting be over.

"We agreed on two things," she later told Josh, "to hire a consultant to determine if the five year old study was still valid, and, if so, how best to turn a dark, grungy, moldy prison complex into a museum that will actually attract visitors. And, before the next meeting in three months, Dylan and Mrs. Stoltz will visit a prison museum in Idaho that has netted a profit every year it's been open."

CHAPTER 10

Lanetia half listened to Juston's plea. "Me and Rachel can do it. All you have to do is show us. You showed us how to milk the cows. Please," Juston argued and pleaded at the same time. She knew they could do it. But the consequences… Was it worth the consequences that would surely flow from Josh and Vonnie Pearl? Lanetia tossed each of them an apple. Cinda, whose legs might be long enough for her feet to depress the tractor's pedals, was obviously in agreement that Rachel and Juston should learn to drive the tractor. If they did, she would not be denied. Vonnie Pearl hadn't said anything about Rachel milking the cows, but driving the tractor?

"Ma's gone to Atlanta," Rachel pointed out, as though she had read Lanetia's thoughts. "Josh gone to therapy. If we all take turns, the fields will be plowed before we leave for Kentucky. Cause when we get back, it will be time to plant. I get bored cooped up in the house."

"Argue for all of us and stop being selfish," Cinda said, stomping her foot. "You never think about anybody but you."

"Don't you touch me," Rachel warned. "You too young. Juston is too. I'll be drivin' next year. I need the practice."

Juston held out his hands. Where did he learn that? Her father always talked about the helping hands. Was this gesture in their genes? After Lanetia showed them how to drive the tractor, she stood on the running board while each of them plowed a couple of rows. Then, she walked along, nervously at first, while each one of them drove solo. Lanetia had stooped to pick up a rock when she heard Josh yell at Cinda to get off the tractor. Cinda glared at her brother and accelerated. "Cinda, stop," Lanetia said, standing up and throwing the rock to the edge of the field.

"Why I gotta stop? Just because he say so? I'm doin' fine. My turn," Cinda muttered, as she shifted to neutral and set the brake before turning off the tractor.

"Nesha, what you doin'?" Josh asked. He frowned, not yet sure he liked the idea of Cinda driving the tractor.

"They wanted to help. Field's almost done. Now, that you're here, you can supervise them and I can cook supper. We've been tossing aside the larger rocks because they get caught in the plow and slow the whole process." Josh and Lanetia stared at each other for a long moment, then Josh slowly nodded and stepped on the running board.

"You so grown. Start it." Cinda, with no hesitation, started the tractor. She again glared at her brother, before releasing the brake. "You done learned all this while I was gone?" Cinda nodded.

"Cinda, you have two more rows before it's my turn again," Juston said. "Don't hog the tractor," he continued, reminding Cinda of their agreement, as he veered away from the tractor, having seen a rock that needed to be tossed out of the field. Rachel, who had been walking ahead of the tractor and had stopped to listen to decide it she needed to intervene, picked up a rock and tossed it to the side.

They were all laughing when they came in for supper. "Showers, then you eat," Lanetia ordered.

"Something smells good. I hope you cooked lots of it cause we are hungry. Got the field finished. Cows in for the night. What about watchin' a movie?"

"Okay. Zeezee called. They're staying for another couple of days. Purlie's surgery went well. Your mother met her cousin, Rev. Goodman, and they've been invited to his home for dinner tomorrow."

Later that night as Lanetia lay on the sofa, writing in her notebook, Josh pushed Brer Rabbit aside as he kneeled by the sofa. “So this is what it would be like without my Ma around. I like it. I don’t want to go back to the way it was…all tense…no laughter…no dancin’.”

“Let’s just enjoy each day. As soon as they return, I will leave for Kentucky. A week, then we’ll be back for the planting. I hear there may be a storm brewing. That’s one reason I wanted to get the last field plowed today.

“Josh, the kids will sleep the sleep of the laborer who has done a good day’s work. We need all the help we can get, especially with you and Mr. Vinton doing Mr. Harmond’s work, too.”

“I know.”

“We could really use Amare, but his parents are trying to work it out for him to stay with his grandparents, so this situation won’t happen to him again. They’ll be back next week from their annual business meeting. We’ll know then whether or not Amare will return. They were excited to be going to Tampa this year and not somewhere in North Dakota.” Just then a clap of thunder shook the house, startling them. Seconds later, rain pelted the windows. “Josh, is Brer Rabbit supposed to be so large? He looks like a raccoon.”

"Nesha…" Joshua couldn't continue. He was laughing too hard.

"What's so funny?"

"Cat… Cat eat anything a cat ever thought was fit to eat. Saw him eatin' some green beans. I ain't never seen no cat eat green beans. Don't make no effort to do nothin' but find a place to sleep. Maybelle try to get him to play and he stalk off like he been insulted. Should've kept his brother. He up at the Turletons being a proper cat. Your cat gonna look like a blimp by this time next year and he won't be sharin' this sofa with you cause you and him won't be able to fit on it. Your cat need to be on a serious diet."

By morning, their world was coated in ice. All through the day, they heard the snapping of tree limbs. "Nesha, you don't need to go to the old home place. You hear what's goin' on. It ain't safe."

"Josh, I will walk in the middle of the driveway. You've cut down the trees around the old home place. I'll be fine."

"Still sleetin'."

"Josh, the kids are studying. I've made sandwiches and soup for lunch. I thought you were looking through those catalogues to figure out what parts you need for the electrical plant.

I will not go for a stroll in the woods. After lunch, ask if they need help with their math. Thanks."

The wind whipped Lanetia's scarf from around her neck. She was almost to the old home place when she stopped to rearrange it. As she tied the ends, she noticed a movement by the windmill. She stared for some moments through the sleet and had almost decided that she hadn't really seen anything. But, then, there it was again. Bears…she'd read a report that the bears were awake and very hungry. A hiker in the mountains had been mauled two weeks ago. Deer were always around. There had also been a sighting of a mountain lion. Could be the sleet. Lanetia felt for the gun that she always carried. She took it out of her pocket and, in the shelter of her coat, slid in a clip. You shouldn't do this, she told herself. She almost turned around when an ice coated branch crashed to the ground in front of her.

The sleet was turning to snow and she could see maybe an arm's length in front of her. Lanetia walked around the windmill and tripped over a wire. She picked herself up and followed the wire to a tree. Wire wound around a tree. Why? She followed the wire back to the windmill. The wire was also wound around one of the steel supports. Didn't make sense. Old home place or the house? *If I tell Josh, I came up here, he will be angry…upset…thoroughly displeased. Old home place.* The wire was hard to unwind because of the cold, but for some reason, Lanetia sensed that she should not leave the wire as she found it. She wound the wire around a stick to carry it back to the old home place.

At the old home place, Lanetia settled in for an afternoon of writing an article about the school system. Then, when that article wrote itself faster than she would have thought and, with the snow piling deeper and deeper, she turned up the heat in the back room and forgot about time.

Lanetia was startled awake when the outer door blew open. "Nesha…" Josh… She hurriedly hid the notebook, just as Josh opened the door to the back room. "No wonder you sleep. This place could roast turkey," Josh declared. "You know what time it is?" *No.* "After six. We cooked supper. Come on. Turn off that heater. I drove the SUV. Snow drifting three to six feet and it ain't stopped." As he picked up her coat that she had draped over the printing press, the gun would have fallen out of her pocket if he hadn't been quick enough to catch it. "Why the gun loaded? Somebody been around here?"

"No. I'll show you what I found." Lanetia said. She held up the wire wrapped stick that she had put beside the metal bin in which she kept an umbrella. "At the windmill…that wire was wrapped around a support and around a tree. I thought I saw something up there, but that's all I found. Did the windmill need the anchorage? I didn't think… Was this something you rigged?"

"No, I ain't been up there in a month. You know what that kind of wire is for, don't you?" At her shake of the head, he continued: "Trip wire for dynamite and shotgun traps…protectin' what shouldn't be grown. This snow should end tomorrow and be mostly melted in a couple of days. Me and Vinton will take a look." While Josh was talking, he removed the clip from the gun and put the clip in one pocket of her coat and the gun in the other. He held the coat open for her. "The wind still blowin'. Tie your scarf."

"How's your Dad," Kaida asked, as she sat back, fanning herself with a piece of cardboard. A thief had stolen the copper tubing from the air conditioner and the repairman would not be able to replace it until tomorrow.

"Franklin persuaded him to participate in some trial. He's determined to see Patrice's baby. What are we to do with this furniture?"

"We? No, you… What are *you* to do with this furniture? *My* furniture is on its way to Louisville. Maya just called to ask when will the truck arrive. Children…" Kaida spritzed her face and neck with ice water and continued fanning. "You bought both houses and the furniture we didn't want. Thank you. The money has been invested so my children's college tuition will be paid. I did not even buy a pair of shoes. That no good man I married... His daughter's tuition was due and he had the nerve to tell me that he's expecting another child. What is wrong with him? Why do I have to take him to court, just to get him to do what he agreed to do—half the college expenses and keep them on his insurance? What is so hard about that?"

"I guess I was lucky only the copper tubing was stolen this time," Lanetia interjected, hoping Kaida would change the topic of conversation to anything or anyone other than her ex-husband. Lanetia knew that Kaida's ex was threatening to take her to court to revise their agreement because of Kaida's inheritance. Lanetia had told Kaida to take the offensive. They'd been on the phone most of yesterday with Kaida's divorce attorney.

"Okay... I'm glad you modernized the heating and cooling system." Lanetia laughed and Kaida joined in. A lot of good a state of the art heating and cooling system was if it never worked. "You need a tenant in Mama's house. They'll make sure no one steals anything from this house. Lanetia, you will have to leave the place furnished if you intend to use this place as a writing retreat.

"It took three men a day and a half to move the furniture back to the house. After two nights in a sleeping bag, I am ready for a bed."

"If I leave this furniture in the house and someone steals it, I will never forgive myself. Aunt Maline trusts me… Where are those children?"

"They were in the fruit orchard," Kaida said, getting up to peer out the window. "Might have a decent crop this year. Frost came at all the wrong times last year. I'll come and help put up the fruit. Is this the year to make…" Lanetia nodded. "We had the best ribs in Louisville. We won awards. The restaurant made money. Sometimes, I wonder why it wasn't enough.

"I see them and I know where they're headed. I went down that path many a summer day. You did, too. Remember? Remember us older cousins telling you babies all those scary stories?"

"The creek?"

"The creek's a kid magnet. Before you ask… Yes, you did warn them. Remember Big Mama telling us the same thing? As soon as she lay down for her nap, we were gone. Can they swim?"

"Yes. Don't you think the water is still too cold?"

"They'll find out. I don't like any of the prospective tenants we've interviewed," Kaida said, frowning at the list that was on the mantel.

"I agree. There's a family coming at six thirty. I'm hot. Let's walk to the creek. Find those children."

"Nesha, Mama wanted you to have the family Bible and her journals. I've been meaning to tell you, but I was upset that she didn't want me to have the Bible… No, I was upset that she wanted you to have her journals. She explicitly said I was not to read them. She knew I wouldn't care about the Bible. I don't like Patrice, but sometimes I see so much of her in me… Knowing that upset me even more.

"She wrote in a journal even with the neuropathy. I don't know if any that she wrote at the last is legible. I tried to get her to use a recorder, but she said her thoughts were for writing. I took all of the boxes home with me, but I couldn't do it. Mama knew me. She didn't want me to read what she wrote for a reason. She doesn't want Jelly Bean or Tasha to read them either. She said she left you some instructions. Must be in one of the journals. I couldn't find anything…other than what I just told you. We can unload the van when we get back."

"I wish she hadn't."

"She said you would say that."

The fields were sprouting green. The farmer who leased the acreage kept the lawns mown and he did some edging. Lanetia kicked a mound of dirt next to a field. A rock caught her eye. "Wait up, Kaida. Look…an arrowhead. Look at the shape."

"There was a quarry somewhere on the property. Indians, from long ago, would make arrowheads and scrapers from the stone. Back in the day, we found them all the time. We gave them to Big Mama. I wonder where they went to?"

"I didn't know that. Any idea where the quarry is?"

"I think it was filled in a long time ago. I remember Big Mama saying that we could walk over it and not know what we were walking across. We would find the prettiest blue stones. Gave those to Big Mama, too. You were what six…seven when Big Daddy died?" *Six.* "For the longest, the place wasn't farmed. Big Mama lived with us, except in the summer. Mama had a time persuading her to keep the lawn mown. You remember when you visited what a jungle this place was? Mama was determined that this place would look like her childhood home. That's why she retired here. She dragged Dad here, kicking and screaming. He told me, after five years, he couldn't imagine living anywhere else. Took him that long to adjust to hearing the hoots of owls rather than police sirens. Did I tell you that he planted the weeping willow they're buried next to?

"The farmer who's leasing the land is probably plowing up all kinds of stuff. See this…" Kaida picked up a grayish flat stone and gave it to Lanetia. "The Indians called it firestone. Flint." Lanetia put the stones in a jeans' pocket to show to the kids.

The creek meandered along a tree lined course across the property. About five years ago, the owners of the adjacent property had decided that the creek was the boundary line of the two properties. Lanetia had had to take them to court to prevent them from selling what wasn't theirs to sell. If they'd asked, the Aunts probably would have given them access to the creek. But, they weren't the type of people to ask. After they lost that lawsuit, Lanetia had heard they sold the property. The new owner had promptly resold the property and now there was a small subdivision about two miles down the road. The Aunts had to erect a fence to keep the children who lived in the subdivision away from the creek.

"Lanetia, I can hear you thinking. I was thinking the same thing. We're going to have to walk the fence to make sure it's in good condition. We need an ATV."

"Might be able to rent one at the Co-Op or a tractor. I saw a sign that said farm equipment for rent."

"How did you three get across the creek?" Lanetia called out, after spotting the children who were so intent on their conversation that they had not seen Kaida and Lanetia.

"Nesha, that tree," Rachel called back, pointing at a scrub tree that had fallen across a narrow bend in the creek. Part of it was underwater. Lanetia and Kaida frowned at each other. *How?*

"What's the matter?"

"A snake crawled on it after we crossed and it's sunning itself," Juston answered. "Look about halfway across. It's almost the same color as the bark of the tree." Lanetia had to really look to make out the huge water moccasin that was curled up on the tree trunk. "We kinda crawled over. And, then, just as Rachel got off the tree, the tree rolled over and now part of it is in the water," Juston continued. "We were wondering how far to the bridge."

"Look out for snakes. There should be a path. There used to be a dirt crossing not far from here. We'll walk along this side."

"Kaida… Hey, guys, wait up," Lanetia called out a few minutes later. "Kaida, look in the water," she said, "the glint of sun between the shadows. Isn't that a blue something?"

"Might be some blue glass," Kaida said discouragingly. "I wish I hadn't said anything about those blue stones. Lanetia, that water is deeper than it looks. Where's a stick?" In response,

Lanetia picked up a half rotted tree branch. She measured the depth of the water near the bank. It was a little above her knees. The blue something was about three feet out.

"Not deep. I know. Sinkholes. Big Mama used to scare us with the stories of the sinkholes around here. Take off your shirt and I'll take off mine. We'll make a rope. You hold on to one end and I'll hang on to the other. Watch the backpack. If I fall in, I don't want my gun to get wet."

"I don't believe we're doing this," Kaida grumbled, as she unbuttoned her flannel shirt. Lanetia smiled and gave Kaida her own flannel shirt. Kaida tied the shirt tails together and tested her knot. It held. She gave the shirt to Lanetia who began to loop one of the sleeves around her hand. "No…twist the shirts into a rope and then tie it…not long enough to go around your waist and…okay, loop it around your hand and make a fist. I'll tie it. I wasn't a troop leader for nothing," Kaida said, sighing.

"Now that I don't have any circulation in that hand…satisfied?" Kaida nodded. "Brace yourself against that tree. Just a little drop. Oh… this water is freezing."

"Hurry up."

Lanetia slowly made her way to the blue object. She didn't want to stir up the mud and obscure whatever it was. She held up the rock for all to see, then as she turned, her foot slipped and the next thing she knew there wasn't any bottom under her feet and she was fighting an eddy that threatened to pull her down into its swirling depths. She heard Kaida shout—*let go of the damn rock and help me*. But her hand wouldn't obey. Lanetia somehow twisted the shirt rope around her other arm and, then, she felt a tug that felt like it dislocated her shoulder. The next thing she knew she was stretched out on the bank…only it wasn't the bank that was there before. The entire bank had caved in and Kaida was clinging to the scrub tree that now was half in the water. Its roots looked like petrified snakes clinging to a deep anchorage. The children were screaming. Lanetia crawled up the bank and only then did Kaida inch backward to where she was. "I told you to let go of that damn rock. Why are you so stubborn? Y'all stop screaming," Kaida shouted. "We're fine. Let me untie this or your circulation will be cut off. Y'all hush. Now, you see why Lanetia told you to stay away from the creek? What is this hung on my foot?" Kaida kicked her foot out of the backpack. Lanetia put the blue stone in the backpack to Kaida's disgust.

The dirt crossing was just as they remembered it, but the children were too afraid to cross it. "I am not walking on the road wearing only my bra," Kaida fussed. "I can't get this knot out because the material's wet and my hands are cold."

"Put your arms through the sleeves." Kaida frowned and gingerly put a hand into a sleeve and immediately withdrew it.

"My bra might not be dry, but it's body temperature," she said, with a grimace and a shiver.

"You can wear the backpack," Lanetia suggested, only half joking.

"And exactly what does that cover?"

"We're even. You didn't let go of the backpack and I didn't let go of the rock."

"Not the same thing. Anyway, I had my foot through the strap. It wasn't going anywhere. We're gonna be cited for indecent exposure. Well, I will. You're wearing mud."

"Let's just get to the other side. We're lucky there's not been much rain, just a couple of showers. It's not that muddy." Lanetia said, testing the top of the dirt bridge with another stick. "Walk slow. The water's deeper here and I don't want another dunking." As soon as she got to the other side, Lanetia hugged the three children. "Kaida, that knot is not coming out. Think of it like we have on our bathing suit tops."

The embankment by the bridge was steep and muddy. Kaida and Lanetia hesitated, trying to remember if the embankment was less steep on the other side of the bridge. Rachel decided for them. She refused to walk the narrow path that went under the bridge. Kaida made Lanetia walk on the outside, but they met no one in the quarter mile they had to walk to the driveway. By the time, they had showered and ate dinner, the prospective renters had arrived.

Mr. And Mrs. Jerry Hudson had four children. She was a cook at the elementary school and he worked in a factory, making stoves. The four children were not well behaved. Lanetia and Kaida were both shaking their heads as the Hudsons drove away. "I'm going to bed," Kaida muttered.

Lanetia pulled the covers around Cinda. Juston was sprawled on top of the covers in the room Franklin always slept in. Lanetia found a light blanket and tucked it around him. Rachel was reading a book. Rachel was enjoying having a room of her own.

Lanetia washed the blue rock and set it on the window sill. Blue…the blue of the sky on a hot, hazy summer's day. The next day, after the air conditioner had been repaired, they went to Nashville. Kaida had to drive. Lanetia's shoulder was too sore. Kaida rolled her eyes, but got interested when they returned and Lanetia clumsily chipped some pieces off the rock and glued the pieces to backings for earrings. Lanetia made Juston a pendant.

"I want a necklace. Let me do it," Rachel said. "You study the stone to determine where you want to chip it. Then, you put the cloth over the stone and position the chisel and tap it with the hammer. That way no flying splinters. I'll make us all necklaces. Now that I know what you did, I can do it," Rachel insisted.

"Don't make your pendant like mine," Juston warned. "Nesha, show me how to cap the end of the leather thong with these silver things."

"Dab a bit of glue on the end, put end in the cap, then mash together the ends of the cap with the pliers. You do the other end. Then take a hook, attach it to this little thingie," Lanetia instructed, picking up a split ring, "just slide it around…there…now you thread the pendant through this end, put around your neck. I like."

"Me, too."

"Me, three," Kaida chimed in. "Lanetia, you'll just have to buy more stuff. The interior of this rock is even prettier than the exterior. We made jewelry in Girl Scouts. I'd forgotten."

'Ma, why you doin' this? I got accepted. Six weeks…not even the whole summer. Why you sayin' I can't go?" Rachel shouted at her mother.

"Don't you shout at me. I be your mother and I say no."

"You should want me to do somethin' that interests me. Keep me busy. Keep me from doin' what you did… Get pregnant at fourteen." Vonnie Pearl slapped Rachel and Rachel just looked her up and down before running up the stairs.

"You done took my son. You ain't takin' my daughter," Vonnie Pearl said to a silent Lanetia. "All your foreign ways. Got my Ma thinkin' I be crazy. Well, I ain't. My cousin said that I didn't do nothin' out of the ordinary. I felt threatened and I did what was necessary to lessen the threat. That be what normal people do."

"Well, since you aren't crazy," Josh said from behind Vonnie Pearl, who whirled around at the sound of his voice. Josh let the door slam. "Hear what I have to say."

"Josh…" Vonnie Pearl began.

"You listen. If you want to be full of hate, that's your business. Can't no one stop you hating. Not good for your soul. Did your cousin tell you that? You don't want us… No, you listen. Lanetia is my wife. We will leave your house. I promised Dad I would stay until Rachel graduated from high school. He did not know about Cinda. I made that promise to myself. I been planning to fix up the old home place for me, Lanetia, and Juston. That will be my priority this summer and we will be out of your house. You can live in this house with your hatred for company. Is there anything I have said that you do not understand?"

"If it be that important to her, she can go."

"Doesn't change anything. Where Zeezee?"

"Diggin' in her herbs. Why y'all keep givin' me a headache?" Vonnie Pearl complained.

"Go to bed. Ain't that what you do when you have a headache?" Josh said, showing no sympathy for his mother who was beginning to cry. "Nesha, come with me. I need you to walk with me."

They walked in silence through the fields that were waiting to be planted. "You were right. But, when it comes to people and their motivation, you usually are. I had to hear it for myself. I'm sorry I subjected you to my mother. Where the kids?"

"I took them to D'Arton's birthday party. He passed. Cinda and Juston have been teaching him to read. So they have a lot to celebrate." At his raised eyebrow, Lanetia continued: "They confessed on the way to the party. That's the reason when he comes to play, they disappear. I was going to volunteer to take Rachel to school. Now, I think you and Zeezee should go, along with Vonnie Pearl, so that Vonnie Pearl knows exactly where Rachel is and what she's doing."

"You do? She won't talk to the doctor, but she'll talk to that adulterous, womanizing cousin of hers. Every word he says is gospel. He doesn't believe in mental illness. He believes in demon possession. Maybe multiple demons. He has a ritual that he performs. That's what she wants to do. But, no…she is not crazy."

"Josh, hold my hand. I like it when you hold my hand." He squeezed her hand and she squeezed back. "It might work for a while. A placebo. It might work forever, if she truly believes. The mind is amazing. You know that."

Zeezee watched them approach and stood up, wiping her hands on her apron. "What done happened?" she questioned, as soon as they were within talking distance. "Josh, you look like you want to kill somebody."

"Rachel has been accepted to that summer arts program. I'll get a check in the mail for the fees tomorrow. Please, talk to your daughter. Rachel is going. No matter how many times Ma changes her mind; no matter what hell she puts us through, Rachel is going. You make her understand that. You also make her understand that I will not participate in your nephew's demon ridding ritual. Tell him his country bumpkin cousin who cannot speak proper English, refuses."

"Josh, calm yourself. I done told Vonnie Pearl that if she want to do it, to do it and don't expect us to do it with her. We ain't got no demons. That be what he diagnosed her with. I told her as long as it was just words and layin' on of hands, she didn't need no support. And if it was somethin' more than that, she was a fool to participate. She don't see that he want to parade her around for his own glorification.

"Nesha, what you gonna plant in that field that ain't been planted in years? Josh said you asked if you could plant somethin', I forget what he called it, in that field y'all was plowin' yesterday."

"Millet. It should grow. An experiment. Josh showed me the mill and it's still set up to grind corn and wheat. Our ancestors grew millet. I acquired a taste for it. I cook it like rice or I grind it and make bread. I thought I'd try growing it. The seed arrived today. It needs a lot less water than corn to thrive, so that field is perfect."

"The market in the States is mostly for birdseed," Josh explained. "It's sold in health food stores. Seed is organic food grade, guaranteed to grow. We'll plant it first of June. I know you said you didn't want no help," he continued, quirking an eyebrow at Lanetia. "From what I read, we gonna have to spread compost at least once a month. I ain't got too much on my plate." Lanetia shrugged. Joshua hadn't wanted her to plant anything in that field. When she had asked why, he had paused for a too long moment and then said he would help her. *Pick your battles, a voice reminded her.*

"Lanetia asked her brother to send her the grinder she had in storage. I picked it up today at Old Bob's. Tomorrow we will taste millet bread, if you will be so kind as to tell your daughter that you will be cooking supper tomorrow." Zeezee shook her fist at her grandson. "You ready to walk back to the house with us?"

"May as well. By the time I get through talkin' to *your mother*, I will be doin' all the cookin' for the next month."

The next day, Lanetia had more help than she needed or wanted. "Is it like the mill?" Juston asked, as he studied the exterior of the grinder.

"No, look… This grinder uses high speed blades. The mill uses two stones to grind the grain into meal or flour. Pour grain to that first line on the hopper. I want a meal, so we'll grind for ten seconds and stop. We repeat until we determine if it's the consistency we want. See that corn meal I poured in the saucer for comparison? That's what I want it to look like."

"Did you do this before? Make your own meal?" Cinda asked. "Yes. Don't fight over who flips the switch. Do rock, paper, scissors, or something." Zeezee could be so contrary… She reached over and flipped the switch to the glares of Cinda and

Juston. Rachel laughed. Joshua was keeping time so he beat Rachel to the switch. Rachel poured a little into a bowl and compared it to the corn meal. Thirty more seconds…some of the grain hadn't ground.

Lanetia had decided to make fried millet bread. Looked just like corn cakes. Zeezee couldn't wait and slathered butter on the first piece of bread Lanetia put into the bread basket. Zeezee passed around a taste.

"Tastes like cornbread," Juston said, disappointed.

"That's why I use it as a substitute for cornmeal," Lanetia said, somewhat exasperated. "If you really taste it, it's not as sweet as cornmeal and the texture is different, but not that different. I like it with lots of butter."

No one expected Vonnie Pearl to eat the millet bread, but she did.

Kaemon arrived on Tuesday night. Nina was not with him. "I came to help with the planting." He brushed aside their questions about Nina. "You know Nina does not like this place. Too backwoods. I'll stay until after Juneteenth. Helene and Nora are still upset they weren't invited to your wedding. They said if it was so rushed, how come me, Nina, and Thea were invited. They're very disappointed that you haven't yet had the baby they were so sure you were expecting. Why else have a rushed wedding? Josh, have you forgotten? It's your year to cook the meat."

Josh and Kaemon sat under a tree, drinking water as Lanetia drove the tractor, with Juston tending the seeder. "Is there anything she doesn't do?" Kaemon asked, with just a hint of bitterness.

"She don't like doin' a lot of things. She has to because of my hand."

"But she does it. She'll compromise. She won't look you in the eye and say it's either me or them."

"She won't go to church with me. Every Sunday, Pope got somethin' to say about a wife being submissive to her husband. And how it's a husband's duty to make sure his wife is doin' the right thing. I've about had enough of him. She done made plenty of enemies. Everybody in the school system done lost their jobs. I saw the advertisement for teachers. To attract teachers, they will pay some kind of supplement. They did decide to let the teachers interview, but the word is they won't be hired back."

"Joshua, I don't know if I can answer the questions you want to ask. My soul needs this place. I don't understand it. Andy said this was the place we first tasted and lived freedom in this land of broken promises and dreams deferred. Maybe a part of me knows that.

"Detroit…I don't even recognize it anymore. Some of the people who live in Detroit are so dangerous that even I don't want to deal with what comes through the doors, asking about the Army. You heard about the recruitment scandals?" Josh nodded. "I was investigated. They didn't find anything, but Josh…I have been tempted. The pressure is so intense that I have wanted to say anything, promise anything to have the numbers. After I was investigated and cleared, I resigned. I've done everything I could to be a good husband, I need to do this for me. Down from the old home place, the clearing… That's where I want to build."

"The site of the old barn? Not across the road on that knoll?"

"Yeah. I know that's the site Andy and I chose, but when I went there this morning, it didn't move me. Where the barn was…called me…spoke to me. You couldn't possibly remember that barn."

"I heard stories about it. I'll get the site surveyed and deed it over to you. You'll be near Nesha and me. In the fall, we'll be movin' into the old home place."

"Do you mind if I go to Atlanta with you when you take Rachel to school?" *No.* "I'd like to meet Zeezee's relatives. I can't believe you allowed Rachel and Cinda to drive the tractor. Never thought I'd see the sight," he said, grinning as Cinda traded places with Lanetia who took over tending the seeder. "This one here… I expected to see driving anything that could be driven," Kaemon said as Juston got a bottle of water from the cooler.

That night… Lanetia slipped out of bed and, in the sitting room, she hurriedly dressed in some old jeans and a flannel shirt. *Thinkin'* that was what Josh had said as he had turned his back to her. She peeked into Juston's room. Juston, who was waiting for her, hopped out of bed, fully dressed, except for shoes. "Mind the steps." Juston nodded. He knew which ones squeaked. They were quiet until they got to the storage porch. "I have everything that we need at the old home place. Put on your shoes, coat, and stocking cap," Lanetia whispered, pointing to the hooks where they kept their coats and scarves. She quietly closed the door to the kitchen. "I hate leaving this porch door unlatched," she whispered more to herself than to Juston. There was no lock on the door…just the latch. There was a full moon and they really didn't need the flashlight. The bright bluish light of the flashlight actually caused the shadows to appear to be more menacing, so Lanetia turned it off. “I found a place above the old home place. A small clearing that’s perfect…

“Juston, do you remember what I said…that you have to tell me how you feel. Is this something you really want to do?”

“I know it’s just something you wrote about… But, yes, more than anything. Closure…that’s what the ceremony is all about and,” he slipped his hand into hers, “it’s what I need. Nesha, they left that day and just didn’t come back. Granddaddy said they were in those caskets, but they wouldn’t let me look. They said the car exploded after the crash. Granddaddy said I wouldn’t recognize what was in there. The nightmares have mostly gone, but the one on Sunday… I don’t like feeling so afraid. I’m glad you knew to come and stayed with me.”

“I’m glad, too.” Lanetia squeezed his hand. Lanetia had been dreaming and the woman in the coral suit had prodded her awake. The woman’s face had gradually changed to Juston’s. Lanetia had found herself opening the door to Juston’s room to check on him. He was sitting up in bed, tears streaming down his face, trembling. She had gotten into bed with him and held him as close as she could. He was so small. Earlier, he and Cinda had been planning his birthday party. Juston was a June baby.

Josh had peeked in and she had gestured for him to close the door and he had backed out. “Talk?” She’d asked Juston. “I came home from school and me and Farley were playing like we always did after school. Mommy and Daddy went to the store. Mommy asked Farley's mother to watch me like she always did. They didn't come back that night. Sometimes they did that and I would stay with Farley and his mother. They always came back. Either the next day or the day after. They never stayed away more than three days. They'd always bring me a present. Farley would get a present and they always had some money for Farley's mother.

"This time…the next day, Farley's mother told us we didn't have to go to school and she didn't go to work. That afternoon…Granddaddy and your father came. Granddaddy cried and I didn't understand. We left that afternoon to go… I don't know where it was. Granddaddy said it was where he grew up. I didn't tell you before. Granddaddy had an argument with Mommy's cousin. She didn't want my Mommy to be buried there. I didn't hear any more. Someone took me to a house down the road, so I wouldn't hear any more.

"After the funeral, Granddaddy told me I would be living with your father. Why didn't they come back?"

"Juston, I don't know if there is an answer to your question." Lanetia heart ached for him. Hadn't she asked the same question when her mother had not come back? No one had an answer then, either. One day, she would tell him that they had felt no pain. No one in either of the cars had survived the impact. The autopsies had shown his parents had alcohol and cocaine in their systems and his father was in no condition to drive. Juston would know that the accident wasn't his father's fault. The other car had run the stop sign. Turned out the other driver had been drinking. No one had insurance. Five grieving families had been left behind to ask the question why.

"Do you remember what one of the characters did in the second AWB book when she needed to say goodbye to her great-grandmother?" Lanetia had felt his nod. "There's a full moon on Wednesday night. You think of what you would like to say to your parents and I'll find a place where you can say goodbye in your own way. Would you like that?" Again, she had felt his nod. Lanetia had crooned to him a song Darly used to sing to herself when she was upset until he had relaxed into sleep.

"Wait for me," Cinda whispered loudly from behind them.

"Cinda, go back to bed," Lanetia ordered. "This…"

"She can come," Juston interrupted. "She's been asking me why I was sad. I didn't know how to tell her. She won't laugh or think I'm weird. She's kind of like you in that way." Juston held up his hand and stood still, waiting, listening. "Rachel's coming.

She must have heard Cinda get up. Knew that shadow was Rachel," Juston said, as Rachel came into view.

"Wonder Cinda didn't wake up the whole house. Don't know how she didn't. She barely missed the three steps that squeak," Rachel said, with a hint of defiance.

"I was quiet. You were sleep when I left. Tell the truth," Cinda protested.

"I woke up as you shut the door. The nightlight in the hall…shines in my face when the door is open. Yes, you were very quiet. What are we doin'?" Lanetia did not answer. Juston must decide whether or not to share his story.

"My parents were killed on this day last year. I'm saying goodbye," Juston said, laying his head on Lanetia's upper arm. "You can come, but I don't need you to comment on how I choose to say goodbye."

"I wouldn't do that. I didn't know it was today."

"Nobody did, but Nesha. Nesha says we need to be quiet because voices carry in these hills."

Lanetia opened the door to the old home place and grabbed the backpack she had packed. Lanetia studied the three to assess their clothing. They all had on hats and coats and socks and outdoor shoes. Lanetia checked the temperature. Mid-thirties. She decided she needed her coat that hung on the hook by the door. She locked the door.

"We have to walk around the construction. Yesterday, I found a path." In the shadows of the trees, Lanetia needed the flashlight to find the path. She had marked the beginning of the path with a bit of silver ribbon tied around the branch of a small redbud tree that was still in blossom. Cinda pointed to the gleaming ribbon when Lanetia swept the flashlight over the area where she thought the path started.

The small clearing was eerily lit by the full moon. Lanetia gave the flashlight to Rachel to hold while she studied her handiwork. Earlier that day, she had found the round, flat stones to make the outer circle. The second circle had been more difficult to create...the wood had to come from a tree struck by lightning. She had walked the forest for an hour before she had found the charred branch of a tree off to the side of the path she was on. She had broken the branch into small enough pieces to fit into her backpack and had to make two trips to have enough for the second circle. The third circle had been easier...there were plenty of weeds that had volunteered in the clearing. The weeds didn't appear to have minded their transplanting. None were wilted.

Lanetia had scoured the forest for a plant with a bloom and finding none...had dug up a blooming purple iris from the iris bed planted in front of the old home place by Josh's great-grandmother. She had planted it in a small pot and, with the waning of the moon, she would transplant to a spot beside the center flat stone.

On that stone, was the purple iris...the gift of beauty; an unripened peach and apple from the orchard...the gift of potential and nourishment; rainwater...the gift of drink; and a picture of Juston's parents...the ones they were here to speak to.

Lanetia placed a candle by each stone of the outer circle and two candles on the center stone. She held up her hand. No breeze. For once, the weather report was right. Lanetia gave Rachel the extra lighter, so she could help light the candles. She, then, took from the backpack a small drum and a small bottle of rainwater. The bottle of water on the flat rock could not be disturbed. Lanetia then turned in a circle, again studying her handiwork. She could almost hear Angilyne's instructions as though Angilyne stood next to her. "The ground is dry. Let's all sit quietly for a few minutes. Juston, sit where you can see the picture of your parents. I will sit behind you. Do you want…"

"Embrace me with your knees," Juston interrupted, "just like the book."

"Okay, but first, I will sprinkle a little of this rainwater on us and around us for extra protection. Sometimes when we perform rituals...it's always best to protect ourselves from the unforeseen," Lanetia explained as she sprinkled them and the ground of the inner circle with rainwater. "We will listen to some music that I have recorded for tonight. From this point on, all words will come from Juston. When he has said what is in his heart to say, then and only then will there be words from the rest of us and only if our hearts demand that words be spoken. Understood?" They nodded.

Lanetia turned on the portable CD player and a soft undulating music backed with a drum that seemed to stir the stillness filled the clearing. "Nesha, turn it up," Juston said. Lanetia turned up the volume until Juston nodded. Toward the end of the music, Lanetia began to drum and she continued to drum as Juston spoke. Words seemed to burst forth… Words that had been suppressed… Lanetia drummed to the rhythm of Juston's words and was surprised when hands were placed over hers and took over. She looked up into Josh's tear streaked face and leaned against him.

"Nesha, they're smiling at me," Juston said and he wasn't looking at the picture on the rock, but into the distance. "They heard me. They really heard me. Bye, Mommy… Bye, Daddy. I know… Nesha's my mommy now and Josh is my daddy. I know… Nesha, tell them."

"Juston, the flesh of your flesh and the flesh of my ancestors by whom we shall forever be joined, is my son and I thank you for his life. He is and always shall be precious to me." Lanetia was surprised again as Joshua said the words with her as though they had been rehearsed. "I pour this water, the tears of our Mother Earth, in honor of you. Go, in peace. Your son, my son, our son shall always be loved by me forever, for death, as you have shown us, does not sever the ties of love. In peace, shall you go, knowing that no thing has been left undone. Peace to you and to all who witness what has been wrought this night." Every candle in the clearing blinked out as though a hand had been poised over each, waiting for that moment. Lanetia remembered to play the last song… a song of joy that filled the small clearing and chased away all fear. Only then did she look around and see Zeezee and Kaemon.

"Maybe if your Ma had had such a ceremony for Andy…" Zeezee whispered. "Girl, why didn't we know you sooner?"

Back at the old home place, Lanetia and Zeezee made chocolate. For a long while they were silent, each of them assimilating the experience in their own way. Kaemon broke the silence. "Thank you, Lanetia, for giving voice to the yearning of my soul. Big John, Andy…they were all there…welcoming me home. My soul is content. I am home to stay."

"We better get back to the house," Zeezee said, looking at the clock on the wall beside the door. "We been talkin' for more than an hour. Kids just about sleep. Almost time to get up. Nesha, put those candles in the sink. Just in case. Juston, you take your mama and daddy's picture. You keep it safe. Hang it in your room or put it on your bureau." Juston nodded, his eyes half-closed. "Nesha, I'm glad I got to attend your service. I heard Rachel get up. I thought she was goin' to her bathroom, but I heard her sneakin' down the steps. I heard that boy Ronnie done come back and I thought she was bein' foolish. I woke Josh and Kaemon. Then, we found out you, Juston, and Cinda was gone. We was just in time to see your light as you went up that path to that clearing. Glad you marked it with that ribbon. At first, we wasn't gonna join you, but I'm so glad we did. Got to say goodbye to my mama. Never had the chance until tonight."

"Josh, was that my daddy? Kind of looked like Uncle Kaemon, but his hair was different," Cinda asked sleepily, as Josh picked her up.

"That was our daddy. I saw him, too. Just as plain as day."

"So it wasn't a dream," Rachel whispered. "It really wasn't a dream and I'm not asleep?"

"Then all of us had the same dream. Can't be a bad thing for family to have the same dream, can it?"

The reddish bronze rays of the rising sun were streaking the horizon by the time Lanetia was ready for bed. Josh was sitting on the sofa, staring into space. "Nesha, I won't laugh at what you do. I know tonight was for Juston, but it was healing for more than him. Like that night after P's cabin burned, our souls met in a place, I can't describe. Like then, we said…haven't we met before and now we meet again. Joy has once again come to us."

Lanetia held out her arms to Josh. She didn't know whether or not she wanted to be held or loved. It didn't matter. Each would follow the other's lead on this morning.

Rachel answered the phone and handed it to Lanetia. Lanetia held the phone away from her ear. "I'll be there on the plane that arrives at seven fifteen. Come pick me up," Nina sobbed and hung up the phone.

"Are you guys too sleepy to help in the fields today? Cinda, you are. You can't keep your eyes open. Let me look at you two. No. Y'all get a book. Read and nap."

For a second, Lanetia wondered what Zeezee had said to Vonnie Pearl to explain the girls' sleepiness. Whatever the explanation, Vonnie Pearl made no comment and went about her morning chores.

"Gonna rain," Josh said, when, at her signal, he had stopped the tractor beside her.

"A word…under the tree. You need a bottle of water. The one you have is empty. Kaemon, we'll bring you a bottle. Be back in a minute." Kaemon nodded and took a sip of water from a bottle that was nearly empty. "Josh, Nina just called. I take it Kaemon has already talked to her."

"Called her as soon as he knew she would be up. He told her he wanted a divorce and that she could file the papers. He said he would be back for his clothes and then he would never, ever set foot in Detroit again."

"She's flying in this evening. I'll pick her up at the airport in Knoxville."

"You're tired," Josh protested. "She can…"

"No, she cannot. I'll be fine. I'll help for an hour or so, then…"

"Go back to the house and take a nap. I'd go with you, but she won't want to see me. She probably thinks I had somethin' to do with his decision."

"Something like that."

Lanetia listened to Nina as she wept and accused everyone but herself of causing her marriage to fail. "Nina, I have listened to you for an hour. You don't even sound like the person I met last summer. What happened?"

"My sister said if I put my foot down that he would come around. She said he would never leave me. She said…"

"Nina, you have to decide. Stop listening to everyone but yourself. What does your heart say? If you can't live in the mountains, then let him go. Be kind to yourself and him."

"I couldn't take the winter. I couldn't do it. It's bad enough in Detroit, especially with all the cutbacks in services. There wasn't enough salt or that salt solution to last the winter. Thea's in on it. Thea told Kaemon that as soon as she retires, she would move to the mountains and keep house for him.

"I love that man."

"Then work out a compromise."

"How do you like this place?"

"Me? I hate the mountains. But Josh made a promise and I will not be the cause of him breaking his promise." Lanetia's words seemed to shock Nina into a contemplative silence, only broken by barely suppressed sighs. For the first time or maybe for the thousandth time, Lanetia considered her feelings. She'd always thought she could think herself into an action that would untangle any web she had woven for herself. Now, she wasn't so confident.

"Josh told you about his promise," Nina said as they turned into the driveway.

"Just as Kaemon told you that he wanted to retire to the mountains. Remember, that's what you told me."

"How do you live somewhere you hate?"

"I keep very busy. I leave when I can. I say to myself over and over again… I love this man enough to do this. When that fails, I shut myself away and write myself into oblivion. Like I said at first, I keep myself very busy. You and Kaemon can decide on your sleeping arrangement. Zeezee has prepared a room for you if it's needed."

Kaemon opened the doors to the SUV and then got Nina's suitcase from the rear seat. "We'll talk. We'll go from there. Are you hungry? We can warm…"

"No, I couldn't eat."

"Nesha, Josh is in the kitchen. By the way, I liked the millet bread."

"You want to take your food upstairs?" Josh asked as he fixed Lanetia a plate.

"No, I'll eat in the kitchen. Who made millet bread?"

"Ma did. Cinda showed her how to use the grinder. She put a little sugar in the mix. You said the slight bitterness wouldn't be noticeable if you used a bit of sugar. And she put more flour in the mix. Taste it. What do you think?"

"Very good."

"You don't like it?"

"I prefer my bread savory, not sweet. When I make bread, which thank goodness was a long time ago…a loaf of bread," she explained at his puzzled expression, "I mix in herbs. I only add enough sugar to activate the yeast. A cake is cake and bread shouldn't be sweet. My preference. That's all."

"You don't like to cook, do you?"

"No. I've told you that before. Was something supposed to have changed?"

"The kids said that you and Kaida had a good time in the kitchen."

"I like to watch Kaida cook. Kaida's a gourmet cook. She trained to be a chef. She worked as a sous chef in D.C., Houston, and Denver. Then, she and her husband moved to Louisville to open a restaurant. It did well until he couldn't keep his pants zipped. Kaida was working for a catering company when her mother became too ill to live alone. Aunt Maline didn't want to move to Aunt Leda's house and Aunt Leda refused to move into the home place. Kaida assessed the situation and decided to move in with her mother. Jelly Bean paid for all the extras. Tasha came when she could. She has three little ones. They really pulled together. Aunt Maline didn't want to admit to herself that Aunt Leda was that ill. When Aunt Maline came to her peace with the severity of Aunt Leda's illness, she spent most of her time at Aunt Leda's house. Didn't I tell you this?"

"The part about your Aunts… Yes…you did. Kaida…no. I didn't know what she did. I was lookin' through Ma's CD's and tapes. She has three of your cousin's CD's. Did you know he has his own syndicated show?"

"He ***had*** his own syndicated show. What's on now are reruns. Got caught with the producer's wife. In his dressing room, during a change of costume. The producer chased him across the stage in front of the audience and he was, shall I say… Do you know what streaking is?" Josh nodded. "The producer shot him. Just in the leg…in front of that audience. All recorded for posterity. That was his last show. It never aired. The producer sent a copy of the video to me as justification for canceling Jelly Bean's contract. I reviewed all of Jelly Bean's contracts. Josh, really, you can laugh. I laugh every time I see Jelly Bean. That's why he glares at me. Then, he looks really sheepish and whispers that I'd better not tell the family why he doesn't have a show. That was two or three years ago."

Josh threw back his head and laughed. "Nesha, your family…"

"Are you beginning to understand why I'm cynical?"

"I think so."

CHAPTER 11

Why am I having this conversation? Déjà vu? Zeezee and Lanetia stared at each other, neither willing to give an inch. Two bison butting heads… Why couldn't Zeezee understand? Sometimes being socially correct did not benefit anyone. Once a stranger, always a stranger…that was Crow Cut Cove's reaction to anyone who dared invade its boundaries. "I will help prepare the food. I will not stay. I won't pretend anymore. They don't like me and I don't care for them. I'll work on the newspaper. Give them something to talk about."

Zeezee sighed. She'd asked Josh if they could skip the Memorial Day cookout. Rachel was getting ready to go to the Summer Arts School for six weeks and she had to be there by six on Friday evening; Lanetia was hosting a bridal shower for her friend Janine on Friday in Nashville; Nina, where ever she was, was crying; Vonnie Pearl, for some reason, wore a puzzled frown; and she was trying to think of an excuse not to stay with the

Reverend Goodman. Vonnie Pearl had said they would. Josh had refused, saying he would stay at Deuce's home and, to be honest, that's where she wanted to stay.

"Can't believe all the stuff they supposed to bring with them," Zeezee said. "You ain't weedin' the herbs. I know you tired. You been to Knoxville, Nashville, and Chattanooga with Rachel, lookin' for the stuff on the list. Ordered stuff off the Internet. Ridiculous. You'd think she was goin' away for a year. School say it supply everything and then put up a BUT in capital letters of what it don't supply. Don't get me started. I know it be a highly rated program. The students win all kinds of awards. They come from everywhere, even out of the Country. I read the school's website. Rachel got in because that pottery teacher wrote a recommendation. Not like the high school has any art classes."

Lanetia pulled up a weed. "Next year, if Rachel decides to attend, she'll have most of what she needs and we won't have to buy as much. She's taken the on-line aptitude tests that the college requires. The tests indicate that she would do really well in the three-D arts. She'll do fine at the school. She'll showcase her work at the end of the session, so we'll get to see what she's created. Your herb garden is so peaceful. There's more water in the lake this year. I walked up to where P's cabin was. It was a year ago… What a year."

"P's cousin finally sold the place to Josh. Josh used to whittle, He won't do it no more because that talent must've come from P and he always thought P was a crazy white man pretendin' to be an Indian. P wasn't pretendin'. He was with his mama, on the reservation, until he was thirteen. Only place she could go. Her parents died when she was really young and the only relative they had was a great aunt who lived on the reservation. When P was thirteen, he went to a boardin' school, paid for by his daddy. He hated that school. Ran away, but his mama made him go back, so he would have a chance to go to college. You the only one who don't mind listenin' when I talk about him. Nesha, don't nobody else want to hear about him. Sometimes, I just want to go in the woods and scream his name. I want him…us to be remembered."

"Zeezee, I've written all the stories you've told me in a journal. One day, I'll read those stories to my children and you'll tell them even more stories and I'll write those in the journal."

"Make me want to cry. I guess we all tired."

"Kind of takes the tiredness away talking about the man you loved, doesn't it?" Zeezee didn't respond. She had snapped off a sprig of purple fennel and she was twirling it under her nose, letting the aroma of licorice take her to another place and time.

"You don't mind not havin' your car?" Zeezee asked, tossing the sprig of fennel into the weed bag.

"Why should I mind? Franklin's coming to get me and the kids. I'll drive one of Dad's old cars while I'm in Nashville. Sometimes you ask the oddest things."

"I done what I was asked to do. I talked to you and you ain't changed your mind. Didn't think you would. Some things with you just ain't negotiable."

Because Rachel was leaving on Friday, Juston had asked if they could celebrate his birthday early. Juston liked the tradition of hiding presents, so Lanetia hid his presents. When Juston awakened on that Memorial Day, there was a teaser present on his pillow. At one o'clock, his birthday party began. By three, the adults were arriving for the cookout.

Lanetia helped with the food. She slipped away after the food was blessed. Halfway to the old home place, Nina caught up with her.

"Can I visit with you? They're talking about both of us and I will cuss one of them and that doesn't make for a pleasant relationship. Did you see Roberta? How do you tolerate her behavior?"

"I ignore it. For some reason, in his heart…Josh wants me to be jealous. He and, only he, can put a stop to Roberta's antics. A part of him wants to, but there's a part that doesn't and Roberta takes full advantage. Josh is conflicted. He doesn't want me to cling, yet he wants me to embody his idea of femininity. I just figured that out. Thank you."

"I think I understood what you said. I really like the plans for the house. I'm trying to wrap my mind around this place. Kaemon wants to live here most of the year, but he's willing to spend the winter elsewhere, but not this coming winter. I'm supposed to be looking for a winter residence. I really, really don't like Florida."

"Would you consider an island in the Caribbean? I know someone you could talk to who lives in a retirement community on a private island."

"I'd never thought of doing that. That might work. I wonder if we could afford it? We could sell the house and the bills… I saw your electric bill. Wouldn't have a water bill. I wonder… Kaemon had the site bush hogged last Friday. It's about two acres. This Thursday…I wasn't, but I will… Kaemon's asked a builder to look at the site."

"Make yourself at home. This is my domain. There's a refrigerator in the back room with water and maybe some fruit."

"Smells newsy," Nina said, wrinkling her nose at the smell of ink and paper.

"I'll turn on the air conditioner. It's so noisy I try not to turn it on, but I can't stand being in a stuffy room. Josh and his father caulked all the windows so they don't open. I'm working on a story about the gated communities on Cherry Hill. Seems like there's infighting in two of the homeowners' associations. Also, there was a shooting last week. No one was killed. Now, the alleged victim wants his side of the story told. Doesn't want the other side told at all." *Why?* "It's all connected. They found out their water is contaminated. They're having to buy drinking and bathing water. They've dug four wells and had to cap them all. Arsenic…mine seepage and runoff. Fish are dying in the lake. I'll be in the back room, listening to the interviews and taking notes.

"Rachel usually helps with the crossword puzzle. Would you like to do that? It's easy. I have a computer program that creates the puzzle. Another thing… Could you man the booth this summer? Next weekend the market opens for the summer. You wouldn't be able to travel on the weekends, but you'd be free the rest of the week. Josh will pay you a percentage of the sales." Nina stared at Lanetia, then turned on the computer.

"I've seen the booth. You think I've decided to stay?"

"You're considering it."

"Why doesn't Josh do what he did last year? I'm sure…Harmond…that's his name, could use the extra money."

“Mr. Harmond is ill. We’ll be helping him this year. Also, part of the proceeds is most of Zeezee’s spending money for the year. She doesn’t like to ask Josh for money. It was just a thought…”

“If I stay, I need something to do,” Nina pointed out. “There’s electricity for the refrigerator. Sometimes, Zeezee sells butter and eggs. She can sell the hair oil. All my friends who use it rave about how soft their hair feels and how good their hair smells. Kaemon says my hair has never felt so alive and he loves that berry scent.

“The booth is under a huge tulip poplar and two dogwoods. I don’t mind the heat, but Andy had a fan. It was the oddest looking contraption. Blew air over a compartment filled with dry ice, for the coolest breeze. I wonder where it is? Can’t remember the last time I visited the booth. Tell Josh, I can do it. I shouldn’t depend on Kaemon for everything. Our eldest can drive my car when he comes for Juneteenth and drive back with Thea. In the meantime, if you don’t mind, I can drive Hoopty.” Lanetia nodded. “Now…crossword puzzle. I know my way around computers. Before my mother needed me twenty-four/seven, I was the resource administrator for a senior citizens’ center. I taught word processing, spread sheets, surfing the Internet. If anyone needed help with a computer program, I would figure out the program, so they could use it without too much frustration." For the first time since Nina had arrived, Lanetia sensed her relax. They worked in silence until Cinda and Juston showed up, each with a stuffed backpack.

"We brought lots of food. Cinda, get the plates and the forks. I'll put the food on the table. There's juice and stuff in the refrigerator. Nesha, I remembered to bring the tea and lots of lemons."

"Isn't it time for the ballgame? Juston…"

"Might be. They talk too much and I don't want to listen anymore and I don't want to play ball with them. D'Arton's mother doesn't know that Cinda and I taught him to read. She thinks Mrs. Symmon, the reading tutor, did, and, if it wasn't for you, she'd be back next year and D'Arton would continue to do as well as he did this year. She's asking everyone to sign a petition saying they don't want the State to take over the school system."

"Juston, she works for the principal of the elementary school."

"As a maid."

"It's honest work."

"And that means, you can't think for yourself, have an opinion, do what's best for yourself?"

"Sometimes. Depends on how desperate you are. You need to feed yourself, your family… You learn how to hold it all in. Sometimes your life depends on knowing when…"

"After we eat, can we play chess in the back room?" Juston said, deliberately interrupting. He knew he was being rude. They shared an intense look. He didn't want to hear about grown-up choices that were less than ideal. "We won't make any noise."

"Sure." Lanetia let it go. One day, he would understand and maybe, one day as he made a less than ideal choice, he would remember this day. "I can't believe you packed all this food in the two backpacks. Did Zeezee help?" Cinda nodded. "Where's the chocolate cake and pecan pie?" Juston pointed to two foil wrapped packages. "It's been a long day. I'm going to pick up some strawberries in a couple of hours. Do you want to go?"

"You're going to pick strawberries?" Nina asked incredulous. "At night?"

"No. There was a sign in Old Bob's store that a farm near Salyna has strawberries. I called and the farmer said he would pick two crates for me. It's not dark until almost nine and that's when he said he should be back from the fields." *Two crates? Nina questioned.* "Have to get enough to make jam, freeze some for ice cream, and the reason I wanted them…cakes."

"You're making a strawberry cake?" Lanetia nodded. "Patrice said your strawberry cake was really good," Juston said. "We'll go. We're not tired. I had the best birthday party. Can we stop at the drug store in Salyna? The one with the picture machine. I can choose the pictures I want printed." Lanetia nodded.

"I'm making a cake for Janine's wedding shower, not for you to eat," Lanetia warned.

"But…don't we get to taste it? I've never had strawberry cake before," Juston protested.

"I'll make a little one for you. Cinda, I think it will be just enough for both of you," Lanetia said, as Cinda almost choked on a piece of fried chicken in her haste to join Juston's protest.

Vonnie Pearl pretended to clear the freezer to make room for the strawberries as Lanetia made the strawberry cakes. She had two shopping bags of ingredients—spelt and oat flours, raw sugar granulated and powdered, pecans for garnishment, vanilla extract, almond milk and yogurt, and Zeezee's homemade butter. Not exactly her grandmother's cake, but just as good. Almost three days for the cakes to ripen as her grandmother would say. Lanetia smiled at the memory. Her grandmother would ripen the cakes for at least two weeks. The yearly ritual of making the strawberry cake—an alcoholic buzz dressed up in strawberry flecked butter cream frosting—that's what her mother said it was. She hadn't been allowed to have but a crumb until she was fourteen. Then, her grandmother had ceremoniously sliced a paper thin slice and presented it to her. She hadn't felt a thing until she stood up and had to hurriedly sit because she was dizzy. Her grandmother and mother had laughed and she had leaned against her mother until she had felt that she could walk.

Zeezee pretended to quilt. She was hurt that Lanetia had refused to use her buttermilk as an ingredient. Zeezee had said she understood about milk intolerance, but almond milk yogurt? Lanetia had the feeling that Zeezee thought she was making up ailments that really didn't exist. *If you can use the butter, why not the buttermilk?* Janine swears that she can taste the buttermilk in a recipe had been Lanetia's response. All of their hands were stained red from hulling the strawberries. The jam simmered on the back elements of the stove and they had filled too many freezer bags to count. The jars and tops were in the canner being sterilized.

Lanetia poured a half-cup of Royal Lee's liquor into the batter, then frowned. Too late…she had intended to make a couple of cupcakes for the kids. Well, the kids could eat a teensy slice of cake. Bundt cake…sheet cake…two Bundt cakes. She had found the Bundt pans in a box at the old home place. These Bundt pans were heavy…steel? Whatever they were made of, they were now uniformly black like a well-used cast iron skillet. Zeezee said the pans had belonged to Josh's grandmother. Lanetia liked the design…the pans were also used to mold jello.

Lanetia had sensed Vonnie Pearl's disapproval… She supposed Vonnie Pearl disapproved of the liquor. Cinda and Juston were checking to see when the cakes would be ready and, each time they did, Lanetia felt a wave of disapproval emanating from Vonnie Pearl.

Lanetia sighed and began to make a small one layer strawberry cake that had no liquor in it. There was no room for that cake in the oven. By the time she had put away the ingredients and washed the bowls and spoons, the jam was ready. She had almost finished filling the jars with the strawberry jam when the two cakes were ready. Lanetia set the cakes on the counter to cool and poured another half cup of the liquor around the sides of each of the cakes. She slid the third cake into the oven. "I'll watch it and finish filling the jars," Zeezee mouthed at her. Lanetia and Brer Rabbit went upstairs. "Brer Rabbit, I am tired. You understand because you're always tired. I don't know if it's physical or mental. I…"

"Nesha, you wake?"

"Now, I am." Lanetia stretched and yawned. She had fallen asleep with Brer Rabbit in her lap.

"Sorry. Ma wanted me to talk to you about those cakes you made. She say they full of liquor and she don't want the girls to have any."

"I understand. I made one with no liquor in it for the kids. At first, I wasn't, but your mother does know how to project disapproval. The two cakes with the liquor in them will be gone Thursday. Satisfied?"

"Why you angry with me? I can't keep them fools from talkin'. Yesterday, I didn't ask no way, no how for Roberta to sign my name on that petition. I got my name taken off. That's all I can do. Zeezee gave me a slice of the kid's cake. The kids couldn't wait for the icing. Almost gone. I'm putting in an order for my birthday." Lanetia sighed. Vonnie Pearl would not be pleased. Vonnie Pearl always made Josh a Snowball cake. The cake was tooth achingly sweet, a half-round of five layers with coconut jam between the layers and coconut icing. "Zeezee and I tasted what was in the rum bottle."

"Really? Why?"

"Cause Larmont was right. You don't need but a taste. Your granddaddy's liquor is potent. Zeezee couldn't believe it wasn't rum. She's always lookin' for somethin' different. I told her about the jelly. She's already thinkin' that liquor might be just the thing for her spiced peaches. She want to know if you have some more liquor and she'd like to taste the jelly."

"Dad might have some jelly. I'll get her a jar or two if he has any left. Patrice has some liquor. She can't drink it and Larmont doesn't need it. The liquor we made year before last will be properly aged this fall. We make jelly every year. This year we'll make jelly and the liquor. Auntie has promised to supervise me and Kaida."

"Why you angry with me? You ain't looked at me once."

"Have I a reason to be angry with you?"

"No, you don't. Maybe, one day, you'll realize it."

Franklin confiscated one of the cakes as payment. "I had to pay for gas…my time. It's stressful driving on the Interstate. Plus…plus…picture this…twenty drunk Black females at the downtown…" Lanetia laughed. There would be lots of desserts. Franklin took pity on Cinda's and Juston's shameless antics and gave them a crumb apiece. "Don't grumble. This is a grown-up cake. Nesha said you ate your cake. Didn't bring me a piece, did you? What's that old song? *Them's the breaks?* Sister, my dear sister, double the icing on mine and don't forget to fill the hole with icing. Keeps the cake fresher…longer…don't you agree? You have to try this tea I found. With this cake…sublime.

"After I take a nap, I'll take you kids to the movies," he continued, pointing to the coffee table cluttered with books, DVD's, and newspapers. "Look on my phone for movies. Pick your poison as long as it's age appropriate. I was at the hospital until after midnight. Then, I had an early morning round. Nesha, stop hovering. They'll be fine. I'm not driving. Dessa fixed up the spare bedroom for them and she'll be over in a couple of hours. Go… You have last minute details to take care of. We'll visit the Adventure Science Center in the morning and, then, maybe another movie."

"Nesha, I cannot believe you took the time to make a strawberry cake," Janine sighed, as she licked the crumbs from her fingers. "No more crumbs or icing," Janine lamented, as she eyed the cake platter which was as clean as if it had just been washed. "Could you give the recipe to Ramilla? She's making the cakes for the wedding and…"

"Janine, all your guests will be drunk. Do you want that?" Janine's mother interjected. "Lanetia, as always…everything was lovely. The food was delicious and the decorations… I haven't decided whether or not to be offended or amused. I knew that you,

Tanya, and Diné collected that memorabilia, but to theme a wedding shower around it… That was creative.

"The fitting is tomorrow at ten. Othene got such a good deal on the dresses. She's flying in from Paris with the dresses. I will pick her up in the morning. Janine, be on time. Your sister has to be back at the airport by six. July will be here before you know it. Your father will pout because he didn't get a slice of that cake," she said as she hurried to speak to a member of the wedding party who was leaving.

"Nesha, the only good thing about you bein' in Nashville and me bein' in Atlanta is that the cell phone works. I know it be late. Rev. Goodman isn't expected to last the night. We got Rachel settled. Her roommate is the same age and from New Hampshire. Her parents are headmasters at a private school. She paints. It's not her first time away from home. She usually goes to summer camp. Her mother went to Spelman. They checked with the college to make sure the dorms were not co-ed and that their daughter would be locked in at night. Makes you wonder. Since you had them e-mailin' each other, it was like they'd always known each other.

"Kaemon and I will drive back tomorrow. Nina must be some saleswoman. She already dippin' into Zeezee's stock. You could come with me to the funeral?"

"No. I'm sorry you're losing a relative, but I'm not changing my plans. I plan to visit Dad, then drive to Kentucky to interview a prospective tenant. I'll be back by Friday. Did you take your black suit to the cleaners? There was some mud on the hem of the pants."

"No. I forgot. I hardly ever wear it. I was thinkin' about the navy blue suit." Josh sounded disappointed. Lanetia pretended that she didn't hear. Josh had learned how to guilt her into doing what he wanted or so he thought. What he didn't understand was that she had to consciously remind herself that compromise was part of any relationship. Usually…what did it matter? She had always known she would not compromise when she truly wanted or didn't want to do something.

"Whichever. Remember sometimes the cell works when I'm in Kentucky and sometimes not. Last time, it seemed like it was in perpetual roaming mode. In the morning, I'll e-mail Rachel. Have a good night."

Lanetia, you have four days and five nights. Franklin will spoil Juston and Cinda. How to explain? Why should I have to explain needing a break? Just me time. First day…sleep. Then, I'll see what writes itself. Lanetia set up her computer on the enclosed back porch of the old house. A window air conditioner noisily did its thing. The yard was mowed. After she tired of sitting, she would weed the flower beds. Some flowers had volunteered.

"Nesha, we went to a movie every night and we went out to eat every day," Cinda said. "I like your brother. His girlfriend's okay. He let me listen to my heartbeat with his stethoscope and then I listened to Juston's and to his and to Dessa's. Awesome. Wasn't it, Juston?"

"Guess."

"Juston, now is the time to tell me why you're so quiet."

"It would've been nice to spend some time in Kentucky."

"Do you really like the place?"

"You can find stuff there. And it's not tense like it is in the mountains. Nashville wasn't tense either. Can I visit my grandfather? I... You would go with me?"

"Janine is getting married the second weekend in July. Rachel's school ends the next weekend. We don't want to miss the exhibit of her work. When we get back from Atlanta, we'll rest a week, then go to Missouri and end up in Kentucky. How's that?"

"Awesome. Can I let my hair grow?"

"If you take care of it. All I can do… I'm not a hair person, but I can plait it after it's a certain length. You want an afro or braids?"

"Braids. I saw a video of this guy with the neatest braids."

"Zeezee can braid your hair," Cinda offered. "Why are we taking your father's car back home? And I… What about my birthday?"

"Cinda, maybe your mama will let you come with us. Either way, we'll be back for your birthday. Didn't you hear? Your mama wants to go to that church for its anniversary. So, Nesha won't have the SUV and Aunt Nina drives Hoopty, because she can't drive Uncle Kaemon's stick shift. Weren't you listening?" Juston repeated. Cinda glared at him. "They decided to leave her car in Detroit because they need a car when they go back to sell the house and get their stuff."

"McCory, another week and you'll be finished," Corina said, excited. "Tani has been working on the artwork and she just needs the last chapters to complete the drawings. The cover is her best work yet. November is a go."

Lanetia sat between Nora and Helene, trapped. Vonnie Pearl had planned this. She was looking everywhere, but in their direction.

Lanetia felt herself reliving the supper from hell. Would it be like this every year? Her stomach cramped. *Even though she knew that Nora and Helene were two very unhappy women, Lanetia did not feel any compassion for them. Damn it, I'm unhappy. The world does not have to cry because I am unhappy. Why couldn't they pretend to find pleasure in something that did not hurt others?* "So you a Marlowe now. I hear the name Marlowe ain't good enough for you. Where's your wedding ring? My nephew should have been able to afford to buy you a nice ring. Got all that insurance money because his daddy got himself murdered. Too small for you?" Nora needed no answers; she had endless commentary and her own answers. "Don't like the food? One thing Vonnie Pearl could always do…cook. Scared she'll poison you? Vonnie Pearl, bring some more fried chicken...the hot... You outdid yourself this year.

Cinda and Thea had pleaded with her to stay. Thea had never stood up to her sisters. Josh had told them both to ignore his aunts and to stay at the old home place until they were ready for bed.

"What're you gonna write about Juneteenth? Or is that too low class for the likes of you? Newspaper used to have a write-up every year. I forget his name. He walked around talking to us foreigners. Too bad Kaemon and Josh missing out on this chicken."

My article is about the origins of a Juneteenth celebration in the mountains of Tennessee. No place in Tennessee had celebrations like Juneteenth. Southern Kentucky had the Eighth of August, but Tennessee having been the first Confederate State to fall to Union forces...did not. Technically, the Slaves in Tennessee had been freed by the first Emancipation Proclamation, but did they know...did anyone bother to tell them...or were they being used by the Union to build railroads...encampments? Maybe, because of the occupation, they were doing their best to put food on the table and one didn't celebrate being hungry.

She had searched and searched for an article in the Newspaper about its origins, but had found nothing in the back issues. There was nothing in Big John's Diary about a celebration. He had mentioned the Fourth of July, but only to say he couldn't bring himself to celebrate a nation that considered his ancestors three/fifths of a person and that would do nothing to stop the lynchings of innocent men, women, and children. Then, in going through the church records for an article about the church and its founders...she had found some old letters...rubber banded together...from Eddie Taylor, Jr. He was writing to his parents, but they had brought the letters to church to read to their friends and his friends. Eddie Taylor had joined the Army on the day after he graduated from high school. He said he had the misfortune and fortune to be stationed at Fort Hood in Texas. He wrote that he had no idea there was a worse place for Black people than the mountains of East Tennessee. "Texas ain't no place for a Black man..." he'd written. However, he'd met his wife there and attended Juneteenth celebrations. He'd enclosed a flyer from one of the celebrations he'd attended. "We should have a celebration like this. Have the kids do speeches...have a ballgame...a vendor's tent. Let people know we exist on that mountain." That was the spark and the next year was the first Juneteenth Celebration. Eddie Taylor...home on leave...spoke at that Juneteenth Celebration.

No escape like last year. There is no Mr. P's cabin. I wonder if either of them would notice if I left. Thea, I wish you could hear me. You don't have to be so embarrassed. There's no one to mediate or to turn their bitterness into laughter. I'm their sport for tonight. Tomorrow, they'll be at the Celebration all day, complaining to anyone who will or won't listen. Sunday...they will attend church all day. Monday...they will go fishing at the dam. Tuesday...they will leave. Like last year, Zeezee is nowhere to be found. I wonder where she disappears to? Just like last year, except no males at the table. They're all at the pit. Even Juston, who'd been torn between staying and experiencing the pit...she'd tossed a light jacket to him and told him to go.

"Mrs. Marlowe, can't you answer to your name?" Helene said, as she deliberately stepped on Lanetia's foot. Instinctively, Lanetia kicked her. Pure hatred emanated from Helene. "Now, that we have your attention. My sister asked you a question and if you would be so courteous as to answer."

"Don't you know the answer? You'll have to excuse me. I have some work to do."

Lanetia took the steps two at a time. Jacket and keys…on the desk upstairs. "I'll get the phone," she called out. "Hello. What… I see. Tell me now. I'll think about it."

Juston was right. One was tense in these mountains. Always looking over one's shoulder, being startled at the song of a bird, having to look down and up and around to make sure one wasn't walking into a trap.

Mericus had promised never to return. Why was he here? Why did he want to talk to her? There was no one on this side of the church. In the distance, loud music played, announcing the beginning of the ball game. People would be jostling for the best seats on the bleachers set up on two sides of the field. Earlier, she had walked through the market tent. In the backpack slung over her shoulder were two hand turned wooden bowls and a Black rag doll…not for Cinda…for her collection. Lanetia had spent most of her time at the booth of some vendors from a small town outside of

Chattanooga who mistakenly called their business an antique shop. The doll had been tucked in a box. Lanetia could tell by the unprocessed cotton stuffing that peeked through a rip in the leg that the doll was old. Its clothes were long gone. The bowls were for Patrice.

Lanetia walked parallel to Mericus until he stopped in the middle of the cemetery, next to a tall tombstone. He motioned for her to come over.

"Still don't know how to make friends." *Guess not.* "I want to take D'Arton back with me. I'm married. I have my business. I'm clean."

"You have been busy."

"Not as busy as you. They really, really want your water, your land, and they ain't give up. I hear they gonna burn that house that's goin' up. You almost caught some folks when they was gettin' ready to blow up the windmill. Takin' that wire was inspired. McNeil the only one sellin' it and he know he one step from the jail. He can't afford to be implicated. The Bureau's just waitin' for him to mess up.

"This be Andy's grave. People really don't see J.L. as being from here. Not like his daddy. Lot of jealousy in these old shacks.

"You know what his mama ask for when I said I would take my boy?" Lanetia raised an eyebrow. "Money. I just want you to know that I got your message. Took me a while to figure out what I should do. You tell Cinda and Juston I thank them for bein' friends with my boy. I heard sense comin' from his mouth when I talked to him yesterday."

"I heard Ronnie has returned."

"True."

"He's your cousin?"

"True."

"He's not welcome on this side of the mountain."

"I'll pass the message to him. They dug another well."

"Contaminated?"

"Worse than the others they dug. Lot of fancy homes with no access to clean water. Only place the poison ain't is on this mountain. The ore wasn't deep like it was everywhere else."

"They could build rainwater catchment ponds. The poison wouldn't leach into the ponds faster than it could be filtered."

"Rich don't like spendin' money for what they think should be free. You know that. Always a pleasure talkin' to you, Mrs.

Marlowe. Thought I'd tell you what certain people talkin' about." He lifted his shades in salute and walked away from the baseball game.

Andy, why couldn't you have hid out somewhere else? Something shiny? Vonnie Pearl will have a hissy if there's trash on your grave. Lanetia bent to pick up the foil and the top of the tombstone exploded. She had the presence of mind to drop and huddle against the tombstone. *Bastard.*

"Roll," somebody...Mericus shouted. "Roll. Don't stand up. The tombstones will give you some protection. Keep rollin' until you get to Sadmia's tombstone." The top of the tombstone, he was behind exploded. Lanetia took off the backpack and wound the strap around her hand. When another tombstone exploded…she rolled.

Lanetia shakily put a clip into her gun. To her left, another tombstone exploded. Whoever it was, was up high. Where would… The church belfry… Josh had told her he didn't remember when the bell had rang out to announce the beginning of Sunday's service. A window, painted white, to blend in with the white painted church… Where was it? They had been standing at Andy's grave. Josh had pointed it out to her. If the window was at that angle, whoever was there could not see Sadmia's tombstone. Leaning… At last year's homecoming, someone had backed into it and the only way it would remain upright was in its current position. But the belfry was not insulated…the wood was thin. Lanetia peeked over Sadmia's tombstone. The sun glinted off the tip of a gun. Whoever it was, impatiently broke one of the panes of glass in order to aim the gun in her direction. No one would hear. That damn music. Someone must have a hit. In the distance, she could hear the roar of the crowd enjoying the ball game. Lanetia huddled against the tombstone, studying the scene in her mind. At that angle, he had to be standing to the left of the window, trying to shoot across the sidewalk. It was a difficult shot from that window, but the wood was thin. The thought meant something. She studied her gun. Shoot through the wood. Anything would be better than waiting for him to knock a hole in the side of the belfry facing her location and then where would she go?

Lanetia aimed, hoping the bullet would penetrate the wood and give the person in the belfry something to think about. She fired. Nothing. She fired again and this time the shadowy figure appeared to sag against the window. The person didn't seem to be aiming at anything as dirt kicked up by the bullets hitting the dry earth caused a brownish haze in the air. Mericus peered from around a tombstone that was nearer the church. "I think he may be wounded. Whatever it is you aimin' at, keep on aimin' at it."

Lanetia peeked again and saw the shadow against the white window. Lanetia fired again and again. The wood surrounding the window must have been rotten, because this time when the shadow sagged against the window it gave away and the person, a man, fell to the ground. "Don't stand up. He might not be alone," Mericus warned.

"I ain't in on this," he continued, "I would never hurt J. L. You just gonna have to believe that. I need to get out of here. Seem like I done forgot what this place be like. I ain't got no friends here either. I'm gonna get my boy and get out of this place. Can you get to me? You shoot and crawl to the next tombstone. You got it…shoot at that window and crawl.

"You a cool one," Mericus said, when she joined him. "Wish my wife… Well, she ain't. She a good woman. We gonna crawl to those tombstones right next to the church. Can't nobody see over the overhang and the cross on top of the vestibule will block their vision, too. I don't think there be anybody else. You bleedin'. Stone got your face."

"Just have to bleed. Got yours, too. Why'd you drop the foil?"

"Didn't drop no foil. Tryin' to think about that old belfry. Ain't no more windows."

"There's no one else in the belfry. Look at that crow on the electric wire," Lanetia said, pointing. "It's looking into the belfry and it hasn't flown away. Crows know guns. They're hunted…for sport." Mericus nodded.

"There's a telephone in the church. You'd best go. I'll make sure D'Arton gets to you. Thank you. I thought you had something to do with this."

"You okay. You ain't scared to admit when you wrong. I'll take my leave, Mrs. Marlowe. You bring my boy to me. I'll get his mama the money."

No one knew anything had happened until the Highway Patrol came screaming up the mountain road. Three patrol cars were in Sycamore…directing traffic.

"My gun carry permit," Lanetia said, holding it out for the Trooper to see. He scanned it and gave it back to her. Her gun lay in full view on the steps beside her.

"I'll unload the gun." Lanetia shrugged. "An ambulance is on its way."

"It looks worse than it is." Another trooper was leaning over the white male who lay at the edge of the cemetery. He shook his head.

"Keep the people away from here. Put up the warning tape. I'll call for backup," one of the troopers said.

Just then Juston came running toward the church. "Mama, Mama… Mama," he screamed. "That's my mama. Mama…"

"Please…my son."

"Let him through." The trooper thought to walk Juston to the church steps, but Juston wrenched away from him and ran to Lanetia.

"Juston, I'm okay. Just got dinged by some stone. Juston, look at me." He nodded, crying too hard to say anything. "I have to give a statement. Put your head in my lap. Are you taping? The blue lights are on." The trooper nodded.

"My name is Lanetia McCory. It's Saturday, the Juneteenth Celebration. I was visiting the grave of my father-in-law at the Crow Cut Cove Missionary Baptist Church, Sycamore, Tennessee when someone started shooting at me. I was in fear of my life. I could not run because the gunfire was coming from a higher elevation. I determined that the shots were coming from the belfry of the church and I returned fire. I am licensed to carry a handgun which I have with me at all times. It appears that I shot the male person who was firing at me. He sagged against the window in the belfry. The window gave way. The male fell to the ground and did not move. After I determined there was no one else…I fired multiple times and there was no return fire…I went into the church and used the phone to call 911. I sat on the church steps until the Patrol arrived. In an attempt to shoot me, the person desecrated the tombstones and the graves that I am pointing to."

"We're taking pictures. Come over here," the trooper said to Hardemon, who was acting in his capacity as the only EMT in the County. "Ms. McCory is hurt. The other one is beyond your help, but check him out."

"Mrs. Marlowe…do you want to go to the hospital?" The trooper frowned at Hardemon. Hardemon noticed and explained: "She's married to Joshua Marlowe and she owns the County newspaper." The trooper nodded and hurried to assist in putting up the warning tape.

"No, not unless you think it's necessary. Do you think I need stitches?"

"No. You got sprayed with the stone. You've got a gash along your jaw that's long and shallow. I'm going to use a sealer…like a glue. You don't want stitches in your face if you can help it. Good thing you had on sunglasses…good sunglasses. They cracked, but did not shatter."

"She's my wife." Lanetia heard Josh say. "You let me pass. That's my wife and son. You let…"

"We're gonna let you pass. These others can't come with you. When the EMT is finished, you can take her home," a trooper said.

"Kaemon, get some boards. Need to board up that window. Get some plywood from the building site." Kaemon nodded and grabbed Nina's hand.

"I'll take care of it. You get Nesha home."

"Nesha…"

"Wait a minute, Mr. Marlowe. Let me tend to her arm and you can take her home. How's that hand?"

"Fine."

"I think they're both in shock. Some of your grandmother's tea and bed. That's it."

"Nesha?"

"We're okay. Juston didn't need to see me like this. But he'll be okay. Juston, time to go home. Juston, we hold our heads up…no matter what. I have my arm around you. We will walk through that crowd. Understand?" Juston nodded. Joshua held Juston's other hand and they walked through the crowd that hadn't parted on its own accord. One of the troopers had to order the people to stand aside. Lanetia felt Cinda slip her hand into hers as they walked to the SUV.

"Juston, drink the tea Zeezee has made for you and I will sit by your bed until you are asleep. Just a sip… I know… It's nasty, but it will help you sleep."

"You had blood all over you. I thought you were leaving me, too."

"I promised your parents…I would stay. I try to keep my promises. Think about seeing Rachel in Atlanta. Did you see the pieces she has posted on the College's website? I don't think Rachel will be an accountant, do you? Mommy loves you."

"I love you…too."

"Nesha, he's asleep," Joshua said.

"He'll know he's alone. I will…"

"I'll sit with Juston," Vonnie Pearl interrupted. "Me and Cinda. Josh, Ma got everything ready. Y'all go to your room and she'll be along."

"Josh, I've been cleared by the police. I don't think I'll be sued…wrongful death. The coroner says that even though I shot him, he believes the cause of death was a heart attack. However, if not treated, he would have eventually bled to death from the wounds I caused. The TBI agent doesn't think I was a primary target. I was an "opportunity". They speculate that he was after Mericus because everyone has figured out that he turned on them and received immunity."

"He wasn't shootin' at Mericus."

"I think rage took over. To him…I was the "if only". Anyway, Bond isn't aware enough to be told and there are no relatives. I need to get away. Thank you… I haven't thanked you for keeping your relatives away from me. I know I wasn't going to Missouri until the end of July. Why are we arguing? I promised Juston that I would take him to see his grandfather. Now…July… Does it matter? I need to get away. My father has decided that he wants to go to Missouri with us. I am not happy about that. Either Cinda can go or she can't. Make up your mind."

"He's gonna try to persuade you to leave me. He said I couldn't protect you from the ignorance that pervades these mountains. He said…"

"Stop. My father has never been able to persuade me to do anything I didn't want to do. While I'm thinking about it…your cousin…the Reverend has hired a private detective to investigate my background. He does not want to go there. Because I will expose him for what he is and I don't need a private investigator to do so. Do me a favor, since he is your cousin. Tell him to back off."

"Didn't know. But that's par for the course."

"That's what Rid…Corina was calling about. The detective came to her house earlier this evening. Whatever your cousin wants to know, he'd best ask me. If I choose to, I will answer him. And you should talk to your mother about her money. It is her money. She can do what she wants with it. Does she really want to give it to her cousin?

"Josh, he charged her five thousand dollars for the demon ridding ritual. He says three or four more are needed. Josh, it's a scam. Your mother is the latest victim. He does not care whose money he steals or the pretext. Stop her if you can. Mr. P's money deserves a better use."

"He told me that he wasn't chargin' her money."

"Isn't asking for a donation each time the ritual is performed a fee?"

"I'll take care of it."

"Josh, I'm not planning on leaving you. Action...reaction... a person is dead. It doesn't matter that he was trying to kill me. I have to cope with the knowledge that I will kill if pushed. You'd think I'd be empowered, but I'm not. I think I've scared myself. Let me cope in my own way. I know you have shot a person. I saw you do it. Have you ever been the cause or a cause of someone's death?" Josh shook his head. "He was a sentient being. I never thought I could do such a thing…for any reason. Can she go with us?"

"She's already packed and so is Zeezee."

"Josh, I forgot…I heard a rumor that someone might try to burn Kaemon's house. I think you should put some alarms around it."

"Who doin' the rumorin?"

"I'd rather not say."

"What a surprise. Why D'Arton goin' with you?"

"I'm taking him to his father."

"Some folks say Mericus was at the Juneteenth Celebration."

"The TBI says he was, but he was halfway home when the ballgame started. He called me a couple of days ago and said he'd gotten it worked out with D'Arton's mother. I'll swing through

Evansville and drop him off. I doubt that he'll be back. Please, I will return. Let me go. Please…"

"Just come back. I need for you to come back."

"Dad, if you don't like the entourage, don't come. I've rented a van…a large van. You can sit up or lie down. I've packed blankets and pillows. You should be comfortable. Make up your mind. We should be in Springfield sometime tonight. We'll stay there. Your cousin lives about twenty miles from Springfield. No decent hotel there…his words. I've told Juston that his grandfather is ill. Juston's still fragile," Lanetia fretted. "Please don't tell him that boys don't cry."

"I'm surprised you recognize that. You're not helping him. He saw… Look at your face."

"If it bothers you…don't go."

"That's not what I meant and you know it. I told you last year that the people in those mountains were ignorant and what does ignorance do when challenged? What does it know to do? Violence. That is always ignorance's response. What did you do to that Bond person?"

"Dad, he lost everything. His glorious future. He blamed me and Mericus. He wasn't raised to cope with adversity. His daddy always made it right." Her father snorted. "I'm not defending him. Those are the facts. Dad, I have listened to a lecture from Franklin. Patrice even had something to say. I've heard it all. Are you ready? I did not want to stop long. You were supposed to be packed and ready."

"I'm packed. I have to eat in two hours."

"I have your schedule. You have your medicine?"

"I'll take good care of my son. Don't you worry, Miz Lanetia." Mericus and Lanetia had agreed that she would not arrive in Evansville until dusk. Mericus had on a hat and his long braids covered his face, hiding the cuts that were healing. D'Arton clung to Lanetia for a moment.

"E-mail us. We have the laptop with us and your father says you can use his computer. Write to your mother. If you need to get a message to her quickly, just e-mail us and we'll give it to your mother. We'll stop by for a long visit on the way back. Your dad will take good care of you. You heard him promise me. He has never yet broken a promise to me." D'Arton smiled and let his father take his hand.

Lanetia's father and Zeezee had eaten breakfast and were sitting on the terrace of the hotel by the time Lanetia and the kids came down for breakfast.

MacClemore Bennett had been diagnosed with end stage cirrhosis of the liver from a lifetime of drinking. The only reason he was not drinking was that the assisted living facility was diligent and vigilant in preventing visitors from bringing liquor into the facility. He and Lanetia's Dad told stories while Lanetia listened and surreptitiously took notes. She had the micro-recorder in her pocket, but she wished she had a video camera. Mac's gestures and his facial expressions made the stories come alive and her notes did not do justice to the show he was putting on for Juston. *I'll transcribe the stories and make a book of them for Juston. We'll come back tomorrow. Maybe he won't mind a video camera, if I tell him he is making a memory for Juston.*

"You didn't talk much," Lanetia commented as she tucked Juston in bed.

"I just wanted to hear him talk. He tells the funniest stories. He can talk his way out of anything. He said your dad had the brains and he had the mother wit. Is he too tired to see us tomorrow?"

"We'll visit after lunch. He said he'll be ready for us."

"Are you going to video him with the camera you bought?" Lanetia nodded. "He'll like that. He likes cameras. He always wanted his picture taken. I kind of wish my name was MacClemore, but he wouldn't let Daddy name me MacClemore. He said the name was cursed. He said every MacClemore that was…drink was his undoing. He said he always wanted to be something. He never knew what, just something. He said it was always there, just out of his reach."

"He is something. Tell him tomorrow that he's a Master Storyteller. We're losing the ones who can tell stories like your grandfather. There's a style, a cadence that you don't hear any more. His stories kept us riveted to our seats, didn't they? Zeezee can do that, too. My generation is too stressed out to notice the little things that color a good story." Juston was asleep. Lanetia stared at her notebook and woke up an hour later. She sleepily checked on Juston in the next bed and turned off the light.

"Nesha, this house feels good. I like this back porch. Your father was in a good temper when we dropped him off. He don't get to see his people that often. Where them kids off to?"

"Looking for blue stones. They know not to go to the creek. Creek's almost dry anyway. Did you get a good feeling about Mericus and D'Arton?"

"Yes and an even better feelin' about that wife of his. She got some good sense. I can see why you come here to get away from everybody."

"The kids told you?"

"They let it slip. All them movies and not one mention of you bein' with them. What you thinkin' on so hard? Sit still while I dab this ointment on them cuts. No need for you to have any scars. Just lean back and relax. Take your arm out of your shirt, so I can see what them cuts look like and dab on some ointment."

"Same things I was thinking on when I came to the mountains. So many things I've done in the past, I couldn't do anymore. Things that at one time I thought were important. I'm finding out that I can do some of those things, but only when it's their time to be done. In the past, I set the time. Now, there's another clock setting the time and I have to honor that clock.

"I wasn't aware of what I call a clock until last summer. And it wasn't until this year that I began honoring it."

"Josh is scared of losin' you." Zeezee washed and dried her hands as she studied Lanetia. Nowadays, she could not read Lanetia. She sensed that Lanetia wanted to be alone and they couldn't allow her be alone. What if Lanetia decided she was better off alone than with them? "I done told you. I spoiled Josh. He use to gettin' his own way. Can't blame Vonnie Pearl for that. I done it. He spoiled, but he ain't mean spoiled. Don't even sulk like he used to. He maturin'…just like you. You two…"

"I know. It's difficult for me. I'm not spoiled and it's really, really difficult for me. Please try to understand." Zeezee nodded. "Have you seen what the builder is doing to the old home place?" Zeezee nodded again and picked up the quilt top she had brought with her. "Do you think it will help matters?"

"Why that man got a private detective investigating your background?" Zeezee asked, instead of answering the question. Today, she did not want to think on her daughter.

"Ask him."

"Josh said the detective gave that man…I just can't think of him as my kin…his money back after talkin' to Corina."

"That's because the detective talked to my father after he talked to Corina. Corina gave him Dad's phone number. The question is what did my father say to him. I can paraphrase what he said…I will destroy you. There's not a prosecutor in this Country that will go forward with a case. I'm dying. State doesn't want the expense of a dying man's medical care. You will be in a cemetery, if you're found. Wild animals, buzzards…doubt you'll be found.

Dad never had stories to tell like his cousin. You always know that he means what he says."

"Short and sweet. Would he really?"

"If pushed, I don't really know what he's capable of. And, now he's dying. What has he to lose? He knows certain people who will do anything for money from when he had that juke joint. I know he never bought liquor from a legitimate wholesaler when he owned it. Mama told me…" *Nesha?* Lanetia returned to the present with a sigh. "Most people sense from his tone…flat, no emotion, chilling… that it's best not to test the owner of that voice. That voice says I will survive and you will not."

"I see."

"My father has many skeletons in his many closets. What would you like for lunch?"

"Nesha, we been here three days and you on the phone half the night and starin' at the computer the other half. What you doin'?"

"The kids found another blue rock. The color is not as intense as the one I found this past spring," Lanetia said, pointing to the rock on the mantel. "I didn't know that Rachel made you and Vonnie Pearl earrings. Vonnie Pearl wore hers to homecoming service. Josh said she received a lot of compliments." Lanetia smiled at Zeezee as if to say I'm just as evasive at answering questions as you are, aren't I? Zeezee sighed.

"Nesha, Vonnie Pearl ain't never gonna thank you for tellin' Josh what she was doin' with her money. I thank you. She was all set to give that piece of you know what five thousand dollars for another ritual. And him laughin' all the way to the liquor store to buy himself another case of champagne. Kaemon almost told her what you done for Juston that night. Josh stopped him. Kaemon don't understand how Vonnie Pearl think. If it ain't in the Bible, then it be of the devil. He was explainin' to her why it be wrong to take money for what that man claim to be doin' in the name of the Lord."

"I think, and I may be wrong, that he hires a private detective to find dirt and he uses that dirt when asking for donations," Lanetia speculated.

"I think you may be right. If it wasn't for Purlie, I wish I didn't know none of them people. Well, maybe a few of them be worth knowin'. Vonnie Pearl said Grace scared her. Lookin' at yourself can be scary. That piece of nothin' just like Winslow. Slicker than black ice. Winslow promised Ma that he wouldn't never kill nobody else. But when you drinkin' and gamblin', what you expect? Camelia told me that Ma just couldn't justify that third murder. Shot that boy in the back. When they told her, she took to her bed and was dead the next day. I went to that jail and told him he killed our Ma. I told him that the hell that was waitin' for him hadn't been created, but when his time came, it would be ready.

"Purlie said he changed to escape the curse I put on him. Lately, I been rememberin' things. Guess cause I talk to Purlie nearly every day. Haven't decided if all this rememberin' be a good thing or not."

"I'm going to walk to the creek with the kids," Lanetia said, grabbing a walking stick from the umbrella stand. "They're looking in that direction. Do you want to come? Or sit out here and nap and quilt?" Zeezee nodded and tested the three remaining walking sticks before choosing one made of hickory.

"Nesha, look," Cinda said, pointing. "What…"

"The sinkhole is a lot larger. There must be an underground stream flowing underneath the creek bed. Might make a good fishing hole once it settles down. Don't go any closer. Look at the ground. It's rippled. I don't think the ground is stable too much beyond where we are." Lanetia poked at the red dirt that was rippling to the surface. "That's red clay percolating up from below. You saw how deep that gully was in the field beyond the stand of trees behind the house and red clay was at the bottom of that gully." Lanetia pushed the tip of the walking stick into the rippled ground. There was a spongy resistance. "There's definitely something going on. I'll get someone to erect a fence around this area."

The next day Lanetia returned from showing Domino Masters, who she had hired to erect the fence, where the fence should be placed and dropped a blue stone and a pinky red stone on the mantel. "It's the same kind of stone, just different colors because of the minerals in the soil," she told Cinda and Juston. "I think I may have found a tenant. Masters's brother needs a place to stay. Just returned from a tour of duty in the Mideast. Navy… Doesn't drink or smoke…no drugs. Would like to have a lady friend. Their family owned a farm about ten miles from here. When their parents died, they sold. Domino said it was the sorriest thing they could have done. Domino's brother is coming by this evening."

Randall Masters… "Ms. McCory, I will look after your property. You should know. I did not leave the Navy by choice. I have a medical discharge. I have PTSD. Not incapacitating, just annoying. We were chasing pirates and I can't get past what happened when we caught up with the pirates. I got my twenty years in. I just have to keep busy until I decide what to do next. Do you mind if I do some landscaping? My dime." Lanetia nodded.

"Next time you see me, my hair will be first stage locks. I know people will talk and say I'm on drugs. I'm not. I want to be free from looking a certain way…know what I mean?" Again, Lanetia nodded.

"Here's the lease." Lanetia handed him a manila folder. "We're not leaving until Sunday, so you have a day to look it over and…"

"I'll read it now, if you don't mind." After Randall Masters finished reading the lease, he signed the lease and handed it to Lanetia. Lanetia signed the lease and gave it to Juston to copy on the multi-function printer that she had set up on the back porch. When Juston returned with the copy, Randall Masters was counting out the security deposit and the first month's rent.

"Lanetia, call your husband and tell him you will stay for one, maybe, two more days. One of my managers was caught with his hand in the till and I set up interviews on Monday for his replacement. I'm really tired. I thought I'd be rested by now. You conduct the interviews. You make that call, get everyone in bed, and come back to the den. I want to talk to you."

Lanetia thought her father was asleep when she returned. He was sitting in his favorite chair and he had dropped the remote on the floor by his feet. It was way past his bedtime. "Dad…Dad, you should go to bed. Do you…"

"Sit. I'm awake. I can't tell stories like my cousin. He said I should take you to that forsaken place where we were born. Late October when the snakes are hibernating would be a good time. You think about it. Just listen.

"You were always researching the family. Remember, I told you to concentrate on your mother's family. Well…I want to tell you about my family. My mother's name was Breella. You know that. I told you what the B stood for when I gave you a copy of the notebook of her herbal remedies. She had a twin named Gabriel. When Gabriel was sixteen, he had a son named MacClemore. I was a late baby. The Mac you met is Gabriel's grandson. Mac's a year, almost two years younger than me. There was fourteen years between me and the brother that was closest in age to me. Mac and I were like brothers. When my mama died, I spent most of my time at his house. But, I want to tell you about Gabriel. Mac made me promise. He wants Juston to know the story when he's older.

"Gabriel witnessed a white man rape a little girl. He was out hunting and heard her screams. White man had an old shack in the woods where he did his dirt. When he came out, Gabriel shot him. He took that little girl to her mother. He promised that little girl that it wouldn't happen ever again. He was twenty-two years old.

"Over the course of the next month, he killed the largest landowner in the County because he cheated his workers and beat them for no reason; the miller who cheated on the weights when they brought their grain in to be sold; the grocer who sold rotten food at inflated prices; the banker who wouldn't lend them money to buy land; the sheriff and the deputy who had killed somebody's son, brother, father, uncle, cousin just for sport; and the doctor who refused to treat them. He posted a letter on the town hall door. He told them…*I a Black man done this to you. When you read, this I will be dead. Evil begets evil. Do evil, harm any of my people and no grave will hold me.*

"They came to the shacks and they were met with a hail of gunfire. No one knows where the gunfire came from. They were too scared to fire on those white people. The undertaker and the interim sheriff died that night.

"When I was growing up, people still said that Gabriel visited, just to check that we were okay. My mother said his spirit told her where to find him. He was sitting with his back against a tree with a smile on his face. I think I saw him once. I was walking in the woods with my mother and, all of a sudden, she started singing and there beside her for just a blink was this much younger man and they were so happy to see each other.

"But from that time on, the time of violence, we were invisible. We worked for them and we got the minimum of our due. Nothing extra. They didn't have a doctor and neither did we. My uncle Phias, another of my mother's brothers, opened a joint…sold everything. They didn't bother it. Found out after I left that my father and some of his brothers were silent partners."

"Your mother knew herbs."

"You think she helped him continue his journey? My father said Gabriel wouldn't run. He also said that Gabriel never wanted to kill anybody and that Gabriel couldn't live with himself for doing so much that he considered wrong. Gabriel had a public fake funeral, then the real private funeral at the time of his death. The books still list the events of that time as an unsolved rampage by Negro unknown.

"There's an old Bible. I'll show it to you. Tomorrow. Pages are crumbling. Gabriel wrote a note to my mother in the margin of one of the pages. Gabriel said his soul belonged near my mother—his twin. They said when she put on a hat and dressed like a man, you couldn't tell who was who. They're buried next to each other. Gabriel and Breella."

"She helped him?"

“Maybe. It was reported that he could be in two places at the same time. My father said that she would never let Gabriel carry such a burden all alone. But she had to stay. She had children and she was pregnant with one of my sisters at the time this happened. Sometimes we have to do awful things in order to survive. We do those awful things and we stay because there are people who need us. I was born when my mother was fifty-six years old. I was thirteen, almost fourteen, when she died.

“Zeezee told me some of what you speculated I told that private detective. I wonder what else you told her. She wanted to say more, but she’s learned the hard way a lesson about me, hasn’t she? Don’t tell me. Not that you would. Just so you know…you pretty much nailed it.

“Thank you,” Lanetia said a short time later when her father had talked himself into a doze. “You do just fine telling a story. Just fine,” she whispered. Lanetia stared into the shadows of her room. Her father seeing what could not have been there to see? Her father…

Lanetia continued to stare into the darkness. A gift. Her father had given her a gift. He’d shown her the way to deal with the events of that hot June day. As she thought on his words, all that happened on Juneteenth receded to a place…always assessable, but transformed. I am the sum total of all of my actions, not any one single action. I will always be a different person because of the events of that day, but there are people who need me. Honor their need. Stay. Breella stayed and, because she did, I am me. A me I am finally beginning to like.

Does one ever know one's parents?

"Best choice. When can she start?" Franklin McCory said, frowning as he read Lanetia's notes on each of the résumés.

"I told her to be at the store at eight and the manager from the Northside store would train her for two weeks. "I'll set her up in the computer with the other employees. I gave her the packet of information about insurance, the rules… She'll complete the paperwork in the morning and Mr. Garrey can take it from there."

"Estelan is getting a divorce," Franklin McCory said, abruptly changing the subject.

"I'm sorry to hear that." Lanetia continued to set up the new employee in the computer.

"I liked him. Even if he did have that accent. Always thought he was laughing at me."

"Dad, the experience with Estelan taught me that even though this society had little to offer me, this Earth had everything to offer. Estelan would visit a place and that place never forgot

Estelan. He never met a person who didn't have a story to tell and that he wanted to hear. My eyes…my ears…all my senses…the darkened mirror became clear and reflected a reality that beckoned. That was my season with him.

"Being with Josh is teaching me the wonders of the spirit this Earth has to offer. This is my season of the spirit. I am where I must be at this stage in my life."

"Zeezee showed me the pictures of Rachel's work posted on the website of that school. I'd like to buy the painting… Zeezee says Rachel won't sell it. The Dean of the School has asked to display it for the next year. She has talent.

"One more thing. I know the origin of your middle name. Your mother would have been happier if she had married Alphonzo. He had much the same background as your mother. He wasn't like me. Your mother never understood why I was so driven. We were married because of Patrice. I wasn't even sure Patrice was mine until she was three. She was having a tantrum and her lower lip curled in a certain way that I had seen many times before. My father's sister, Aunt Patty Gail, had a temper. When her lip curled like that, you'd better run because she would pick up whatever was in reach and throw it at you and she rarely missed her target.

"You were born the next year and your middle name was payback for the three years of hell I put your mother through.

"Let Juston cling. He needs it. Mac says Juston's been benignly neglected up until now. Drink, drugs, and disorder… Last year, I saw Mac in his eyes. This year…not a trace. Mac saw it, too. Draw up a will for Mac. Here's the information. Send it to me and I'll make sure Mac signs it. And a copy of Mac telling the stories and the video. Make two copies of the video. I want Mac to have a copy. Fix it so it looks like a one man show." Lanetia nodded. *There was only one person she would trust this video to.*

"Mac doesn't want Juston to lose the name Bennett. He has no problem with him taking the name McCory. He doesn't want any other change."

"I understand."

"Juston can be a Bennett-McCory."

"Dad, I really do understand what you've said. I intend to keep your name."

"Good. Have a safe trip. I will not get up to see you off."

CHAPTER 12

J*osh, will you please come with me to Janine's wedding?* A simple question that was difficult to ask. Josh had asked why he should go which she perceived as a challenge to her decision not to attend his cousin's funeral.

"I said I would."

"But you don't want to. Why?"

""'You're gonna be busy being the matron of honor. The kids want to go. They asked Franklin to take them to the movies and he agreed. I guess I just be tired. We been tryin' to get two more windmills situated and just one thing after another."

Joshua and Larmont were in an animated conversation about the presidential election when Lanetia found them. The videographer had tagged along because he did not have a picture of her with her significant other. "Picture with my husband." She sat in Joshua's lap and they mugged for the camera for a couple of minutes. "Time to dance. Are you rested?"

"Very rested."

Lanetia, along with Cinda and Juston, wandered the exhibits of the students' art. Josh, Kaemon, Vonnie Pearl, and Nina were helping Rachel pack. Rachel had twice as much stuff as she had come with. They had decided to rent a small U-Haul.

"Tani, you startled me. Meet Cinda and Juston. Miss Tani and I went to school together. She illustrates children's books." Lanetia smiled. Cinda and Juston had quickly glanced at each other and were now trying to be polite and not stare at Tani. Tani had feathers, cowries and strings of different kinds of semi-precious stones intertwined in her braids which reached past her hips. She had on a bright purple silk top, with strings of beads around her neck, and silver bracelets that reached to her elbows on each arm. She had more than one ring on each of her fingers, toe rings on each of her toes, and too many ankle bracelets to count. No earrings. Tani said earrings interfered with her drawing. Lanetia made a note to herself to ask Tani where she had bought her jeweled sandals. In college, Tani was always covered with paint. Tani said she was a throwback to the time when women wore their wealth for all to see. Tani was someone to stare at and she expected the stares.

“Have you seen your sister-in-law’s exhibit?” Tani asked, after an air kiss.

“Haven’t gotten to it yet.”

“I couldn’t believe what she painted. Much better executed than…”

“Tani,” Lanetia interrupted. “Not here. Come by Ridnour’s about six. It’ll be the three of us. Everyone else will be attending the awards ceremony.”

“I didn’t think you would finish it,” Corina murmured. “But that was always one of the ways you coped. Lose yourself in the oblivion of writing. Once you got going… I’ll edit these last chapters and I’ll do the grunt work. You are so lucky.” Lanetia frowned. “I know… You don’t want to talk about it.

“Kellon, how long will it take for you to finish the illustrations?”

“Ridnour, you should have gone to the Exhibit,” Tani responded.

“I did. Yesterday evening when it first opened.”

“Did you see it?”

"Yes. She had the opportunity to actually participate in a ceremony. You were too much of a fraidy cat. Roll your eyes all you want. You were. Angilyn wouldn't have let anything happen to you. Lanetia is still here. For someone who is whack…you have the weirdest superstitions."

"I do have limits."

"If you say so. I really liked Rachel's jewelry. Isn't that what she's winning an award for? That stone…that blue…"

"If there's any of that rock left…I had no idea she had taken it with her…you'll each get a pair of earrings. I don't think too many people will recognize what Rachel has referenced in that picture. There's too much other stuff in it."

"I'm waiting to be fired," Tani commented.

"Kellon, she has no idea. Why would I fire you? I need your criticism. Feel warm and fuzzy, now?"

"McCory, you are full of it," Tani laughed.

"I have an idea for another book. Maybe it won't take five years to write."

"Aunt Maline, when…how? I'm so glad to see you. You'll stay awhile?"

"Month or so. I called and you weren't here. Vonnie Pearl told me to come on. Kaemon and Nina met me at the airport yesterday. I hear Franklin had something for you to do. He's finally allowing you to be a part of his business. Let me see your face?" Lanetia turned and Aunt Maline studied her face. "Healed. Very little scarring. Are you using the honey, aloe, and a little bit of witch hazel paste?"

"No, Auntie. I would attract too many insects."

"Do you know the reason I have beautiful skin? Yes, you do. You will do as I say. I don't think you're using your sunscreen. I see a little line around your hairline, so you're wearing a hat."

"Auntie, if my skin looks half as good as yours when I'm your age, I will count myself lucky." Aunt Maline preened for a second. She did not have a wrinkle and her skin was just as smooth as it had been when she was twenty-five. "You remember Juston?"

"Yes, I do. I'm your Aunt Maline. Middle sister of three, just like your mama. You are a handsome one. I wanted to tell you that at the wedding, but we didn't get a chance to talk. And these two…Rachel…and Cinda.

"Zeezee, Lanetia has told me about your salve. I know that's why there's no scarring. But, I do want Lanetia to use our old family remedy for what ails the skin. Lanetia used it when she lived in New York and D.C. and this climate in the winter is something like that, isn't it?" Zeezee nodded, but she looked skeptical.

After supper, the two of them walked to the old home place. "I did it, Auntie. After all these years, I did it," Lanetia said, doing a little dance around her aunt.

"These mountains have been good and horrible to you, Lanetia. Do they have any idea how much you hate this place?"

"No. We'll keep it that way."

"I hated Chicago. Lived there for thirty years. But Fizzy Lee was there. You remember Fizzy Lee?" Lanetia nodded. *She and Fizzy Lee, even though Fizzy Lee was eighty-five, that's what she admitted to, had loud, raucous conversations about anything and everything every couple of months. She was another one who read every copy of the Paper. She was a second or third cousin whose father, as the story went, laughed when he should have been ducking. The white man he laughed at gathered his friends and came for him, but his mother outsmarted them and hid him until the sorghum harvest. They took the sorghum to a town ten miles away to be turned into syrup. She dressed like the white war widows and, because of her light skin, she wasn't stopped and her borrowed wagon, hitched to borrowed horses from some folk in the next county who happened to be away, wasn't searched. There was a train pulling out of the station, going in the right direction. She pulled up alongside the train and before he jumped into an open boxcar, she thrust a cloth sack into his hands. Once on the train, he opened the sack and found some bread, boiled eggs, and all the money his mother had saved from selling eggs and vegetables. And a name and a city written on a scrap of paper. Carson Bailey Chicago. Carson Bailey owned a bar that never closed. He owed her a favor. What favor, we don't know and there was only one letter from Carson Bailey and it was about a recipe for a liquor he wanted her to make. Either she or my grandfather added to it, because it appeared to be the basic recipe for Grandad's liquor. Carson Bailey took in her son. Made him go to school and write to his mother once a month, using a made up name. Grandmother had his letters and Aunt Maline has them now. Fizzy Lee thinks he burned his mother's letters. He didn't want his wife to read them. I read his letters when I wrote the family history. He taught at a boys' school for five years and when Mr. Bailey died he took over the business. He bought houses and fixed them up as either boarding houses or rentals. He was known to be a fair landlord and his properties were clean and well maintained. That was because of his mother. When he began buying houses, his mother set out one ground rule for him...if you wouldn't live there, don't you rent it to nobody. Cousin Fizzy Lee showed me the sites of the properties he had owned. Next to the bar, he opened a shop called*

Sorghum's which sold things from home that weren't readily available in Chicago. Fizzy Lee's brother lost it all. Aunt Maline said Fizzy Lee could have grown the business, but their mother insisted that her brother run the business. Her brother liked the liquor and gambling.

"I have an ulterior motive." *Tell.* "You gave away the peaches, but I want some pear preserves and we need dried apples for the Recipe. If there are any persimmons… Those trees haven't produced a persimmon in six years. They added a subtle flavor that no one could guess. Well, no one's ever guessed the medlars either. I'll have to come back in late October for a week. Around Halloween?" It was a rhetorical question that did not require an answer. Aunt Maline had grown up with medlars and she could tell by looking if they were ripe. "That's when the medlars will have done their bletting and Fizzy Lee's daughter can bring her for a visit."

"I'll mark my calendar." Lanetia and Aunt Maline linked arms and walked the rest of the way in silence.

"Why are you cussing an e-mail?" Aunt Maline asked, looking up from a box of fabric. "You really shouldn't hide your notebooks in the fabric. From what I heard at supper, Zeezee will be down here this week looking for some fabric to start another quilt. You should encourage her to sell that quilt with the purple border. Nina says that the price has been bid up to three thousand dollars. That's a nice chunk of change. Worth every penny. She does beautiful work. I'd like a quilt made of that border pattern."

"Sometimes it's really difficult to let go of a part of one's self."

"Most artists have that problem. I'm glad you told me about this fabric. We have an African festival at church and all the fabric stores have the same selection of African prints. I want something unique. I've never seen these prints before. I'll have to look through all of the boxes before I make a final choice. Though, there is such a thing as too much choice."

"Do you really, really like San Diego?"

"Love it. Warm…dry…the ocean… What's not to love? We won't talk about the wild fires. Cussing?"

"They're not supposed to know the test scores of the individual students. Range…yes. The principal at the elementary school who was hired by the State wants to meet with me and Josh concerning Juston's and Cinda's attendance at school this coming school year. He says they had the highest scores in their age cohorts and asks what assurances do I need to feel comfortable they are getting a quality education."

"From your tone of voice, I take it Juston will never set foot in that school again."

"You take right. If I had my way neither would Cinda or Rachel, but if this educator pushes the right buttons, Josh will send them back. His civic duty."

"Take these notebooks and hide them…"

"In this cabinet…my archives… Nobody ever opens this cabinet, but me. Behind the bottom stack of newspapers."

Stedham Trahern was not only the principal of the elementary school, he would also be the lead in turning around all of the public schools in Grotman County. "So, we can count on them returning to school this term? We need good students. Other students will follow their lead and everybody wins. I'm amazed at their scores. We might want to skip them a grade…challenge them."

"Juston will not be returning."

"We have teachers who understand the importance of diversity…who are eager to teach…who want every pupil to do the very best he or she can. No one will hold back your son because of his ethnicity, color, or religion. I have hired teachers who want your child to learn."

"All you say may be true. He will not return."

"Mrs. Marlowe, we need…"

"I'm not concerned with what you need. I'm concerned with his needs. He is not fodder for your elementary school football team, basketball team, or whatever team you have planned."

"That is just an idea. I may not…"

"You have at every other school you've allegedly turned around. The overall test scores did not increase that much, if at all. You do believe in discipline and order. My son does not need your brand of educating. Yes, Mr. Trahern, I do my research. I do not agree with your curriculum. I don't believe that children should take standardized tests every week to prepare them for the yearly tests. There's no love of learning, just the exercise of taking tests."

"Mr. Marlowe, your sisters will…"

"I agree with my wife. They won't be returning. I was prepared to give you a chance, but their minds, their spirits are too precious for me to take a chance with. No exercise period… No arts… Regulated bathroom breaks… Corporal punishment for the smallest infraction. You have to read between the lines… I'm not sending my sisters to a prison."

"Once you see the results, I hope you will change your minds. The formula works. I've shown you the proof." Lanetia closed her notebook. As far as she was concerned, the meeting was over. "Mrs. Marlowe, what will you be writing in your newspaper?"

"An analysis of your proof." Stedham Trahern paled and he dropped the pen he was fiddling with. He bent to pick it up. Before he could settle back in his seat, they had gone.

"Nesha, people don't understand this doublespeak, he and the State people be talkin'. I wouldn't understand it if your Aunt hadn't taken the time to translate for me. She said she used to write policy statements for the Chicago School Board. I'm sorry I wouldn't listen to you. We're just goin' from worse to worst in this County."

CHAPTER 13

Nesha studied the card that D'Arton had sent. "He sent me a card and a gift card. D'Arton… He wrote a note," Cinda repeated for the fifth time.

"He e-mails you," Lanetia pointed out. The short paragraph that D'Arton had written actually made sense. And it was his handwriting. Sometimes, his stepmother addressed the envelopes in which he sent his drawings. The three, Cinda, D'Arton, and Juston had created a comic strip that Lanetia printed in the Newspaper. D'Arton and Juston did most of the illustrations and D'Arton had illustrated the card with one of the comic strip's characters.

"This is different. I'm gonna e-mail him and tell him I'm a gonna save it forever," Cinda said, all in a whirl as she prepared for her birthday party.

"Save one of the bags of party favors for him. Send it to him when you write him a proper thank you note. And remember to fill in the dialog bubble he drew on your card. Have you found all your birthday presents?"

Cinda nodded, then shook her head. "I have too much on my mind. Ma would know. That's who I was lookin' for. Nesha, Juston wrote me a poem. Now, I know why you and Aunt Maline made me a scrapbook. I love makin' memories."

"Lanetia, where are you going?"

"To work on the newspaper." Aunt Maline pointed to the festive table in the dining room. "It's best I'm not around. Vonnie Pearl will feel like she has to share her daughter with me and that causes tension which could erupt at the most inconvenient of times."

"I'll walk with you. Really hot. Why did people come to the mountains in the summer?"

"Night breezes. Temperature's just right for sleeping."

"Lanetia, when do you plan on telling Josh about your love? Eventually, he will find out. He will be really hurt that you didn't tell him."

"Auntie, I want…no…need to see Estelan."

"That's not what I meant. Is that a good idea?"

"Not to engage in what might have been. He's not my love any more. He's my friend. He's hurting. He e-mailed me and he says he can't do it anymore. The firm could close. We communicate maybe twice a year. We never talk about anything but business, pleasantries. This time…he said things that I never thought he would say. Then, Oz who never communicates with me…told me more. I regain and I lose; regain and lose. I still helped out…"

"But not in the last two years," Aunt Maline reminded her gently. "You were too stressed to help even yourself. Nella shouldn't have put the burden of looking after Frankie on you. But she knew she couldn't trust sink or swim Franklin to do it. I respect Franklin's ability to make money and his political skills, but he has never had a clue about being a husband or a father. It was something that was expected, so he did it." Aunt Maline sighed. "People always said we looked like identical triplets, but Nella was the pretty one. Leda and I had to work at pretty. Nella just was."

"Sometimes I don't recognize her pictures."

"Because your last memory of her was of her frailness. Sometimes we are so bewildered by our choices and you can't build a life on bewilderment. The millet bread makes a tasty stuffing. I will have Tasha try Vonnie Pearl's recipe at Thanksgiving. Josh says the millet will be ready to reap by the end of September. I might stay for that.

"I'll have you accompany me on my annual visit to Paul's palace. I mean Jelly Bean. Everyone gives me this blank look when I say Paul. We called him Paul, which is the name my sister gave him at birth, until he went to college and gave himself that ridiculous nickname and refused to acknowledge us unless we called him Jelly Bean. I hope I'm doing the right thing," she fretted. "That way, you can see Estelan."

"Lanetia and I will be visiting Jelly Bean," Aunt Maline announced at supper. Josh laid down his fork and everyone became very quiet. Aunt Maline continued as though she did not notice. "I thought we would leave the day after Labor Day and return the next Monday or Tuesday. I don't like flying alone. When I flew to Knoxville, one of Tasha's church members who was flying to Raleigh was my companion. Tasha is flying out when I'm ready to return to San Diego."

"Where does Jelly Bean live? I don't remember," Josh stared at Lanetia. She wasn't looking at anyone, but she was frowning at her plate. *Had her Aunt even asked her if she wanted to visit Jelly Bean?*

"Philadelphia. He's just returned from a European tour. Lanetia, I thought we could fly back into Nashville. I think I'm ready to visit my old home and see the renovations. I'd also like to visit with your father and your sister and brother. I'll call Kaida and ask her to meet us at the house.

“I remember the Masters. I never knew any of their children,” she commented, sighing at the memory of her home.

“Domino is the only one who stayed in the County and I think he is the youngest or next to the youngest. Randall is older than Domino. I do know that. I’ve decided to enlarge the back porch and make it into a work area. The light is fantastic and the maple tree will shade it.” Lanetia was no longer frowning, but neither was she eating. *I hope I’m doing the right thing.*

“I like that. Lanetia, when you buy the tickets…I like the aisle seat.”

“To make this work, you must be committed and disciplined. If you do not want this to work…tell me now. I will not waste my time. Juston, just so you know, you will not attend that school…ever. I will find a boarding school for you.” *No.* “Yes, I will. It would be a last resort, but I have a responsibility to ensure you have options. At your age, you have certain skills and knowledge to master. And…you will…either at this table or in a boarding school. Do you understand? Whether or not I am here, you have lessons.

“Each of you has your lessons. You have your books. You have your exercises. You also have a schedule. I expect your lessons to be completed per your schedule. When I return, I will check your work. You will be tested. If you have questions, ask…Josh, Kaemon, Nina…e-mail me…look it up on the Internet."

"What does Jelly Bean want?" Juston muttered. "Why do you have to go?"

"To accompany Aunt Maline. Jelly Bean…no one ever knows what he wants. Jelly Bean doesn't know what he wants."

"Oh, the tangled webs," Jelly Bean sang in greeting to them. Lanetia pointed out Aunt Maline's luggage to him as it came around on the baggage carousel. "Lanetia…"

"I don't want to hear it. I have a flight to catch. Take care of Auntie."

"Of course. Be back in time for my party. I have a surprise. And, just so you know…I didn't tell Estelan about your incident."

"Thanks. Are you engaged again?"

"How'd you know?" Jelly Bean looked disappointed that his surprise was no surprise.

"Smile, hitch up the pants… You look too pleased with yourself. Bye. I will return in time and in fashion."

The intimate retail area built around a cul-de-sac was alive with people. There were no empty storefronts. The on street parking spaces were all taken. The park had more flowers than before and the trees actually provided shade. Children played in the fountain. She and Estelan had fought and fought for that park. The City had wanted to build a parking garage on the site.

Lanetia had not returned to this cul-de-sac for almost four years. She looked up at the second floor of the renovated warehouse. She would turn away from her desk when she tired of reading or writing at her desk and gaze at the fountain, daydreaming.

Renèe's eyes widened in surprise when Lanetia walked in. Renèe had started out as a receptionist. She was now the firm's paralegal. The firm couldn't keep a receptionist. One receptionist had returned to school and was now a lawyer, specializing in mediation, and another owned a business selling exotic writing paper. Her business, *The Art of Writing*, was on the first floor. "Am I glad to see you. When did you get in?"

"Yesterday…late."

"Well, it's been hell around here for the past year. Oz…" Lanetia grimaced. Estelan's partner is how she always thought of Oz. Oz was an excellent attorney when he worked. Oz was the product of wealth and privilege. Unfortunately, just as Oz was all set to play at working as his father's attorney, Oz's father's business had declared bankruptcy and never recovered. Oz sometimes forgot he actually had to work for a living. However, he was Estelan's friend.

A decent friend. He had e-mailed, then called and poured out what was happening with the firm, with Estelan… For once, it wasn't about him. *I'm afraid for him. Help.*

Lanetia had considered ignoring his plea, but Estelan… She didn't hate Estelan. She didn't want to avenge the loss of their relationship. She had begun to think of him as a friend, not as a lover she wanted to reclaim. There would always be an ache that accompanied her memory of that time…that phase of her life. He had nurtured a part of her she had not known existed. Now, that part of her was hers to do with as she chose…or not…as the past four, or was it five years, had made apparent.

"Loyna, you may not know me. My name is McCory. At one time, I worked with Estelan."

"Yes. His former partner," Loyna said with a sneer that said he didn't marry you. He married me.

"May I come in?"

"Why?"

"We have some business to discuss. No, don't close the door. We really do have some business to discuss. Would you rather I discuss your business with Estelan? We don't have to do this the hard way, do we?"

"I heard you were a bitch," Loyna said, in a tone where she did not have to add...now I know what I heard is true. "Do come in."

"Estelan is too much the gentleman. I am not a gentleman. Estelan is my friend. Do you remember your first marriage?" Loyna took a step back and turned to stare out a window.

"What do you want?" Loyna said to her image in the window.

"Nothing for myself. You do what you did before. You give up custody. No one need know why. You have until ten in the morning to inform your attorney of your change of heart. Once you sign the papers, you will never again contact Estelan or your daughter. If your daughter ever wants to contact you, she will find you."

"I can leave and he will never find me."

"Then all you will have is a child you do not want. Do it my way, and Estelan, the gentleman that he is, will pay you what he offered, but nothing more."

"Who are you to come into my home and threaten me?"

"I find that threats to a person like you are ineffective. You are welcome to read what I have." Lanetia laid a large yellow envelope on the coffee table. "Also, there are pictures. Some people like to keep a record of their activities." Loyna stared at the yellow envelope as though a snake lay on the table. "Your first husband..."

"Get..." Loyna could not take her eyes from the envelope. She knew it contained pictures of the practice of San-du, a jumble of African and Island religions that was not true to either or recognizable by the practitioners of the much maligned parent religions. Her mug shot? Estelan had met Loyna when she was supposedly reeling from a divorce. Oz had thoroughly researched Loyna and a friend of his who was in law enforcement had supplied him with her criminal record. Loyna was a member of a religious sect that was in the process of sacrificing a child when the child's screams penetrated one of the participants' drug induced haze. That woman fled with the child to a hospital. Luckily, the child only had superficial ritual cuts. They drank the blood of chickens that had been fed a diet of psycho-active mushrooms. Oz believed that Loyna had adulterated Estelan's food with the mushrooms. Sometimes, Estelan was not himself, and now

that they no longer lived together, Estelan did not have those episodes.

"Did Estelan ever tell you? I do not bluff. Don't read, look, or think too long or this information will find its way to Estelan. Then, you will get nothing."

"Get out. Take..."

"You should look at the contents. 10 a.m."

"Is Estelan in?"

"He's here, but he's not in," Renèe warned. "Loyna is taking him to the cleaners in more ways than one. Just a spiteful bitch. He wasn't cheating on her. The private detective was a better witness for Estelan than he was for her. All Estelan does is work. Every female he met was a client and either Oz or I was with him. Can you believe it? Oz, at this moment, is in court, or, at any rate, that's the lie he told me."

Estelan Wenderford barely looked up when the door opened. When he saw Lanetia, he slowly rose from the executive chair they had chosen when furnishing the office, a chocolate brown leather for his and a cordovan red leather for hers. They stared at each other for a long moment. "Did Renèe call you?" Hostility emanated from him, his voice, his stance, and the hand that clutched the pen she had given him so long ago.

“No. Oz called. I should have trusted you. He is a good friend to you. He elaborated on what you said. Can the firm be saved or…?”

Estelan seemed to wilt into the chair. “I think this office is bugged,” he interjected, with a tired wave of his hand that said he did not care.

“I have nothing to say to you that a third party cannot hear. Is the firm in financial trouble? Mind if I sit?”

“My manners. Of course. I can’t concentrate on work. There is no reason for that woman to do what she has done, is doing. Why destroy me? I was willing to pay her anything… Dorolea is my daughter.

“I haven’t seen my daughter in three months. I am her father. At the hearing, that woman lied and said I had abused my daughter. She had no details. I could not defend myself. I could only say I would never harm my daughter. Why are these people so quick to believe such evil? The judge grilled me after the attorney finished with me.

“I’m sure you didn’t come to hear me vent. I always bared my soul to you, didn’t I? Angilyn told me not to marry that woman. She said she would say what my mother would not. Angilyn is staying with me.”

"That's good. I'd like to see her while I'm here."

"I'll call her. What did I do wrong?"

"Sometimes you're too honest."

"You liked that about me, even when you didn't like what I said."

"You cared if I was doing something that would harm me. I appreciated that."

"My attorney says the most I can hope for is supervised visitation. I will never see my daughter. When I arrive to pick her up per the court order, that woman has taken her elsewhere. The court always accepts her excuses. If I wait an hour, then I should have waited two hours. Nothing I do will ever be enough in their eyes. Why?"

"You love your daughter. And you look upon her with love. You have never once looked upon your wife with love." *Because if you had, she would never have wanted to leave you or to hurt you. I know that I did not.*

"She trapped me."

"You were supposed to love her once she presented you with that bit of yourself."

"It doesn't work that way. It just doesn't work that way."

"It's a fantasy. You see it played out on television every night."

"Are you happy?"

"I have my moments. Mostly no. I can deal with it."

"He does not treat you well?"

"He is a wonderful loving husband. I love him, but I don't love where we are. Sometimes the feelings I have about that place overwhelm my feelings for him. He doesn't deserve my unhappiness." Estelan nodded his understanding.

"I would hate for the firm to go under. I just spent most of my money buying the family property, but I can mortgage it."

"No. That's not necessary. It's not money. I have no heart for this. Twice…now…I've lost my heart. Living… Why live when there is no hope?"

"Estelan…you are not a bitter person. You're one of the few persons I have been graced to know who can give so much love and understanding to others. To be in your presence is joy. Don't lose that."

"My Lanetia. You were too naïve to be aware of or even fear your stalker that sunny fall day in Greenwich Village." The beginnings of a smile began to tease his lips. "I've wanted to tell you. I regret my selfishness. How could I possibly know if I could live in Tennessee? I refused to try. I thought you would return, especially when I told you I was involved with another. My mother had never before called me a fool. She did when I told her we were no longer together. I've had to grow up. Angilyn says it's about time. Now, you are married and I am divorced and in the middle of a custody battle for my daughter.

"I will call Angilyn. She can meet us at Mèrage. No more pretending to work on this day. We will sit on the balcony at our favorite table and make up stories about the people who walk the sidewalk."

"Is your nephew with you, too?"

"Children grow up fast. He's in college. Angilyn's only chick. Her only spoiled chick. I think he talks to her at least twice a day."

Angilyn and Lanetia hugged each other and stood apart for a second to get a good look at each other. "If only you were my sister and not that piece of trash. Estelan said you are married. Is he a good man?"

"Very." Angilyn was one of Estelan's older half-siblings. Estelan's father had been busy before he married Estelan's mother. He had children by four different women that they knew of.

Estelan's mother then had three daughters by her second husband. Estelan said that was one of the reasons he got along so well with everyone—he was the youngest of his father's children and the eldest of his mother's children.

When his father's former lovers had confronted Estelan's mother regarding her marriage to his father… What potion had she used? His mother had simply told them…he asked me. From then on, those women became her closest friends.

"My brother is devastated. I told the judge I would care for Dorolea as my own. He acted as if he did not believe me. I wanted to say a bad word, but I did not. That attorney insinuated that I was in the United States illegally. I was so glad I had my green card. He then implied it was a fake. Estelan says I cannot sue that attorney for slander because he made the statement as part of his cross examination. That judge just sat there and did nothing to stop his character assassination of me or my brother. I wish I could invoke the Vodun."

"Since when didn't you?" Lanetia asked, trying not to laugh.

"You know what I mean. If one invokes the Vodun for harm to another, no matter what the provocation, one must pay a hefty price. I will not tempt fate. My grandmother taught me too well. Sometimes one must endure what must be."

"Oz…"

"Do not mention that one. He is very intelligent, but no commitment. His father raised a fool."

"Jelly Bean's yearly bash is tomorrow. I know you both have been invited."

"I've been trying to persuade my brother to attend. Take his mind off things best not dwelled on. Maybe you can persuade him to attend."

Lanetia glanced at Estelan. He wasn't listening to them. His eyes were following a family passing by below. "What happened to your real estate practice?"

"Two years…two hurricanes. There is no real estate being sold on the island. We have tourists. Tourists do not buy houses and, if they did, they would not buy houses that no insurance company will insure." *But…* "Hurricanes come and go? These hurricanes are different. They strike the same island(s). There is no recovery. The same building would be built again and again, only to be destroyed again and again. My grandmother says the Ancestors are troubled and they send a message we have not the sense to understand.

"Estelan says I should open a restaurant…authentic island food. I do not know why he suggested it. I cannot cook. Usually he will laugh and have a story about me and my mother's burned cooking pots. Today, he does not even hear our conversation.

"Estelan, my brother, Estelan…answer the phone. It is vibrating. I can feel it. It is in your pocket next to me."

Estelan did not say anything…just listened, with eyes bright with tears. He dropped the phone on the table. Lanetia gave it to Angilyn. "Estelan?"

"My attorney. I am needed in court. Why must I hear the judge say the words that will take my daughter from me?"

"We are here. Come," Angilyn said. "We do not show the enemy that she has won. You will appeal."

They took a taxi to the courthouse. Estelan's attorney met them outside the judge's chambers and rushed Estelan inside. Thirty minutes later, Estelan, his face streaked with tears, walked out of the judge's chambers with a little girl clinging to his neck.

My attorney, Jonathan Chatham…my partner, Lanetia McCory, and you know my sister."

"I've heard of you. Have you returned?" Jonathan Chatham smiled a greeting as he had a file in one hand and a suitcase in the other.

"No, I'm just visiting."

"May I ask what you did?" At Estelan's indrawn breath, Jonathan Chatham continued: "When I got the call this morning… We have been signing papers… I heard a voice in the background say tell him to inform that bitch, excuse my language, that I am here, doing what I agreed to do. I asked who the ***B*** was and her attorney said Estelan's former partner. He said he would call you." Lanetia nodded. The call had come at 9:58. "I'll get my car and drop you off at your office."

"Estelan will tell you that I was never a gentleman." Lanetia responded and Jonathan Chatham knew there would be no further explanation. He shook his head, still amazed at what had just happened, and went to get his car.

"Lanetia…"

"You will always be my friend. I think you know that. Will she turn around?" The little girl turned and smiled. Lanetia smiled back. The little girl looked like her daddy. "Hello, Gorgeous."

"Meet your Aunt Lanetia…your godmother." Lanetia nodded. She'd always felt she could not bear to be in the presence of Estelan's child, but now, today, she knew that she and Estelan were truly friends. She had said it and now she knew it was true.

"I…"

"No…I will drive you to Jelly Bean's residence," Estelan said, anticipating that Lanetia would now return to Philadelphia. "We will attend the dinner and then, Angilyn, we will leave and Lanetia will retreat to the second floor. There will be a children's table at the dinner. The dinner is formal. My daughter and my sister need dresses. We are going shopping and Miss, no Mrs. Marlowe, is it not?, you will come with us."

Lanetia turned, checking herself in the mirror. She hadn't worn a formal gown in years. Her aunt shared the mirror with her. Their eyes met in the mirror. "Auntie, you look divine."

"I feel guilty. Your husband should be here."

"Don't. A father and daughter… reunited. Is my hair…"

"I don't know how you went from cornrows to that mop you have on your head, but the style suits you. And that necklace… I remember when you bought it or did Estelan give it to you? You never really said."

"A gift…" Aunt Maline tweaked the sapphire necklace so that it was perfectly centered.

"So…Oz was in the attorney's office when the Ex came and she never saw him. After you and Estelan left to meet Angilyn, Oz called Renèe looking for you, in a panic because the judge refused to come to his chambers. Estelan says Renèe lit a fire under that judge. Never know what someone knows about you, do you? You do good work."

"Renèe said it felt like old times."

"My necklace…a little help, please." Lanetia clasped the diamond necklace around Aunt Maline's neck. "I'm leaving all my jewelry to you."

"What?"

"You heard me. You look so much like Nella. I know you've never thought so. Leda and I used to talk about how much you reminded us of Nella."

"Patrice looks like Mama."

"Patrice does in a way, but not in the way you do."

"Tasha…"

"I've set up a trust fund for Tasha's children's education. I can't leave too much to Tasha. Her husband means well, but he will spend it and they will have nothing to show for it. I've paid off their mortgage. I told Tasha what I would do when I accepted her invitation. Tasha is so naïve. She asked me, just because she knew how much I liked it when her mother and I visited. She wasn't really looking for anything in return. Kaida's getting some money. I've got it all divided…just the way I want it."

"Aunt Maline, please… I need you to stick around for a while."

"Oh, I plan on it. You haven't presented me with a great nephew or niece. We middle children have to stick together. We look lovely. Photos on the stairs. Take my arm."

"Juston, what is your problem? Just say what you have to say."

"We saw your picture on the Internet. You and Aunt Maline with Jelly Bean and his fiancée."

"And?"

"You didn't even look like yourself."

"Juston, make-up doesn't make me a different person."

"You had on a dress that showed everything," he blurted out.

"Really. Who told you that? You listen…really listen to what I say. You will not be a narrow minded, rigid, judgmental prig…not my son. My dress was appropriate for the occasion."

"But…"

"But nothing. Do I need to explain further?"

"No ma'am."

"Your lessons…are you working on your lessons?"

"Yes. No."

"Which is it?"

"Josh is sad."

"Why?"

"Because you didn't want him with you."

"Is he there?" *Yes*. "Give the phone to him."

"Josh, you are correct. I did not want you with me. I had an errand. I knew if you found out that you would be hurt, but I hope you can forgive the hurt I've caused. No part of me wants you to hurt because of something I've done, but I had to do what I did. I don't know what you've read about Jelly Bean's bash, but it's not what it's touted to be."

"What is it?"

"There's a very sedate formal dinner for family and certain business acquaintances. After the dinner, those of us who are Jelly Bean's house guests who want no part of the after party retreat to the upstairs theater room and lock the door. The after party is an orgy of sex, drugs, and fundamentalism."

"Say what?"

"He's a gospel singer; not a saint. He's in it for the money. This year, Jelly Bean did not start partying early and he was upright at the dinner and quite amusing. Showboating for his fiancée. Some years…we had to persuade him not to attend the dinner. Fundamentalism—downstairs, on the doors, there is a sign with a Bible verse printed thereon. Whatever the Bible verse refers to, that is what they do in that room."

"That's sick."

"Aunt Leda told him a long, long time ago that he was going to hell. Didn't bother him. Their night of fun. You've nothing to be sad about."

"You looked very beautiful."

"You're too kind. Thank you. I miss all of you."

"I miss you…very…too."

CHAPTER 14

Nesha, that was a stunner dress and an even more stunning necklace. Is it yours?

"Mine?" Lanetia looked up from the computer, blinking. She was only half listening to Nina who had wandered in.

"The necklace."

"Yes."

"Can we see it? We saw you at your wedding, maybe marriage really agrees with you. I…we forget how pretty you are since you never wear makeup or dress in anything but jeans and a flannel shirt or a tee shirt."

"No. It's in a safety deposit box in Nashville."

"The dress?"

"In storage in Nashville. I cleaned out the storage unit in D.C. I intended to give everything to Goodwill or the Salvation Army and I couldn't. Well, Angilyn wouldn't let me." Angilyn had pointed out the benefits of being a packrat. After their shopping trip, she and Angilyn had gone to the storage unit so Estelan could have some bonding time with Dorolea and so that she could find a dress. They had ended up filling up a portable pod that a friend of Angilyn would transport to Nashville. The next morning, Lanetia had emptied her safety deposit box. One day she would sell most of the jewelry, but not now and the sapphire necklace she never wanted to sell. Even if she never wore it again, she wanted to be able to hold it and remember that time of her life. She knew she didn't need it to remember, but she wanted to be able to touch it…hold it up to the light and smile at the rush of memory. "I now have three storage units in Nashville. Sorry…what were you saying?"

"You aunt also had on some serious bling."

"When you're single, you can buy bling. When you're married…have children, bling's not on the grocery list. How much did you get for the quilt?"

"$5,500.00. Zeezee said it was crazy. On the Tuesday after Labor Day, we had a conference call with the people who had left their names and telephone numbers and told them they could bid on it. They bid it up. Zeezee asked for cash. The next day, the winning bidder flew in… Drove up here and counted out the money in hundred dollar bills. We packed the quilt for her. Everyone was happy."

"You like selling, don't you?"

"I seem to have a flare for it. Who's coming up the driveway in a huge, high dollar SUV?"

"Huh?"

"Georgia license plates. I was heading to the house. Our house just might be finished late next month. This place is almost finished. You might tell Josh you like what's being done." *Uh-huh.* "You coming?"

"I have to finish this. I'll be up for supper."

The alarm pinged. Lanetia looked at the time on the computer, startled. She had promised Josh to return for supper. She shut down the computer and locked up.

Josh stopped her at the kitchen door. "Deuce, Rev. Goodman, and his wife are here. They're stayin' for supper."

"Rachel told me when I called. Do I need to change?"

"Up to you."

"Whose tray?" Lanetia pointed to the covered tray on the kitchen table.

"Your aunt said she wasn't feelin' well."

"I'll take it to her."

"Auntie, what's the matter? What do you need?"

"Nothing. The tension in that room. I don't know who they are, but they brought the devil with them. There are toxic people on this Earth. They make my flesh crawl. Armor, girl."

"I'd like for Brother Paul to give a concert at the church," Reverend Goodman repeated for the third time.

"I will give you his manager's number," Lanetia responded for the third time.

"I've never gotten a response. I'm sure he would take your call."

"No."

"An even more uncomfortable silence settled over the dining table. Lanetia noticed the flicked glances of the Reverend Goodman. It was as though he was undressing her.

"We're having the yearly Church Festival. A concert by Brother Paul would make it even more successful than it has been in the past. Cousin Vonnie Pearl is coming. Are you coming with her?"

Armor. "If you're still speaking to me, no, I am not."

"You can bring the children… A fine Christian experience for all the family. I…"

"Mr. Goodman, I'm not interested in your church affairs. If you want a personal introduction to Brother Paul, I cannot help you."

"I would think you would want to be in someone's church asking for…"

"I'll ask the question. Why?"

"Brother Paul's parties are well known in certain circles."

"It's also well known in certain circles that an eighteen year old has alleged that you impregnated her. Seems like you would be in church with rumors like that in certain circles." Reverend Goodman's fork clattered to his plate. Lanetia had called Corina who had called a friend who attended the Reverend's church who was also a friend of Sister Ibrahima. Sister Ibrahima was known to know all the gossip. Reverend Goodman stared at Lanetia just like a deer does when a car is about to hit it.

"If I hear any rumors of Brother Paul's party with my name attached, I will know the source. People who know me know my character and I do not take kindly to slander. Do we understand each other?" Reverend Goodman began to eat.

"Mrs. … I really don't know what to call you," Eleanor said, faking a laugh. "We're cousins-in-law." Lanetia stared at her. "I see. I think you understand I'm in a precarious position. I have never worked. A concert would excite the church members and…"

"Did you not understand what I said? You chose to marry your husband and you chose not to work. If your husband is voted out, I'm sure he will survive. I'm sure you will survive. You have all the money you've stolen over the years, don't you?"

Now, neither of the Goodmans was eating. "Now, who's committing slander?" Eleanor said, looking not at Lanetia, but at her husband.

"I have facts. Your church is being audited and you have no explanation for the missing funds. But a concert with kickbacks would satisfy the demands of the auditors. Wouldn't replace the missing funds. But you don't care about the missing funds unless someone informs on you, do you? I would hope you were intelligent enough to put some away in an offshore account." Lanetia knew they had not. They had used every cent of the money to support their extravagant lifestyle. "I have work to do. Deuce, good to see you looking so well. Have a safe trip back to Atlanta."

Zeezee followed Lanetia. “Stop, Nesha. Let’s go to the oak tree.” Zeezee sat in the tractor tire that hung from a branch with red-gold leaves that matched the rays of the setting sun that streaked the sky. “Tell me,” she ordered. Lanetia sighed and sat in the lawn chair that Kaemon had positioned under the oak tree.

“My cousin will perform for anyone, anywhere if the money is right. I made a few calls after I called the house to find out who was visiting. Seems like Jelly Bean couldn’t stomach the deal your nephew proposed to his manager. One of Jelly Bean’s friends took the offer and is now looking at some very heavy fines and possible jail time. Tax evasion. This was three, four years ago and Jelly Bean’s manager will not take Goodman’s calls. My cousin has a great aversion to the IRS and the criminal justice system. He says the Bible says give Caesar his due and he does. I’d say your nephew’s church will implode within the next year.”

“The eighteen year old?”

“She has e-mails, notes, credit card receipts… Not looking good for your nephew. He can screw around with the adult females, but not a child who’s not out of high school. Her mother, who does not attend the church, wants him arrested, but in Georgia her daughter is over the age of consent. So the mother intends to sue him civilly. He doesn’t have his father to smooth over his indiscretions anymore.”

"Just like that Winslow. Nesha…just an observation. You got a cruel streak in you."

"Yes, I do."

"I can tell you what I see, cause I got me one, too."

CHAPTER 15

What do you want to do for our anniversary? Josh was turned away from Lanetia and his voice was muffled by his pillow. What would be the color, the expression of his suppressed anger? I will be the catalyst. And I have to ensure that his anger, if he cannot contain it, will be turned toward me and only me. He will hurt no other because I could not be his expectation.

"Hadn't thought of doing anything. Do you want to do something?"

"I asked you. What would be your fantasy first year anniversary?"

"I've never given it a thought. The millet is ready…"

"I'm not talkin' about millet," Joshua snapped. "Anniversary…first year…paper."

"We don't **have** to do anything. It can be a day like any other. You can exercise the male prerogative of forgetfulness for all I care. Are we arguing?"

"Somethin's wrong when a wife don't know if she's arguin' with her husband."

Lanetia didn't respond. She took herself and her book to the sitting room and wrapped herself in a quilt. She scooted Brer Rabbit off the sofa and sat in the warm spot he had made. Brer Rabbit glared at her as he turned around and around. He thumped the rug with his bushy tail, curled up, and settled back into sleep. Josh hadn't talked to her since she and Aunt Maline had returned from Kentucky. I am making a mess of things. Aunt Maline and she had taken a long walk in the woods. Aunt Maline had said Joshua's male pride was wounded. You'll have to wait for him to initiate the conversation. If he only knew what you did. Lanetia, I would never tell him. He would say he understood, and all the while it would eat away at your relationship until you have a hole like that sinkhole by the creek. Try not to challenge him until he is secure in your love. Lanetia had shrugged. I know it will be difficult for you, but if you want your marriage to survive this rocky patch, try… Try really hard. Lanetia, you might consider selling that necklace. Men aren't like us. You know that it evokes a memory that does not affect your feelings for Joshua. All he will ever see or rather imagine is the male who gave it to you. In a roundabout way, he asked me about it. I told him you'd had it for some time and that he'd best ask you if he wanted to know more. I've been thinking. I really miss that old house. I love what you're done to it. Would you mind if I came back and just stayed with Tasha during the winter? Think about it. Fizzie Lee said I was a fool not to live in the only place I really feel at home. She said she would stay a month with me, maybe two, if I didn't put her to work.

I don't have to think about it. I gave you a key for a reason. It's your home. And, Fizzie Lee will put you to work." They both laughed. Fizzie Lee didn't know how to sit still. "I've been thinking, too. What about a family reunion? We haven't had one in years. If Tasha can't fly home with you in the spring, I'll come.

"What are you reading?" Joshua asked, waking her from her half-sleep.

"How to reap millet."

"Small field like that, you have to do it by hand. That why you went to the mill? Lookin' at the dryin' room?"

"Yes. I put down some traps to see if there were any mice. So far…nothing."

"I can't sleep. I wanted to talk, not argue. You just seem so wrapped up in your projects." Lanetia held open the quilt and he settled in beside her.

"I'm not averse to celebrating our first anniversary. Where?" Lanetia interrupted herself. The laptop was on the coffee table. She gestured for Joshua to give the computer to her. "Let's do a search to see if there are any shows within a three hundred mile radius that we would like to see."

"Laugh…" Lanetia muttered at her work crew that consisted of the kids, Aunt Maline, Zeezee, and Nina. She held the book so they could see the pictures of the people reaping millet. "Aunt Maline, Zeezee, y'all sit and supervise," Lanetia finally said, giving the book to Zeezee. They both had chairs with umbrellas attached to shade them from the sun. Kaemon and Josh were working on the heating and cooling systems at both houses.

Two days later, Tasha arrived. Lanetia met her at the Nashville airport. Tasha wanted to leave before she got to the house, because the steep, sinuous road made her dizzy and carsick. Lanetia had to stop four times along the way. In the living room, Tasha sat next to Aunt Maline and moaned. Then, Tasha decided she would call the airline to see if she could change the tickets. After complaining about the outrageous change fee, she settled in for a two day visit. "They call you Nesha? You'd try to brain us when we did that. Really pretty country. Just in the middle of nowhere. Auntie's pear preserves arrived and not one jar was broken. So…you're going to celebrate your first year anniversary after you drop us off at the airport? I can't remember the last time I went to the theater.

"Do you mind if I salivate over your hubby? Don't look at me like I've lost it. Auntie told me; I saw his picture, but it's not the same. Can a woman really be so used to being around a man who looks like that to the point she doesn't see him anymore? Lanetia, your husband is ripped. My hubby, bless his chubby heart, never looked like that. I can't complain…look at me after three babies. I vaguely remember having a figure."

In the dim light of the theater, Lanetia studied the program. She wished she could find a hole and hibernate until she was rested. Compromise. She fought against sleep. She could feel Joshua glancing her way to reassure himself that she was enjoying the show. She rearranged the shawl that had slipped off her bare shoulder. Josh leaned over and whispered. She shook her head. The theater's chilly temperature was the only thing keeping her awake.

The next day, as soon as she got home, she took a nap. Josh shook her awake. "Ma want to talk to us. We can listen. Please?"

"I have something for you. I meant to give it to you earlier, but I was too sleepy to think of it. It's on the coffee table."

Joshua slowly untied the blue and purple ribbon and unwrapped the album without tearing the wrapping paper. He held the album, then opened it. He turned a page. “I thought you hadn’t thought about our anniversary.”

“I hadn’t thought about celebrating it. That’s your paper.”

“You got pictures of us all through the year.”

“The kids helped.”

“Tomorrow we’ll do a walk-through of the renovation. Come on. Let’s hear what Ma has to say.”

Vonnie Pearl was waiting for them in the kitchen. “Y’all sit. I’m finishin’ supper.” She stirred the green beans, adjusted the heat so the beans would simmer, and sat at the table with them. “Y’all don’t have to leave. I done said I was sorry. What else you want me to do?”

“Ma, it be best for us to have our own place. This be your home. I want you to be comfortable in your home. We’ll be back and forth. The kids will have their lessons here most days. We’ll probably eat here most days. I set up an intercom system for the three houses.”

“We’ll be here by ourselves. Just me, Ma, and the girls. Josh, no intercom can make up for you not being here. I been tryin’. Why can’t Nesha try?”

“Why should she?”

“Your aunt described the porch to me. She thought you’d like the fireplace.”

“I do. Josh, thank you. We have a home. The plans… You changed the plans, didn’t you?” He nodded. “I love it. Josh, do you think we could keep the bed we sleep in now and get another…” Josh hugged her so hard that she couldn’t speak.

“I love you. I was hopin’ you liked that bed.”

“Nesha, Nesha, telephone…Miss Corina,” Cinda sang out. “She say she be tryin’ to reach you all day and she appreciate if you would bother to read your e-mails. I told her you were at the mill, sacking the grain. She told me to run down here and tell you to call her back yesterday.”

Lanetia nodded. She was sifting the millet to rid it of inedible debris and she was wondering why she had ever thought this would be a fun thing to do. Juston and Rachel held the sifting rack and moved it back and forth over the container while she poured the millet. Cinda found a place to sit and watch.

"Some things…it be very good to be too little to do," she observed. "Can we go to the movies this weekend? The new *Danger Ranger* movie starts."

"I already asked," Juston responded. *Well, Cinda demanded. Sometime, you talk too slow.* "Yes. Saturday afternoon. And we can't argue over where to eat."

"Then I get to decide."

"And why is that," Rachel demanded. "Why you always got to have your way?" *Rachel…keep moving the screen.* "Juston, you can move the screen without my help," Rachel snapped, putting her hands on her hips.

"Okay, that's enough for today. We're all hot and tired. Let's go home and cool down with a shower," Lanetia said.

"I hate you havin' your own house. Can I come visit?" Cinda complained.

"Who can stop you?" Juston said. "Nesha, we're almost finished. There's one more bag. Rachel, come on. I don't want to come back tomorrow."

"Then let's do it. I like the porch the best of all. It's almost exactly like the one at your house in Kentucky. Here…you got a fireplace. And you got a closet as big as a room. Nesha, can't you pour a bit faster? Next year, if you just have to grow this stuff, we'll know not to sack it before we sift it. Stupid book," Rachel fussed.

Joshua was talking on the phone when they got back to the house. "Nesha, come here," he called out from the living room. "Don't go down to our place just yet. I'll be off the phone in a minute."

"Zeezee, what are you cooking?"

"I was making some chowchow. Guess I still am. Josh, tryin' to work out with Deuce to come halfway and pick up Vonnie Pearl so she can go to that church festival."

"I thought he was driving. Purlie's looking forward to seeing you."

"Things change," Zeezee said enigmatically.

"Nesha, Zeezee…I got it worked out. Junior will meet us a couple of exits past the last Chattanooga exit. Nesha, we got an invitation for this Friday night. Short notice. I told Johannsson no, but he's insisting."

"Josh, who's the little girl in the dining room with the coloring book?"

"Minnie's grandbaby. Her mama couldn't keep her, so she's been here since school started. Today, I went with Minnie to the school. School has stressed Quinya. Her name is Quinya. She just started school this year. She got hives, havin' nightmares, and the teacher won't let them use the bathroom when they have to go. It's a mess. Minnie signed the papers for you to homeschool Quinya."

"Anyone think of asking me?" Lanetia asked, dismayed at the prospect of dealing with another child. She would rather have someone like Amare who was now in school in Birmingham.

"Nesha, what else was Minnie to do? School is makin' Quinya ill and Minnie didn't finish high school. Minnie's out on the side porch with Ma. Quinya's got to stay out of the sun because of the medicine she's takin'. Please, talk to Minnie. Not today," he added hastily. "We got an invitation. Johannsson just dropped it off."

"There's no County Board Meeting until the third week in October."

"Not about a Board Meeting. We…me, you, Nina, and Kaemon been invited to the Walnut Hill Mountain Club. They have a dinner and dance every year."

"Why?"

"Johannsson says that you should get to know all aspects of the people living in the mountains. Maybe you wouldn't be so critical.

"Nesha, I told him no when he first suggested it. I told him no today. Kaemon told him no. Now, if we don't go, Kaemon says we'll be the bad guys."

"How? It's an invitation. Invitations can be declined."

"You own the County newspaper."

"Any one of them could have bought it. Holzer had it on the market for six years. They don't want us there. I don't want to be there. Why?"

"I guess we go and find out. Zeezee gonna stay with the kids."

"Maybe they tryin' honey, since vinegar ain't workin'," Zeezee speculated, from the door where she was listening.

◆◆◆

"Nina, I'll drop you off at the Mall. I'm not buying a dress for a function I don't want to attend. I have plenty of clothes. I'll find something suitable in the storage unit."

"If I had some notice, I could have gotten my daughter to send me something. I take it you're going for maximum coverage?" Lanetia nodded. "What really gets me is that Kaemon and Josh both knew about this and didn't say a word. Kaemon said they thought they had taken care of it. Men. Bet you a dollar, this has something to do with that picture of you and Jelly Bean. We just passed the place we took the gun safety class to get our permits. I never touched a gun until I came to Tennessee." *Tennessee…the ignorance in this State would cause one to do many things one would not have thought one would or could do. Such serene beautiful country to harbor so much ignorance and hate. Do the people who are full of ignorance and hate even see the beauty?*

"Kaemon said you received your permits. If he hasn't gotten you a backpack to sling over your shoulder, there's a store near here that sells camping gear. That's where I bought mine. This is Green Hills," Lanetia said, coming to a stop in front of one of the anchor department stores. "You should find something. I'll call you when I get back."

At one time or another, Lanetia had interviewed each of the males who sat at the table with them. Their wives…she had never met. When the waiter tipped the wine bottle toward her glass, Lanetia stopped him and asked for seltzer, with a slice of lime. Josh followed her lead. Kaemon and Nina accepted the wine.

"I find wine relaxing," Christa Johannsson commented to Lanetia. "You know, I've met your father. He and my husband served on some committee together. Funny, how small this world is. I'm president of the garden club. Mr. Holzer used to write up our meetings."

"I accept submissions from any organized group in the County. You can write up your meetings and e-mail it to me. I'll be glad to print it."

"I hadn't thought of doing that. Sally…Mrs. Holzer took care of that. She was the club. I'm trying to get the club going again. Now, the water is killing everything. All my lovely plants will have to be replaced. But, we've promised not to talk about water tonight. We don't want anyone to start shooting.

"I enjoy the Paper. Makes my husband angry. Since you came, seems like the State has taken over all of our institutions. Trahern is out. He just got word, He's only here for a year. Someone else will be assigned to this district next school year. Scores must show an improvement for three consecutive years before the State will return control to the local school board. After, you wrote that article about his track record and his methods, we decided to start a private school, located at the Baptist Church since it is the largest facility. We've hired the teachers who were terminated. Should be up and running by the middle of November.

That comes as no surprise to you, does it? In one of your articles, you speculated that would be our response to the State takeover. That waiter was supposed to leave the bottle of wine on the table.

"Joey, find the waiter. We're dry." Johannsson looked around and raised his hand when he caught the eye of a waiter. Another waiter arrived at the same time with their seltzers. Mrs. Johannsson positioned the wine bottle in front of her. Her husband moved the bottle to the center of the table. She moved it back to where it would be within easy reach. "And we all enjoyed your cousin's singing at the Southern Baptist Regional Convention last year. I have all of his CD's."

The man across the table winked at Lanetia. She stared back at him. He looked familiar, but she couldn't place him.

"You don't know who I am, do you?"

Lanetia smiled. She recognized the voice. "Bob."

Old Bob laughed. "I dress up nicely. I grew up spending my summers on Walnut Hill. I dropped out of the rat race over thirty years ago. I will warn you. The Warfordys plan to monopolize you once they're introduced. They're sitting at what we call the lawyers' table. You've been quite successful at avoiding the few attorneys who practice in our corrupt County."

"Used to be an Economics professor at Sewanee, didn't you Bob?" Andersen, the Mayor of Tiny Town said, with a laugh. His laugh said that Bob was talking too much.

"I try not to remember that time of my life. It was not a success."

"Now, you own all of Sycamore and Marlowe owns everything else worth owning on the Peak. Bob's boy flew over the Peak and he says you're building something beside where you dammed the creek. What have you thought up now?" Andersen said, raising his glass to Josh.

"Electrical plant. Electricity's not reliable in the winter. This past year, from November to March, more often than not we didn't have electricity from the Co-Op. That's not acceptable. I won't pay a bill for something I'm not getting. So I'll make my own."

"I see," Johannsson responded. He was not pleased. He was also president of the electrical co-op. "We're doing the best we can. The storms we've been having are more severe and last longer. We get the lines back up as soon as we can."

"We're the last on your list."

"You've been getting a credit," Johannsson pointed out. "Your alternative sources are more efficient than in the past. Your neighbor, Vinton, just went live with his solar array and windmill that you installed. You're not making it worthwhile to maintain the lines."

The food was horrible.

"We all need the *Danger Ranger* movie after last night. Get me out of here to the 21st century or is *Danger Ranger* set in the future? I can't believe I was being grilled because of that quilt. Who does Mrs. Thing think she is? Sell to the locals, my ass. I sell to the highest bidder. She offered one hundred dollars. I told her next year, Zeezee, your quilts are starting at $500.00. Hello…Nina's in the house, now. And Nina ain't from here."

"Nina, we were all grilled about something. I was in the Army. Yes, I know guns. Most I ever shot at anybody was here." Nesha, stop laughing. "But it is funny. Johannsson's expression when Josh said he was building a power plant… I wish I'd had a hidden camera. And they were too interested in Nesha's SUV. That nurse told them you got off the mountain and back up the mountain in this SUV. You shouldn't have been able to do that without calling for some kind of assistance, which unfortunately they wouldn't have been able to provide. And, yes…Nesha…what *do* you think about Brother Paul performing at a fundraiser for their private school?"

"I gave Andersen Brother Paul's manager's phone number." *I don't think you've heard the last of that, Kaemon muttered.* "They're going to close down the school system," Lanetia commented, shrugging. "How many kids do we have?"

"Eleven," Rachel, said, naming them. "Nobody's graduating this year."

"Nesha, we found another of these SUV's. Seems like they were a limited edition meant for the Canadian market. The only way you can tell if it is one of these SUV's is by the VIN. Yours came from an estate sale in North Dakota. The one we found, the man had two and was getting rid of the one his wife drove. She died and he couldn't bear to have it around. It should be delivered to Nashville, next week. We've got the car lot looking for another, but people don't get rid of these SUV's," Kaemon said. "I think I'll call some guys I know in Detroit. One of them might be able to find another one."

"Josh, Nesha, I know it ain't in your plans, but I don't see any other way," Zeezee said, "I been thinkin' on what I been hearin'. You gonna have to turn that porch of yours into a school room. Can't do it at the church… It ain't insulated and you can't keep it warm. Ain't gonna have no electricity. Our dining room table ain't big enough. Nesha, you and me was going to see Minnie on Monday. May as well make the rounds." *I…* "Yes, you do.

Their kids gonna be in your home. You tell the Baptist Church, nice of them to say their school open to our kids. How they gonna get to Tiny Town when it be stormin'? Just an empty offer."

"Y'all go in." Lanetia said. "I have some telephone calls to make. Josh, enjoy the movie. Give me the keys. I might go to the mall. If I do, I'll be back by the time the movie ends." Josh raised an eyebrow. "I may not go anywhere. I may just sit in the SUV and talk on the phone. Go. Enjoy."

Lanetia was still sitting in the front passenger seat of the SUV, with the door open, when Juston ran back to get his jacket. He opened the passenger door just in time to hear Corina scream *Hollywood. Let me get Koki on a three-way. She thinks she's got a go. We need to invest...*

"Ridnour, don't get too excited. Most projects die at this stage. I want Estelan to talk to Koki. If he's says it's excitement time, I'll get excited."

"Nesha..."

"Juston, get your jacket. They're waiting for you."

"But...your book...a movie?"

"One for each book, Juston," Corina yelled. "I will call Estelan. Oh, I almost forgot...can you make some appearances at the military bases around the Country? Do your remember Renetta Bearden? ROTC…? She was a senior when we pledged. We didn't see that much of her. She's a Major or something. She wants… Not that she knew it was you or us. She thought it was a white writer. She's at Fort Benning. If you can come down in the next two weeks, you can talk to her, appear at the base schools, and decide on the terms. I talked to the printer. I can get some advance copies. Renetta says don't expect any sales. That's why they've started this program. The base schools are filled with illiterate children with no books, magazines, or newspapers in the home. She likes your books and she's put in a requisition to buy copies for every base. She says she needs one more signature before it's approved. McCory, you have to do this. It's exposure. Which I know you hate."

"Juston, go. Josh is coming to see why you're dawdling. Juston, me and you."

"Me and you." He ran to meet Joshua who was almost to the SUV.

CHAPTER 16

Lanetia knocked on Minnie's door. Minnie opened the door and stood there as though she was guarding the crown jewels. "Minnie, Zeezee and I would like to talk to you about Quinya."

"What about her?"

"She can't learn, if she's frightened. She says she hears someone trying to break into the house."

"That's just this old place creakin'. I done told her to pay it no mind. She too big to be blubberin' about imaginary monsters."

"She's six. She's in a strange place. Her mother…"

"In jail. Too hard headed to listen to anybody with any sense. But that ain't neither here nor there."

"Josh can fix some of the creaks and the windows. I think it's the rattling of the windows that frightens Quinya the most."

"How I'm supposed to pay for this? I ain't got no newspaper or cousin who's a fancy gospel singer."

"I'm sure Josh would accept one of your cobblers as payment. Maybe two if you thought his work was worth it."

"You eat my cobbler?" Minnie's swept Lanetia from head to foot with a glance that said you don't know what a cobbler tastes like.

"Of course. I especially like the blackberry cobbler and the peach cobbler. I only eat the crust of the cherry cobbler. I don't like cooked cherries."

"You want to see them windows, so you can tell him what need to be done?" Minnie's house was clean and neat. Like so many other people who lived on the Peak, Minnie's only income was from SSI. She did not have the money to maintain her home and pay the bills. Now, she had Quinya. Lanetia raised the window in Quinya's room. It reminded her of the windows in Mr. P's cabin. Lanetia wrote notes detailing the repairs for each window in the house.

"You done good, Lanetia," Zeezee said. "Keep it up."

"Why'd she take Juston and not us?"

"Because he threw a hissy. I ain't never seen the like in my life," Josh said, shaking his head at the memory of the scene between Nesha and Juston. Juston had known for a week that Nesha was going to visit Corina. As Nesha had cooked breakfast, Juston had burst into tears. He wanted to go with her. “Don’t leave me here,” he’d cried. Nesha had looked at Juston as though he were an alien from outer space which had made the outburst worse. Nesha had listened for all of two minutes before she had told Juston to pack some clothes and not to complain if he was bored.

Corina had cleared her dining room table. Estelan, Angilyn, and Dorolea arrived shortly after Lanetia and Juston. Koki and Tani did not arrive until an hour later.

Lanetia had met Koki in New York. Then, Koki had made her living by drawing sketches of people and places. She was more often than not homeless, because she couldn’t pay her rent. Lanetia would never have looked at Koki’s artwork if she had not met Estelan. One day, when a north wind from Canada blew bitterly cold, she had bought three of Koki’s sketches. Koki had followed her a little way seemingly talking gibberish until Lanetia had stopped to listen. On a cold, cold day, Koki was telling the world of a hot summer day where anything was possible. *A way to think one’s self warm, Lanetia had thought, fascinated at the possibilities of mind over environment.*

There had been a coffee shop across the street and she had bought Koki a meal and listened. On that day, she had learned that there was an actual person bundled inside the rags. The church she attended irregularly had a program to help the homeless. She had persuaded Koki to go with her to talk to the coordinator.

Lanetia had forgotten about Koki, until one day, on a hot August morning, this middle aged woman with a wild afro had appeared in her office. Renèe had whispered that the woman did not have an appointment and had insisted on waiting for her to return from a motion hearing. The woman had pointed to the sketches on the wall of Lanetia's office…*I did those. I asked the coordinator your name and I always thought it was such a pretty name. I think that's why I remembered it. I got in a program where you were given a video camera and told to film your life. I was hooked from the moment I looked through the lens of the camera. The bio I did won an award. I used the money to move to L.A. Now, I direct…mostly cable shows. I find myself in need of an attorney. I have traveled from L.A. to ask you one question. Will you be my attorney?*

"Koki…my son, Juston." *Pleased to meet you. I have something for you and, if I say so myself, I did a fantastic job. Your father will be pleased and so will your cousin.* Lanetia smiled. "Can't wait. Juston is holding Dorolea, Estelan's daughter. You know Estelan. Sitting beside him is his sister, Angilyn. You've been talking to Corina and Tani. Juston, play with

Dorolea…quietly. I know she's a baby. You can read her a story or color some pictures for her and let her choose the pictures and the colors. We won't be long. Estelan says she may be two, but she talks a mile a minute. Kahla should be home from school in a couple of hours." Juston smiled and he and Dorolea settled in front of the big picture window with a pop-up book.

"I don't recall ever telling you that I wrote those books."

"You never did, but Estelan did," Koki laughed. "Here's the deal. If we can raise the money for the actual filming, I can get the money to do everything else. Just to let you know, any estimate of costs that we come up with, double it and we might be in the ballpark. The reason I want to do it like this is to retain creative control. No investment, no creative control. It would be movie of the week type deal. I have that agreement. I just need to produce the movies. All will be aired. I've already talked to some actresses and actors about being in the production for scale. Some have walked as soon as I said the word *scale*. Others are interested. Once it airs, we'll package it as a DVD and that's how we'll recoup our investment.

"Lanetia, I would rather not hire a screenwriter, but I will if you can't do it. I think a screenwriter would screw up the characters." Lanetia frowned. "Okay, I hired a screenwriter to write a draft and it was horrible. Will you and Estelan please refrain from giving me dirty lawyer looks? I thought if I had something to present to you, and you liked it, you would just ask me *where do I sign my name*." As if by agreement, Lanetia and Estelan shook their heads and said…*it doesn't work like that*. "I've learned my lesson. Approval first."

"Why do you think I would do any better? I've never written a screenplay."

"Lanetia, a graphic novel is almost a screenplay. I'm glad you continued in that format and didn't listen to Corina. No offense."

"None taken. Once I read the finished manuscript, I knew it had to be another graphic novel."

"We'll go through the first book and mark the scenes that will play well on the small screen. If there needs to be added dialogue, you will write it and I will review it. By now, I should know what works and what doesn't," Koki asserted. No one disagreed and she continued.

"Estelan, we need you to create a production company. AWB Productions will do."

"Okay. Am I looking at the Board of Directors?"

"Estelan, it's late. These drafts can wait. I have to drive to Fort…"

"I'm driving. Did you not hear Corina? Lanetia, we work too well together for us not to. Why can't we do as we did in the past? I overnight or e-mail you what I need you to do."

"I was in Nashville then. There's no reliable overnight mail in the mountains from December and, maybe November, until the last snowstorm in April. Sometimes if the Dish is coated with ice and snow, there is no Internet. During the winter, I live in a world that I had no idea existed in this day and age. You already know…there is no cell phone service. Sometimes the landline doesn't work.

"We've written the draft of the prospectus. That's enough for tonight."

"Think about it. I should have stayed at the hotel when I took Angilyn and Dorolea for the night. But, I knew we could get most of this done tonight."

"You take the master bedroom downstairs. I'll get my suitcase and sleep upstairs."

"Sure?"

"Remember to call Angilyn and let her know."

Morning came too soon. Lanetia smelled breakfast and stumbled out of bed to the bathroom. A shower did little to awaken her. Corina had cut up a honeydew melon and a cantaloupe. Lanetia could not stomach the eggs and sausage, so she nibbled on the melon.

Estelan returned from picking up Angilyn and Dorolea while Lanetia was idly flipping through her books and making notes in the margins. They had one box of each of the four books.

"Everyone…sit," Estelan ordered, as they settled into their seats and Angilyn strapped Dorolea into her car seat. "Corina, is this your van? It is…"

"No," Corina said, laughing. "This belongs to a friend of mine who transports children for a daycare. I have a van, but it's too small for all of us and boxes of books. I'll sit up front and show you where Mickey's school is. Kahla gets to play hooky."

"Koki, why the camera?" Lanetia asked.

"Presentation. You, as A. Hartley, are an unknown. Authors can sell their work when no one else can. Forget, I am there. Just talk to your audience."

"Josh, I went by Corina's to give Nesha Vonnie Pearl's jacket," Deuce said. "Lanetia's SUV was in the driveway, along with three other vehicles. Corina's neighbor happened to be outside. She said they left early this morning in a van. Then she said something…

She thought I knew what she was talking about. She said she really enjoyed Lanetia's and Corina's performances at the club and wished they would return. Something about looking at the performances on the Internet. Her phone rang before I could ask any questions. Do you know what she was talking about?"

"No."

Major Renetta Bearden was not in uniform. "Makes the children nervous," she explained. "The contract is in the manila folder on the table," she said, pointing. Lanetia nodded and sat on a thinly padded chair at the round table that had an arrangement of multi-colored silk tulips in the center. Lanetia gestured for Juston to sit on a bench in front of the window. Soon, he and Kahla were immersed in a whispered conversation. Dorolea, in her stroller, chaperoned. Renetta only had enough chairs for the adults. "I don't remember you. I was trying to graduate, not deal with pledges. You don't know how surprised I was that we attended the same school, pledged the same sorority. You even have your own videographer. Actually, we will be filming also. Once you prepare the prospectus, send me a copy. I can walk it to the PR Corps and smooth your access to the bases…in any branch. We can help each other."

"Major…"

"Renetta..."

"I've scanned the first couple of paragraphs. I live in a place that is mostly inaccessible from November or December until April. I may be able to do this one appearance and that's it until next year. However, as this is written, I cannot sign it. Granted, last winter may have been an anomaly. If there are blizzards like there were last year, nothing gets off the mountains."

"We can work with your schedule. If you can give me two days notice, I can set you up. You'll be speaking to a captive audience...the children in school. Mr. Attorney, are you listening?"

"And writing," Estelan shot back. He held out his hand for the contract. Corina, not too gently, tapped Lanetia's left foot with her right foot. *Do it*, she mouthed when Lanetia turned to glare at her. Estelan was smiling. He knew she didn't want his input. Only a fool acts as her own attorney—Aura had always said that as a prelude to asking for help. Aura had ordinarily known when to ask for help, but not the one time she really needed it. Lanetia passed the contract to Estelan and he accepted with a nod and a wink that said thank you for not making a scene. "Corina will be traveling with Lanetia and sometimes the children might have to travel with them. I think there should be some provision for that."

"I'll call the JAG who wrote the contract. Why don't you talk to him and find us when you've hammered out an agreement?"

"Sounds like a plan."

"We have three schools to visit. They're in the same complex of buildings. He'll direct you." Estelan nodded. "Is A. Hartley ready?"

Tani and Corina had created a slide show…three versions for three different age groups.

After the reading at the high school, Lanetia sat on the edge of the stage and talked and talked and talked, until Renetta strong armed her into the hallway. "I know what I told you, but I wish you had brought more books. You sold out. We're eating with the officers. Food is decent. I am surprised. Some parents heard you were here and came. Some civilians heard you were here and came. You know, everyone thinks you're an Army brat."

"You told them I wasn't. Tell me you did?" Renetta laughed.

Corina softly knocked on the bedroom door and opened it a crack. "You sleep?"

"Almost. What's up?"

"My next door neighbor left a message on my phone that some man came by, looking for you. Was anyone supposed…"

"No one I know of."

"McCory… You're going to be around Estelan. You still care a great deal for him. Your eyes…their expression…so sad. Josh loves you and you love him. You've got to let what you had with Estelan remain in the past. Just like he does. Even though, his expression was just as sad as yours."

"Why does life create all these parallel pathways after permitting the pathways to cross?"

"I wish I knew. Maybe I'd be over Mr. Party instead of hoping that one day, magically, he will grow up and truly want only me."

"Ridnour, there's a poem in those words."

"'Night, McCory."

"Nesha, how will you tell Josh?" Juston asked as they drove through Sycamore.

"Do I have to?"

"I think it's time. I liked everyone."

"You were wonderful. Juston, I know some really good people and they've helped me a lot. I never thought I had much to offer them in return."

"Miss Koki said that if a person takes the time to get to know you that you're the kind of person most people wish they were."

Lanetia and Juston returned in time for supper. As Lanetia got plates for them, she sensed the chill. Beef stew and cornbread would not chase away the coldness of their expressions. She and Juston liked to butter the cornbread and ladle the beef stew on top. The Marlowes thought it a peculiar way to eat beef stew. For them, the cornbread was on a small plate to the side of the bowl of beef stew. There was an apple betty for dessert. Juston liked apple betty.

The Marlowes were ranged against them or maybe just against Lanetia. Nina was the only one who spoke to her. Even Zeezee stared at her accusingly. "Will someone tell me what I've done or alleged to have done?" Lanetia sat in an empty chair next to Nina and pushed her bowl away. Juston sat next to Rachel who glared at him. Juston stared at his bowl before he began to mix the cornbread with the beef stew. He tested the stew with his tongue and decided the stew was too hot to eat. How many mealtimes with

Nora and Helene would she have to endure? “I don’t know how any of you can eat. Why not talk instead of seethe?”

“What you playin’ at?” Josh said, pushing his plate away.

“I don’t play. Be specific,” Lanetia responded, not looking at him. It only took seconds to go from hunger to feeling like she never wanted to eat again.

“Is this specific enough?” Josh took a folded piece of paper from his pocket. He unfolded the paper and turned it so she could see a picture of her and Juston with a caption—A. Hartley and son, Juston. Reclusive author, A. Hartley, made a rare appearance at Fort Benning. She will be traveling to the bases around the Country to assist the Armed Forces in their Literacy campaign. The latest in the AWB series is on sale on the AWB website. Sources say a movie is in the works.

“The power of the Internet. Kaemon, you still get updates. It had to come out sooner or later. I would rather it be later. That’s one of the reasons I came here. To find out if I could still write after all that I had gone through. In the past year, I started writing again. Hartley is my mother’s maiden name. A. is my middle initial.

“Why not tell you? Writing, to me, is very private. I rarely tell anyone I write. When I first began to write, too many people laughed. So it's something I keep to myself, because it's too precious to me for someone to make light of. Is that all? Any other specific?"

"What did you and Corina do at the club?"

"We did spoken word performances like we did at college. Or rather she did spoken word; I read… There's a difference."

"Why not tell me?"

"I just told you why I did not."

"I've never laughed at what you do."

"You've also never pretended to understand why I needed to be something more than your wife," she said, turning to look in his direction, but not at him. "I have some understanding of your lack of understanding. Your mother… Her husband…your father was her life. You wanted the same. I can't give that to you.

"Juston went with me to make sure I came back. Yes, Juston, I figured that out. This is a good place for you. I've always come back, haven't I?" Juston nodded.

"Josh, I think we need space. The first year is the hardest… I suppose every year could be the hardest. Depends on one's perspective."

"No. We don't need space. We need to understand each other."

"Well understand this. I am an attorney. I have decided to work with the firm I co-founded. I will not be running for D.A. I've started two more books and I'd rather concentrate on them. That means I will go to Kentucky more often. Not in the winter, but maybe in the winter. I suppose I'm stuck on that museum committee. When Mona has a project, I may or may not accept it.

"I haven't decided whether or not to sell the newspaper or just close it down."

"Why would you do either?" Their eyes finally met and Josh sat back in his chair. Lanetia was furious and his fury was no match for the fury that raged in her eyes. A fury that would burn bridges and anyone in her path. A fury that did not know regret.

"Because I'm in my don't care mode. This County can burn in hellfire and brimstone for all I care. Joshua, you can judge me by Vonnie Pearl, Roberta, whomever. Love doesn't conquer all. I wish it did." In saying that, Lanetia, knew what she had willed herself not to think about. She was in love with the thought of being in love. *I, who could not believe in another love had fallen in love with the idea of loving again…a plot in an unrealized book.* She did not love Joshua and she certainly didn't like the man she was talking to.

"Keeping secrets is no way for us to be. I just don't want us to have secrets."

"Like you don't…or is it because I'm female, I shouldn't worry my little head about what you do? You're a lot smarter than your daddy, but maybe not in a good way."

"Dad didn't see the big picture." Josh balled up the picture. "Nesha…"

"We can agree on that."

"Before you get the wrong idea. I didn't do anything illegal. Immoral…but not illegal."

"I agree."

"I fell in love with you. Changed things. Look at me, Nesha."

"Why? I fell in love with you." She wished she could laugh. *If only you knew what I defined as loving you.* "Does change things, doesn't it?"

"I never agreed to sell. I said I would think about it. I made sure they understood that I would only think about it."

"They understood that you would sell. They feel cheated."

"I know. I never lied to them. I used them. I admit that I used them. My Daddy said nothin' up here belonged to them. They had Cherry Hill and Walnut Hill. We know what they did…they fouled what they had. Daddy said they weren't comin' here to do the same thing. I honored his commitment, but I really didn't understand what he was sayin' until you came."

"What are you two talking about?" Kaemon demanded.

"Mericus was always telling me he would never hurt J.L. Until the dinner at the Club, I didn't understand what he was saying. Mericus…good friend to J.L.…amoral Mericus."

"I had help in bidding successfully on all this property," Josh said in the silence that followed Lanetia's comment. "I had almost persuaded myself to sell. Daddy would understand. Then Lanetia showed up and they tried to hurt her."

"Why? After Andy…" Kaemon protested, looking at his nephew as though he had never seen him before.

"Because like Lanetia…I hate this place. There…I said it. Nesha, you think I don't know? You've been doin' the same thing I do. You keep yourself so busy…you forget you in these mountains. Took me a while to recognize myself. Uncle Kaemon, I love the land, but I hate the location. This past year, because Nesha and I have been together, has been the first bearable year since I came back. Daddy never meant for me to come back."

"If we all agree we hate this place," Rachel, said, looking around the table, why don't we leave?"

"Rachel, we're the only ones who live in Crow Cut Cove who have somewhere else to go," Joshua said, staring straight ahead at nothing. "If we leave, this place will be as foul as Walnut Hill and Cherry Hill There be coal in this mountain. All those years ago, it wasn't economical for them to mine it. Now, it is. They'd have to shear off the top of the mountain to get to it. That's what they would do. The coal is the kind in short supply. They been tryin' to find a way around the Federal Government. The three different species of endangered plants in the forest…not found anywhere else. They been tryin' to introduce those plants in the Park, but haven't met with success.

"Then, they have to contend with the land grant our ancestors received when they moved here. They were so sure there wasn't anything under this land. That was part of the lure—mineral rights. Didn't have the technology to find what was in this mountain. Phosphate…that was on the surface. Once they took that, the land was divided among the families. That was part of the land grant. They started bidding on the properties up here and Dad always outbid them. He had to go. Mericus told me what Dad had done. He wasn't helpin' Dad. Mericus said Old Bob was Dad's source of information. To this day, they just suspect Old Bob helped Dad. If he'd helped me in the same way, they would've known it was him. But Mericus did odd jobs for all the businesses in Tiny Town and no one ever thought he was listenin' to them. He became my source of information."

"You lied..."

"No, I didn't, Uncle Kaemon. I just didn't disagree with you. You truly love this place. Dad truly loved this place. Dad made sure I had what I needed never to need this place. He told me that he wanted more for me than this place."

"How did Nesha figure out what was going on?"

"That field where the millet was planted. Too late, I discovered that Nesha looks at rocks. Most women don't. But Nesha...always on the lookout for an unusual rock. Field is full of lumps of coal. The seam is near the surface where the field is. Lanetia had read enough to know that no coal should be on the Peak. Am I right?"

"You are."

"I think you would keep the newspaper. The power in this County don't like you, but they respect you. You ownin' the newspaper has protected us more than you know.

"Certain people sittin' at this table need to know somethin'. Nesha did not marry me for my money or Ma's money. Nesha has never asked me for a cent. We signed an agreement that our assets would remain separate. I…I didn't know it meant my wife would never... Are we okay? Nesha… Okay?"

Control...she knew well the kind of control Josh was trying to exert. The subtle undermining that never let you rest...always on the lookout...the innocence of the controller...your best interests their goal or so they said. It was all a lie. "I... No. I won't live the life of my mother. I won't live a life of bewilderment. I made a mistake. I can't live with your need for control. What you've just said is despicable and your motivation is even more despicable. I don't need to be married to you." *Free…to walk and preserve my illusions of…self.*

"Mama…" *No, I wasn't free.*

"Juston, we adults make mistakes. Joshua can't fix me. I don't need fixing. Joshua, you stay here tonight and, tomorrow Juston and I will leave. I don't want to see you. This is my last meal with Nora and Helene."

"Nesha, stop," Zeezee pleaded.

"Zeezee, I'm a lot of things and if your grandson had not said that about the money, I would have tried. Did you hear what he said?" *She wouldn't understand what I heard. Control. Why must males control? How dare he? When the mind, the body tires of fighting...it sickens and dies. I won't let that happen. I've seen it. I've seen the withering. I won't let that happen to me.*

Such a little thing...really. But it's the little things that hurt the worse. I remember the Guide telling us of the ant and the elephant. Once infected with an ant, an elephant will commit suicide in its distress at being unable to rid itself of the itch it could not scratch. We had come upon a circle of destruction...trees uprooted, the earth pounded into mounds with deep hollows between, the undergrowth torn and tossed willy-nilly...all in the circle of destruction...all caused by the ant. Ants have a scent and the elephants avoid areas that are infested with ants...that's what the Guide said.

"Josh got his faults. He do like control. You ain't give in to him. He done got so much better since you been with him."

"I'm tired of fighting him."

"I understand, but don't throw away somethin' I done seen is good. You two together are good."

"Always his defender. I do like that about you, Zeezee. But…there's a problem. What he's saying is not defensible. And his actions certainly aren't. Not from my perspective. Juston, we have packing to do. There's some food in the refrigerator. I'll make you breakfast for supper."

"Don't do this to us." Lanetia looked at Joshua, his tear-filled eyes, and felt nothing, not even the rage that had blinded her when he had mentioned their agreement.

"If it makes you feel better to think I did this to us, then so be it."

Juston grabbed Nesha's hand as she quietly closed the door to the porch. For a moment, he rested his head on her chest and she stroked his hair. In a couple of months, he would have an afro and then, they'd work on the braids.

Nesha sat on the bed…Joshua's grandparents' bed…stroking Brer Rabbit. *I didn't see it. Not until tonight. I just didn't see it. In love with the thought of being in love. I married a man like my father. How could I have been so blind? Did I think I could fix him? Lanetia, how could you have been so stupid? I wish I could cry. Why didn't I stop myself from making a fool of myself? Aunt Maline…she warned me. You remind me of your mama. Why didn't I hear what she was saying? Hadn't Aunt Leda tried to warn her? He's used to having his way, isn't he? Just that question and still I didn't hear.*

How could I have been so blind? Now I know who Juston was talking to before we left Atlanta. I knew it hurt, but I thought I had worked through the hurt of Dad's ridicule. I thought… I have not. I've shoved it to a very leaky place. Although, to give Dad his due, he has not openly ridiculed me since our truce—just the eyes, the tone of voice.

Why did I permit Frankie to hide behind his made up reality? I was not running from anywhere or anyone when I came back to Nashville, just as I was not running from anything when I came here. He still doesn't want to admit that his need upended my life—his need that triggered that long ago promise to Mama.

I've always known why I would never have married Estelan. He and I are too alike in all the wrong ways. We both cherished our secrets. But Estelan pushed me to write…to be creative. The practice of law can sap one's soul and I wonder that I chose such a profession, he said. Estelan loved to entertain. He loved the production that was his idea of entertainment. He was like Jelly Bean in that respect. I thought one day I'd wake up and enjoy the lifestyle he was creating.

Shouldn't have rushed into marriage. But for once, I wanted to experience going over the waterfall. And, Joshua, the chameleon, fascinated me. But we all are…I knew that about myself and it was as though I was learning about an aspect of myself that made me slightly uneasy through studying Joshua. She felt a presence.

"Juston, please go to bed."

"It's me…Cinda."

"You know where Juston is."

"I don't want to stay here without you. Everybody's arguin'. I was mad because you didn't take me. I…"

"Kahla?"

"She likes Juston," Cinda said, digging the toe of her left shoe into the hand-braided rug that covered the hardwood floor. "Uncle Kaemon said you're gorgeous."

"Gorgeous? Your uncle needs glasses. Cinda, I've made a mess of things. Could you visit with Juston? On nights like tonight, one needs friends. Call Zeezee and tell her you're here. Go."

Lanetia woke up as the sun rose in the eastern sky. She blearily studied the suitcases she had packed before falling asleep, fully clothed.

Juston's door was open and Cinda was asleep in the twin bed. Juston had let her sleep with his stuffed dog, Wild Wover. Practice for the puppy he wanted.

On the kitchen table, a note was propped against a vase with a single red mum in it.

I'm on the porch.

Please…I have to be civil…Lanetia told herself on the way to the porch. Josh hadn't lit a fire. He sat in the chair by the window that faced the rising sun. He had on his coat and he was staring at nothing. His eyes were red from lack of sleep. "It's freezing. Come to the kitchen. Can we be civilized?" Lanetia asked as she peered into the refrigerator. Oatmeal…Juston would have oatmeal for breakfast. She poured the water from the kettle and filled it with fresh water.

"We can. I didn't stand a chance once you found out your Ex was available, did I?"

"What's his status got to do with me? He's my friend. He respects that I am married." Joshua stared at his hands. His Ex had not respected his wife…or him.

"Then why?"

"You don't respect me. I knew you didn't when you didn't stop Roberta. I wondered how you could say you loved me, but yet, you didn't respect me. A friend of mine once said there're all kinds of love. I thought I loved you, but I can't be what you need. And, I finally realized last night that you can't be what I need. So where does that leave us? Two people in love with phantoms, ghosts, a dream?

"Yesterday, in front of those children and parents, there was a part of me that was terrified. And I remembered you kissing me on my nose and I remembered to do and not analyze. I have a lot to thank you for."

"Why don't you sit and we talk? I don't know what to say. I shouldn't have said anything about our agreement. I thought I was… I thought I was telling you I didn't need to fix you. I wanted you to be so proud of me that you would want to sit next to me, go places with me. I wasn't somebody you only wanted to be with in the dark or hidden away in these mountains.

"I didn't think you'd take it as disrespect. I wanted you to be jealous. Then, you'd claim me as your own. If I had known what Ma had tried to do, then I might have understood more. One of the times when I was in Atlanta, I talked to Grace's psychiatrist. He said that when you're in a place where you have no control or perceive you have no control, then you control what or who you can. He said a certain type of woman would see me as manly. He said a woman who could take care of herself would see me as flawed. He said some women want to be taken care of and some women want a partner. Partners supply what the other lacks to make a whole. Would you agree to marriage counseling?"

"Wouldn't it be a waste of our time? You'd want Bible based counseling and I'd want secular. Do you see the disconnect? I'm not interested in being the neck that turns the head or whatever that analogy is when the preachers talk about the good wife, the pearl beyond price. I have a face…with two eyes, two ears, a nose, a mouth. I even have a brain. I am not a pliant, brainless neck. I don't want to control you. I have a hard enough time with me.

"Claim you…claim you… Like the mother lode? I stood in front of my family and friends and married you. What other claiming do you need?" Burning tears threatened to slide down her cheeks and Lanetia hid her face in her hands. Josh fiddled with the note he had written.

"Then let's not unclaim each other. I'm gonna screw up with you. You're gonna screw up with me. Why can't we talk until we understand each other?"

"Because your idea of talking is to make a pronouncement. You then sit or stand and wait for *all hail Joshua*. If I disagree with you, it's a personal attack on your manhood. Do you want to count the nights you've slept with your back to me?"

"No. I figured it didn't bother you too much. You use those times to be as far away from me as you can. One night, you didn't notice me… You were sittin' on the sofa, gigglin' at an e-mail or maybe an article you were readin'. You don't ever try to talk to me when I'm angry, except to say that you know that I'm angry and if I want to talk about it, you'll listen. You just let me be angry because I don't know how to talk to you when I'm angry. But…that's what grown-ups do, isn't it? An adult recognizes that another adult's feelings are to be acknowledged and, if the other adult wishes to talk about his feelings, then you're there to listen and discuss resolutions, if that's what's needed. A child's feelings are treated the same, except one might be able to pacify a child because the child doesn't have the maturity to deal with all of his feelings.

"Dr. Beauchron gave me some books to read. You've treated me like an adult and I've wanted to be the child who could be pacified."

"Your coffee's ready. I thought it was later," Lanetia said, referring to the coffee maker that was on a timer. Josh would get up and drink a cup of coffee before tending to the animals. "Josh, I didn't marry you expecting you to change. Compromise …yes… I expected compromise. I was willing to compromise. You want me to change and, for me, the change you want is not possible."

""Nesha, I read in one of the books that what we're doin' now is a sign that, if we work at our marriage, we have a good chance of succeedin'."

Their eyes met. Lanetia nodded. Joshua returned the nod.

CHAPTER 17

That night, of my own free will, I slid my wedding ring on my heart finger. I had wondered if Joshua had noticed that I did not wear my wedding ring. I had prepared so many explanations if he had asked. I will never tell Josh the real reason I agreed to stay. Before Juston went to bed, we had a long talk. At some point in the conversation, Juston named me *Mama* which he only did when he was truly upset and frightened. With the utterance of that one word, Juston reminded me that he was a child who needed security and stability. After Juston went to bed, I called Josh and asked him to come down in the morning…to talk. At that time, I felt nothing for Josh, for in the place in my being where I had nurtured what I believed to be love was an ugly, purple bruise that was spreading.

I'd taken off the ring the day after Josh had cut his hand. Because of his work, Joshua rarely wore his wedding ring. The ring looked too new. The ring bore no signs that it had endured a year of marriage. Maybe that's what Josh and I needed…a clean slate.

We agreed that we would each make a list of marriage counselors and choose the one who was the least offensive to each of us. We chose a counseling practice in Nashville that had a female and a male partner. She was a minister and he taught psychology at Meharry. One of the first things they suggested, independent of each other, was that Josh travel with me to the military bases, because I had such a difficult time sharing me with him and the travel would help him to understand that there are many things that one cannot control. As the kids had no intention of being left behind, it turned out well. We all learned lessons in patience and accepting frustration.

Patrice had a baby girl in late October. Patrice asked Aunt Maline to come. Aunt Maline was coming anyway, so she accepted. The week after Baby Nella made her appearance, Kaida, Aunt Maline, and I made the liquor and medlar jelly. I stayed for another week, but Patrice did not need my help. Larmont's mother decided that she would tolerate Patrice for the sake of her granddaughter. Aunt Maline traveled between the home place in Kentucky and Patrice's until after Christmas. She became great friends with Randall who drove her everywhere she wanted to go. Randall is looking forward to Aunt Maline's return and has volunteered to fly to San Diego and escort her home.

I wish I could say that motherhood has mellowed Patrice, but it has not. Baby Nella is teaching her a thing or two. Baby Nella… Patrice knew that I always wanted to name my daughter, if I had one, Nella. Aunt Maline said to let it go. So I have…sort of. Aunt Maline says Baby Nella is what my mother was not…a stubborn little girl.

Dad has responded well to the drugs used during the trial. He is comfortable. His cancer is in remission. This past spring, he and I traveled to the huddle of shacks on the Mississippi/Louisiana border where he was born. I never want to go back there, but, I know, one day I will…if only to take Juston to visit the graves of his parents. Dad said Juston's cousin didn't have the money to bury Juston's mother in Minnesota with her parents and he told her, the only place he would pay for a burial would be in his family's cemetery. I asked him if he heard what he was saying. He gave me the look that said I am oblivious to anyone's opinion, but my own. I wrote to Juston's cousin and asked her if she would like for Juston to visit. She wrote back that she would like that. She did not want to be a stranger to Juston. We spent the 4th of July week with her.

I found the conch shell packed away in one of Aunt Leda's boxes marked *Journals*. I had forgotten it existed. When I was little, the conch shell was always on the mantel and its coral interior and the sound of the sea within had fascinated me. Aunt Maline reminded me that the old, old woman who was my great grandmother would hold it to my ear and tell me stories of her adventures with my great grandfather and sing songs that no one today knew the words to. Every story was accompanied by a song… Charlette, my great grandmother, died the year I was nine. When I saw the shell, I understood that the memory I have of Charlette is a subconscious construct of an old woman, with a coronet of gray braids, wearing a suit the color of the interior of the conch shell, who had the look of Zeezee. Funny…I found the album with her pictures and she looks nothing like Zeezee, but the hair…I remembered the braids and their skin tones…almost an exact match. Aunt Maline told me the story of the conch. Estelan had told me much the same story as we sat on the beach on the island where he was born. The roar one hears when one holds the conch shell to one's ears are all the stories of all the peoples of the world. If one listens with the ears of a storyteller, one might be gifted with a story.

The conch shell travels with me from Tennessee to Kentucky and back again. Whenever I have writer's block, either with the Paper or my novels, I listen to the roar of the conch shell and whatever I am writing seems to write itself.

In another of the boxes marked *Journals*, I found the blue stones and arrowheads and scrapers that Kaida remembered. I spread them out on the kitchen table during one of Kaida's visits to the home place and she chose the ones she wanted.

If only Franklin would end his engagement and get married. Neither he nor Dessa are in any hurry.

The first AWB movie will air in November.

This second winter in the mountains… We were lucky that Nina and Kaemon had to care for their granddaughter while their daughter attended school. They homeschool the children when Josh and I are away. Their daughter graduates from the med tech program in the spring, so next year they will spend from November to April on the island where Telman James lives. We visited the island in May, after the school year was officially over, and Telman James told me many things. He has learned to use his intuition well which is one of the reasons that his investments are so profitable.

Miz Treena says I should name my quilt *Mountains Conquered*. Zeezee hung the quilt in her room so she could study it and, after two weeks, she took it down. Zeezee said that Miz Treena got the name right, even though when she created the pattern, she didn't have mountains in mind.

I took a picture of the quilt for Zeezee's quilt album and that's its official name. I hung the quilt on my living room wall. I look at the quilt and see my failure to please Zeezee in making a perfect point. I know. I am too hard on myself.

Josh and I have been through ten months of counseling. We were fortunate that Zeezee agreed to participate in six weeks of the counseling, as did Rachel, Juston, and Cinda. I had a long talk with Juston's grandfather and my father. Juston's grandfather met Josh and decided that yes Josh could be Juston's father. Juston is now a Bennett-Marlowe and I am a McCory. Maybe one day, I will be known as Mrs. Marlowe, but not for a long while.

One day, I will feel peace within at the thought of Vonnie Pearl. I strive for neutrality when in her presence. She keeps a scrapbook of my appearances, because, more often than not, Rachel and Cinda are with me and Josh. Rachel will be in college soon and Vonnie Pearl appears to have accepted that Rachel will return only for the holidays. Rachel has made plans for her summers and they do not include Crow Cut Cove.

This second year of marriage has been more of a year of adjustment than our first year of marriage. I recognize that, in many ways, Josh and I are fragile, but our foundation is solid. Josh and I are discussing having a baby. Cinda and Juston are lobbying for a baby. I think I'm ready. I think **we** are ready.

I dreamed of she who wears the coral suit. She sits beside a vast waterfall, staring into the distance. She is smiling. She trusts me. More so, I understand—went to the mountains to hide my face…the mountains cried out **no hiding place**.

• ~AfterWord~ •

Funny, I'd forgotten how many times I've reread and, to be brutally honest with myself, changed this written accounting of my first years of marriage. My scribbled notes in the margins are telling. I've never been able to change that I was and am stubborn and unyielding, even when I knew I was wrong or not completely in the right. Josh pointed out what we both knew, but hadn't articulated. We argue when we're navigating change. Then, I understood…we're trying to find that place where we can move forward with some degree of sanity, not certainty, but sanity. That's the truth I have for Juston.

• ~About The Author~ •

Writing a sequel to Crow Cut Cove has taken more than twenty years. I have enjoyed revisiting the mountains and its inhabitants. A special thanks to Book-Pros for formatting this novel and to Rhealisticdesign for the cover. Enjoy!

D.M. Martin

Made in the USA
Columbia, SC
16 October 2022